FLOWER O' THE HEATHER

FLOWER O' THE HEATHER

A STORY OF THE KILLING TIMES

BY ROBERT WILLIAM MACKENNA

AUTHOR OF "THE ADVENTURE OF DEATH," "THE ADVENTURE OF LIFE," "THROUGH A TENT DOOR"

Dumfries
T.C. Farries & Co. Limited in
association with Octocentenary Committee
of Nithsdale District Council

First edition 1922
New edition 1985

ISBN 0 948278 04 8 (Paper)
ISBN 0 948278 05 6 (Cloth)

The publisher acknowledges subsidy from the Scottish Arts Council towards the publication of this volume.

Printed in Great Britain by Penwell Limited, Parkwood, Callington, Cornwall.
Bound by Booth Bookbinders, Mabe, Penryn, Cornwall.

TO

JAMES MACKENNA, C.I.E., I.C.S.

CONTENTS

FLOWER O' THE HEATHER

CHAPTER I

ON DEVORGILLA'S BRIDGE

It is a far cry from the grey walls of Balliol College to the sands at Dumfries, and there be many ways that may lead a man from the one to the other. So thought I, Walter de Brydde of the City of Warwick, when on an April morning in the year of grace 1685 I stood upon Devorgilla's bridge and watched the silver Nith glide under the red arches.

I was there in obedience to a whim; and the whim, with all that went before it—let me set it down that men may judge me for what I was—was the child of a drunken frolic. It befell in this wise.

I was a student at Balliol—a student, an' you please, by courtesy, for I had no love for book-learning, finding life alluring enough without that fragrance which high scholarship is supposed to lend it.

It was the middle of the Lent term, and a little band of men like-minded with myself had assembled in my room, whose window overlooked the quadrangle, and with cards, and ribald tales, and song, to say nothing of much good beer, we had spent a boisterous evening. Big Tom had pealed five score and one silvery notes from Christ Church Tower, and into the throbbing silence that followed his mighty strokes, I, with the fire of some bold lover, had flung the glad notes of rare old Ben's "Song to Celia." A storm of cheers greeted the first verse, and, with jocund heart, well-pleased, I was about to pour my soul into the tenderness of the second, when Maltravers, seated in the window-recess, interrupted me.

"Hush!" he cried, "there's a Proctor in the Quad, listening: what can he want?" Now when much liquor is in, a man's wits tend to forsake him, and I was in the mood to flout all authority.

"To perdition with all Proctors!" I exclaimed. "The mangy spies!" And I strode to the window and looked out.

In the faint moonlight I saw the shadowy figure of a man standing with face upturned at gaze below my window. The sight stirred some spirit of misrule within me, and, flinging the window wide, I hurled straight at the dark figure my leathern beer-pot with its silver rim. The contents struck him full in the face, and the missile fell with a thud on the lawn behind him. There was an angry splutter; the man drew his sleeve across his face, and stooping picked up the tankard. In that moment some trick of movement revealed him, and Maltravers gasped "Zounds! It's the Master himself."

And so it proved—to my bitter cost. Had I been coward enough to seek to hide my identity, it would have been useless, for the silver rim of my leather jack bore my name. Thus it came to pass that I stood, a solitary figure, with none to say a word in my behoof before the Court of Discipline.

I felt strangely forlorn and foolish as I made obeisance to the President and his six venerable colleagues. I had no defence to offer save that of drunkenness, and, being sober now, I was not fool enough to plead that offence in mitigation of an offence still graver: so I held my peace. The Court found me guilty—they could do none other; and in sonorous Latin periods the President delivered sentence. I had no degree of which they could deprive me: they were unwilling, as this was my first appearance before the Court, to pronounce upon me a sentence of permanent expulsion, but my grave offence must be dealt with severely. I must make an apology in person to the Master; and I should be rusticated for one year. I bowed to the Court, and then drew myself up to let these grey-beards, who were shaking their heads together over the moral delinquencies of the rising generation, see that I could take my punishment like a man. The Proctor touched me on the arm; my gown slipped from my shoulders. Then I felt humbled to the dust. I was without the pale. The truth struck home and chilled my heart more than all the ponderous Latin periods which had been pronounced over me.

The Court rose and I was free to go.

Out in the open, I was assailed by an eager crowd of sympathisers. Youth is the age of generous and unreasoning impulses—and youth tends ever to take the side of the condemned, whatever his offence. Belike it is well for the world.

I might have been a hero, rather than a man disgraced.

"So they have not hanged, drawn, and quartered you," cried Maltravers, as he slipped his arm through mine.

"Nor sent you to the pillory," cried another.

I told the crowd what my punishment was to be.

"A scurrilous shame," muttered a sympathiser. "What's the old place coming to? They want younger blood in their Court of Discipline. Sour old kill-joys the whole pack of them: nourished on Latin roots till any milk of human kindness in them has turned to vinegar."

I forced a laugh to my lips. "As the culprit," I

said, "I think my punishment has been tempered with mercy. I behaved like a zany. I deserve my fate."

"Fac bono sis animo: cheer up," cried Maltravers, "the year will soon pass: and we shall speed your departure on the morrow, in the hope that we may hasten your return."

I went to my rooms and packed up my belongings, sending them to the inn on the Banbury Road, where on the morrow I should await the coach for Warwick. Then I made my way to the Master and tendered him my apology. He accepted it with a courtly grace that made me feel the more the baseness of my offence. The rest of the day I spent in farewell visits to friends in my own and other colleges—and then I lay down to rest. Little did I think, as I lay and heard the mellow notes of Big Tom throb from Tom Tower, that in a few weeks I should be lying, a fugitive, on a Scottish hill-side. The future hides her secrets from us behind a jealous hand.

Morning came, and I prepared to depart. No sooner had I passed out of the College gateway than I was seized by zealous hands, and lifted shoulder high. In this wise I was borne to the confines of the City by a cheerful rabble—to my great discomfort, but to their huge amusement. The sorrow they expressed with their lips was belied by the gaiety written on their faces, and though they chanted "*Miserere Domine*" there was a cheerfulness in their voices ill in keeping with their words.

When we came to the confines of the City my bearers lowered me roughly so that I fell in a heap, and as I lay they gathered round me and chanted dolorously a jumble of Latin words. It sounded like some priestly benediction—but it was only the reiterated conjugation of a verb. When the chant was ended Maltravers seized me by the arm and drew me to my feet: "Ave atque vale, Frater: Good-bye, and good luck," he said.

Others crowded round me with farewells upon their lips, the warmth of their hearts speaking in the pressure of their hands. I would fain have tarried, but I tore myself away. As I did so Maltravers shouted, "A parting cheer for the voyager across the Styx," and they rent the air with a shout. I turned to wave a grateful hand, when something tinkled at my feet. I stooped and picked up a penny: "Charon's beer money," shouted a voice. "Don't drink it yourself," —at which there was a roar of laughter. So I made my way to The Bay Horse, sadder at heart, I trow, than was my wont.

The follies of youth have a glamour when one is in a crowd, but the glamour melts like a morning mist when one is alone. I seated myself in the inn parlour to await the coach for Warwick, and as I sat I pondered my state. It was far from pleasing. To return disgraced to the house of my uncle and guardian was a prospect for which I had little heart. Stern at the best of times, he had little sympathy with the ways of youth, and many a homily had I listened to from his sour lips. This last escapade would, I knew, be judged without charity. I had disgraced my family name, a name that since the days when Balliol College was founded by Devorgilla had held a place of honour on the college rolls. For generations the de Bryddes had been *alumni*, and for a de Brydde to be sent down from his Alma Mater for such an offence as mine would lay upon the family record a blot that no penitence could atone for or good conduct purge. So my reception by my guardian was not likely to be a pleasant one. Besides there was this to be thought of: during my last vacation my uncle, a man of ripe age, who had prided himself upon the stern resistance he had offered all his life to what he called the "wiles of the sirens," had, as many a man has done, thrown his prejudices to the winds and espoused a young woman who neither by birth nor in age seemed to be a suitable wife for him. A young man in love may act like a fool, but an old man swept off his feet by love for a woman young enough to be his granddaughter can touch depths of foolishness that no young man has ever plumbed. So, at least, it seemed to me, during the latter half of my vacation, after he had brought home his bride. She was the young apple of his aged eye, and there was no longer any place for me in his affections.

I turned these things over in my mind, and then I thought longingly of my little room at Balliol. To numb my pain I called for a tankard of ale. As I did so my eye was caught by a picture upon the wall. It was a drawing of my own college, and under it in black and staring letters was printed: "Balliol College, Oxford. Founded by the Lady Devorgilla in memory of her husband John Balliol. The pious foundress of this college also built an Abbey in Kirkcudbrightshire and threw a bridge over the Nith at Dumfries. *Requiescat in pace.*"

A sudden fancy seized me. Why need I haste me home? Surely it were wiser to disappear until the storm of my guardian's wrath should have time to subside. I would make a pilgrimage. I would hie me to Dumfries and see with my own eyes the bridge which the foundress of Balliol had caused to be built: and on my pilgrimage I might perchance regain some of my self-respect. The sudden impulse hardened into resolution as I quaffed my ale. Calling for pen and paper I proceeded to write a letter to my uncle. I made no apology for my offence, of which I had little doubt he would receive a full account from the college authorities; but I told him that I was minded to do penance by making a pilgrimage to Devorgilla's bridge at Dumfries and that I should return in due time.

As I sealed the letter the coach drew up at the door, and I gave it to the post-boy. With a sounding horn and a crack of the whip the coach rolled off, and, standing in the doorway, I watched it disappear in a cloud of dust. Then I turned into the inn again and prepared to settle my account. As I did so I calculated that in my belt I had more than thirty pounds, and I was young—just twenty—and many a man with youth upon his side and much less money in his purse has set out to see the world. So I took courage and, having pledged the goodman of the house to take care of my belongings against my return, I purchased from him a good oak staff and set out upon my journey.

Thus it was that a month later I stood, as I have already told, upon the bridge at Dumfries. A farm cart, heavily laden, rolled along it, and lest I should be crushed against the wall I stepped into the little alcove near its middle to let the wagon pass. It rattled ponderously over the cobbled road and as it descended the slope towards the Vennel Port there passed it, all resplendent in a flowing red coat thrown back at the skirt to display its white lining, the swaggering figure of a gigantic soldier. He stalked leisurely along the bridge towards me, and as he passed I looked at him closely. His big, burnished spurs clanked as he walked and the bucket tops of his polished jack-boots moved to the bend of his knees. From his cocked hat a flesh-coloured ribbon depended, falling upon his left shoulder, and touching the broad cross-strap of his belt, which gripped his waist like a vice, so that he threw out his chest—all ornate with a blue plastron edged with silver lace—like a pouter pigeon. In his right hand he carried a supple cane with which ever and anon he struck his jack-boot. Behind him, at a prudent distance, followed two boys, talking furtively, lip to ear. As they passed me I heard the one whisper to the other:

"Liar! It's the King richt eneuch. My big brither tellt me, and he kens!"

"It's naething o' the kind," said the other. "I'll hit ye a bash on the neb. He's only a sergeant o' dragoons," and without more ado the lads fell upon each other.

What the issue might have been I cannot tell, for, hearing the scuffle behind him, the sergeant turned and began to retrace his steps. At the sound of his coming the combatants were seized with panic; their enmity changed to sudden friendship, and together they raced off towards the town. The sergeant descended upon me, and tapping me on the chest with the butt of his stick, said:

"You're a likely young man. What say you to taking service wi' His Majesty? It's a man's life, fu' o' adventure and romance. The women, God bless them, canna keep their een off a sodger's coat. Are ye game to 'list? There are great doings toward, for the King wants men to root out the pestilent Whigs frae the West country. Will ye tak' the shilling?"

The suggestion thus flung at me caught me at unawares. I turned it over rapidly in my mind. Why not? As a soldier, I should see some of the country, and if the worst came to the worst I had money enough in my belt to buy myself out.

Moreover I might do something to redeem myself in the eyes of my uncle—for had not the de Bryddes fought nobly on many a stricken field for the King's Majesty. So, without more ado, I stretched out my hand, and the King's shilling dropped into it.

"Come on," said the sergeant brusquely, "we maun toast the King at my expense," and he led the way to the Stag Inn near the Vennel Port. In the inn-parlour he called for drinks, and ogled the girl who brought them. We drank to His Majesty—" God bless him : " and then the sergeant, after toasting " The lassies—God bless them," became reminiscent and garrulous. But ever he returned to wordy admiration of a woman:

" I tell ye," he said, " there's no' the marrow o' the Beadle o' St. Michael's dochter in the hale o' Dumfries ; an' that's sayin' a lot. The leddies o' the King's Court—an' I've seen maist o' them—couldna haud a candle tae her." He threw a kiss into the air ; then he drank deeply and called for more ale. " By the way," he said, " what dae ye ca' yersel' ?—and whaur did ye get sic legs ? They're like pot-sticks, and yer breist is as flat as a scone. But we'll pu' ye oot, and mak' a man o' ye."

" My name is de Brydde," I replied, ignoring his criticisms of my person.

" De Brydde," he repeated. " It sounds French. Ye'd better ca' yersel' Bryden. It's a guid Scots name, and less kenspeckle. Pu' yer shouthers back, and haud up yer heid."

Two dragoons entered the tavern, and the sergeant was on his dignity.

" Tak' this recruit," he said, " to heidquarters, and hand him ower to the sergeant-major. He's a likely chiel."

I rose to accompany the men, but the sergeant tapped me on the shoulder :

" Ye've forgotten to pay the score," he said. " Hey, Mary," and the tavern maid came forward.

The King's shilling that was mine paid for the sergeant's hospitality. It's the way of the army.

So I became Trooper Bryden of Lag's Horse.

CHAPTER II

TROOPER BRYDEN OF LAG'S HORSE

After the cloistered quiet of Balliol I found my new life passing strange.

Sir Robert Grierson of Lag, our Commanding Officer, was a good soldier, a martinet and a firm believer in the power of the iron hand. He was, we knew, held in high favour by the authorities, and he had been granted a commission to stamp out, by all means in his power, the pestilent and bigoted pack of rebels in Dumfriesshire and Galloway who called themselves Covenanters. He was quick of temper, but he did not lack a kind of sardonic humour, nor was he without bravery. A King's man to the core, he never troubled his mind with empty questionings ; his orders were to put down rebellion and to crush the Covenanters, and that was enough for him.

My fellow-troopers interested me. Some of them were soldiers of fortune who had fought upon the Continent of Europe—hard-bitten men, full of strange oaths and stranger tales of bloody fights fought on alien soil. In their eyes the life of a soldier was the only life worth living, and they held in contempt less bellicose mortals who were content to spend their days in the paths of peace. Of the rest, some were Highlanders, dreamy-eyed creatures of their emotions, which they reined in with a firm hand in the presence of any Lowlander, but to which they gave free vent when much liquor had loosened their tongues. Brave men all—from their youth accustomed to hardship and bloodshed—fighting was as the breath of their nostrils. To me, accustomed to the milder ales of England, their capacity for the strong waters of the North was a revelation. They could drink, undiluted, fiery spirits of a potency and in a quantity that would have killed me. I never saw one drunk; and at the end of an evening of heavy indulgence there was not a man among them but could stand steady upon his feet and find his way unaided back to billets. So far as I could see the only effect of their potations was that after the fourth or fifth pot they became musical and would sing love-songs in the Gaelic tongue with a moisture gathering in their eyes like dewdrops. After that they tended to become theological, and would argue angrily on points of doctrine too abstruse for me to follow. The Lowlanders were a curious mixture of sentimentality and sound common-sense. They carried their drink less well than the Highlanders, but they too were men of unusual capacity—at least to my way of thinking—and always passed through a theological phase on their way to a condition of drunkenness.

I do not know whether my companions found as much interest in studying me as I derived from observing them. Probably they pitied me, as the Highlanders did the Lowlanders. I had not been born in Scotland: that, in their eyes, was a misfortune which almost amounted to a disgrace. My incapacity to rival them in their potations, and my inability to take part in their theological discussions, made them regard me with something akin to contempt. Once I overheard a Highlander whisper to a Lowlander, "Surely she iss a feckless creature," and I guessed with a feeling of abasement that he was speaking of me. On the whole, they treated me with a rude kindliness, doing all they could to make me acquainted with the elements of the rough-and-ready discipline which was the standard of the troop, and protecting my ignorance, whenever they dared, from the harsh tongue of the sergeant-major.

We were mounted men, but our weapons were those of foot-soldiers. Our horses, stout little nags, known as Galloways, were simply our means of conveyance from place to place. If we had been called upon to fight, we should probably have fought on foot, and we were armed accordingly, with long muskets which we bore either slung across our shoulders or suspended muzzle-downwards from our saddle-peaks.

Equipped for rapid movement, we carried little with us save our weapons: but under his saddle-flap each dragoon had a broad metal plate, and behind the saddle was hung a bag of oatmeal. When we bivouacked in the open, as many a time we did, each trooper made for himself on his plate, heated over a camp fire, a farle or two of oat-cake, and with this staved off the pangs of hunger. It was, as the sergeant had said, a man's life—devoid of luxury, compact of hardship and scanty feeding, with little relaxation save what we could find in the taverns of the towns or villages where we halted for a time.

In my ignorance, I had thought that when we set out from Dumfries to march through Galloway we should find, opposed to us somewhere, a force of Covenanters who would give battle. I had imagined that these rebels would have an army of their own ready to challenge the forces of the King: but soon I learned that our warfare was an inglorious campaign against unarmed men and women. We were little more than inquisitors. In the quiet of an afternoon we would clatter up some lonely road to a white farmhouse—the hens scattering in terror before us—and draw rein in the cobbled court-yard.

Lag would hammer imperiously upon the half-open door, and a terrified woman would answer the summons.

"Whaur's the guid-man?" he would cry, and when the good-wife could find speech she would answer:

"He's up on the hills wi' the sheep."

"Think ye," Lag would say, "will he tak' the Test?"

"Ay, he wull that. He's nae Whig, but a King's man is John,"—and to put her words to the proof we would search the hills till we found him. When found, if he took "The Test," which seemed to me for the most part to be an oath of allegiance to the King, with a promise to have no dealings with the pestilent Covenanters, we molested him no further, and Lag would sometimes pass a word of praise upon his sheep or his cattle, which would please the good-man mightily.

But often our raids had a less happy issue. As we drew near to a house, we would see a figure steal hastily from it, and we knew that we were upon the track of a villainous Covenanter. Then we would spur our horses to the gallop and give chase: and what a dance these hill-men could lead us. Some of them had the speed of hares and could leap like young deer over boulders and streams where no horse could follow. Many a sturdy nag crashed to the ground, flinging its rider who had spurred it to the impossible; and if the fugitive succeeded in reaching the vast open spaces of the moorland, many a good horse floundered in the bogs to the great danger of its master, while the fleet-footed Covenanter, who knew every inch of the ground, would leap from tussock to tussock of firm grass, and far out-distance us.

Or again, we would learn that someone—a suspect—was hiding upon the moors, and for days we would search, quartering and requartering the great stretches of heather and bog-land till we were satisfied that our quarry had eluded us—or until, as often happened, we found him. Sometimes it was an old man, stricken with years, so that he could not take to flight: sometimes it was a mere stripling—a lad of my own age—surrounded in his sleep and taken ere he could flee. The measure of justice meted to each was the same.

"Will ye tak' the Test?" If not—death, on the vacant moor, at the hands of men who were at once his accusers, his judges, and his executioners.

Sometimes when a fugitive had refused the Test, and so proclaimed himself a Covenanter, Lag would promise him his life if he would disclose the whereabouts of some others of more moment than himself. But never did I know one of them play the coward: never did I hear one betray another. Three minutes to prepare himself for death: and he would take his bonnet off and turn a fearless face up to the open sky.

And then Lag's voice—breaking in upon the holy silence of the moorland like a clap of thunder in a cloudless sky—"Musketeers! Poise your muskets! make ready: present, give fire!" and another rebel would fall dead among the heather.

The scene used to sicken me, so that I could hardly keep my seat in the saddle, and in my heart I thanked God that I was judged too unskilful as yet to be chosen as one of the firing party. That, of course, was nothing more than sentiment. These men were rebels, opposed to the King's Government, and such malignant fellows well deserved their fate. Yet there began to spring up within me some admiration for their bravery. Not one of them was afraid to die.

Sometimes, of a night, before sleep came to me, I would review the events of the day—not willingly, for the long and grisly tale of horror was one that no man would of set purpose dwell upon, but because in my soul I had begun to doubt the quality of the justice we meted out. It was a dangerous mood for one who had sworn allegiance to the King, and taken service under his standard: but I found myself beginning to wonder whether the people whom we were harrying so mercilessly and putting to death with as little compunction as though they had been reptiles instead of hard-working and thrifty folk—as their little farms and houses proved—were rebels in any real sense. I had no knowledge, as yet, of what had gone before, and I was afraid to ask any of my fellows, lest my questioning should bring doubt upon my own loyalty. But I wondered why these men, some gone far in eld and others in the morning of their days, were ready to die rather than say the few words that would give them life and liberty. Gradually the light broke through the darkness of my thoughts, and I began to understand that in their bearing there was something more than mere disloyalty to the King. They died unflinching, because they were loyal to some ideal that was more precious to them than life, and which torture and the prospect of death could not make them forswear. Were they wrong? Who was I, to judge? I knew nothing of their history, and when first I set out with Lag's Horse I cared as little. I had ridden forth to do battle against rebels. I found myself one of a band engaged in the hideous task of exercising duress upon other men's consciences. The thought was not a pleasant one, and I tried to banish it, but it would come back to me in the still watches when no sound was audible but the heavy breathing of my sleeping companions,—and no sophistry sufficed to stifle it.

Day after day we continued our march westward through Galloway, leaving behind us a track of burning homesteads, with here and there a stark figure, supine, with a bloody gash in his breast, and a weary face turned up to the eternal sky. The sky was laughing in the May sunshine: the blue hyacinths clustered like a low-lying cloud of peat-smoke in the woods by the roadside, and the larks cast the gold of their song into the sea of the air beneath them. The whole earth was full of joy and beauty ; but where we passed, we left desolation, and blood and tears.

As the sun was setting we rode down the valley of the Cree, whose peat-dyed water, reddened by the glare in the sky, spoke silently of the blood-stained moors which it had traversed in its course. A river of blood : a fitting presage of the duties of the morrow that had brought us to Wigtown!

CHAPTER III

BY BLEDNOCH WATER

SHARP and clear rang out the bugle notes of the reveille, rending the morning stillness that brooded over the thatched houses of Wigtown. We tumbled out of our beds of straw in the old barn where we had bivouacked—some with a curse on their lips at such a rude awakening, and others with hearts heavy at the thought of what lay before us. To hunt hill-men among the boulders and the sheltering heather of their native mountains was one thing: for the hunted man had a fox's chance, and more than a fox's cunning: but it was altogether another thing to execute judgment on two defenceless women, and only the most hardened among us had any stomach for such devil's work. Inured to scenes of brutality as I had become, I felt ill at ease when I remembered the task that awaited us, and, in my heart, I nursed the hope that, when the bugle sounded the assembly, we should learn that the prisoners had been reprieved and that we could shake the dust of Wigtown from our feet forever.

It was a glorious morning: and I can still remember, as though it were yesterday, every little event of these early hours. I shook the straw from my coat and went out. There was little sign of life in the street except for the dragoons hurrying about their tasks. My horse, tethered where I had left him the night before, whinnied a morning greeting as I drew near. He was a creature of much understanding, and as I patted his neck and gentled him, he rubbed his nose against my tunic. I undid his halter and with a hand on his fore-lock led him to the watering trough. The clear water tumbled musically into the trough from a red clay pipe that led to some hidden spring; and as my nag bent his neck and dipped his muzzle delicately into the limpid coolness, I watched a minnow dart under the cover of the green weed on the trough-bottom. When I judged he had drunk enough I threw a leg over his back and cantered down the street to the barn where we had slept. There, I slipped the end of his halter through a ring in the wall, and rejoined my companions who were gathered round the door.

We had much to do; there was harness to polish, bridles and bits to clean, and weapons to see to—for Sir Robert was a man vigilant, who took a pride in the smartness of his troop.

"It's a bonnie mornin' for an ugly ploy," said Trooper Agnew, as I sat down on a bench beside him with my saddle on my knees. From his tone I could tell that his heart was as little in the day's work as mine.

"Ay, it's a bonnie morning," I replied, "too bonnie for the work we have to do. I had fain the day was over, and the work were done, if done it must be."

"Weel, ye never can tell: it may be that the women will be reprieved. I've heard tell that Gilbert Wilson has muckle siller, and is ready to pay ransom for his dochter: an' siller speaks when arguments are waste o' wind." He spat on a polishing rag, and rubbed his saddle vigorously. "They tell me he's bocht Aggie off: and if he can he'll buy off Marget tae. But there's the auld woman Lauchlison: she has neither siller nor frien's wi' siller, and I'm fearin' that unless the Royal Clemency comes into play she'll ha'e tae droon."

" But why should they drown ? " said I, voicing half unconsciously the question that had so often perplexed me.

" Weel, that's a hard question," replied Agnew, as he burnished his bit, " and a question that's no for the like o' you and me to settle. A' we ha'e to dae is to carry oot the orders of our superior officers. We maunna think ower muckle for oorsel's."

I was already well acquainted with this plausible argument, and indeed I had heard Lag himself justify some of his acts by an appeal to such dogma ; but I was not satisfied, and ventured to remonstrate :

" Must we," I asked, " do things against which our conscience rebels, simply because we are commanded to do so ? "

Agnew hesitated for a moment before replying, passing the end of his bridle very deliberately through a buckle, and fastening it with care.

" Conscience ! " he said, and laughed. " What richt has a trooper to sic' a thing ? I've nane noo." He lowered his voice—and spoke quickly. " Conscience, my lad ! Ye'd better no' let the sergeant hear ye speak that word, or he'll be reporting ye tae Sir Robert for a Covenanter, and ye'll get gey short shrift, I'm thinkin'. Tak' the advice o' ane that means ye nae ill, and drap yer conscience in the water o' Blednoch, and say farewell tae it forever. If ye keep it, ye'll get mair blame than praise frae it—and I'm thinkin' ye'll no' get ony promotion till ye're weel rid o't."

" Whit's this I hear aboot conscience ? " said Davidson, a dragoon who was standing by the door of the barn.

" Oh, naething," said Agnew. " I was just advising Bryden here to get rid o' his."

" Maist excellent advice," said Davidson. " A puir trooper has nae richt to sic a luxury. Besides, it's a burden, and wi' a' his trappings he has eneuch to carry already." He paused for a moment—looked into the barn over his shoulder and continued: "To my way o' thinkin', naebody has ony richt to a conscience but the King. Ye see it's this way. A trooper maun obey his officers: he has nae richt o' private judgment, so he has nae work for his conscience to do. His officers maun obey them that are higher up—so they dinna need a conscience, and so it goes on, up, and up till ye reach the King, wha is the maister o' us a'. He's the only body in the realm that can afford the luxury: and even he finds it a burden."

"I'm no surprised," interjected Agnew. "A conscience like that maun be an awfu' encumbrance."

"Ay, so it is," replied Davidson. "They do say that the King finds it sic a heavy darg to look after his conscience that he appoints a man to be its keeper."

Agnew laughed. "Does he lead it about on a chain like a dog?" he asked.

"I canna tell you as to that," replied Davidson, "but it's mair than likely, for it maun be a rampageous sort o' beast whiles."

"And what if it breaks away," asked Agnew, laughing again, "and fleshes its teeth in the King's leg?"

"Man," said Davidson, "ye remind me: the very thing ye speak o' aince happened. Nae doot the keeper is there to haud back his conscience frae worrying the King, but I mind readin' that ane o' the keepers didna haud the beast in ticht eneuch, and it bit the King. It had something to dae wi' a wumman. I've forgotten the partic'lers: but I think the King was auld King Hal."

"And what happened to the keeper?" asked Agnew.

"Oh, him," replied Davidson. "The King chopped his heid off. And that, or something like it, is what will happen to you, my lad," he said, looking meaningly at me, "if Lag hears ye talk ony sic nonsense. If thae damnable Covenanters didna nurse their consciences like sickly bairns they would be a bit mair pliable, and gi'e us less work."

I would gladly have continued the conversation, but we were interrupted by the appearance of the cook, who came round the corner of the barn staggering under the weight of a huge black pot full of our morning porridge.

"Parritch, lads, wha's for parritch?" he called, setting down his load, and preparing to serve out our portions with a large wooden ladle. We filed past him each with our metal platter and a horn spoon in our hands, and received a generous ladleful. The regimental cook is always fair game for the would-be wit, and our cook came in for his share of chaff; but he was ready of tongue, and answered jibe with jibe—some of his retorts stinging like a whip-lash so that his tormentors were sore and sorry that they had challenged him.

Soon the last man was served and all of us fell to.

When our meal was over there was little time left ere the assembly sounded. As the bugle notes blared over the village, we flung ourselves into our saddles, and at the word turned our horses up the village street. The clatter of hoofs, and the jingle of creaking harness brought the folks to their doors, for the appeal of mounted men is as old as the art of war. We were conscious of admiring glances from many a lassie's eye, and some of the roysterers among us, behind the back of authority, gave back smile for smile, and threw furtive kisses to the comelier of the women-folk.

Near the Tolbooth Sir Robert awaited us, sitting his horse motionless like a man cut out of stone. A sharp word of command, and we reined our horses in, wheeling and forming a line in front of the Tolbooth door. There we waited.

By and by we heard the tramp of horses, and Colonel Winram at the head of his company rode down the other side of the street and halted opposite to us. Winram and Lag dismounted, giving their horses into the charge of their orderlies, and walked together to the Tolbooth door. They knocked loudly, and after a mighty clatter of keys and shooting of bolts the black door swung back, and they passed in. We waited long, but still there was no sign of their return. My neighbour on the right, whose horse was champing its bit and tossing its head in irritation, whispered: "They maun ha'e been reprievit."

"Thank God for that," I said, out of my heart.

But it was not to be. With a loud creak, as though it were in pain, the door swung open, and there came forth, splendid in his robes of office, Sheriff Graham. Followed him, Provost Coltran, Grier of Lag, and Colonel Winram. Behind them, each led by a gaoler, came two women. Foremost was Margaret Lauchlison, bent with age, and leaning on a stick, her thin grey hair falling over her withered cheeks. She did not raise her eyes to look at us, but I saw that her lips were moving silently, and a great pity surged up in my breast and gripped me by the throat. Some four paces behind her came Margaret Wilson, and as she passed out of the darkness of the door she raised her face to the sky and took a long breath of the clean morning air. She was straight as a willow-wand, with a colour in her cheeks like red May-blossom, and a brave look in her blue eyes. Her brown hair glinted in the sunlight, and she walked with a steady step between the ranks of horsemen like a queen going to her coronal. She looked curiously at the troopers as she passed us. I watched her coming, and, suddenly, her big child-like eyes met mine, and for very shame I hung my head.

Some twenty yards from the Tolbooth door, beside the Town Cross, the little procession halted, and the town-crier, after jangling his cracked bell, mounted the lower step at the base of the cross and read from a big parchment:

"God save the King! Whereas Margaret Lauchlison, widow of John Mulligan, wright in Drumjargon, and Margaret Wilson, daughter of Gilbert Wilson, farmer in Penninghame, were indicted on April 13th, in the year of grace 1685 before Sheriff Graham, Sir Robert Grierson of Lag, Colonel Winram, and Captain Strachan, as being guilty of the Rebellion of Bothwell Brig, Aird's Moss, twenty field Conventicles, and twenty house Conventicles, the Assize did sit, and after witnesses heard did bring them in guilty, and the judges sentenced them to be tied to palisadoes fixed in the sand, within the floodmark of the sea, and there to stand till the flood overflows them. The whilk sentence, being in accordance with the law of this Kingdom, is decreed to be carried out this day, the 11th of May in the year of grace 1685. God Save the King."

When he ceased there was silence for a space, and then Grier of Lag, his sword scraping the gravel as he moved, walked up to the older prisoner, and shouted:

"Margaret Lauchlison, will ye recant?"

She raised her head, looked him in the eyes with such a fire in hers that his gaze fell before it, and in a steady voice replied:

"Goodness and mercy ha'e followed me a' the days o' my life, and I'm no' gaun back on my Lord in the hour o' my death,"—and she bowed her head again, as though there was nothing more to be said, but her lips kept moving silently.

Lag turned from her with a shrug of the shoulders, and approached the younger prisoner. She turned her head to meet him with a winsome smile that would have softened a heart less granite hard; but to him her beauty made no appeal.

"Margaret Wilson," he said, "you have heard your sentence. Will ye recant?"

I can still hear her reply:

"Sir, I count it a high honour to suffer for Christ's truth. He alone is King and Head of His Church."

It was a brave answer, but it was not the answer that Lag required, so he turned on his heel and rejoined the Sheriff and the Provost. I did not hear what passed between them, but it was not to the advantage of the prisoners, for the next moment I saw that the gaoler was fastening the old woman's left wrist to the stirrup leather of one of the troopers who had been ordered to bring his horse up nearer the Town Cross. Many a time since I have wondered whether it was ill-luck or good fortune that made them hit on me to do such a disservice for Margaret Wilson. It may have been nothing more than blind chance, or it may have been the act of Providence—I am no theologian, and have never been able to settle these fine points—but, at a word from Lag, her gaoler brought the girl over beside me, and shackled her wrist to my stirrup leather. I dared not look at her face, but I saw her hand, shapely and brown, close round the stirrup leather as though she were in pain when the gaoler tightened the thong.

"Curse you," I growled, "there's no need to cut her hand off. She'll not escape," and I would fain have hit the brute over the head with the butt of my musket. He slackened the thong a trifle, and as he slouched off I was conscious that my prisoner looked up at me as though to thank me: but I dared not meet her eyes, and she spoke no word.

There was a rattle of drums, and we wheeled into our appointed places, and began our woeful journey to the sea. Heading our procession walked two halberdiers, their weapons glistening above their heads. Followed them the Sheriff and the Provost: and after these Winram and the troopers in two lines, between which walked the prisoners. Lag rode behind on his great black horse. It was a brave sight for the old town of Wigtown—but a sight of dule.

Down the street we went, but this time there were no glances of admiration cast upon us: nothing but silent looks of awe, touched with pity. Ahead I saw anxious mothers shepherding their children into the shelter of their doors, and when we came near them I could see that some of the children and many of the women were weeping. I dared not look Margaret Wilson in the face, but I let my eyes wander to her hair, brown and lustrous in the sunshine. My hand on the reins was moist, my lips were dry, and I cursed myself that ever I had thrown in my lot with such a horde of murderers. Agnew's words about conscience kept ringing in my ears, and I felt them sear my brain. Conscience indeed! What kind of conscience had I, that I could take part in such a devilish ploy? If I had had the courage of a rabbit I would have swung the girl up before me, set spurs to my horse, broken from the line and raced for life. But I was a coward. I had no heart for such high adventure, and many a time since, as I have lain in the dark before the cock-crowing, I have been tortured by remorse for the brave good thing I was too big a craven to attempt.

The procession wound slowly on, then wheeled to the left and descended to the river bank. I believe the Blednoch has altered its course since that day.

I have never had the heart to revisit the scene, but men tell me so. Then, it flowed into the sea over a long stretch of brown sand just below the town. It was neither broad, nor yet very deep: but when the tide of Solway was at its full it flooded all the sand banks, and filled the river-mouth so that the river water was dammed back, and it became a broad stream.

Far out on the sand I saw a stake planted: and another some thirty paces nearer shore. They led the old woman, weary with her walk, to the farther stake, and tying her to it left her there. Down the channel one could see the tide coming in—its brown and foam-sprinkled front raised above the underlying water. Cruel it looked, like some questing wild beast raising its head to spy out its prey. A halberdier came and severed the thong that fastened Margaret Wilson to my stirrup leather, and led her away. My eyes followed her, and as she passed my horse's head she looked at me over her shoulder and our eyes met. I shall see those eyes until the Day of Judgment: blue as the speedwell—blue, and unafraid.

They led her to the nearer stake, and bound her there. There was a kind of mercy in their cruelty, for they thought that if the younger woman should witness the death of the elder one she might be persuaded to recant before she herself was engulfed. Quickly, as is its wont, the Solway tide rushed over the sand. Before Margaret Wilson was fastened to the stake, the water was knee-deep where Margaret Lauchlison stood: and soon it was at the maiden's feet. As the first wave touched her there was a murmur like a groan from some of the town folk who had followed us and stood behind us in little knots upon the river bank. The tide flowed on, mounting higher and higher, until old Margaret Lauchlison stood waist deep in a swirl of tawny water. She was too far out for us to hear her if she spoke, but we could see that she had raised her head and was looking fearlessly over the water. And then the younger woman did a strange thing. Out of the fold of her gown over her bosom she drew a little book, opened it and read aloud. A hush fell upon us: and our horses, soothed by the music of her voice, stopped their head-tossing and were still. She read so clearly that all of us could hear, and there was a proud note in her voice as she ended: "For I am persuaded that neither death, nor life, nor angels, nor principalities, nor powers, nor things present, nor things to come, nor height, nor depth, nor any other creature, shall be able to separate us from the love of God, which is in Christ Jesus our Lord." Then she kissed the open page, and returned her testament to her bosom, and in a moment burst into song:

"My sins and faults of youth
Do Thou, O Lord, forget!
After Thy mercy think on me,
And for Thy goodness great."

She sang like a bird, her clear notes soaring up to the blue vault of heaven, out of the depths of a heart untouched by fear. I heard Agnew, who was ranged next me, mutter "This is devil's work," but my throat was too parched for speech. Would she never cease? On and on went that pure young voice, singing verse after verse till the psalm was finished. When she had ended the tide was well about her waist, and had already taken Margaret Lauchlison by the throat.

"What see ye yonder, Marget Wilson?" shouted Lag, pointing with his sword to the farther stake.

She looked for a moment, and answered: "I see Christ wrestling there."

Then there was a great silence, and looking out to

sea we saw a huge wave sweep white-crested over the head of the older woman, who bent to meet it, and was no more seen. The law had taken its course with her.

There was a murmur of angry voices behind us, but a stern look from Lag silenced the timorous crowd. Setting spurs to his horse he plunged into the water, and drew up beside the nearer stake. He severed the rope that bound the girl, whereat a cheer rose from the townsfolk who imagined that the law had relented and that its majesty was satisfied with the death of one victim. He turned his horse and dragged the girl ashore. As they reached the bank, he flung her from him and demanded:

"Will ye take the oath? Will ye say 'God Save the King?'"

"God save him an He will," she said. "I wish the salvation of all men, and the damnation of none."

Now to my thinking that was an answer sufficient, and for such the town folk took it, for some of them cried: "She's said it! She's said it! She's saved!"

Lag turned on them like a tiger: "Curse ye," he shouted, "for a pack o' bletherin' auld wives! The hizzy winna' recant. Back intil the sea wi' her," and gripping her by the arm he dragged her back, and with his own hands fastened her again to the stake. Her head fell forward so that for an instant her face lay upon the waters, then she raised it proudly again. But a halberdier, with no pity in his foul heart, reached out his long halberd, and placing the blade of it upon her neck pushed her face down into the sea.

"Tak' anither sup, hinny," he said, and leered at the townsfolk: but they cried shame upon him and Lag bade him desist.

On came the waters, wave after wave, mounting steadily till they reached her heart: then they swept over the curve of her bosom and mounted higher and higher till they touched her neck. She was silent now—silent, but unafraid. She turned her face to the bank, and, O wonder, she smiled, and in her eyes there was a mystic light as though she had seen the Invisible. The cruel waves came on, climbing up the column of her throat until, as though to show her a mercy which man denied her, the sea swirled over her and her face fell forward beneath the waves. Her brown hair floated on the water like a piece of beautiful sea-wrack, and the broken foam clung to it like pearls. Justice—God forgive the word—justice had been done: and two women, malignant and dangerous to the realm because they claimed the right to worship their Maker according to the dictates of their conscience, had been lawfully done to death.

There was a rattle of drums, and we fell into rank again. I looked across the water. Far off I saw a gull flash like a streak of silver into the waves, and near at hand, afloat upon the water, a wisp of brown seaweed—or was it a lassie's hair?

CHAPTER IV

THE TAVERN BRAWL

It was high noon as we clattered up the hill, back to our camping-place. Our day's work was done, but it was not till evening that we were free to go about our own affairs. Try as I might I could not blot out the memory of the doings of the morning, and when night fell I took my way with half a dozen companions to the inn that stood not far from the Tolbooth in the hope that there I might find some relief from the scourge of my thoughts. In the sanded kitchen, round a glowing fire—for though it was May the nights were still chilly—we found many of the towns-folk already gathered. Some were passing a patient hour with the dambrod, seeking inspiration for crafty moves of the black or white men in tankards of the tavern-keeper's ale. Others were gathered round the fire smoking, each with a flagon of liquor at his elbow.

I sat down at a little table with Trooper Agnew, and called for something to drink. I was in no mood for amusement, and spurned Agnew's suggestion that we should play draughts. The inn-keeper placed a tobacco jar between us.

"Ye'll try a smoke?" he queried. "It's guid tobacco: a' the better, though I hardly daur mention it, that it paid nae duty."

Nothing loth, Agnew and I filled our pipes, and the inn-keeper picking up a piece of red peat with the tongs held it to our pipes till they were aglow. It was, as mine host had said, good tobacco, and under its soothing influence and the brightening effect of his ale my gloom began to disappear. From time to time other troopers dropped in, and they were followed by sundry of the townsfolk with whom, in spite of the events of the morning, we red-coat men were on good terms. Close by the fire sat one of the halberdiers—the man who had pushed the head of the drowning girl under the water with his halberd. The ale had loosened his tongue.

"I dinna ken," he said, "but the thing lies here: if thae stiff-necked Covenanters winna' tak' the oath to the King, it is the end o' a' proper order in the country." He spat a hissing expectoration upon the glowing peat. "I'm a man o' order masel'. I expect fowk to obey me in virtue o' ma office just as I'm ready to obey them as God and the King ha'e set abune me."

He spoke loudly as though challenging his audience; but no one made answer.

The silence was broken by the clatter of draughts as two players ended a game and set about replacing the men for another joust. The halberdier took a long draught from his mug.

"Tak' anither sup, hinny," he said, reminiscently, as he set the tankard down. Then drawing the back of his hand across his mouth he continued: "It was a fine bit work we did this mornin', lads. I rarely ta'en pairt in a better job. There's naethin' like making an example o' malignants, and I'm thinkin' it will be lang before ony mair o' the women o' this countryside are misguided enough to throw in their lot wi' the hill-preachers. She was a thrawn auld besom was Marget Lauchlison. I have kent her mony a year—aye psalm-singing and gabbling texts. Will ye believe it, she's even flung texts at me. Me! the toon's halberdier! 'The wicked shall fall by his own wickedness,' said she: 'The wicked shall be turned into Hell'; 'The dwelling place of the wicked shall come to naught.' Oh, she had a nesty tongue. But noo she's cleppin' wi' the partans, thank God. Here, Mac, fill me anither jorum. It tak's a lot o' yill tae wash the taste o' the auld besom's texts off ma tongue."

The inn-keeper placed a full tankard beside him.

"Tak' anither sup, hinny," he said with a laugh, and drank deeply. "Lag was by-ordnar' the day; I thocht he was gaun to let the bit lassock off when he dragged her oot o' the water. But nae sic thing, thank God! Ma certes, he's a through-gaun chiel, Lag. The women-fowk thocht she had ta'en the aith when she said 'God save him, an He will.' But Lag kent fine what was in her black heart. She wanted only to save her life. She was far better drooned—the young rebel! Naethin' like makin' an example o' them when they are young. Certes, I settled her. Tak' anither sup, hinny."

A peal of laughter rang through the kitchen. It was more than I could stand; for notwithstanding all I had seen and done as a trooper some spark of chivalry still glowed in my heart, and I was under the spell of her blue and dauntless eyes. I sprang to my feet.

"Curse you for a black-hearted ruffian!" I shouted. "None but a damned cur would make sport of two dead women."

A silence absolute and cold fell upon the gathering at my first words, and as I stood there I felt it oppress me.

"Whit's this, whit's this," cried the halberdier. "A trooper turned Covenanter! I'm thinkin' Lag and Winram will ha'e something to say to this, an they hear o't."

" Be silent ! " I thundered. " I am no Covenanter, but it would be good for Scotland if there were more such women as we drowned this morning, and fewer men with such foul hearts as yours."

It was an ill-judged place and time for such a speech, but I was on fire with anger. The halberdier rose to his feet, flung the contents of his tankard in my face, roared with laughter, and cried, " Tak' anither sup, hinny."

This was beyond endurance. With one leap I was upon him and hurled him to the ground. He fell with a crash ; his head struck the flagged floor with a heavy thud, and he lay still. I had fallen with him, and as I rose I received a blow which flung me down again. In an instant, as though a match had been set to a keg of powder, the tavern was in an uproar. What but a moment before had been a personal conflict between myself and the halberdier had waxed into a general mêlée.

Some joined battle on my side, others were against me, and townsmen and troopers laid about them wildly with fists, beer-pots, and any other weapons to which they could lay their hands. The clean sanded floor became a mire of blood and tumbled ale, in which wallowed a tangle of cursing, fighting men.

Just when the fray was at its hottest the door of the kitchen was thrown open, and the sergeant of our troop stood in its shadow.

" What's this ? " he shouted, and, as though by magic, the combat ceased.

None of us spoke, but the inn-keeper, finding speech at last, said : " A maist unseemly row, sergeant, begun by ane o' your ain men, wha wi' oot provocation felled ma frien' the halberdier wha lies yonder a'maist deid."

The sergeant strode to the body of the halberdier and dropped on his knees beside it.

"What lousy deevil has done this?" he cried.

"The Englishman," said the inn-keeper; "Nae Scotsman would ha'e felled sic a decent man unprovoked."

I looked at the halberdier, and saw with relief that he was beginning to recover from his stupor.

"Fetch us a gill o' your best, Mac," said the sergeant. "We'll see if a wee drap o' Blednoch will no' bring the puir fellow roon'. And you, Agnew, and MacTaggart, arrest Trooper Bryden. Lag will ha'e somethin' to say aboot this."

Agnew and MacTaggart laid each a hand on my shoulder, but my gorge was up and I resented being made a prisoner. I looked towards the door; there were four or five troopers in a knot beside it and escape in that direction was impossible; but behind me there was a stair. One sudden wrench and I tore myself from my captors and raced wildly up it. At the top, a door stood open. I flung it to in the faces of Agnew and MacTaggart, who were racing up behind me, and shot the bolt. Frail though it was, this barrier would give me a moment's respite. I found myself in an attic room, and to my joy saw, in the light of the moon, a window set in the slope of the roof. Rapidly I forced it open, and threw myself up and out upon the thatched roof. In a moment I was at its edge, and dropped into the garden at the back of the inn. As I dropped I heard the door at the stair-head crash and I knew that my pursuers would soon be upon me. Crouching low I dashed to the bottom of the garden, broke my way through the prickly hedge and flew hot-foot down the hill.

In the fitful light I saw the gleam of the river, and knew that my escape was barred in that direction. I saw that I must either run along the brae-face towards the sea, or inland up-river to the hills. As I ran I came to a quick decision and chose the latter course. I glanced over my shoulder, and, though I could see by the lights in their windows the houses in the main street of the town, I could not distinguish any pursuers. Behind me I heard confused shoutings, and the loud voice of the sergeant giving orders. Breathless, I plunged into a thick growth of bracken on the hill-side and lay still. I knew that this could afford me only a temporary refuge, but it served to let me regain breath, and as I lay there I heard the sergeant cry: "Get lanterns and quarter the brae-side. He canna ford the water."

I lay in my hiding-place until the lights of the lanterns began to appear at the top of the brae, then I rose stealthily and, bent double, hurried to the edge of the bed of brackens. Here, I knew, I was sufficiently distant from my nearest pursuer to be outside his vision, while his twinkling light gave me the clue to his whereabouts. Then I turned and tore along the hillside away from the town. When I had covered what I thought was the better part of a mile, I lay down under the cover of a granite boulder. Far behind me I could see the wandering lights, and I knew that for the moment I had outdistanced my pursuers; and then to my great relief I heard the notes of the Last Post rise and fall upon the night air. I smiled as I saw the scattered lights stop, then begin to move compactly up the hill. At least half an hour, I judged, must elapse before the pursuit could be renewed, and I felt with any luck that interval ought to suffice for my escape. It was too dark—and I was not sufficiently acquainted with the country-side—to take my bearings, but I knew that the river Cree flowed past the town of Newton-Stewart, and behind the town were the hills which had afforded many a Covenanter a safe hiding-place from pursuit. Caution prevented me from making for the high road, though the speed of my progress might there be greater. Caution, too, forbade my keeping to the brink of the river. My greatest safety seemed to lie along the tract between them, so I set boldly out.

CHAPTER V

IN THE DARK OF THE NIGHT

I HAD not gone far when my ears caught a familiar sound—the beat of hoofs on the high road. I paused to listen, and concluded that two horsemen were making for Newton-Stewart. I guessed the message they carried, and I knew that not only was I likely to have pursuers on my heels, but that, unless I walked warily, I was in danger of running into a cordon of troopers who would be detailed from Newton-Stewart to search for me. I was a deserter, to whom Lag would give as little quarter as to a Covenanter. The conviction that there was a price on my head made me suddenly conscious of the sweetness of life, and drove me to sudden thought.

By some means or other, before I concealed myself in the fastnesses of the hills, I must obtain a store of food. The hiding Covenanter, I remembered, was fed by his friends. I was friendless; and unless I could manage to lay up some store of food before I forsook the inhabited valleys nothing but death awaited me among the hills. As I thought of this, an inspiration of courage came to me. Though it would be foolishness to walk along the high road I might with advantage make better speed and possibly find a means of obtaining food if I walked just beyond the hedge which bordered it. Sooner or later I should in this way come to a roadside inn. With this thought encouraging me, I plodded steadily on. The highway was deserted, and no sound was to be heard but the muffled beat of my own steps upon the turf. If pursuers were following me from Wigtown, I had left them far behind. It might be that Lag, thinking shrewdly, had decided that no good purpose was to be served by continuing the pursuit that night, for he knew that a man wandering at large in the uniform of a trooper would have little opportunity of escaping. So, possibly, he had contented himself by sending the horsemen to Newton-Stewart to apprise the garrison there. Perhaps at this very moment he was chuckling over his cups as he thought how he would lay me by the heels on the morrow. In fancy I could see the furrows on his brow gather in a knot as he brooded over my punishment.

Then, borne on the still night air, I heard the click and clatter of uncertain footsteps coming towards me. I crouched behind the hedge and peered anxiously along the road: then my ears caught the sound of a song. The wayfarer was in a jovial mood, and I judged, from the uncertainty of his language, that he was half-drunk. I waited to make sure that the man was alone, then I stole through the hedge and walked boldly to meet him.

"It is a fine night," I said, as I came abreast of him. He stopped in the middle of a stave and looked me up and down.

"Aye, it's a fine nicht," he replied. "Nane the waur for a drap o' drink. Here! Tak' a dram, an pledge the King's health." He searched his pockets and after some difficulty withdrew a half-empty bottle from the inside of his coat and offered it to me. "The King, God bless him," I said, as I put it to my lips.

"It's a peety ye're no' traivellin' my road," said the wayfarer. "A braw young callant like you wi' the King's uniform on his back would mak' a graun convoy for an auld man alang this lanely road."

"No," I answered, as I handed him his bottle, "My way lies in another direction."

"Ye'll no' happen to be ane o' Lag's men, are ye ?" He did not await my reply, but continued : "He's a bonnie deevil, Lag ! He kens the richt medicine for Covenanters : but I ken the richt medicine for Jock Tamson," and putting the bottle to his lips he drank deep and long. Then he staggered to the side of the road and sat down, and holding the bottle towards me said : "Sit doon and gi'es yer crack."

Now I had no wish to be delayed by this half-drunken countryman ; but I thought that he might be of service to me, so I seated myself and pretended once again to take a deep draught from his bottle. He snatched it from my lips.

"Haud on," he said, "ye've got a maist uncanny drouth, and that bottle maun last me till Setterday."

"Unless you leave it alone," I said, "it will be empty ere you reach home."

"Weel, what if it is ?" he hiccoughed. "The Lord made guid drink and I'm no' the man to spurn the mercies o' the Creator."

"Well," I said, "your drink is good, and I'm as dry as ashes. Can you tell me where I can get a bottle."

"Oh, weel I can, an' if ye're minded to gang and see Luckie Macmillan, I'll gi'e ye a convoy. The guid woman'll be bedded sine, but she'll rise tae see to ony frien' o' Jock Tamson's. Come on, lad," and he raised himself unsteadily to his feet and, taking me by the arm, began to retrace his steps in the direction from which he came.

We followed the high road for perhaps a mile, and as we went he rambled on in good-natured but somewhat incoherent talk, stopping every now and then while he laid hold of my arm and tapped my chest with the fingers of his free hand to emphasise some empty confidence. He had imparted to me, as a great secret, some froth of gossip, when he exclaimed:

"Weel: here we are at Luckie's loanin' and the guid-wife is no' in her bed yet; I can see a licht in the window."

We turned from the high road and went down the lane, at the bottom of which I could discern the dark outline of a cottage. As we drew near I was startled by the sound of a restless horse pawing the ground and, quick in its wake, the jangle of a bridle chain. A few more steps and I saw two horses tethered to the gatepost, and their harness was that of the dragoons. I was walking into the lion's den!

"So Luckie's got company, guid woman," hiccoughed my companion. "I hope it's no' the gaugers."

I seized on the suggestion in hot haste:

"Wheesht, man," I hissed, "they are gaugers sure enough, and if you are caught here with a bottle of Luckie's best, you'll be up before Provost Coltran at the next Session in Wigtown."

"Guid help us! an' me a God-fearin' man. Let's rin for't."

As he spoke, the door of the cottage was thrown open and in the light from it I saw one of the troopers. Placing a firm hand over my companion's mouth I dragged him into the shadow of the hedge, and pushing him before me wormed my way through to its other side.

Here we lay, still and silent, while I, with ears alert, heard the troopers vault into their saddles and with a cheery "Good night, Luckie," clatter up the lane to the high road to continue their way to Newton-Stewart.

We lay hidden till the noise of their going died in

the distance, then we pushed our way back through the hedge and made for the cottage. Jock beat an unsteady tattoo on the door.

"Wha's knockin' at this time o' nicht ?" asked a woman's voice from behind the door.

"Jock Tamson, Luckie, wi' a frien'."

"Jock Tamson !—he's awa' hame to his bed an 'oor sin'."

"Na, Luckie, it's me richt eneuch, and I've brocht a frien', a braw laddie in the King's uniform, to see ye."

The King's uniform seemed to act as a charm, for the door was at once thrown open and we entered.

With a fugitive's caution I lingered to see that the old woman closed the door and barred it. Then, following the uncertain light of the tallow candle which she carried, we made our way along the sanded floor of the passage and passed through a low door into a wide kitchen. Peat embers still glowed on the hearth, and when Luckie had lit two more candles which stood in bottles on a long deal table I was able to make some note of my surroundings. Our hostess was a woman far gone in years. Her face was expressionless, as though set in a mould, but from beneath the shadow of her heavy eyebrows gleamed a pair of piercing eyes that age had not dimmed. She moved slowly with shuffling gait, half-bowed as though pursuing something elusive which she could not catch. I noticed, too, for danger had quickened my vision, that her right hand and arm were never still.

She stooped over the hearth and casting fresh peats upon it said: "And what's yer pleesure, gentlemen ?"

"A bottle o' Blednoch, Luckie, a wheen soda scones and a whang o' cheese ; and dinna forget the butter—we're fair famished," answered Jock, his words jostling each other. Our hostess brought a small table and set it before us, and we sat down. Very speedily, for one so old, Luckie brought our refreshment, and Thomson, seizing the black bottle, poured himself out a stiff glass, which he drank at a gulp. I helped myself to a moderate dram and set the bottle on the table between us. Thomson seized it at once and replenished his glass, and then said as he passed the bottle to the old woman:

"Will ye no tak' a drap, Luckie, for the guid o' the hoose?"

She shuffled to the dresser and came back with a glass which she filled.

"A toast," said Thomson. "The King, God bless him," and we stood up, and drank. The potent spirit burned my mouth like liquid fire, but my companions seemed to relish it as they drank deeply. I had no desire to dull my wits with strong drink, so, as I helped myself to a scone and a piece of cheese, I asked Luckie if she could let me have a little water.

"Watter!" cried Thomson. "Whit the deevil d'ye want wi' watter? Surely you're no' gaun to rot your inside wi' sic' feckless trash."

"No," I said, "I just want to let down the whisky."

"Whit!" he shouted, "spile guid Blednoch wi' pump watter!—it's a desecration, a fair abomination in the sicht o' the Lord. I thought frae yer brogue ye were an Englishman. This proves it; nae stammick for guid drink; nae heid for theology. Puir deevil!"—and he shook his head pityingly.

I laughed as I watched my insatiable companion once more empty his glass and refill it.

"An' whit are ye daein' on the road sae late the nicht, young man?" said Luckie, suddenly. "Lag's men are usually bedded long afore noo. Are ye after the deserter tae, like the twa dragoons that were here a bittock syne?"

I had made up my mind that my flight and identity would best be concealed by an appearance of ingenuous candour, so I replied without hesitation :

" Yes, I am. He has not been here to-night, has he ? "

" Certes, no," exclaimed the old woman. " This is a law-abiding hoose and I wad shelter neither Covenanter nor renegade King's man."

My words seemed to disarm her of any suspicion she might have had about me, and she busied herself stirring the peat fire.

Its warmth and the whisky which he had consumed were making Jock drowsy. He had not touched any of the food, and his chin had begun to sink on his chest. Soon he slipped from his seat and lay huddled, a snoring mass, on the flagged floor. Luckie made as though to lift him, but I forbade her.

" Let him be: he'll only be quarrelsome if you wake him, and he's quite safe on the floor."

" That's as may be," said Luckie, " but ye're no' gaun to stop a' nicht, or ye'll never catch the deserter, and ye canna leave Jock Tamson to sleep in my kitchen. I'm a dacint widda' woman, and nae scandal has ever soiled my name ; and I'll no' hae it said that ony man ever sleepit in my hoose, and me by my lane, since I buried my ain man thirty years sin'."

" That's all right," I replied, " have no fear. If Jock is not awake when I go, I'll carry him out and put him in the ditch by the roadside."

The old woman laughed quietly. " Fegs, that's no' bad ; he'll get the fricht o' his life when he waukens up in the cauld o' the mornin' and sees the stars abune him instead o' the bauks o' my kitchen."

I had been doing justice to the good fare of the house, but a look at the " wag-at-the-wa' " warned me that I must delay no longer. But there was something I must discover. I took my pipe from my pocket and as I filled it said: "I should think, Luckie, that you are well acquainted with this countryside."

"Naebody better," she replied. "I was born in Blednoch and I've spent a' my days between there and Penninghame Kirk. No' that I've bothered the kirk muckle," she added.

"Then," I said, "suppose a deserter was minded to make for the hills on the other side o' the Cree, where think you he would try to cross the river?"

"If he wisna a fule," she said, "he'd ford it juist ayont the Carse o' Bar. Aince he's ower it's a straicht road to the heichts o' Millfore."

"And where may the Carse o' Bar be?" I asked. "For unless I hurry, my man may be over the water before I can reach it."

"It's no' far," she said, "and ye canna miss it. Ony fule could see it in the dark."

"Well, I must be off," I said. "Grier o' Lag is no easy taskmaster and I must lay this man by the heels. I'll haste me and lie in wait by the Carse of Bar, and if my luck's in, I may catch him there. What do I owe you, and may I have some of your good scones and a bit of cheese to keep me going?"

She brought me a great plateful of scones, which I stowed about my person with considerable satisfaction; then I paid her what she asked, and, picking up Jock, bore him towards the door. He made no resistance, and his head fell limply over my arm as though he were a person dead, though the noise of his breathing was evidence sufficient that he was only very drunk. Luckie opened the door and stood by it with a candle in her hand. I carried Jock down the lane and deposited him underneath the hedge. Then I went back to the cottage to bid my hostess good night.

" If ye come through to the back door," she said, " I'll pit ye on the straicht road for the Carse o' Bar."

I followed her through the kitchen, and she opened a door at the rear of the house and stood in its shadow to let me pass.

" Gang richt doon the hill," she said, " and keep yon whin bush on yer left haun; syne ye'll come to a bed o' bracken,—keep that on yer richt and haud straicht on. By an' by ye'll strike the water edge. Haud up it till ye come to a bend, and that's the place whaur the deserter will maist likely try to cross it. Ony fule can ford the Cree; it tak's a wise body to ken whaur. Guid nicht to ye."

" Good night," I answered, as I set out, turning for a moment for a last look at the bent old woman as she stood in the dancing shadows thrown by the candle held in her shaking hand.

CHAPTER VI

IN THE LAP OF THE HILLS

As I set out I saw that the moon was rapidly sinking. Much time had been lost, and I must needs make haste. I hurried past the whin bush, and by-and-by came to the bed of brackens. Just as I reached it the moon sank, but there was still enough light to let me see dimly things near at hand. I judged that the river must lie about a mile away, and to walk that distance over unknown ground in the dark tests a man in a hundred ways. I did not know at what moment some lurking figure might spring upon me from the shelter of the brackens, and, clapping a hand on my shoulder, arrest me in the King's name. I had no weapon of defence save a stout heart and a pair of iron fists. Even a brave man, in flight, is apt to read into every rustle of a leaf or into every one of the natural sounds that come from the sleeping earth an eerie significance, and more than once I halted and crouched down to listen closely to some sound, which proved to be of no moment.

Conscience is a stern judge who speaks most clearly in the silences of the night when a man is alone, and as I groped my way onward the relentless pursuing voice spoke in my ear like some sibilant and clinging fury of which I could not rid myself. The avenger of blood was on my heels: some ghostly warlock, some awesome fiend sent from the pit to take me thither! The horror of the deed in which I had taken part in the morning gripped me by the heart. I stumbled on distraught, and as I went I remembered how once I had heard among the hills a shrill cry as of a child in pain, and looking to see whence the cry had come I saw dragging itself wearily along the hillside, with ears dropped back and hind-limbs paralysed with fear, a young rabbit, and as I looked I saw behind it a weasel trotting briskly, with nose up and gleaming eyes, in the track of its victim. I knew enough of wood-craft to realise that the chase had lasted long and that from the time the weasel began the pursuit until the moment when I saw them, the issue had been certain; and I knew that the rabbit knew. Such tricks of fancy does memory play upon a man in sore straits. I saw, again, the end of the chase—the flurry of fur as the weasel gripped the rabbit by the throat; I heard its dying cry as the teeth of its pursuer closed in the veins of its neck; and there in the dark, I was seized with sudden nausea. I drew a long breath and tried to cry aloud, but my tongue clave to the roof of my mouth; fear had robbed me of speech. Then a sudden access of strength came to me and I began to run. Was it only the fevered imaginings of a disordered brain, or was it fact, that to my racing feet the racing feet of some pursuer echoed and echoed again? Suddenly my foot struck a boulder. I was thrown headlong and lay bruised and breathless on the ground—and as I lay the sound of footsteps that had seemed so real to me was no more heard.

I was bruised by my fall and my limbs were still shaking when I struggled up, but I hurried on again, and by and by the tinkle of the river as it rippled over its bed fell on my ear like delicate, companionable music. When I reached its edge I sat down for a moment and peered into the darkness towards the other side; but gaze as I might I could not see across it. It looked dark and cold and uncertain, and though

I was a swimmer I had no desire to find myself flung suddenly out of my depth. So, before I took off my shoes and stockings, I cut a long wand from a willow near, and with this in my hand I began warily to adventure the passage. I stood ankle deep in the water and felt for my next step with my slender staff. It gave me no support, but it let me know with each step the depth that lay before me. By-and-by I reached the other side, and painfully—because of my naked feet—I traversed it until I came to the green sward beyond. Here I sat down in the shelter of a clump of bushes and put on my shoes and stockings. The cold water had braced me, and I was my own man again.

As I set out once more I calculated that the sun would rise in three hours' time, and I knew that an hour after sunrise it would be dangerous for me to continue my flight in the open. For, though the country-side was but thinly peopled, some shepherd on the hills or some woman from her cottage door might espy a strange figure trespassing upon their native solitude. To be seen might prove my undoing, so I hurried on while the darkness was still upon the earth.

When day broke I was up among the hills. Now I began to walk circumspectly, scanning the near and distant country before venturing across any open space; and when the sun had been up for an hour, and the last silver beads of dew were beginning to dry on the tips of the heather, I set about finding a resting-place. It was an easy task, for the heather and bracken grew luxuriantly. I crawled into the middle of a clump of bracken, and drawing the leafy stems over me lay snugly hid. I was foot-sore and hungry, but I helped myself to Luckie's good provender, and almost as soon as I had finished my meal I was fast asleep.

When I awoke I was, for a moment, at a loss to

understand my surroundings. Then I remembered my flight, and all my senses were alive again. I judged from the position of the sun that it must be late afternoon. Caution made me wary, and I did not stir from my lair, for I knew that questing troopers might already be on the adjacent hill-sides looking for me, and their keen eyes would be quick to discern any unusual movement in the heart of a bed of bracken, so I lay still and waited. Then I dozed off again, and when I awoke once more, the stars were beginning to appear.

Secure beneath the defence of the dark, I quitted my resting-place. So far, fortune had smiled upon me ; I had baffled my pursuers, and during the hours of the night the chase would be suspended. The thought lent speed to my feet and flooded my heart with hope. Ere the break of morn I should have covered many a mile. So I pressed on resolutely, and when the moon rose I had already advanced far on my way.

As I went I began to consider my future. My aim was to reach England. Once across the border I should be safe from pursuit : but in reaching that distant goal I must avoid the haunts of men, and until such time as I could rid myself of my trooper's uniform and find another garb, my journey would be surrounded with countless difficulties. I estimated that with care my store of food would last three days. After that the problem of procuring supplies would be as difficult as it would be urgent. I dared not venture near any cottage : I dared not enter any village or town, and the more I thought of my future the blacker it became. Defiantly I choked down my fears and resolved that I should live for the moment only. There was more of boldness than wisdom in the decision, and when I had come to it I trudged on blithely with no thought except to cover as many miles as possible before the day should break.

When that hour came I found myself standing by the side of a lone grey loch laid in the lap of the hills. On each side the great sheet of water was surrounded by a heather-clad ridge, from whose crest some ancient cataclysm had torn huge boulders which lay strewn here and there on the slopes that led down to the water edge. Remote from the haunts of man, it seemed to my tired eyes a place of enchanting beauty; and I stood there as though a spell were upon me and watched the sun rise, diffusing as it came a myriad fairy tints which transformed the granite slabs to silver, and lighted up the mist-clad hill-side with colours of pearl and purple and gold.

I watched a dove-grey cloud roll gently from the face of the loch and, driven by some vagrant wind, wander ghost-like over the hill-side. The moor-fowl were beginning to wake and I heard the cry of the cock-grouse challenge the morn. Pushing my way through the dew-laden beds of heather, I ascended to the crest of the slope which ran up from the loch, and looked across the country. Before me rolled a panorama of moor and hill, while in the far distance the morning sky bent down to touch the earth. There was no human habitation in sight; no feather of peat-smoke ascending into the air from a shepherd's cot; no sheep or cattle or living thing; but the silence was broken by the wail of the whaups, which, in that immensity of space, seemed charged with woe. I descended from the hill-top and passed round the end of the loch to reconnoitre from the ridge on the other side. My eyes were met by a like expanse of moor and hills. Here, surely, I thought, is solitude and safety. Here might any fugitive conceal himself till the fever of the hue and cry should abate. For a time at least I should make this peaceful mountain fastness my home.

When I came down from the ridge I walked along

the edge of the loch till I came upon a little stream which broke merrily away from the loch-side and rippled with tinkling chatter under the heather and across the moorland till the brown ribbon of its course was lost in the distance. Half-dreaming I walked along its bank. Suddenly in a little pool I saw a trout dart to the cover of a stone. With the zest of boyhood, but the wariness of maturer years, I groped with cautious fingers beneath the stone and in a few seconds felt the slight movements of the little fish as my hands closed slowly upon it. In a flash it was out on the bank—yards away, and soon other four lay beside it. I had found an unexpected means of replenishing my larder. With flint and steel and tinder I speedily lit a handful of dry grass placed under the shelter of a boulder, and adding some broken stems of old heather and bits of withered bracken I soon made a pleasant fire over which I cooked my trout on a flat stone. I have eaten few breakfasts so grateful since.

The meal over, I took care to extinguish the fire. Then, in better cheer than I had yet been since the moment of my desertion, looking about for a resting-place I found a great granite boulder projecting from the hill-side and underneath its free edge a space where a man might lie comfortably and well hidden by the tall bracken which over-arched the opening. Laying a thick bed of heather beneath the rock, I crawled in, drawing back the brackens to their natural positions over a hiding-place wonderfully snug and safe.

I judged from the position of the sun that it was near six of the morning when I crawled into my bed, and soon I was fast asleep. It was high noon when I awoke and peered cautiously through the fronds of the bracken on a solitude as absolute as it was in the early hours of the morning. I felt sorely tempted to venture out for a little while; but discretion counselled caution, and I lay down once more and was soon fast asleep. When I awoke again I saw that the sun was setting.

I rose and stretched my stiffened limbs. The loch lay in the twilight smooth as a sheet of polished glass. I went down to its edge and, undressing, plunged into its waters, still warm from the rays of the summer sun. Greatly refreshed, I swam ashore, dressed, and ate some food from my rapidly diminishing store. I had found in the burn-trout an unexpected addition to my larder, but it was evident that very soon I should be in sore straits.

Suddenly, I heard a shrill sound cleave the air. Quickly I crawled under the shelter of the nearest rock and listened. The sound was coming from the heather slopes on the other side of the loch and I soon became aware that it was from a flute played by a musician of skill. I was amazed and awed. The gathering darkness, the loneliness of the hills, the stillness of the loch, gave to the music a weird and haunting beauty. I could catch no glimpse of the player, but now I knew that I was not alone in this mountain solitude. The music died away only to come again with fresh vigour as the player piped a jigging tune. It changed once more, and out of the darkness and distance floated an old Scots melody—an echo of hopeless sorrow from far off years. It ceased.

I waited until the darkness was complete, and, taking a careful note of the bearings of my hiding-place, I set out with silent footsteps to the other side of the loch to see if I could discover, without myself being seen, this hill-side maker of music. Slowly I rounded the end of the loch, and stole furtively along its edge till I came to a point below the place from which I judged the melody had come. There, crouching low, and pausing frequently, I went up the slope. Suddenly I heard a voice near me, and sank to the ground. No man in his senses speaks aloud to himself! There must be two people at least on this hill-side, and my solitude and safety were delusions! I cursed myself for a fool, and then as the speaker raised his voice I knew that I was not listening to men talking together, but to a man praying to his Maker—a Covenanter—a fugitive like myself—hiding in these fastnesses. Silently as I had come I stole away and left the moorland saint alone with his God.

CHAPTER VII

THE FLUTE-PLAYER

THE moon was breaking through a wreath of clouds when I came to the end of the loch again, and its light guided me to my hiding-place. As I had lain asleep all day, I was in no need of rest, so I set out along the hill-side to stretch my limbs and explore my surroundings further. All was silent, and the face of the loch shone in the moonlight like a silver shield.

The unexpected happenings of the last hour filled my mind. I had been told once and again that the Covenanters were a dour, stubborn pack of kill-joys, with no interests outside the narrow confines of their bigotry. A flute-playing Covenanter—and, withal, a master such as this man had shown himself to be—was something I found it hard to understand. And more than once since that fatal day at Wigtown I had thought of winsome Margaret Wilson, whose brave blue eyes were of a kind to kindle love in a man's heart. She, the sweet maid, and this soulful musician of the hills, made me think that after all the Covenanters must be human beings with feelings and aspirations, loves and hopes like other men, and were not merely lawless fanatics to be shot like wild cats or drowned like sheep-worrying dogs.

I wondered whether this Covenanter had been hiding on the other side of the loch long before I came; or whether he had been driven by the troopers from some other lair a few hours before and was but a passer-by in the night. No man, in flight, resting for a time would have been so unwary as this flute-player. He must have been there long enough to know that his solitude was unlikely to be disturbed by any sudden arrival of troopers, and, if so, he must have some means of supplying himself with food. An idea seized me. If he, like myself, was a fugitive in hiding I might be able to eke out my diminishing store by procuring from him some of the food which I imagined must be brought to him by friends. But then, how could I expect that one, whose enemies wore the same coat as I did, would grant me this favour. Even if I told him my story, would he believe me ?

However, I resolved that, when the morning broke, I would try to make friends with this man : but—my uniform ? From his hiding-place he would doubtless observe my approach, and either conceal himself the closer or escape me by flight. Turning the matter over in my mind, I continued my walk along the loch-side, and suddenly, because I was not paying full heed to the manner of my going, my feet sank under me and I was sucked into a bog. A "bottomless" bog so common in these Scottish moors would quickly have solved my difficulties. With no small effort I raised my head above the ooze and slime, withdrew my right arm from the sodden morass, out of which it came with a hideous squelch, and felt all round for some firm tussock of grass or rushes. Luckily finding one, I pulled upon it cautiously, and it held—then more firmly, and still it held. Clinging to it I withdrew my left arm from the morass, and, laying hold on another tussock, after a prolonged and exhausting effort I succeeded in drawing myself up till I was able to rest my arms on a clump of rushes that stood in the heart of the bog. Resting for a little to recover myself, I at last drew myself completely out ; and as I stood with my feet planted firmly in the heart of the rushes, I saw a clump of grass, and stepped upon it, and from it, with a quick leap, to the other side. As I stood wet and mud-drenched, it suddenly flashed upon me that this untoward event might turn to my advantage. The brown ooze of the bog would effectually hide the scarlet of my coat. Even if the fugitive on the other side of the loch should see my approach, he would not recognise in this mud-stained wanderer an erstwhile spick-and-span trooper of Lag's Horse.

I made my way carefully to the water edge and washed the bitter ooze from my face and hands. Then I took off my tunic—having first carefully taken from its pockets the remains of my store of food, now all sodden—and laid it on a boulder to dry. Then I paced up and down briskly, till the exercise brought a grateful warmth to my limbs.

I sat down and looked wonderingly over the broad surface of the loch. A wind had sprung up, warm and not unkindly, which caught the surface of the water and drove little plashing waves against the gravel edge. As I listened to their chatter I suddenly heard footsteps close at hand. Throwing myself flat on the ground I waited. Who was it ? The Covenanter ought to be at the other side of the loch. Was there another refugee as well as myself on this side, or was it a pursuer who had at last found me, and had I escaped death in the bog only to face it a few days hence against a wall in Wigtown with a firing party before me ?

CHAPTER VIII

A COVENANTER'S CHARITY

THE footsteps drew nearer and stopped. I had been seen. There was a long pause, then a voice in level, steady tones said: "Are you a kent body in this country-side?"

I rose quickly to my feet and faced the speaker. I could see him as a dark but indistinct figure standing some yards from me on the slope of the brae, but I knew from the lack of austerity in his tones that he was no trooper, and I thought that in all likelihood he would prove to be the player of the flute.

"Need a man answer such a question?" said I. "What right have you to ask who I am?"

"I have no right," he replied, as he drew nearer—"no title but curiosity. Strangers here are few and far between. As for me, I am a shepherd."

"A strange time of night," said I, "for a shepherd to look for his sheep."

"Ay," answered the voice, "and my flock has been scattered by wolves."

"I understand," I said. "You are a minister of the Kirk, a Covenanter, a hill-man in hiding."

He came quite close to me and said: "I'm no' denying that you speak the truth. Who are you?"

"Like you," I replied, "I am a fugitive—a man with a price on his head."

"A Covenanter?"

"No; a deserter from Lag's Horse."

"From Lag's Horse?" he exclaimed, repeating my words. "A deserter?"

Uncertain what to say, I waited. Then he continued:

"May I make so bold as to ask if your desertion is the fruit of conviction of soul, or the outcome of some drunken spree?"

I have not the Scottish faculty for analysing my motives, and I hardly knew what to say. Was I a penitent, ashamed and sorry for the evil things in which I had played a part, or did I desert merely to escape punishment for my part in the drunken brawl in the tavern? I had not yet made a serious attempt to assess the matter; and here, taken at unawares in the stillness of the night among the silent hills, I was conscious of the near presence of God before whose bar I was arraigned by this quiet interlocutor.

"I am wet to the skin and chilled to the bone, for only an hour ago I foundered in a bog, but if you will walk with me," I said, "I will tell you the story and you shall judge."

"It is not for man to judge, for he cannot read the heart aright, but if you will tell me your story I will know as much of you as you seem already to know of me," he said, as he took me by the arm. "Like you," he continued, "I am a fugitive; and if you are likely to stop for long in this hiding-place, it were well that we should understand each other."

As we paced up and down, I told him the whole shameful tale.

When I had finished he sat down on the hill-side and, burying his face in his hands, was silent for a space. Then he rose, and laying a hand upon my shoulder peered into my face. The darkness was yet too great for us to see each other clearly, but his eyes were glistening.

"It is not," he said, "for me to judge. God

knows! but I am thinking that your desertion was more than a whim, though I would not go the length of saying that you have repented with tears for the evil you have done. May God forgive you, and may grace be given you to turn ere it is too late from the paths of the wicked."

As I told him my story I had feared that when he heard it he would have nothing more to do with me: but I had misjudged his charity. Suddenly he held his hand out to me, saying:

"Providence has cast us together, mayhap that your soul may be saved, and mine kept from withering. I am ready to be your friend if you will be mine."

I took his outstretched hand. I had longed for his friendship for my own selfish ends, and he, who had nothing to gain from my friendship, offered me his freely.

The night had worn thin as we talked, and now in the growing light I could see my companion more clearly. He seemed a man well past middle life; before long I was to learn that he was more than three score years and ten, but neither at this moment nor later should I have imagined it. He was straight as a ramrod, spare of body and pallid of face, save where on his high cheek-bones the moorland wind and the rays of the summer sun had burned him brown. The hair of his head was black, streaked here and there by a few scanty threads of silver. His forehead was broad and high, his nose was well-formed and somewhat aquiline, and his brown eyes were full of light. It was to his eyes and to his mouth, around which there seemed to lurk some wistful playfulness, that his face owed its attraction. He was without doubt a handsome man—I have rarely seen a handsomer.

As I peered into his face and looked him up and down, somewhat rudely I fear, he was studying me with care. My woebegone appearance seemed to amuse him, for when his scrutiny was over he said :

"Ye're no' ill-faured : but I'm thinking Lag would be ill-pleased if he saw one of his dragoons in sic a mess."

"I trust he won't," I said with fervour, and my companion laughed heartily.

He laid a hand upon my arm, and with a twinkle in his eye said : "The old Book says : 'If thine enemy hunger, feed him.' Have you anything to eat ?"

I showed him what I had and invited him to help himself, as I picked up my tunic and slipped it on.

"No, no," he replied, "I am better provided than you. The Lord that sent the ravens to Elijah has spread for me a table in the wilderness and my cup runneth over. Come with me and let us break our fast together. They do say that to eat a man's salt thirls another to him as a friend. I have no salt to offer you, but"—and he smiled—"I have plenty of mutton ham, and I am thinking you will find that salt enough."

The light was rapidly flooding the hill-side as we took our way round to his side of the loch.

"Bide here a minute," he said, as he left me beside a granite boulder.

I guessed that, with native caution, he was as yet averse to let me see his resting-place, or the place in which he stored his food. In my heart of hearts the slight stung me, and then I realised that I had no right to expect that a Covenanter should trust me absolutely, on the instant. In a few moments he was back again, and I was amazed at the quantity of food he brought with him. It was wrapped in a fair cloth of linen, which he spread carefully on the hill-side, arranging the food upon it. There were farles of oat-cake, and scones, besides the remains of a goodly leg of mutton. When the feast was spread he stood up and taking off his bonnet began to pray aloud. I listened till he had finished his lengthy prayer, refraining from laying hands upon any of the toothsome food that lay before me. When he had ground out a long " Amen," he opened his eyes and replaced his bonnet. Then he cut a generous slice of mutton and passed it to me.

" I never break my fast," he said, " without thanking God, and I am glad to see that you are a well-mannered young man. I dare hardly have expected so much from a trooper."

" Ah," I answered, " I have had advantages denied to most of the troopers."

He nodded his head, and lapsing into the speech of the country-side, as I had yet to learn was his wont whenever his feelings were stirred, he said :

" That reminds me of what once befell mair than thirty years sin' when I was daunnerin' along the road from Kirkcudbright to Causewayend. It was a summer day just like this, and on the road I foregathered wi' a sailor-body that had come off a schooner in Kirkcudbright. We walked along and cracked, and I found him, like every other sailor-man, to be an interesting chiel. By and by we cam' to a roadside inn. I asked him to join me in a bite and sup. The inn-keeper's lass brocht us scones and cheese and a dram apiece, and when they were set afore us, I, as is my custom, took off my bonnet and proceeded to thank the Lord for these temporal mercies. When I opened ma een I found that my braw sailor lad had gulped doon my dram as weel as his ain, while I was asking the blessing. ' What dae ye mean by sic a ploy ? ' says I ; but the edge was ta'en off ma anger when the sailor-man, wiping his moo' wi' the back o' his haun', said, ' Weel, sir, the guid Book says ye should watch as weel as pray.' "

At the memory of the trick played upon him my companion burst into laughter, and I have rarely heard a happier laugh.

He was a generous host, and pressed me to take my fill.

" There is plenty for us both," he said. " Dinna be blate, my lad, help yersel'." Then as he offered me another slice of mutton, he said : " I am thinking that the ravens are kinder to me than they were to Elijah, for, so far as I know, they never brocht him a mutton ham. But who ever heard o' a braxy sheep in the wilds o' Mount Carmel ! " and he laughed again.

When our meal was over he looked me up and down again. I could see that he was distressed at the condition of my clothing, but I explained to him that I considered my fall into the bog a blessing in disguise, since it toned down the bright colour of my garments and would make them less easily seen upon the moorland.

" That's as may be, but ye're an awfu' sicht. However, I've no doubt that when the glaur dries it winna look so bad."

As he talked I was divesting myself of my uniform, and as I stood before him in my shirt he looked me over again and said : " You might disguise yourself by making a kilt out o' your coat, but twa sic' spindle shanks o' legs would gi'e you awa' at once. I know well, since ye're an Englishman, ye werena' brought up on the carritches, and I can see for myself ye got no oatmeal when ye were a bairn."

I laughed, as I tossed my last garment aside, and running to the edge of the loch plunged into its depths. He watched me as I swam, and when I came to the shore again I found him drying my outer garments over a fire which he had kindled.

" It'll be time for bed," he said, " in a few minutes.

You take your ways to your own hidie-hole and I will take my way to mine; and may God send us sweet repose. No man can tell, but I am thinking there will be no troopers up here the day. They combed this loch-side a fortnight sin', and when they had gone I came and hid here. Maist likely they'll no' be back here for a long time."

I thanked him for his hospitality, and as I turned to go I said: "Where shall I find you to-night, for I should like to have more of your company?"

"Well," he answered, "I always sleep on this side of the loch; and when night falls and a' thing seems safe, it is mair than likely ye'll hear me playing a bit tune on the flute. When ye hear that, if ye come round to this side and just wait a wee, ye'll likely see me again. Good morning! and God bless you!"

CHAPTER IX

THE STORY OF ALEXANDER MAIN

I MADE for my hiding-place, and, snugly covered up in my lair, I was soon asleep. In the late afternoon I awoke. What it was that woke me I know not, but as I lay half-conscious in the dreamy shallows that lie around the sea of sleep, I heard something stir among the brackens not far from me. I raised myself on an elbow, and separating the fronds above me gazed in the direction from which the sound came. Less than a score of paces away a winsome girl was tripping briskly along the hill-side. Her head was crowned with masses of chestnut-brown hair which glistened with a golden sheen where the sunlight caught it. Over her shoulders was flung lightly a plaid of shepherd's tartan. Her gown was of a dull reddish colour, and she walked lightly, with elastic step. I was not near enough, nor dare I, lest I should be seen, crane my neck beyond my hiding-place to see her features clearly, but I could tell that she was fair to look upon. My eyes followed her wistfully as she rapidly ascended the slope, but in a moment she was out of sight over its crest. I wondered who she could be. This mountain fastness was a place of strange surprises. I pondered long but could find no light, so I settled myself to sleep again; but ere I slept there flitted through my waking dreams the vision of a winsome maid with hair a glory of sun-kissed brown.

On waking, my first thought was of her, and anxiously and half-hopefully I peeped into the gathering darkness to see if she had come back again; but there was nothing to see except the beds of heather, purple in the gathering twilight, and the grey shadows of the granite rocks scattered along the hill-side.

I judged that the time had come when I might with safety issue from my hiding-place, so I ventured forth. Sitting down upon the hill-side I helped myself to some of my rapidly diminishing food. As I did so, I thought with gratitude of the hermit on the other side of the loch, who, of his large charity, had made me free of his ample stores.

And then the truth flashed upon me—the little bird which brought his food was no repulsive, croaking raven, but a graceful heather-lintie—the girl whom I had seen that afternoon.

When I had finished eating, I went down to the edge of the loch and, stooping, drank. Then I returned to my seat and waited. The stars were coming out one by one, and the horn of the moon was just appearing like the point of a silver sickle above a bank of clouds when I heard the music of the flute. It pulsated with a haunting beauty, like some elfin melody which the semi-darkness and the intervening water conspired to render strangely sweet. Evidently the player was in a happy mood, for his notes were instinct with joy, and, though they lacked that mystic sadness which had so thrilled me a night ago, they cast a glamour over me. When the music ceased I tarried for a space, for I had no desire to break in upon the devotions of my friend; but by and by I made my way round to the other side of the loch.

I found the hermit awaiting me. He bade me "Good e'en" and asked if I had had anything to eat. I told him that I had already satisfied my hunger.

"That is a pity," he said, "for the ravens have been kind to-day and have brought me a little Galloway cheese forby twa or three girdles-fu' o' guid, crisp oatcake; by the morn they'll no' be so tasty, so just try a corner and a wee bit o' cheese along with me."

Little loth, I assented, and soon I was enjoying some of his toothsome store. I ate sparingly, for I had already blunted the edge of my hunger and I had no wish to abuse his generosity. As I nibbled the crisp oatcake I thought of the girl I had seen on the hill-side, and in a fit of curiosity said: "I have been thinking that though the Lord sent the ravens to feed Elijah, he has been sending somebody bonnier and blither to feed you—in fact no raven, but a heather-lintie!"

He looked at me quickly, and replied: "I am no' sayin' yea or nay; and at any rate you have no call to exercise your mind with what doesna concern you."

The rebuke was a just one and I was sorry for my offence.

When our meal was over, he took me by the arm. "What say you to a walk by the light o' the moon?" he asked. "I'll guarantee you will fall into no more bogs, for I know every foot of these hills as well as I know the palm of my hand."

"Your pleasure is mine," I said. So we set out, and as we went he talked.

"Last night," he said, "you told me your story; to-night, if you care to listen, I will tell you mine.

"I am an older man by far than you are, and I will never see the three-score and ten again. As my days so has my strength been. I have seen a feck of things and taken part in many a deed that will help to make history. You may think I boast myself, but listen.

My name is Alexander Main, and, as you ken, I am a minister of the Kirk of Scotland. The year 1638 saw me a student in the Glasgow College—that is long syne, and they were stirring times. Ye may have heard of that great gathering in the Greyfriars Kirk at Edinburgh on the last day of February 1638, when we swore and put our names to the National Covenant. It was a great day. The crowd filled kirk and yard. Well do I mind the gallant Warriston reading the Covenant, much of which had come glowing from his own pen—but most of all I mind the silence that fell upon us when the reading was over. Then the good Earl of Sutherland stepped forward and put his name to it, and man followed man, each eager to pledge himself to the bond. Some of us, I mind well, wrote after their names the words 'Till death,' and others signed it with their blood."

"And what might this Covenant be?" I asked.

"Ah," he said, "I had forgotten. Briefly the bond was this: 'to adhere to and defend the true religion of Presbyterianism, and to labour to recover the purity and liberty of the Gospel as it was established and professed in the Kingdom of Scotland.' It was to put an end to all endeavours to foist prelacy upon us and to signify our adherence to the Presbyterian form of Church-government which King James himself had sworn to uphold in this Kingdom of Scotland, that we put our names to the bond. Not that we were against the King, for in the Covenant it was written plain that we were ready with our lives to stand to the defence of our dread sovereign, the King's Majesty. The wave of fervour spread like a holy fire from that old kirkyard through the length and breadth of Scotland, and the noblest blood in the land and the flower of its intellect signed the Covenant. Later on there came a day when those who stood for liberty of conscience in England as well as Scotland made a compact. That was the Solemn League and Covenant, whereby we bound ourselves to preserve a reformed religion in the Church of Scotland. The memory of man is short, and it has almost been forgotten that the solemn league was a joint Scottish and English affair, and that it was ratified by the English Parliament. These things were the beginning, but since then this puir kingdom has passed through the fire."

He paused and sighed deeply, then picking up the thread of his words again he told me the chequered history of the Covenanters for close on fifty years. It was a story that thrilled me—a record of suffering, of high endeavour, of grievous wrong. Of his own sufferings he made little, though he had suffered sore, and I, who had never felt the call to sacrifice myself for a principle, was humbled to the dust as I listened. He spoke in accents tense with emotion, and sometimes his voice rang with pride. I was too spell-bound to interrupt him, though many questions were upon my lips.

At last he ceased, as though the memories he was recalling had overwhelmed him, then he resumed:

"So, in some sort, my story is the story of puir auld Scotland, for the past fifty years. It is a tragedy, and the pity is—a needless tragedy! If the rulers of a land would study history and human nature, it would save them from muckle wrong-doing and oppression. It has been tried before and, I doubt not, it will be tried many a time again, but it will never succeed—for no tyrant can destroy the soul of a people by brute force. They call us rebels, and maybe so we are, but we were not rebels in the beginning. Two kings signed the bond: the Parliament passed it. We remained true to our pledged word; the kings forgot theirs, and they call *us* the law-breakers. And some call us narrow-minded fanatics. Some of us may be; for when the penalty of a man's faith is his death, he may come to lay as much stress on the commas in his creed as on the principles it declares. No man has the right to compromise on the fundamentals.

" Sometimes I wonder if I had my life to live over again whether I would do as I have done. Maist likely I should, for all through I have let my conscience guide me. I have no regrets, but only a gnawing sorrow that sometimes torments me. I have been in dangers many, and I have never lowered my flag, either to a fear or to a denial of my faith, and yet the Lord has not counted me worthy to win the martyr's crown." His voice broke, and he hesitated for a moment, then went on : " I have fought a good fight ; I have almost finished my course, but whether I have kept the faith is no' for me to say. I have tried.

" The night of Scotland's woe has been long and stormy ; but the dawn of a better day is not far off, and she will yet take her place in the forefront of the nations as the land in which the battle for liberty of conscience was fought and won.

" Look ye," and he pointed to the east, where the darkness was beginning to break as the sun swung up from his bed.

CHAPTER X

THE FIELD MEETING

A WEEK passed uneventfully. Each night I joined my friend and the glad notes of his flute were still our signal: each morning we parted to sleep through the daylight hours each in his own hiding-place.

I was strangely attracted by this old man. He was a gentle spirit, quick to take offence, often when none was meant, but equally quick to forget. He had a quaint humour, flashes of which lightened our converse as we walked together in the night, and he had all the confidence of a little child in the abiding love of God. As I parted with him one morning, he said:

"I doubt you'll no' ken what day of the week this is."

I was quick to confess my ignorance.

"Well," he said, "it is Saturday, and ye'll no' hear me playing the nicht. On such a nicht one is too near the threshold of the Sabbath day lichtly to engage in sic a worldly amusement. However, if ye'll come round to my side of the loch about the usual time, we'll tak' a bite o' supper together—after that ye'd better leave me to my meditations in view of the Lord's Day, for I am preaching the morn."

"In which church, may I ask?" I said, forgetting for a moment where I was.

"In the kirk of the moorland," he answered, "which has no roof but God's heaven, and no altar but the loving hearts of men and women!"

A sudden desire sprang up in my heart. " Sir," I said, hesitatingly, " I do not consider myself worthy, but I should count it a high honour if I may come with you."

He paused before he answered : " The House is the Lord's, He turns no man from His door : come, an you wish it." Then he laughed, and looking me up and down said : " Man, but you're an awfu' sicht if you are coming. Ye wadna like to appear before Lag in sic unsoldierly trappings : daur ye face God ? " Then he laid a hand on my shoulder, and looking into my face with his piercing eyes, said : " The Lord tak's nae pleasure in the looks o' a man, and belike he pays little heed to claes or the beggar at the rich man's gate wouldna have had much of a chance; it is the heart that counts, my lad, it is the heart, and a contrite heart He will not despise." Then he gripped me by the hand, and said : " Awa to your bed and come an' look for me by and by, and syne we'll set out for the kirk. It is a long road to travel and ye'll need a good rest before we start."

So I left him and made my way back to my own side of the loch. There I undressed and looked ruefully at my mud-bespattered garments. They certainly were far from that soldierly spotlessness of which I had been so proud when first I donned them. But the mud on them was quite dry, so I made a heather brush, and brushed them well. Then I took them down to the loch-side and washed out some of the more obstinate stains, then laying them to dry among the brackens I sought my bed.

When I awoke night had fallen, so, leaving my hiding place, I sought my garments and put them on.

I judged that it must be nearly ten o'clock as I went round the head of the loch to seek my friend. I found him awaiting me at our trysting-place and we ate our meal in silence. When we had finished, he said :

"Wait for me here; I will come again ere long," and disappeared into the darkness. I sat in the starlit silence watching the moon's fitful light move upon the face of the waters. Many thoughts passed through my mind. I wondered what reception I, in a trooper's uniform, would receive at the hands of the hill-men whom I was shortly to meet. Would the guarantee of the minister be credential sufficient: then a doubt assailed me. I knew that as a deserter I was under penalty of death—but even a deserter, if captured, might still be pardoned; but to have, as a further charge in the indictment against him, that of consorting with proscribed hill-men and taking part in a Conventicle would rob me of the last chance of pardon if I should ever fall into the hands of my pursuers. For a moment I was tempted to withdraw from this new adventure. Then I spurned myself for a coward. I owed my life to the friendliness of this old man, who daily gave me so ungrudgingly of his store, and I felt that it would be base and ungrateful to withdraw now, since, after all, the invitation to accompany him was of my own seeking.

The moments passed slowly, and I judged that more than an hour had elapsed since he left me. I began to grow uneasy. Had he lost me in the dark, or had he judged me unworthy to accompany him, and gone off alone? I rose to my feet, determined to make a search for him, when I heard the rustle of his footsteps, and in a moment he was beside me.

"Did you think I wasna comin' back?" he queried. "I have just been wrestling with a point o' doctrine; but I've got the truth o't now. Come!" and he set out along the hill-side.

He walked slowly, absorbed in deep meditation. I followed close on his heels, seeking to make sure of my footsteps by keeping as near him as possible. He seemed in no mood to talk, and I held my tongue.

When we had walked for two hours, he stopped suddenly and said: "We are half-way there now. I think that we might take a rest," and he sat down on a hummock on the hill-side.

I sat down beside him, and more by way of breaking the silence than from any special desire to talk—for I had little to say, I remarked: "What a beautiful night!"

He grunted, and in spite of the darkness I could see him shrug his shoulders with displeasure.

"Wheesht, man," he said. "This is nae time to speak about sic things. Have ye forgotten it is the Sabbath day?"

I was unprepared for such a rebuff, and a hot reply sprang to my lips, but I felt unwilling to hurt his feelings, so I held my tongue.

He sat with his knees drawn up towards his chin, his clasped hands holding them, and his eyes fixed on the distance.

I stretched myself lazily upon the hill-side and awaited his pleasure.

We rested for a long time, and then, as the eastern sky began to break into light, he rose to his feet and saying, "It is time to go on," he set out again. I followed close behind him as before. He walked with his hands clasped behind his back, his two thumbs revolving ceaselessly round each other.

Out of the ebb of night, day rose like a goddess. Before me was beauty unspeakable. The moorland was covered by a thin vale of mist. Here and there, where the sun was reflected from it, it shone like silver, and where some mischievous hill-wind had torn a rent in it, a splash of brown heath or a tussock of purple heather broke colouringly through. The world was waking up from its slumber. A hare, startled, sprang along the hill-side before us—its ears acock, its body zig-zagging as though to evade some apprehended missile. The whaups called to each other mournfully, and, high above us, unseen, a lark poured out its soul in sparkling song.

I was beginning to wonder when we should arrive at our destination, when my companion turned suddenly to the left and walked downhill into the valley. Here, for a time, we followed what had been the bed of an ancient stream, long since dried up, until we came to a cleft between the hills which gradually widened out into a kind of amphitheatre. Almost for the first time since we had left our hiding-place, my companion spoke.

"This is the trysting-place," he said. "The folk will be here ere long. I ll leave ye while I complete my preparations," and saying "Rest ye," he walked on through the amphitheatre and disappeared.

I stretched myself upon my back and drew my bonnet over my eyes. I know not how long I lay thus, but suddenly I was conscious that someone was standing beside me, and opening my eyes I saw the minister at my side.

"They are beginning to come," he said, as he looked out through the cleft by which we had entered the hollow. My gaze followed his, and I saw at some distance a man of middle age, followed by two younger men, coming in single file towards us. My companion left me and hurried to meet them. I saw him approach the eldest with outstretched hand which was taken and shaken vigorously; then he greeted the two younger men, and the four stood, a little knot in the morning light, talking earnestly.

From glances that were cast from time to time in my direction, I knew they were talking of me. The colloquy lasted for some time. My friend was apparently vouching for my trustworthiness with many protestations, for I could see him strike the palm of his left hand with his clenched right fist. At last the minister and the elder man came towards me. The two younger men separated, one climbing to the top of the ridge on one side of the amphitheatre and the other ascending the slope upon its other side.

I surmised that these two younger men were to play the part of sentinels to give timely warning, if need arose, of the coming of the dreaded troopers. They had no weapons but shepherd's crooks.

As the two elder men approached me, I rose, and as they drew nearer I heard my friend still pleading for me. " I believe that, at heart, he is no' a bad young man, but being English, his opportunities have been few, and he is strangely lacking in a knowledge o' the fundamentals, but I am hoping that he may yet prove to be a brand plucked from the burning."

With difficulty I restrained a smile, but I took a step towards them and, bowing to my friend's companion who stood straight-backed and stalwart before me, I said : " My uniform is but a poor passport to your trust, but the heart beneath it is not a false heart and none of your people need fear ill from me."

The old man offered me his hand. " Young man," he said, " I hae little cause to trust your coat, but if your creedentials satisfy the meenister, they're guid enough for Tammas Frazer."

" That's richt, Thomas ! " cried the minister, " that's richt. As the Buik says : ' Charity suffereth long and is kind ' ! "

We stood silent for an embarrassed moment, until the hill-man said : " And noo, Meenister, ye'll gi'e us a word afore I set the kirk in order," and lifting their bonnets the two men closed their eyes.

I followed their example, and then the minister lifted up his voice and, in tones of pathetic earnestness, besought the blessing of God upon all the doings of the day ; sought, too, for divine protection for all who at the hazard of their lives should come to worship there that Sabbath morning.

When the prayer was over, Thomas turned to me, and said: "You are a likely young man and a hefty; we had better leave the man o' God to his meditations. Come and lend me a hand."

For a moment I was at a loss to understand what he meant, but I followed him, and when he picked up a small boulder I did likewise and together we carried the stones to the sloping hillside and arranged them at short intervals from each other. Altogether we gathered some thirty or forty stones, which we set in semicircular rows. Opposite to these, on the other side of the amphitheatre, we built a little mound of boulders and laid upon the top of it a great flat rock. This was to be the preacher's pulpit, and I was struck with the care that Thomas devoted to its building. When it was finished he stood upon it and tested it. Satisfied, he descended from it, saying: "It'll dae fine. There's naething like a guid foundation for a sermon," and in his austere eyes a light flickered.

By this time other worshippers had begun to gather and were thronging round the minister in little clusters. From the looks cast in my direction I knew that I was the object of more than one inquiry, and while my recent companion went forward to greet some other of the worshippers, I hung back a little shamefacedly. Seeing my hesitation the minister beckoned me, and when I came near he placed a hand upon my shoulder and said:

"My friends, here is the prodigal. He has eaten of the husks of the swine, but, I think, he has at last set his foot on the road to his Father's house."

It was a strange introduction, received in silence by the little group, and with a mounting colour I looked at the people and they looked at me. There was a glint of challenge in the eyes of some of the men and a hint of suspicion in others. The older women looked at me with something I took for pity; the younger ones pretended not to look at all. The silence was embarrassing, but it was broken by the minister who said:

"And now, my friends, it is time to begin our service. Will you take your places?" and turning to me he said, "Young man, I think ye'd better come and sit near the pulpit, where I can see that ye behave yersel'!"

In silence, and with a demure sobriety as though they were crossing the threshold of a holy place, they stepped across the dip in the amphitheatre and seated themselves upon the stones laid ready for them. I walked behind the minister towards his pulpit. A couple of paces from it he stopped and raised his right hand high above his head. On the top of the hill that faced us I saw one of the sentinels spring erect and hold his hand aloft, and turning, we saw that the sentinel on the other hill top had made a like signal. It was a sign that all was well, and that the service might safely begin.

The minister mounted his pulpit and I sat down a little below it. In a voice which rang melodiously through the silence he said: "Let us worship God by singing to His praise the 121st psalm." He read the psalm from beginning to end and then the congregation, still sitting, took up the refrain and sang slowly the confident words. It was a psalm which to these hill-folk must have been charged with many memories.

There was more of earnestness than of melody in the singing, but suddenly I was aware of one voice that sounded clear and bell-like among the jumble of raucous notes. My ears guided my eyes and I was able to pick the singer out.

CHAPTER XI

FLOWER O' THE HEATHER

SHE was a girl of some twenty years who sat on the slope opposite to me. Her features were regular and fine and in strange contrast to the rugged countenances that surrounded her. From underneath the kerchief that snooded her hair a wanton lock of gold strayed over the whiteness of her high forehead. I caught a glimpse of two pink ears set like wild roses among the locks that clustered round them. She sat demurely, unaware of my rapt scrutiny. Her lips were red as ripe cherries, and as she sang I saw behind them the glint of white and regular teeth. Her eyes I could not catch; they were lifted to the distant sky over the hill-tops; her soul was in her singing. One hand rested in her lap, the other hung down by her side, and almost touched the grass beside her rough seat. The open book upon her knees was open for form's sake only. She was singing from her heart and she knew the words without appeal to the printed page. I took my eyes from her with difficulty and let them wander over the little congregation of which she was a part, but I found no face there which could hold them, and quickly they turned again to look upon this winsome maid.

She had lowered her eyes now, and as I glanced across at her I met their level gaze. There was a glint of light in them such as I have seen upon a moorland tarn when the sunbeams frolic there, and as I looked at her I was aware that something within me was beating against my ribs like a wild caged bird.

When the psalm was ended the minister behind me said solemnly, " Let us pray," and over against me I saw the heads of the congregation bend reverently. Some sat with clasped hands, others buried their faces in the hollow of their palms. My devotions were divided, and before the preacher had completed his sentences of invocation I found myself peeping through my separated fingers at the girl. Her eyes were closed, her dainty hands were clasped delicately. I had never, till that moment, known that the human hand may become as subtle an instrument for expressing the feelings as the human eye. In her clasped hands I saw the rapture of a splendid faith: I saw devotion that would not shrink from death; I saw love and sacrifice.

The preacher prayed on, embracing in his petitions the furthest corners of the universe. His words fell on my ears, but I did not hear them, for at that moment my whole world centred in this alluring daughter of the Covenant.

Once again I was conscious that my heart was thumping wildly, and I was selfish enough to wonder whether my presence was disturbing her devotions as much as hers was destroying mine. But she gave no sign. The lustrous pools of her eyes were hidden from my gaze behind the dropped lids. So long as she was unaware of it, I felt no hesitation in letting my eyes dwell upon her, to drink in the beauty of her soul-filled face.

I was still gazing upon this vision when suddenly the prayer ended. I can tell no more of the service. I only know that in that little band of worshippers I was one of the most fervent—but I fear that I was worshipping one of God's creatures rather than God Himself.

After the benediction had been pronounced over the standing congregation, I looked up at the sky and judged that well-nigh three hours must have elapsed since we sang the opening psalm, and to me it had passed in a flash. Never before had I known the minutes fly upon such winged feet.

I shook myself out of my dream and turned towards the minister. He had dropped on his knees and was engaged in silent prayer. Unwilling to disturb him, I turned once more toward the congregation which had already arisen from its stony pews and was standing clustered in little knots. I hesitated for a moment, and as I hung uncertain I felt an arm slip through mine. It was the minister.

"Come," he said, "you must get to know some of my flock. I could tell, my lad, as ye sat at my feet during the service that you were strangely moved."

Good honest man! I had been strangely moved, but by other emotions than those for which he gave me credit!

As he talked, we had descended the slope and stood in the hollow. The congregation gathered round us; many of the men, and some of the older women, grasped the preacher warmly by the hand. There was no effusiveness in these salutations, but a quiet earnestness that bespoke their love for him.

"Ye were michty in prayer the day," said one, while I heard another exclaim: "Ye divided the word maist skilfully, sir. The twalfth heid micht ha'e been expanded wi' advantage, but your fourteenth was by-ordinar'. I never heard finer words o' grace, no even frae godly Samuel Rutherford himself. God keep ye, sir." "Ay," said another. "When ye gied oot yer sixth heid says I tae masel', 'Noo, how will he handle that ane: but, sir, ye were maisterfu', an' I was mair than satisfied."

These words of praise were accepted by the minister with a modest derogation: "I am but a frail mouthpiece," he said. "The message has suffered through my poor imperfections."

In the press around him I was suddenly conscious of *her* presence. I saw his face light up with a smile as he stretched his hand out to her: "Mary, lass," he said, as he drew her towards him, "ye're a woman grown. It seems but yesterday that I baptised you."

My eyes were on her face, and I saw the colour mount beneath her healthy brown as she smiled. I felt I would have given all of life that might lie before me had that smile been for me. With ears alert I waited to hear her speak. Softly, and in sweet accents, within whose music there was a note of roguery, she answered:

"If the wee ravens didna grow up, wha would bring food to Elijah?"

The minister laughed. "It was a fine cheese, Mary, and your oatcakes couldna be bettered in the shire. What say you, young man?" he said, turning to me.

The moment I had dreamed of had come, and the eyes of the girl were turned expectantly upon me, and then, fool that I was, any readiness of wit I had, oozed through the soles of my feet and left me standing in the adorable presence, an inarticulate dolt. I mumbled I know not what, but she laughed my confusion aside.

"If there are twa mouths to fill," she said, "the ravens will ha'e to fly into the wilderness a wee oftener. I maun tell mither."

She looked at me, and then with a glint in her beautiful eyes that made me think she had not been altogether unaware of my scrutiny during the service, said: "For a trooper, ye behaved very weel," and then lest I might imagine that I was more to her than the merest insect that hides among the heather, she turned once more to the minister.

I was too young then to know that, be she Covenanter's daughter or Court lady, woman is ever the same, with the same arts to provoke, the same witchery to allure, the same artfully artless skill to torture and to heal the heart of man. She had turned away from me, but in doing so she had drawn me closer to herself, and I was rivetted to the ground where I stood, ready to stand there for ever—just to be within sound of her voice, within arm's length of her hand. Suddenly she disentangled herself from the little group and going to its outskirts placed her hand upon the arm of a middle-aged bearded man and brought him to the minister. There was something in the shape of the forehead and eyebrows of the man that made me think he might be her father, and my thought was confirmed when the minister, taking him by the hand, said:

"Andrew, you have a daughter to be proud of. Her mither's ain bairn, and a bonnie lass."

Her father paid no attention to the compliment, and as though to bring back the thoughts of the man of God from such a worldly object as a pretty girl, said:

"And when may we expect ye tae honour our hoose by comin' for the catechisin'?"

"God willing, I shall be at Daldowie on Friday next, and, Andrew, I'll expect ye to be sounder in the proofs than ye were last time."

"And now," he said, turning to me, "we must be going. We have a long road before us. God keep you all. Good-bye," and without another word he strode away. I followed him, and as I passed the girl she glanced at me and her lips moved. I hesitated and stopped, and O wonder! she had stretched out her hand to me.

"Good-bye," she said. "Tak' care of the minister. Maybe you'll convoy him to the catechisin'."

"Trust me," I said. "No harm shall touch a hair of his head if I can fend it off."

"Thank you," she replied. "I think I can trust you, in spite o' your coat," and she dropped my hand.

That was all: but her words and the trust she was ready to place in me had made my whole world glow. I hurried after the minister, walking on air, and felt sorely tempted to burst into song, but I knew that, on such a day, to have done so would have rendered me suspect of wanton godlessness and I restrained myself; but it was only outwardly. My heart was singing like a clutch of larks, and the rugged hill-side was covered with springing flowers. Once before I had felt the spell of a woman, but never till now had any daughter of Eve cast such a glamour over me. Was it love? Was it love? And if it were—was it love on my side alone? It must be, for how dare I think that a renegade trooper, hall-marked by a uniform that to these simple folk meant blood and death, could awaken in the sweet soul of that innocent girl feelings such as she had stirred within my breast. I pictured her again: I saw her sweet brown eyes, and I remembered the glory of her hair, which for a moment I had seen in all its beauty when her kerchief had slipped back. It was chestnut-brown, coiled in great masses, save just above her brow, where in some mood of whim nature had set a golden curl like an aureole. And as I fondly recalled her features one by one I found myself thinking that behind the demure repose of her face there lurked some elfin roguishness—something elusive that gave her a mysterious charm.

I walked on in a maze of dreams, but was called sharply back to earth by the voice of the minister.

"Where are you going, my lad? Are you making

for the border, or where ? Our road lies up the brae face," and turning I discovered that, in my dreams, instead of following the minister I was walking obliquely away from him. I ran to rejoin him, but I had no excuse ready to explain my error, nor did he ask for one. We resumed our walk together and in a moment or two he said :

" Well, what think you o' a Conventicle ? "

There was no mental reservation in my reply : " Never, sir, did I so enjoy a religious service."

" Enjoy ? " he repeated, questioningly. " Enjoy ? that is a worldly word to use concerning such a privilege."

I looked at him sharply, half suspecting that he had guessed the cause of my appreciation of the field-meeting ; but there was nothing in his solemn countenance to make me think he suspected me of duplicity.

" You English folk," he continued, " have queer ways of using your own language. I can understand a hungry man enjoying a hearty meal ; but enjoying a privilege seems wrong. One accepts a privilege with a thankful and humble heart." Then he stopped suddenly, stamping his foot upon the ground. " Alexander Main," he said, " ye're wrong. You are misjudging the young man ; ye're growing old, and the sap in your heart is drying up. Shame on you that you should ever doubt that a man may rejoice at being privileged to enter the presence of God." Then he stretched out his hand : " Forgive me, young man. We Scots have perhaps lost our sense of joy in our sense of duty, but we are wrong, wrong, wrong ! "

His wonted kindliness of heart was bubbling over. My joy had come from a very human source and sorely was I tempted to explain myself : but I held my peace.

We took the path again and plodded along the hillside until we came to the top of a long ridge. As we drew near it the minister signalled to me to crouch down, and on his hands and knees he crawled up and peered long and earnestly over the other side. I knew the reason of his caution. If he stood erect on the brow-top his dark figure, sharp-cut against the sky, might be seen by some patrol of troopers on the moorland. His caution brought me back sharply from the land of dreams. He and I were hunted men.

Apparently his scrutiny satisfied him, for he turned round and, sitting down, said: "We may rest here awhile." I sat beside him and together we scanned the valley that lay below us. It seemed to be a vast solitude, but as I looked I began to pick out here and there a moving figure, and startled, I called his attention to them. He looked and, after a pause, made answer: "They are only the moorland folk making their ways home. See yonder, that is no trooper, but a woman. Poor, harried sheep! May the Great Shepherd guide them all to the fold of home, and in His own good time to the fold abune." I looked again, scanning the moorland with sharpened eyes in the hope that afar I might catch a glimpse of her whose life had touched mine so tenderly that day; but I could not discern her.

I was stirred by a strange desire to talk, and I began to put to my companion questions about some of his flock, and by devious paths I led him to the subject that was really in my heart.

"Mary," he said, "what would you know about Mary?" and then he smiled. "Oh, that is how the land lies, is it? Well, I'm no' surprised. She's a bonnie lass, and as good as she is bonnie, and a likely lass to take a young man's eye. But put her out of your mind. She's no' for you. The dove maunna' mate wi' the corbie."

"She must be a brave woman," I said, "for I understand that she brings us our food."

" Wha tell't ye that ? " he exclaimed, turning upon me sharply and lapsing into the fashion of speech which was ever his refuge when he was moved.

" Well, sir," I answered, " you said as much, and I put two and two together."

" Did I ? " he exclaimed. " Well, ye maun guess nae mair ; dinna forget this is the Sabbath day."

CHAPTER XII

THE GREATER LOVE

IDLY I pulled a little sprig of thyme which grew beside me, and crushing it between my fingers inhaled its perfume.

My companion watched me, saying: "Wonderful! wonderful! what glories there are in creation. Many a time I've lain awake at nights and thought about it all. Flowers on the moor, far bonnier than anything that ever man fashioned; birds in the air lilting sweeter melodies than man can make; the colour spilled across the sky when the sun sets; the mist on the hills. Glory everywhere; but nothing to the glory yonder"—and he raised his eyes to the heavens.

When we had rested for a time, my companion rose and we set out again.

The sun was setting when we came within sight of our hiding places.

"Come to my side of the loch," he said. "Ye'll want your supper before ye make for your bed," and together we made for the place where we had already enjoyed so many meals together. I went to the little stream to see if haply I might discover a trout there, but he forbade me sternly.

"Must I tell ye again that it is the Sabbath day? Ye maunna catch fish the nicht."

He left me for a moment, and sought his little store, and when he came back, we took our meal in silence. When we had finished he said: "I am wearied to-night; God send us sweet repose," and kneeling down he commended us both and "all good hill-folk" to the protection of the Almighty. He prayed too for his little congregation, and as he did so I wondered if another prayer might at that hour be ascending like incense from the lips of the girl who had begun to haunt my heart; and I wondered if in her petitions there would be any thought of me.

When his prayer was over the old man rose to his feet, and laying a hand upon my shoulder while I bowed my uncovered head he lifted his face to the sky and gave me his blessing. There was a catch in my voice as, touched at heart and humbled, I bade him "Good night."

I walked round the end of the loch and sought my hiding-place, but though I was fatigued I could not fall asleep. The stars were glittering afar, and I wondered if at that moment she, too, were looking up at their beauty. I lived through once again all the incidents of the day in which she had played a part. I heard her sweet voice singing, I saw the light upon her hair, the glint in her eyes and, once again, I felt the pressure of her hand. There in the darkness I lifted my own right hand to my lips and kissed it—for had she not touched it? Then I fell asleep, but even as I slept she walked, an angel, through my dreams.

When I awoke my first thought was of her: then, as I looked up at the sky, I judged that the day was already some hours past the dawn. Cautiously I separated the fronds of brackens and looked along the moor. What I saw made me draw back in horror: then, with a beating heart, I took courage and peeped carefully through once more.

The troopers were upon us, and on my side of the loch there were some twenty who, scattered about, on horseback, were quartering and requartering the whole hill-side. I looked warily across to the other side of the loch. There I could see none. I knew that my safety lay in absolute stillness. A movement of one of the bracken stems beneath which I lay might betray me—even my breathing might be heard, and I knew the uncanny instinct with which a trooper's horse was sometimes aware of the presence of a fugitive when his rider might be ignorant. As I listened to the voices of the troopers, and heard the hoofs of their horses, I felt a sudden love for all the timorous hunted creatures of the earth. In imagination I saw a hare, with ears laid back, and eyes dilate with fear, lying clapped in her form.

In my extremity I thought of Mary, and wondered if she knew of my peril. My lips were dry as sand, my hands were moist, and my heart was beating loudly, so that I thought the sound of it must be heard by my pursuers. Would it be a speedy death there on the moorland, or would I be taken to Wigtown and given a trial? Life had never seemed sweeter than in that morning hour, and now fate was about to dash the cup of happiness from my lips. I dared not stir to look again through the brackens, but I knew from the sound of the voices that some of the troopers were now close to my hiding-place. With ears alert I listened. Surely that was Agnew's voice. I heard the jangle of bridle chains, and the creak of stirrup leathers: I could hear the heavy breathing of the horses—they were closing in upon me on every side. One minute more and I should be discovered, and then, death! And I, because I had learned to love, had grown afraid to die.

Suddenly, clear and shrill, the sound of a flute came from the far side of the loch. What madness was this? Did not the old man know that the troopers were upon us? In the very teeth of danger he was calmly playing a tune that I had heard more than once in the moonlit hours of the night. O fool! What frenzy had seized him?

The sound reached the troopers. I heard a voice shout, "What the devil is that?" and the tramp of the horses ceased. The player played on. . . . There was a sharp word of command: the horses were spurred to the gallop, and raced to the other side of the loch. As they passed my hiding-place one of them almost brushed my feet with its hoofs. The player played on. . . . There was no tremor in his notes; clear and shrill they cleft the moorland air. I took courage and peered out. Look where I might I could see no trooper on my side of the loch, but on the other side I saw them rapidly converging to the place from which the music came. The player ceased as suddenly as he had begun, and lying there in my hiding-place I cursed him for his folly. Never before had I heard his flute save in the hours of darkness. And then the truth flashed upon me. It was not madness: it was sacrifice! He had seen my danger, and to save me, with no thought of self, he had done this thing.

Would they find him? I, with no skill in prayer, found myself praying fervently that he might escape. Then something within me cried: "You can save him—show yourself." It was the voice of Mary, and, startled, I peered through the brackens to see if she could be near, but there was no one to be seen on my side of the loch and nothing to be heard but the trailing of the wind along the tops of the heather. "Save him!" cried the voice again. I sprang to my feet and shouted, but the wind carried my voice away over my shoulder. Then I heard loud cries on the other side of the loch and I knew that the troopers had found the Minister. . . . Could I save him now? . . . Was any good purpose to be served by my surrender, or did it mean simply that two lives would be taken in place of one? Again I heard the voice: "Too late," it said, "too late," and it was the voice of Mary, choked with tears.

I threw myself down again, and cursed myself for a coward. I could not see what was happening on the other side of the loch. For a time there was the tumult of many voices, and then all was still. I knew what that meant. Lag or Claver'se or whatever devil incarnate might be at the head of the troop was putting my friend to the test. Would he take the oath? I knew that to him allegiance to his God was far more precious than fealty to an earthly king. I could see the whole scene: he, calm, in the circle of his accusers, with the firing party charging their weapons. I could hear the bullying voice of the commander trying to break his spirit, and then I knew—for I had seen it—that he would be given five minutes to make his peace with God. Little need for that! . . . The crash of muskets tore the silence and I knew that Alexander Main, hillman, and Saint, had won his crown of glory at the last.

I felt the tears brim in my eyes, and trickle scalding down my cheeks. Then I was seized with dread once more. Would the troopers be content with this one victim, or would they come again to my side of the loch and continue their search? I knew not; I could only wait for whatever might happen. In a few minutes I should know.

I could hear the sound of the troopers' voices and their laughter, and peering through the brackens I saw the little cavalcade go back to the edge of the loch where they gave their horses to drink. In a body they marched to the end of the loch. If they swung round to the left and came again to quarter my side of the hill, my fate was sealed. With hands clenched I waited, watching. I was taut as a bow-string with suspense. The string snapped: I was free !—for when they reached the end of the loch, they set their horses to the ascent that led to the top of the hill, and in half an hour the last of them had disappeared. And there on my bed of heather beneath the brackens I lay and cried like a child.

I lay there till the sun went down ; then in the gloaming I stole round to the other side of the loch to look for my friend. I found him at last. He was lying on his back, with eyes open, looking into the depth of the sky. There was a smile upon his face, a smile of pride and unspeakable joy. A great bloody gash, where the murderous bullets had struck him, lay over his heart. Beside him, face downward, lay an open book. I picked it up reverently. It was his Bible, and a splash of blood lay upon the open page across these words : "They shall hunger no more, neither thirst any more ; neither shall the sun light on them, nor any heat." Gently I closed the book, and sat down beside him. I had lost a friend ; a friend who had shown me the greater love ; he was a Covenanter, and I—God help me !—I had been a persecutor. My heart was torn by shame and remorse : but in the dim light his quiet pale face was smiling, as though he was satisfied.

Suddenly a thought struck me. I must give him burial, and quick on the heels of the thought came another : The dead need no covering but the kindly earth ; would it be sacrilege to strip him of his clothes ? He had no further need of them, while I was in sore straits to get rid of my uniform. I knelt down and peered into his face. The smile there gave me courage. In life he had been shrewd and kindly, and I knew that in death he would understand. So, very gently, I began to strip him. As I took his coat off something fell from the pocket. It was his flute. I put it beside his Bible. I have kept both till this day.

Then when I had stripped him, I cast about in my mind for some means to give him burial. Not far away I knew there was a gash in the hill-side where once some primeval tarn had been. Reverently I lifted his body and bore it thither. Gently I laid it down, and standing with bowed head under the starlit sky, I pronounced over that noble dust all I could remember of the English burial service. Did ever Covenanter have a stranger burial ? I trow not. Then reverently I happed him over with heather and brackens and turf which I tore from the hill-side, and laboured on until the trench was filled and I had built a cairn of stones over it.

So I left him sleeping there, and, as I turned away, I was overwhelmed by a sense of loss and loneliness.

I gathered up the clothing which I had taken from his body, and bore it to the side of the loch. There, from the coat, I washed the stains of blood, and laid it on the sward to dry.

Occupied as I had been, I was unconscious of the flight of time ; but I was reminded by a sudden access of hunger. A problem faced me, for I had no food of my own. For days I had been depending on the charity of my friend ; and I did not know where his store lay hidden. In that wilderness it was well secreted lest any questing bird or four-footed creature of the moorlands might find it. A sudden apprehension seized me, and, with its coming, my hunger disappeared. I hurried to the place where we were wont to take our evening meal together, and then I walked in the direction which he had usually taken when he went to fetch the provender. I sought beneath likely tussocks of heather and under the shadow of boulders and beneath the shelves of overhanging turf, where some sheep, aforetime, had had a rubbing place. But nowhere could I find a trace of his store. Baffled, I determined that I would seek my hiding-place and lie down to sleep for the rest of the night. In the morning, with the help of the light, perhaps my quest would be rewarded. So I betook myself to my heather bed, and as I crawled under the bracken—and laid myself down, I thought how, but for the divine charity of my dead friend, I should at that hour have been sleeping the sleep of death.

CHAPTER XIII

PURSUED

MORNING came, clear and bright, and as I stepped out from my hiding-place I was conscious that the air of the dawn had served to whet my hunger. I hurried to the other side of the loch and renewed my search. Crouching down I ferreted in every likely nook and corner, but found nothing. Was it that there was nothing to find? Was the larder already empty, or had the troopers discovered it after they had done their deed of blood, and rifled it of its poor contents? Whatever the case, my search, repeated over and over again during the course of the morning—till I knew every blade of grass and bracken-frond on that side of the loch—revealed nothing. While I searched, my hunger abated; when I paused I was painfully conscious of it, and then, suddenly, I remembered the little trickling stream and in a moment I was bending over it seeking for trout. My search was rewarded and ere long I had caught enough to make a meal. Hunger made me forget discretion, and I lit a fire to cook them.

While the stone on which I was to broil my meal was warming in the flames, I went to the loch side and picked up the garments of my dead friend. Hastily I divested myself of my uniform, and filling the pockets, which I had emptied of my possessions, with large stones, I swam into the middle of the loch and let the heavy burden drop into its depths. Then I made for the shore, and ran in the sunlight till the air had dried me, and then aglow and breathless I donned the clothing of the dead preacher. I felt the flute in the pocket of his coat and drew it out, looking at it with fond eyes, and placed it to my lips—but as I was about to blow, I stopped. It would be sacrilege for unclean lips like mine to call one note from this the plaything and the solace of the dead saint, so I replaced it in my pocket.

I cooked my fish, and, forgetful of the risk I ran, omitted to extinguish my fire. I stretched my hands out to enjoy its warmth and watched the silver grey spirals of smoke coil like ghostly things into the blue atmosphere.

I sat in a reverie, and after awhile I rose to make another search for the undiscovered hiding-place of the old man's hoard.

I had wandered afield, and had come to the brow of the hill. When I rose from my crouching position to stretch myself, I saw a sight that chilled me. Less than half a mile away was a company of troopers who were riding at a gallop. I flung myself upon my face and prayed that my dark figure against the horizon had escaped notice, and then the thought flashed upon me that they were coming direct to the place where I was, and the fire which I had left burning was the beacon that had attracted them. Doubtless they had been continuing their search for me in another quarter of these mountain fastnesses, and now through my own folly I had shown them where to find me.

Crouching low, I raced to the loch side. Then, remembering that the loch was in the cup of the hills, and that until they reached the summit of the slope they could not see me, I rose erect and raced with all my speed to the end of the loch and on. Fear lent wings to my feet. To be safe at all I must put many miles between my pursuers and myself before I thought of hiding. The country was practically unknown to me, but I remembered roughly the way we had taken when we went to the hill-meeting, and I imagined that somewhere in that direction my greatest safety would lie.

Never stopping to look back, but with panting breath, hot-foot I ran, leaping over boulders and crashing through the heather, until my limbs almost refused to respond to my desires ; then I flung myself down into a deep bed of bracken and turned to scan the way I had come. Already I had travelled far, and, when I looked back, piercing the distance with eager eyes, I could see no trace of my pursuers.

Though there was no sign of them, I dared not count on safety till I had placed a much greater distance between us or until night should fall. So, when I had recovered my breath, I left my shelter and hurried on. As I went I recognised some of the landmarks I had passed two days before, and by and by I came to the gorge in the hills where the service had taken place As I entered the little amphitheatre my eyes wandered instinctively to the stone where Mary had sat, but, to my surprise, the stones were no longer there in orderly array. I looked to where the pulpit had been, but it was scattered. Then I knew that some of the worshippers before they left that hallowed spot had, with crafty foresight, scattered the stones that might have been a witness to some band of troopers that a "field preaching" had taken place. Wearily I ascended the slope on one side of the amphitheatre and crouching low among the heather I scanned the surrounding country. The afternoon was now far advanced, and the evening shadows were beginning to gather. Look where I might I could see no sign of my pursuers, and, glad at heart, I decided that here I should rest for an hour or two and then continue my flight when the darkness fell. There was something holy about the place, for *she* had worshipped here.

My long run had exhausted me, so I crawled into a clump of bracken and was soon asleep, my last waking thoughts being of Mary, and not of my danger.

When I woke the moon was high in the heavens. I was conscious of hunger and thirst, but I had not the wherewithal to appease them: but I hoped that on my way I might stumble upon some moorland rivulet, or at the worst a pool of brackish water among the moss-hags. Hunger a man can bear, but thirst is torture to a fugitive.

Somewhere an owl hooted drearily and the eerie sound in that place of desolation startled me, alive in every sense to anything unexpected.

As I began my flight once more I was conscious that my limbs were stiff, but in a few moments, as movement began to warm me, the stiffness disappeared. On a trackless moor it is ever a hard thing for a man unacquainted with the country-side to make much speed, and I had to go warily lest I should stumble, as once before, into some treacherous bog.

The wind had risen and was bringing with it an army of clouds that swept, a dark host, across the sky. Suddenly the darkness was rent by a flashing blade of light which shook like a sword of molten metal held by some giant in the skies, and then, as though a thousand iron doors were flung against their doorposts, the heavens crashed round me. The wild peal of thunder rolled through the night air. Caught by every trembling hill-top, it reverberated and reverberated again till it pulsed into silence. My ears ached. The lightning and the thunder had brought me to a standstill, when again the sky was torn by a blaze of fire. Hard on its heels came another thunderclap and with it a deluge of rain. Every drop was a missile, stinging my face like a whip-lash. Startled, I made haste to seek cover from the storm, but I had left the hills behind me and there was no friendly boulder near at hand.

I turned to look to the hill-side, when, again, a shaft of lightning like a mighty javelin hurtled earthward from the sky. The whole hill-side was lit up by its blaze, and I saw its point strike a great rock of granite that stood on the slope and cleave it in twain. The darkness closed like a door and ere the following peal hammered upon my ears I heard the crash of the shattered boulder as headlong it roared down the hill-side.

The air was heavy with the smell of sulphur; the earth was sodden beneath my feet. My clothes hung heavily upon me and at every step the water oozed from my shoes.

Remembering a trick of the moor men I dropped on my knees and tore up a piece of turf and scooped away some of the underlying earth with my hands. Quickly the water oozed into the bowl from the ground round about it, and when I had given it a moment to settle, I bent and drank deeply. Then I rose and hurried on and, in the hope of discovering some shelter ere long, I broke into a run. It was a foolish thing to do, for save when a lightning flash lit up the ground I could not see more than a yard or two ahead.

Suddenly, as though a red-hot knife had struck me, I felt a stab of pain in my right ankle, and I fell upon my face. The fall winded me, and as I lay while the pitiless rain beat upon me, I tried to realise what had happened. I had trodden upon a stone which had betrayed my foot; my foot had slipped on its edge, and I knew from the pain that I had done myself an injury.

I tried to gather myself up, but every effort sent a

pang to my heart. Slowly I raised myself upon my hands and knees, and then with a great effort I lifted myself to my feet, but I found that I could not bear the pressure of my injured foot upon the ground. I tried to raise it, but the movement only redoubled my agony, and, bemoaning my fate, I lowered myself gently to a sitting posture on the wet earth.

CHAPTER XIV

IN THE SLOUGH OF DESPOND

It was too dark to see the injured part, but from the increasing pressure on the edge of my shoe I knew my foot was swelling. Soon the pain of the pressure became intolerable, and with an effort I leaned over and undid the lace. This gave me some relief, but when I tried to remove the shoe the pain compelled me to desist. But, taking courage, I made trial once more and succeeded at last in getting it off. Then I removed my sock. Very gently I passed a hand over the injured part. I could feel that it was greatly swollen. My foot lay at an angle which led me to think that one or other of the bones of my leg had been broken. My heel dropped backwards, and the inner edge of my foot was twisted outward. If I kept the limb at rest the pain was tolerable; if I moved it the agony was more than I could support. The falling rain upon it was like a cooling balm, and gave me relief, but as I sat there—sodden, helpless—alone amid the desolation of that vast moorland, I was overwhelmed by a sense of my misfortune. Twice already had I escaped from the troopers' hands, and now, unless succour, which seemed outside the range of hope, should come to me, I was doomed to a lingering death.

I prayed for the dawn to break, and then I realised that dawn could bring me no hope, and I ceased to care whether it were light or dark. But the dawn came nevertheless, and with it a wind that swept the rain-clouds out of the sky. I tore up some tufts of heather and made a soft couch upon which to rest my injured limb; then, wet though I was and cold, I lay down and ere long had fallen asleep. I know not how long I slept, but when I woke my head was on fire and I was aching in every limb. My tongue was parched like a piece of leather and I was tortured by a burning thirst, so that I was fain to pluck the grass and heather that lay within my reach and suck from them the scanty drops of moisture that still clung to them. To add to my distress, I was seized with a violent shivering which shook my whole body and caused my injured limb to send stabbing darts of pain all through my being. I laid a hand upon my forehead and found that it was burning hot, and I knew that I was in the grip of some deadly fever. I called for help in my extremity, but my voice was weak as a child's and the only reply that came to me was the cry of a startled whaup. Well, what did it matter if I had to die? Surely it were better to be freed by a speedy death, than to lie there a helpless log until I should die of starvation.

I closed my eyes again and drifted into a dreamy state of partial comfort, from which I was awakened by a violent pain in my right side. My breathing had become difficult. Every movement of my chest was torment, and, to add to my miseries, I began to cough. I opened my eyes and looked into the depths of the sky as though to summon help out of the infinite; but all I could see was a pair of carrion crows that were circling above me, waiting, I had little doubt, for the moment when the breath should leave my body and their foul feasting could begin.

So this was to be the end of it—a week or two, and all that would be left would be a heap of bones, bleaching in the wind and rain of that vast moor.

I closed my eyes again, and drifted once more into

a pleasant state of drowsiness, and suddenly I was my own man again, strong and sound in limb as I had ever been: free from pain, and without a care in the world. I was walking gaily along a road that stretched before me into infinite distance. Birds were singing around me and in the sweet air of the morning there was the scent of hedgerow flowers. Far off, near the summit of the hill where the road seemed to end, a woman was waiting for me. She was beckoning to me to make haste, and though I hurried fleet-foot towards her, she remained as far away as ever. The woman was Mary. Try as I might, I could not reach her. Then a miracle happened: she came towards me. A radiant welcome shone in her face: her arms were outstretched I called to her and held out eager hands towards her: but she drifted past me, and was gone, and, heavy at heart, I fell back, a sodden, tortured thing, on the cold wet moors. My eyes opened. The carrion crows still circled above me: but not for long.

Once more I was on a journey, moving, a formless mass, beneath a leaden sky with no moon or sun or stars to guide me; myself a part of the darkness that surrounded me. In this strange world in which I found myself there were other formless shapes like my own, each drifting noiselessly and without contact through infinite leagues of space. The mass that was me was not me. It was separate from me, yet indissolubly united to me. I was perplexed. Was I the mass or was the mass some other being? I had no being of my own apart from the mass, and yet the mass was not me. Where was I?—What was I?—Who was I? I had no pain, no hands or feet, no torturing thirst, no fever-racked body. Was I disembodied? If so, what was I now? In agony of mind, I, who had no mind, struggled to puzzle the problem out; and then, suddenly, the grey mass that had perplexed me rolled from my sight, and I found myself once more lying upon the moor in pain, alone. The sky above me was sprinkled with stars; night had come again: the day had brought me no succour.

If I lay here any longer, surely the troopers would find me. I must up and on. It seemed to me that a great hand came out of the sky and blotted out my pain as someone might blot out an error upon a child's slate. I was strong again. I sprang to my feet. My limb was sound once more. I ran across the moor like a hind let loose and in the darkness I stepped over a precipice and fell unendingly down. The minutes passed, and I saw them gather themselves into little heaps of hours that stood like cairns of stone on the top of the precipice. The hours piled themselves into days and the days into weeks, till the top of the precipice was covered with stones, and still I was falling through unending space. Some time—I know not when—I must have come to the bottom of the precipice. I felt no crash, but the heaped-up cairns of the minutes and hours and days disappeared from my sight, and I ceased to know anything. I cannot tell how long this deep oblivion lasted. Once only did I wake from it partially. I felt a twinge of pain as though someone had moved me, and then all was dark again.

CHAPTER XV

IN THE HAVEN OF DALDOWIE

A MAN may go to the very gate of death without knowing that he has stood within its shadow till he returns once more to the sunshine of life. I know not how long I lay, an unconscious mass, at the foot of the dream precipice of my delirium, but an hour came when I opened my eyes again. I opened them slowly, for even to lift my lids was an effort, and I looked above me to see if the carrion crows were still watching me. Instead I saw a low thatched roof, and in amazement I let my eyes wander to every side. I was lying on a soft mattress laid on a garret floor. My head was pillowed on a snowy pillow of down. Beside my couch stood a three-legged stool and on it there was a bowl of flowers. I stretched out a weak hand to take one. I picked up a buttercup that flaunted its proud gold before me, and I pressed it to my lips. I lay in a reverie and tried to gather together all I could remember of the past. I recollected my flight from the troopers, the thunderstorm and the rain, and then I remembered my injured limb. I tried to move it and found that it was firmly bound. I was too weak to raise myself and turn down the bedclothes to examine it, but there was further food for thought in the fact that my injury had been cared for.

Where was I ?—and who had brought me here and nursed me back to life again ?

Perplexed I could find no light to guide me, and weary with fruitless thoughts I fell asleep.

When I woke up again my eyes rested upon a woman who was just beginning to appear through a trap-door in the floor. She entered the garret, bearing a cup whose contents gave off a generous odour. She came to my bedside and, carefully removing the flowers from the stool, sat down upon it, and looked at me. My wide-awake eyes met her astonished gaze.

"Thank God," she said, "ye're better. Ye've been queer in the heid for mair than a fortnicht, and me and Andra' had lang syne gi'en ye up."

She dropped on her knees beside me and, slipping her left arm gently under my pillow, raised me and put the cup to my lips.

"Here," she said, "drink some o' this."

I drank a long draught, and never have I tasted anything with savour so exquisite.

All too soon the cup was empty and the warmth of its contents sent a glow through my wasted body. I was about to ask where I was and how I had come there, when I remembered that I had another duty to perform. So, in a voice that shook from weakness and emotion, I said:

"I know not who you are, but you have saved my life, and I would thank you."

"Wheesht," she said. "You are far ower weak to talk yet. When you have had a guid nicht's sleep and a wee drap mair nourishment, it will be time enough. Haud yer wheesht the noo like a guid bairn and gang to sleep," and she drew the coverlet up round my neck and tucked it about me. Some old memory buried in the margin of my consciousness stirred within me. Just so had my mother tucked me to sleep many a time and oft, when I was a little lad, and the memory brought the tears to my eyes. I said nothing, for the will of the woman was stronger than mine at the moment, and I must needs obey it. I watched her place the bowl of flowers upon the stool: then, after smoothing my pillow, she went to the trap-door, passed through it and disappeared.

For a time I lay looking up at the straw roof. My eyes followed the black rafters that supported it, and I tried to count the knots in the beams: but the light which trickled through the window had begun to fade, and as I tried to count I fell asleep.

When I woke again it was dark, but a faint beam from the moon made a pool of silver on the coverlet that lay over me. I heard a voice in the room beneath me. I listened eagerly, but could not distinguish any words, and as I listened it dawned upon me that the voice was that of someone reading aloud. Then there was a pause: and in the silence that followed I heard a grating sound as though a chair were pushed a little, over a sandstone floor, and again the voice spoke. Then I knew that in the kitchen beneath me the people under whose roof I rested were worshipping their God. I, a trooper and deserter, had been succoured by some of the moorland folk, and had found refuge in a Covenanter's cottage!

I lay and thought long of all that I owed to these hunted hill-folk. Twice had I, one of their persecutors, been succoured from death through their charity.

Some time soon after dawn I was wakened by sounds in the room beneath me. I heard a creak as though a hinge were moved, and the clank of a chain, and I knew that the good wife had swung her porridge-pot over the fire and was preparing breakfast for her family. The delicious aroma of slow-cooked porridge began to assail my nostrils and I was conscious that I was hungry.

I wondered if by any chance I should be forgotten; then I banished the uncharitable thought. By and by I heard the sound of footsteps in the kitchen and then a confused murmur of voices. I knew that the family had gathered to break their fast, and I waited with all the patience I could command. The minutes passed slowly and every moment my hunger grew more and more intolerable: but at last the time of waiting was over. I heard footsteps ascending the ladder to my garret. The trap-door was thrown open, the top of a head appeared, a hand reached up and placed a bowl on the floor, and the head disappeared once more. Then again I heard footsteps ascending the ladder, and this time the woman came into the room bearing a second bowl. She picked up the one she had laid upon the floor and came to my bedside.

"Ye've sleepit weel?" she said, inquiry in her voice. "Ye're lookin' somethin' like a man this mornin'. See, I ha'e brocht you your breakfast."

She laid her burden down, and clearing the bowl of flowers from the stool, placed a hand adroitly behind my pillow and propped me up. For a moment the room spun round me. Then she placed the bowl of porridge in my lap and poured a stream of milk over it, saying: "Can ye feed yersel', or maun I feed ye like a bairn?" She gave me a horn spoon, and with a shaky hand I fed myself. She sat watching me, but did not speak again till I had finished my meal.

"That's better," she said. "You'll soon be yersel' again. It's the prood woman I am. I never yet knew a man sae ill as you ha'e been pu' through. Man, but for the grace o' God and our Mary, the craws on the moor would ha'e picked yer banes white long ere noo."

Startled, I looked at her. She had said "Mary." Could it be that this Mary was the Mary of my dreams? I ventured to speak.

"I cannot thank you enough for all you have done for me. But I do not know where I am nor how I came here. I remember nothing since I lay upon the moor, waiting for death."

"Weel," she said, "to make a long story short, ye're in the laft o' Andrew Paterson's fairm-hoose at Daldowie. Mary fand ye lyin' on the moor, in a kin' o' stupor. She got an awfu' fricht, puir lassie. First she thocht ye micht be ane o' the hill-fowk, and then she thocht ye had a kent face, and lookin' again, she minded that she had seen ye wi' the meenister at the field-meeting, the Sabbath afore. She saw ye were gey near deid, but she jaloused ye werena' quite, because ye kept muttering tae yoursel'. So she raced hame like a hare and wadna' rest till she had ta'en her faither oot to fin' ye. They carried ye here on the tail-board o' a cairt, and that's three weeks sin'; and here ye lie and here ye'll bide till ye're a weel man aince mair."

As the full meaning of her words dawned upon m I was uplifted with joy. Mary had found me! Sh had known me! She had cared enough for me to think that I was worth saving! Her big heart had pitied my necessity, and to her I owed my life! A sudden access of strength ran through my being. The blood coursed in my veins; I felt it pulse in my temples. It must have brought a glow to my cheeks, for the woman said:

"Ye're better—a lot better the day. The parritch has put a bit o' colour in your cheeks."

I found my tongue. "Will you," I said, "please thank your husband and your daughter"—I had fain said Mary with my lips: I said it in my heart—"for what they have done for me. Later, I hope to thank them myself."

"Oh, aye," she said, "ye'll be seein' them later on when ye're better. But I'll tell them. Meantime, maybe the nicht, when his work's dune, the guid-man'll be comin' up to see ye himsel'. He's got a wheen questions he wants to ask ye. For instance, we're sairly troubled because you were wearin' the meenister's claes when Mary found ye, and in ane o' your pockets ye had the meenister's Bible. And though ane or twa o' the hill-fowk hae been up to look for the guid man in his hiding-place, naebody has seen him and we're mair than a wee troubled. We ken ye were a trooper, and though the meenister vouched for ye himsel' at the meeting, Andra says that ye canna make a blackfaced tup into a white ane by clippin' its 'oo', and we hope ye haena dune the guid man a mischief. To tell ye the truth, when we got ye here and found the meenister's claes on ye, my guid-man was for puttin' ye oot on the moor again and leavin' ye to dee. But Mary pleaded for ye, and I minded my ain lad, so we hid ye here and nursed ye."

She said no more, and before I could explain she had descended the ladder and shut the trap-door.

The day passed rapidly; I slept and woke and slept and woke again. The good woman came to me more than once with food, but she did not talk to me again nor would she let me talk to her.

"The morn is the Sabbath day. I ha'e nae doot Andra' will come up to see ye sometime, and ye can tell him your story then." That was her good night to me, and when she had descended I heard again, as on the previous evening, the sound of these devout folk at their evening prayer.

Then all was silent and I slept.

CHAPTER XVI

ANDREW PATERSON, HILL-MAN

THE shrill crowing of a cock woke me, just as the first rays of the sun were stealing through the skylight. I lay adrowse, half sleeping, half awake, listening for the first sound of the house coming to life. The cock sounded his bugle again. Somewhere a hen cackled, and then all was still.

My eyes wandered round the garret. A mouse had stolen out of some cranny and was examining the room. He seemed unaware of my presence, for he sat solemnly in the middle of the floor with his tail curved like a sickle and proceeded to preen himself, till some unwitting movement of mine startled him and he scampered to his hole.

Slowly the minutes passed, then I heard movements in the kitchen beneath me. I knew that the day might be a difficult one for me, for sometime during its course I had to explain to the master of the house how I came to be disguised in the garb of the minister. My tale was a plain enough one, and I thought it would not be hard to clear myself of any suspicion of having had a hand in his death; but I could not be sure. Kind though my succourers had been, I knew that they were likely to be distrustful of one who had once been a trooper. The minister had been their friend, and it was but natural that they should feel his death keenly and be all too ready to suspect me of complicity in bringing it about. I determined to tell the tale simply, and I trusted that my words would carry conviction. If not, what then? I knew the fanatic spirit with which the hill-folk were sometimes charged. Would the master of the house, in his wrath, lay hands upon me and wring the life from my body? The evil, uncharitable thought was crushed down. They had shown me such love in the hours of my weakness that they were hardly likely to sacrifice me to their suspicions now.

As I pondered, the trap-door was raised, and, bearing my breakfast, the master of the house entered the garret. "Hoo are ye the day?" he asked.

"Better, I thank you, much better;—I owe my life to you and yours;—I shall never be able to repay you."

He set the food upon the stool before he answered. "Ye're gey gleg wi' your tongue. Naebody was talkin' aboot payin'. Haud your wheesht, and sup your parritch. I jalouse ye need them. Later on I'll be comin' up for a crack. There's a wheen things that are no' clear in my min'. The thing lies here: hoo did ye come by the minister's claes and his Bible?" and he looked at me with a steely glance, that, had I not been guiltless, would have covered me with confusion.

"I am ready," I said, "to tell you the whole story as soon as you are ready to listen."

"Weel," he answered, "I'm comin' back sune," and he went to the trap-door and descended, closing it behind him.

I made a hearty meal and was pleased to discover my strength was coming back to me. When I had finished I must have dropped into a sleep, from which I was wakened by hearing footsteps in the room once more. The man had returned, and under his arm he was carrying a bundle of heather, while in his hand there was a mass of wool. He knelt beside my bed and, turning up the blankets, said:

"Afore we begin to talk I think I'd better see aboot this leg o' yours."

He undid the bandages, and looking down I saw that beneath them the ankle had been carefully padded with wool and heather. I knew now the purpose of the things he had brought with him, for he stripped off the pad with which the ankle was surrounded and began to make a fresh one. Apparently he had some knowledge of the healing art. He ran his fingers gently over the joint and then bade me try to move the foot. I found that movement was difficult, but that though it was painful it did not provoke such suffering as that which I remembered having experienced upon the moor.

"It's daein' fine," he said. "It was a bad break, but by and by ye'll be able to walk again, though I fear ye'll aye be a lamiter. But Jacob himsel'—a better man than you—hirpled for the maist pairt o' his life."

As he talked he was binding my foot again, and when he had finished, it felt most comfortable.

"And noo," he said, "let me hear what ye ha'e to say for yersel'. The facts are black against ye. We fand you on the moor in the meenister's claes: ye had the guid man's Bible in your pocket: when last he was seen you were in his company: and nocht has been heard o' him frae that day to this. What say ye?" and he looked at me piercingly.

Without more ado I told him how the brave old saint had given his life that mine might be saved, and how I had buried his body in the silence of the hills, taking his clothes to disguise myself and bringing away his Bible as a precious possession.

As I talked I watched the changing emotions chase each other across his face. At first his eyes were watchful with suspicion, but as I continued he seemed thrilled with a tensity of expectation, and when I told him how the end had come with the rattle of muskets I saw his strong, gnarled hands clench, and, through his tightened lips, he muttered, " The black deevils," and then the tears stole down his weather-beaten cheeks.

When I had finished there was a silence which at last he broke :

" A man o' God, a saint if ever there was ane. We'll miss him sairly here I'm thinkin', but they will be glad to ha'e him on the other side." Then he rose from the stool and gripping my right hand, crushed it in his own. " I believe you, my lad, I believe you, and if Alexander Main counted you worthy to die for, Andrew Paterson o' Daldowie may count you worthy o' a share of his kail and saut. I maun gang and tell the wife ; her and Mary are anxious to ken the truth " : and he made for the trap-door and began to go down. But just before his head disappeared he turned and called : " Maybe I'll come back the day to see ye again, but if I dinna', the wife'll be up to look after ye, and if I'm spared I'll be up masel' the morn. This is nae day to talk aboot the dambrod. I'll speir ye aboot it some ither time."

CHAPTER XVII

AN ADOPTED SON

It is needless to trace day by day the events of the next fortnight. Each morning found me with increasing strength. The good wife of the house was continually solicitous for my welfare, and had I been son of hers she could not have bestowed more care upon me. She took a pride in every sign of returning strength. Daily she brought me shreds of family gossip; news of the crops; news of the cattle; told me, with housewifely pride, how many chickens had come from her last sitting of eggs.

More than once, in our talk, I tried to turn the conversation to Mary; but never with much success. Shyness kept me from advances too direct. Sometimes she would tell me of the hill-men; and once she told me, with pride flashing in her eyes, of her son.

"He died," she said, "at Drumclog. It was a short, sharp fecht, and the dragoons reeled and fled before the Bonnets o' Blue. My laddie was sair wounded, and died in the arms o' guid Maister Main. His last words were: 'Tell my mither no' to greet. It's been a graun' fecht, and oor side's winnin'.'" There were no tears in her eyes as she told me the tale, but when she had finished she laid a hand upon my head and gently stroked my hair. "He was sic' anither as you, when he fell," and she turned and left me. Of an evening the farmer would sometimes come up, bringing with him a dambrod, and many a well-fought game we had together. He played skilfully and usually won, which gave him considerable satisfaction.

"Ye canna' beat Daldowie on the dambrod," he would say, with a twinkle in his eyes. "Scotland owes little enough to Mary Stuart, the Jezebel, but she or some o' her following brocht this game wi' them, and that is something they'll be able to say for themselves on the Judgment Day. They'll mak' a puir enough show that day, or I'm mistaken, but the dambrod will coont on their side."

When we had played for a week, and Saturday night came, he brought up a slate with a record of the score.

"It's like this, ye see," he said. "We've played a score and half o' games. I ha'e won a score and seven, and you won three—which ye shouldna' ha'e done ava' if I had opened richt and no foozled some o' the moves wi' my king. So ye're weel bate, and it's as weel for you that I dinna' believe in playin' for money, or it is a ruined lad ye'd be the nicht."

There was a gleam of satisfaction in his grey eyes, and I could see that to have beaten me so soundly had given him great pleasure.

"We'll no play the nicht; it's gettin' ower near the Sabbath," he continued, "but I'll bate ye even better next week."

I should have been lacking in gratitude if I had not begun to develop a warm affection for my friends. Simple folks, their joys were simple ones, but they were both filled with the zest of life; and in spite of the daily peril in which they lived, sunshine, rather than clouds, seemed to overhang their dwelling.

There came a day when, after examining my ankle with care, the old man said: "I think we micht try to get ye on your legs," and he raised me in his arms and set me on my feet. The garret spun round me, and the floor rose like the billows of the sea and would have swept me down had it not been for his strong arm.

"Steady lad, steady," he said. "Ye'll fin' your feet in a wee. Just shut your een for a minute and then open them again. I'll haud ye fast; dinna' be feart!"

I did as he bade me and found that the floor had become steady again; then, supported by his arm, I essayed to walk. To my joy I discovered that, though the effort cost me pain, I was able to walk from one end of the room to the other. The old man was delighted.

"Jean," he cried, "come awa' up to the laft. Bryden can walk," and I saw the trap-door rise to admit her.

She stood with her hands on her hips: "It bates a'," she said. "The nicht ye cam' I never thocht to see you on your legs again, but ha'e a care, Andra, the lad's weak yet; help him back intil his bed and I'll fetch him a bowl o' sheep's-heid broth for his supper."

And when I was comfortably settled once more, she was as good as her word.

Next day she brought me a strong ash stick, and with its help and the aid of her arm I was able to walk round the loft in some comfort.

Day by day my strength grew and I began to look forward to the hour when I should be able to join my friends in the kitchen below, when I hoped to see Mary face to face. It may have been nothing more than a coincidence—though, as I listened eagerly, I flattered myself it might be for joy that I was so far recovered—that on the night I first began to walk again, I heard Mary singing a song.

As the hour drew nearer when I should meet her,

I began to be covered with confusion. How would she receive me ?

At last the great day came. In the late afternoon Andrew brought me a suit of clothes.

" The wife sent ye them," he said. " She thocht they were nearer your size than the meenister's," and he laid them on the stool beside my bed and turned his back upon me : then brushing a sleeve across his eyes, he said : " I'm thinkin' it cost Jean a lot to tak' them oot o' the drawer ; ye see they were Dauvit's."

Had I needed any proof of the love they bore me, I had it now. I was to enter the circle round their hearth clad in the garments of their dead son. I had learned enough of the quiet reserve of these hill-folks to know that any words of mine would have been unseemly, so I held my peace, and with the help of the good man put the garments on. Then leaning on my stick and aided by his strong arm I walked to the trap-door. Slowly I made my way down the ladder, guided at every step by Andrew who had preceded me, and by and by my feet touched the flagged floor of the kitchen. The old woman hurried to my side, and between them they guided me to a large rush-bottomed chair set in the ingle-nook beside the fire.

" Nae sae bad, nae sae bad," said the good wife. She looked at me when I was seated and with a sudden " Eh, my! " she turned and shoo'd with her apron a hen that had wandered into the kitchen.

Eagerly I looked round, but there was no sign of Mary. The peat smoke which circled in acrid coils round the room stung my eyes and blurred my vision, but I was able to take note of the things around me. The kitchen was sparsely furnished and scrupulously clean. Against one wall stood a dresser with a row of china bowls, and above them a number of pewter plates. A " wag-at-the-wa' " ticked in a corner near. A settle stood on the other side of the peat fire from that on which I was seated, and a table, with well-scoured top, occupied the middle of the floor.

The good man having satisfied himself that I was all right, went out, and his wife, taking a bowl from the dresser, filled it with water. I watched her as she proceeded with her baking. As she busied herself she talked briskly.

" Ye ken," she said, " you ha'e been under this roof weel ower a month, and yet ye've never tellt us a word aboot yersel', mair than we fand oot. Hae ye got a mither o' your ain, and hoo did you, an Englishman, fin' yer way to this pairt o' the country ? Weel I ken that, ever since Scotland gi'ed ye a king, Scotsmen ha'e been fond o' crossin' the border, but I never heard tell o' an Englishman afore that left his ain country to come North, unless," she added, with a twinkle in her eye, " he cam' as a prisoner."

It was an invitation to unbosom myself, of which I was ready enough to avail me, and I told her some of my story. " So ye're College bred," she said. " That accounts for your nice ceevility.

" They tell me," she continued, " that England's a terrible rich country, that the soil is far kindlier than it is up here and that farmer bodies haena' sic' a struggle as we ha'e in Scotland." She did not wait for my reply, but added : " I am thinkin' maybe that is why, as I ha'e heard, the English ha'e na' muckle backbane, and are readier to listen to sic' trash as the Divine Richt o' Kings."

I tried to explain to her that it was the strain of monarchs whom we had imported from Scotland who laid most stress upon this right, but, as I talked, a shadow filled the doorway, and, looking up, I saw Mary. With a struggle I raised myself to my feet.

" Sit doon, sit doon," said the good-wife, " it's only oor Mary."

" You forget," I answered, " it is to your daughter,

who found me, that I owe my life. By rights I should kneel at her feet."

" Hear to him ! If it hadna' been for Mary's mither and the wey she looked efter ye and fed ye wi' chicken soup and sheep's-heid broth, forby parritch and buttermilk and guid brose made by her ain hand, ye wadna' be sittin' there ! "

" Wheesht, mither, wheesht," said Mary : and with a smile in her eyes that made me think of the stars of the morning in a rose tinged sky, she held out both her hands to me. I took them and bent to kiss them, but they were hastily withdrawn, and looking up I saw a flush upon her cheeks, but I did not read resentment in her eyes.

" Ha'e ye fetched in the kye, Mary ? " asked her mother.

" Aye," she replied, " they're a' in their stalls."

Indeed, one could hear the rattle of chains and the moving of hoofs on the other side of the wall.

" Weel, ye'd better start the milkin'. I'll be oot in a wee to help ye," and without a word more Mary took her departure. My ears were all alert, and, in a moment, I heard her slapping the flank of a cow. Then her stool grated on the cobbles, and I caught the musical tinkle of the milk as it was drawn into the pail ; and to my delight Mary began to sing.

I listened eagerly. She was singing a love song ! The old woman heard her too, for she said : " Dae ye ken ocht aboot kye ? " I hastened to tell her that I knew nothing. " Weel," she said, " it's a queer thing, but ye can aye get mair milk frae a coo if ye sing at the milkin'. If ye sing a nice bricht tune ye'll get twa or three mair gills than if ye dinna sing ava. Noo, that's Meg she's milkin', and Meg has got near as muckle sense as a human being. On Sabbath, ye ken, it would be a terrible sin to sing a sang to the coo when ye're milkin' her, so I've got to fa' back on the psalms. But ye've got to be carefu'. For instance, if ye sang the 'Auld Hundred' to Meg, ye wadna' get near sae muckle milk, because it's solemn-like, than ye wad if ye sang her a psalm that runs to the tune o' 'French.' Forby, I aince had a servant-lass that sang a paraphrase when she was milkin' Meg, and the puir cratur' was that upset that she was milked dry before the luggy was a quarter filled, and when I went masel' to strip her, she put her fit in the pail—a thing I've never kent her dae afore or since."

I laughed.

"Ay," she continued, "an' waur than that, the lass poured the luggy that she had drawn frae Meg among the other milk, and the whole lot turned. Sic' wastry I never kent afore, and ye may be sure that nae paraphrase has ever been sung in my byre since. The guid man was that upset—no' wi' the loss o' the milk—but at the thocht that a paraphrase had been sung in his byre to his coo on the Sabbath day that on the Monday he gi'ed the wench notice."

"I should have thought," I said, "that Mary's voice would persuade the milk from the most reluctant cow."

"I dinna' ken aboot that," she answered: "She's no as guid a milker as her mother, and though my voice is timmer noo I'll guarantee to get mair milk at a milkin' than ever Mary'll fetch ben the hoose."

I would fain have continued the conversation, but the baking was over, and the good woman left to join her daughter. Mary still sang on and I sat in rapture, my heart aglow.

CHAPTER XVIII

THE WISDOM OF A WOMAN

I SAW no more of Mary that day, for ere the milking was over Andrew returned from the fields and after studying me for a moment said: "I think it's time for your bed." Whereat he helped me carefully up the ladder, and left me to disrobe myself. That night, when the moon came out and filled my room with a glory that was not of this earth, I lay and dreamed of Mary, and through the silence of my dream I could hear once again the witching notes of her song.

Day after day I was gently assisted down the ladder, and each day I spent a longer time sitting by the peat fire. Most often my only companion in the kitchen was the good wife, and between us an intimate understanding began to spring up. I felt she liked to have me sitting there, and more than once she would look wistfully at me, and I knew from the sigh with which she turned again to her work that she was thinking of her dead boy .

Her face was attractive, though time had chiselled it deeply—and her eyes were shrewd and kindly. In repose her features were overcast by a mask of solemnity, but at each angle of her mouth a dimple lurked, and a ready smile, which started there or in her eyes, was perpetually chasing away all the sterner lines.

Mary came and went, busy at times on duties about the steading, sometimes on duties further afield, and more than once she set off laden with a well-filled basket and I knew that she was taking succour to some fugitive hill-man hidden on the moors. Always she treated me with kindness—with those innumerable and inexpressible little kindnesses that mean nothing to most people, but which to one in love are as drops of nectar on a parched tongue. Sometimes she would bring me flowers which she had gathered on the moor, and proud I was when on a day she fastened a sprig of heather in my coat.

Sometimes of a night the dambrod was brought out and the old man would beat me soundly once again.

But an evening came when he had no heart to play. He had been moody all day long, and when I suggested a game he said with a groan: "No' the nicht! no' the nicht! I ha'e mair serious things in mind."

I was at a loss to understand his reluctance, for hitherto he had always been eager for a game, but when I began to urge him to play, his wife interrupted me saying:

"Na, na, leave the man alane. If ye want to play, ye can play wi' Mary."

I needed no second invitation, nor did the suggestion seem unwelcome to Mary, who brought the board and the men and set them upon the table. Hers were the white men, mine the black: but after the first move or two the grace of her hand as it poised above the board cast such a spell over me that I began to play with little skill, and she was an easy victor. We played several games, all of which she won: and the only sound that disturbed our tourney was the tinkle of her laugh when she cornered me, or the click of her mother's needles as she knitted in the ingle-nook. But every now and then the old man groaned as though he were in great distress, and looking at him I saw that his head was buried in his hands.

When our tourney was over Mary gathered up the

men and restored them to a drawer, and as she did so she turned to her mother and said:

"Oh, mother, you ha'e never given the minister's Bible and his flute back to the gentleman."

"Nae mair I ha'e," said her mother. "Fetch them here," and Mary brought them to her. She took the Bible and handed it to me. It opened at the blood-stained page. Mary had come behind my chair; I was conscious that she was leaning over me. I could feel her hair touch my face, and then when she saw the stain a hot tear fell and struck my hand. I lifted my face towards her, but she had turned away. Without a word I handed the open book to her mother.

"Eh, dear, the bluid o' a saint," she said, and she closed the book reverently and gave it back to me.

The silence was broken by the good man. "Ay, the bluid o' a saint," he groaned—"ane o' the elect."

And that night for the first time I was present at the "taking o' the Book." Evening after evening as I had lain in the garret, I had heard these good folk at their worship. To-night I was permitted to take part in the rite, and though I have worshipped in the beautiful churches of Oxford and the storied Cathedrals of my own native land, I was never more conscious of the presence of God than in that little farm kitchen on the Galloway moors.

One afternoon as I sat watching the good wife at her baking, I asked her how it was that her husband and she had succeeded in escaping the attentions of the troopers.

"Oh," she said, "we ha'e na' escaped. Lag often gi'es us a ca', but there's a kin' o' understandin' between him and me. It's this way, ye see; before she got married my mother was a sewing-maid to his mother, and when my faither deid and she was left ill-provided, and wi' me to think o', she went back to Mistress Grierson and tellt her her trouble. Weel,

Mrs. Grierson liked my mother and she took her back, and she said: 'Mrs. Kilpatrick,' says she, 'if you will come back, you can bring wee Jean wi' ye. What a bairn picks will never be missed in a hoose like this, and the lassie can play wi' my Robert. Ye see he has neither brither nor sister o' his ain, and is like to be lonely, and your lassie, bein' six or seeven years aulder than him, will be able to keep him oot o' mischief.'

"And so it cam' aboot, and for maybe eight years I was as guid as a sister to him. But he was aye a thrawn wee deevil—kind-hearted at times, but wi' an awfu' temper. Ye see his mother spoiled him. Even as a laddie he was fond o' his ain way, and he was cruel then tae. I min' weel hoo he set his dog on my white kittlin, but I let him ken aboot it, because when the wee thing was safe in the kitchen again I took him by the hair o' the heid and pu'd oot a guid handfu'. My mither skelped me weel, but it was naething to the skelpin' I gie'd him the first chance I got. His mother never correkit him; it was 'puir Rob this, and puir Rob that,' and if it hadna' been that every noo and then, when my mither's patience was fair worn oot, she laid him ower her knee, I'm thinkin' Lag would be a waur man the day than he gets the blame o' bein'. There's guid in him; I'm sure o't, for even the de'il himsel' is no' as black as he's painted: but his heid has been fair turned since the King sent for him to London and knighted him wi' his ain sword.

"I bided in his mother's hoose till I was maybe seventeen years auld, and then my mither got mairrit again and left Dunscore to come and live near Dalry. Weel, I had never seen Lag frae that day till maybe a year sin', when the troopers began to ride through and through this country-side. Ae day I was oot-bye at the kirn when I heard the soond o' horses comin' up the loanin', and turnin', I saw Lag ridin' at the heid o' a company o' armed men. There was a scowl on his face, and when I saw him and minded the ill wark that I heard he had done in ither pairts, I was gey feart. He shouted an order to his troop and they a' drew rein. Then he cam' forrit tae me. 'Woman,' he said, 'Where's yer man?'

"'Fegs," says I, 'Rab Grier, that's no' a very ceevil way to address an auld frien'. Woman indeed! I am Mistress Paterson that was Jean Kilpatrick, that has played wi' ye mony a day in yer mither's hoose at Dunscore.' 'Guid sakes,' he cried, vaultin' oot o' his saddle, 'Jean Kilpatrick! This beats a'.' And he pu'd aff his ridin' gloves and held oot his hand to me. Then he shouted for ane o' his troopers to come and tak' his horse, and in he walks to the kitchen. Weel, we cracked and cracked, and I minded him o' mony o' the ploys we had when we were weans thegither.

"Syne, Mary cam' in wi' a face as white as a sheet. She had seen the troopers, and was awfu' feart: but I saw her comin' and I said: 'Mary lass, tak' a bowl and fetch my auld frien' Sir Robert Grier a drink o' buttermilk.' And that gie'd the lassie courage, for she took the bowl and went oot-bye to the kirn, and in a minute she cam' back wi' the buttermilk; so I set cakes and butter afore him and fed him weel, and as he ate he said: 'Ay, Jean, ye're as guid a baker as your mither. D'ye mind how you and me used to watch her at the bakin' in the old kitchen at Dunscore, and how she used to gie us the wee bits she cut off when she was trimming the cake, and let us put them on the girdle ourselves?' And as he talked he got quite saft-like and the scowl went aff his face a' thegither.

"Then he began to tak' notice o' Mary. 'So this is your dochter,' he said. He looked her up and doon: 'I see she favours her mither, but I'm thinkin' she's better lookin' than you were, Jean. Come here, my pretty doo!' he says, and as Mary went towards him I could see she was a' o' a tremble. He rose frae his chair an' put his arm roon' her shoulder and made as though to kiss her. Weel, I could see Mary shrinkin' frae his touch, and the next minute she had gie'd him a lood skelp on the side o' his face wi' her haun, and wi' her chin in the air, walked oot o' the door. I looked at Lag. There was anger on his broo, but he pu'd himsel' thegither and dropped back in his chair, sayin': 'Jean, ye've brocht her up badly. That's puir hospitality to a guest.' 'Weel, Rob,' says I, 'the lassie's no' to blame. It maun rin in her blood, for mony a guid skelpin' my mither has gi'en ye,—I ha'e skelped ye masel', and noo ye've been skelped by the third generation.' Whereat he let a roar o' laughter oot o' his heid that shook the hams hangin' frae the baulks. And that set his memory going, and he said, 'D'ye mind the day I set my dog on your kitten, and you pu'd a handfu' o' hair oot o' my heid?' and he took his hat off, saying, 'I am thinkin' that is the first place on my pow that is going bald.' 'Ay,' says I, 'weel I mind it, and the lickin' I got.' 'Yes,' says he, laughin', 'but ye paid me back double.' And he roared wi' laughter again.

"We were crackin' as crouse as twa auld cronies, when he said: 'And noo, Jean, a word in yer lug. I had nae thocht when I cam' up here I was gaun to meet an auld frien'. I cam' to ask you and your man, will ye tak' the Test. But I am no' gaun to ask the question o' ye. For the sake o' the auld days, this hoose and they that live in it are safe, so far as Robert Grierson o' Lag is concerned. But that is between you and me. Dinna be lettin' your man or your dochter, the wee besom, consort wi' the hill-men. The times are stern, and the King maun be obeyed. But ye can trust me that I will not do your hoose a mischief. Whaur's your guid man ?' 'He's oot on the hills wi' the sheep,' says I, 'but he will be back before lang,' and I went to the door to look, and there he was comin' doon the brae face. He had seen the troopers and I'm tellin' ye he was gey scared. I waved to him to hurry, and he, thinkin' that I was in danger, cam' rinning. 'Come awa ben the hoose,' says I. 'There's an auld frien' o' mine come to see us,' and I brocht him in, and presented him to Lag.

"Lag was gey ceevil to him, and said naething aboot oaths or tests, but talked aboot sheep and kye, and syne said: 'And noo I'll ha'e to be awa'. I will tak' anither sup o' your buttermilk, Jean,' and then he shook me by the haun' and would ha'e shaken Andra's tae, but Andra wadna tak' a haun' that was stained wi' innocent blood. It was an affront to Lag, but a man like that aye respects anither man wi' courage, and he walked oot o' the door. He sprang into the saddle and the troop formed up and clattered doon the loanin', and the last I saw o' Lag he had turned his heid and was wavin' his haun as he gaed roond the corner at the brae-fit."

"And what of Mary," I said. "What was she doing in the meantime ?"

Her mother laughed. "We looked high and low for her and at last we found her in a hidie-hole in the haystack, greetin' like a wean. She had made up her mind, puir lassie, that Lag would shoot baith her faither and me, because she had boxed his lugs."

"And have you had no trouble since ?" I asked, for I knew that the promise given by Lag would be binding on none but himself, and should a troop Captain like Winram or Claver'se come to Daldowie, disaster might fall on the household.

"Oh, ay," she said, "we've seen Lag mair than

aince since then. He was here twa or three weeks sin' when you were lyin' up in the laft, and he asked aboot you. He speired whether we had seen ocht o' a young man in a trooper's uniform wanderin' aboot the moors. Ye were up in the laft sleepin' as cosy as a mowdie, but I telt him I'd seen nae young man in ony trooper's uniform. I wasna fule enough to tell him that I'd seen a trooper in the meenister's claes. 'Weel,' he said, 'should ye see sic an ane, dinna forget there's a price upon his heid. He is a deserter, and Rab Grier mak's short work o' deserters.'

"So, ye see, so far as Lag's concerned, Daldowie's safe enough. But Andra, puir stubborn buddy, is no' sure o' the richts o't. He is a queer man, Andra, and like lots mair o' the hill-men he wad sooner wear the martyr's crown than his ain guid bannet. But I'm no' made that way. I find the world no' a bad place ava, and I'm content to wait in it till it pleases the Almichty to send for me: and I'm no' forcin' His haun by rinnin' masel' into danger when a bowl o' buttermilk and a farle o' oatcake serves wi' a jocose word to mak' a frien' o' ane that micht be a bitter enemy. That was a wise word o' Solomon's—maybe he learned it frae ane o' his wives—'Every wise woman buildeth her house: but the foolish plucketh it down with her hands.' Even Andra daur'na say that Jean Paterson, his wife, is a fule."

CHAPTER XIX

THE MAKING OF A DAISY CHAIN

A DAY came when at last I was considered strong enough to venture out-of-doors, and on that day, to my joy, I had Mary for a companion. Lending me the support of her arm, she guided me to a grassy hillock beside a little stream that ran down the face of the brae. Many a time I had dreamed of this moment when I should be alone with her—but now that it was come I found myself bereft of words. Apparently, she did not notice my silence but talked merrily as she sat down beside me. Yet, though my tongue was holden so that I could not speak, the scales had fallen from my vision and Mary looked more beautiful than ever. I looked into her eyes and for the first time saw the secret of their loveliness. They were brown as a moorland stream—but a moorland stream may be a thing of gloom, and in her eyes there was nothing but glory. I saw the secret. The rich, deep brown was flecked with little points of lighter hue, as though some golden shaft of sunlight had been caught and held prisoner there, and when she smiled the sleeping sunshine woke and danced like a lambent flame.

Daisies were springing all round us, and as she talked she began to weave a chain. The play of her nimble fingers as she threaded the star-like flowers captivated me. I offered my clumsy aid, and she laughed merrily at my efforts; but every now and then our hands touched, and I was well content.

When the chain was completed I doubled it, and said: "Now, Mary, the crown is ready for the Queen."

She bent her head towards me playfully and I placed the daisies on her glistening hair, nor could I resist the temptation of taking that dear head of hers between my hands, making as my excuse the need to set the garland fair.

"Ay," she said, "I am thinkin' it is no' the first time that you ha'e done this. Tell me aboot the English lassies. Are they bonnie?"

"I know very little about them," I replied, and she, with twinkling eyes, returned:

"Ye dinna expect me to believe that, dae ye?"

With mock solemnity I laid my hand upon my heart and swore I spoke the truth, but she only laughed.

"Tell me," she said, "are they bonnie? I've heard tell they are."

"Well, Mary," I answered, "there may be bonnie lassies in England, but I've seen far bonnier ones in Scotland."

She plucked a daisy and held its yellow heart against her chin. "Oh ay," she said, "I've heard that the Wigtown lassies are gey weel-faured. Nae doot, when ye were a sodger there, ye had a sweetheart."

"No," I said, "I had no sweetheart in Wigtown, although I saw a very bonnie lass there."

"I knew it, I knew it," she cried. "And maybe ye helped her to make a daisy chain?"

"No, Mary," I said, "I never had a chance. I saw her only for an hour."

"But ye loved her?" and she looked at me quickly.

"No," I answered, "I had no right to love her. If I had loved her I should have tried to save her.

She's dead now, but I do not think I can ever forget her."

"Oh," she said, "then you canna forget her. You're never likely to love anither lassie? But ye speak in riddles. Wha was she? Tell me."

It was a hard thing to do, but there was nothing for it. So I told her the story of Margaret Wilson. She listened breathlessly with mounting colour. Her eyes dilated and her lips parted as she sat with awe and pity gathering in her face.

When I had finished she turned from me in silence and looked into the distance. Then she sprang to her feet and faced me, with glowing eyes.

"And you were there! You!" she cried. "You helped the murderers! O God! I wish I had left you on the moor to die!"

This was my condemnation: this my punishment; that this sweet girl should turn from me in horror, hating me. I bent my head in shame.

She stood above me, and when I dared to lift my eyes I saw that her hands, which she had clasped, were trembling.

"Mary," I murmured, and at my voice she started as though my lips polluted her name, "Mary—you cannot know the agony I have suffered for what I did, nor how remorse has bitten into my heart torturing me night and day. It was for that I became a deserter."

"You deserted, and put yoursel' in danger o' death because you were sorry," she said slowly, as though weighing each word.

"Yes," I answered, "that is why I deserted," and I looked into her eyes, from which the anger had faded.

"I'm sorry I was so hasty. I didna mean to be cruel. Forget what I said. I meant it at the meenute, but I dinna mean it noo," and she held out both her hands impulsively. I clasped them, and drew her down beside me again, and she did not resist. For a moment or two she sat in silence pulling at the blades of grass around her. Then she laid a hand upon my arm, and said quietly:

"Tell me aboot her again. Was she really very bonnie?"

"Yes," I replied, "very bonnie."

"The bonniest lassie you ever saw?"

"Yes, the bonniest lassie I had ever seen till then."

"Oh," she exclaimed, "then you've seen a bonnier? And where did ye see her?"

A woman versed in the wiles of her sex would not have thrown the glove down so artlessly. Unwittingly she had challenged me to declare my love—and I was sorely tempted to do so: but I hesitated. A riper moment would come, so I answered simply:

"Yes, I have seen a bonnier lassie among the hills."

"Oh," she exclaimed, and looked at me questioningly, "and what was she daein' there?"

I laid a hand upon hers as I replied: "Now, little Mistress Curiosity, do not ask too much."

She drew her hand away quickly, and brushed it with the other as though to rid it of some defilement. I fear the taunting name had given her umbrage.

"I think you are a licht-o'-love," she said.

"Mary!" I exclaimed, offended in my turn. "What right have you to say such a thing?"

"Weel," she answered, "what else would you ha'e me think. Ye lo'ed Margaret Wilson: ye tell me ye've seen a bonnier lass amang the hills, and when I found you on the moors you were repeatin' a lassie's name ower an' ower again—and her name wasna Margaret."

"I was repeating the name of a lassie?" I exclaimed dubiously.

"Ay, ye were that," she made answer, "or ye wadna be here the day. It was that made me tak' peety on you. I was sorry for the lassie, whaever she micht be, and I thocht if I had a lad o' my ain I should like him to be croonin' ower my name, as you were daein' hers. So I ran hame an' fetched faither, an' we cairried ye to Daldowie."

"And what was the name of the lassie?" I asked, looking at her eagerly.

"Oh! ye kept sayin'—Mary—Mary—Mary—in a kind o' lament."

My heart bounded: there was riot in my veins. "It was your name, Mary—yours—and none other. There is no other Mary in my life."

She looked at me in amazement—her eyes alight. "Surely ye dinna expect me to believe that? You'd only seen me aince—and hardly spoken to me. It couldna be me ye meant."

I made both her hands captive. "Mary, it was. I swear it."

She drew her hands sharply away: "Then you had nae richt tae tak' sic' a liberty. Ye hardly kent me,"—and she sprang up. "I maun fetch the kye," she cried as she hastened off.

I watched her drive them in; then she came for me and led me carefully back to the house. It seemed to me that there was some message tingling from her heart to mine through the arm with which she supported me—but she spoke no word.

As we drew near the door, her mother came out to meet us and catching sight of the forgotten chaplet, exclaimed: "Mary, whatever are ye daein' wi' a string o' daisies in your hair? Ye look like a play-actress."

Laughingly Mary removed the wreath. "It was

only a bairn's ploy," she said; then to my great cheer, she slipped the flowers into her bosom.

"Come awa' in," said Jean: and she assisted me to my place by the fire.

An adventurous hen with a brood of chickens—little fluffy balls of gold and snow—had followed us, and with noisy cluckings from the mother, the little creatures pecked and picked from the floor. Jean clapped her hands at them: "Shoo! ye wee Covenanters!" she cried.

I laughed, as I said, "Why do you call them Covenanters?"

"Weel," she replied, "I often think that chickens and the hill-men ha'e muckle in common. Ye see maist Covenanters tak' life awfu' seriously. They ha'e few pleasures frae the minute they come into the world. A kitten will lie in the sun playin' wi' a bit o' 'oo', and a wee bit puppy will chase its tail for half an hour on end: but wha ever saw a chicken playin'? They dinna ken the way. It's scrape, scrape, pick, pick, frae the day they crack the shell till the day their necks are wrung. And your Covenanter's muckle the same. He's so borne doon wi' the wecht o' life that he has nae time for its joys. They're guid men, I'm no' denyin', but I sometimes think they've got queer notions of God. They fear God, and some o' them are feart o' Him. There's a difference—a big difference. I aye like to think o' the Almichty as a kind-hearted Father: but to hear some even o' the best o' the hill-men talk o' Him, ye micht weel think He was a roarin' fury chasin' weans oot frae amang the young corn wi' a big stick. But there are others. Now godly Samuel Rutherford and your frien' Alexander Main were brimfu' o' the joy o' life. They kent the secret; and it warmed their hearts and made them what they were. I like to think o' the love of God spread ower the whole earth like a May mist on the moors—something that is warm, that has the dew in it and that comes wi' refreshment to puir and lowly things.

"I was brocht up on the Catechism—strong meat and halesome—but it seems to me that noo and then we lose our sense o' the richts o' things. Now there's Andra; he believes that the Catechism hauds a' the wisdom o' man aboot God; and it is a wise book; but to my way o' thinkin', God is far bigger than the Catechism, and some o' us haena learned that yet. Ye canna shut God in a man-made book that ye can buy for tippence."

I laughed as I said: "Mistress Paterson, you interest me greatly, but I fear that some of the things you say to me would shock the good men of the flock."

She laughed heartily as she replied: "Fine I ken that. Ye maunna' say a word o' this to Andra, for if he heard tell o' what I ha'e been sayin', he would be prayin' for me like a lost sheep every nicht when he tak's the Book, and it would be a sair affront for the guid-wife o' the hoose to be prayed for alood by her ain man, afore strangers."

I laughed. "You may trust me," I said, and she continued:

"I ha'e my ain ways o' thinkin'. I've aye had them and in my younger days I ha'e nae doot I was a sair trial to Andra. He had juist to get used to it, however, and noo he lets me alane and maybe I am a better woman for that. At ony rate, I am quite prepared to dee for the Cause if the Lord wills, but I'm no' gaun to look for my death as Andra is sometimes ready to dae in ane o' his uplifted moods, by daein' onything silly. Ye've seen him sit by the fireside sometimes, wi' his heid in his haun's, groanin'. He is a guid man, as naebody kens better than I dae: but every noo and then he gets terrible upset aboot himself. Maist days he is quite sure that he is ane o' the elect. But every noo and then, if he tak's haggis to his supper, he's in a black mood next day and is quite sure that he is ane o' the castaways. Mony a time I ha'e heard him wrestlin' wi' the spirit, wi' mony groans, and when I ha'e gane to him he has been moanin'—' I'm no' sure. Am I ane o' the elect or am I no' ? ' I ken weel it's no his conscience but only the haggis that's tormentin' him. So I juist gi'e him a dish o' herb tea, and next day he is that uplifted that he thinks he's fit to be ta'en like Elijah in a chariot straicht to heaven."

Her face melted in a smile, and for the first time I saw that the winsomeness of Mary's smile was a gift from her mother: then she continued:

" You're very ceevil. You aye ca' me Mistress Paterson, and I suppose that's only richt, but it's a wee bit stiff. It makes me think o' the meenister at a catechisin'. My name's Janet, but naebody ever ca's me that but Andra—and only when he's no' weel pleased wi' me. I'm Jean to them I like, and to them that like me, an' ye can ca' me Jean if it pleases ye."

CHAPTER XX

LOVE THE ALL-COMPELLING

As the days passed I began to be able to go further and further afield. I needed no support save the good ash stick which Andrew had given to me, but for love's sweet sake I dissembled if Mary was at hand to help me.

A day came when I gave serious thought to my future. I was unwilling to tear myself away from Daldowie, for the spell of love bound me, but I felt that I could not continue to trespass indefinitely upon the hospitality of my friends.

And there was another matter of grave moment. Apparently, from what Jean had told me, Lag was in the habit of visiting Daldowie from time to time. So far, he had learned nothing of my presence there ; but a day might come when I should be discovered, and that would expose my friends to deadly peril. I dared not think of that possibility, and yet it was real enough. I turned these things over in my mind, but always hesitated on the brink of decision, because I could not live without Mary.

We were thrown much together. Sometimes I would accompany her when she went about her duties on the farm ; and many a pleasant hour we spent together on the green hill-side. Almost daily I discovered some new and beautiful trait in her character. To know her was to love her. No words can paint her. Vivid, alluring, she was like a mountain stream

—at one time rippling over the shallows of life alive with sunny laughter, or again, falling into quiet reflective pools, lit by some inner light—remote, mysterious. Her haunting variety perplexed me while it charmed me.

Sometimes I was tempted to throw ardent arms about her and pour my love into her ears in a torrent of fervid words. That is the way of the bold lover, but I feared that to declare my love in such cavalier fashion might defeat its end. None but a woman with some rude fibres in her being can care to be treated in such fashion—and I imagined that Mary's soul was delicate and fragile as a butterfly's wing, and would be bruised by such mishandling.

My love for her grew daily, but I hesitated to declare it till I should know whether it was returned. And Mary gave me no clue. If on a day she had lifted me to the heights of bliss by some special winsomeness, she would dash my hope to the earth again by avoiding me for a time so that I was thrown back on my thoughts for companionship. And they gave me little solace. Over and over again I remembered the warning of the dear old saint of the hills: "She's no' for you. The dove maunna mate wi' the corbie."

At nights I lay awake distraught. Was her kindness to me, her winning sweetness, no more than the simple out-pouring of a woman's heart for a man she pitied? I had no need of pity: I hated it: my heart hungered for love. I had yet to learn that there is always pity in a woman's love.

At last I brought my fevered mind to a resolute decision. I would speak. For the sake of those who had succoured me I must leave Daldowie, but before I went I must try to find out the secret in Mary's heart.

The hour came unsought, and took me almost unaware.

We had wandered further afield than was our wont, and on a mellow autumn afternoon we sat by the side of a burn. We had been chatting gaily, when, suddenly, silence fell between us like a sword.

I looked at Mary. Her eyes were fixed on distance, and my gaze fell from the sweet purity of her face to the rich redness of the bunch of rowan berries set in the white of her bodice.

"Mary," I began, "I have something to say to you." She turned and looked at me quickly, but did not speak.

I drew an anxious breath and continued: "I am going away."

Her pointed little chin rose quickly, and she spoke rapidly: "You're gaun away. Whatever for?"

"It is not my will," I said, "but need that urges me. Your mother, your father, and, more than all, you have been kind to me—you found me in sore straits and succoured me. My presence at Daldowie means danger to you all, and for your sakes I must go."

Pallor swept over her face: the red berries at her breast moved tremulously.

"Danger," she said—"the hill-folk think little o' danger: that needna' drive ye away. Is there nae ither reason?"

Before I could speak she continued: "I doot there's some English lassie waiting for ye ayont the Border," and turning her face away from me she whispered, "It maun e'en be as ye will."

"Mary," I said, "you wrong me. If you could read my heart you would know what I suffer. I hate to go. I am leaving friendship and love behind me——"

I paused, but she did not speak. " Before God," I said, " I shall never forget Daldowie, and—you."

Her hands were folded in her lap—and I took them gently in mine.

" Our lives have touched each other so delicately, that I shall never forget you. Dearest, I love you."

She uttered a little startled cry and drew her hands away. " Love you with all the fire of my heart," I said, " and if I succeed in escaping across the border I shall dream always of the day when I may come back and ask you to be my wife. Mary—tell me—have you a little corner in your heart for me ?—You have had the whole of mine since first you spoke to me."

Her face was a damask rose : her lips curved in a smile, and a dimple danced alluringly on her left cheek : her eyes were lit as though a lamp were hidden in their depths, but all she said was,—" I daur say I can promise ye that."

I drew her towards me and took her, gently resisting, into my arms. " O Mary mine," I whispered. Her hand stole up and gently stroked my hair, and as she nestled to me I could feel a wild bird fluttering in her breast. " I love you, Mary," and bending over her dear face I kissed her where the dimple still lingered.

" Sweetheart," she murmured, as her arms closed about my neck, and her lips touched mine.

The old earth ceased to be : heaven was about us, and above us a high lark sang :—my love was in my arms.

A little tremor, as when a leaf is stirred, stole over her. I held her close, and bent to look at her. Twin tears glistened on her eyelids. " Flower o' the Heather," I whispered, " little sweetheart—what ails you ? "

She took a long breath—broken like a sigh.

" I am feared," she said.

" Afraid ? dearest, of what ? "

Her lips were raised to my ear.

" Afraid o' love," she whispered : " for when you kissed me a wee bird flew into my heart and whispered that nae woman ever loved without sorrow."

" Dearest," I said. But she stopped me, and continued :—" But I wouldna lose the love for a' the sorrow that may lie in its heart—for it's the sorrow that makes the love worth while."

" My own Mary," I whispered, " in my arms no sorrow shall ever touch you. I will protect you ! "

" My love, my love," she murmured brokenly, " ye canna thwart God."

So still she lay that I could hear the beating of my heart. I looked at her sweet face half hidden against my coat. There was upon it a beauty that I had never seen before. Reverence that was half awe swept over me, and I bowed my head, for I had seen into the holy place of a woman's soul.

Suddenly she let her arms fall from my neck, and freeing herself gently from my embrace she seated herself by my side.

" I'm sorry," she said gently. " I ha'e spoilt your happy moments wi' my tears. But they're no tears o' sorrow : they're juist the joy bubbling up frae a heart ower fu'. I can let ye go noo—since I ken ye love me. Love can aye surrender, selfishness aye clings."

" Are you sending me away, Mary ? "

" Oh no ! No ! No ! It's because I love you I wad ha'e you go. You're in danger here, and I ken—oh, I ken ye'll come back."

" And now," I answered proudly, " I do not wish to go. I cannot go."

"But you're in danger here. If they find you they'll kill you."

"Beloved," I whispered, "to leave you now would be worse than death."

She buried her head on my shoulder, and sat silent. The door had swung back and shown us the kingdom of love with its laughing meadows and enchanted streams. But amid all that beauty each of us had caught a glimpse of the shadow that lay across our lives.

Suddenly she lifted her face and gazed at me with troubled, wistful eyes. "I ken ye ought to go: but an ye winna it's no for me to send you. My heart cries for you, and," she added slowly, "I've got a notion. About this time o' year my faither aye hires a man. Ye could ha'e the place for the askin'. Ye're strong enough noo to help him, and naebody would ever jalouse that the hired man at Daldowie was Trooper Bryden o' Lag's Horse."

Her ready wit had found the way out.

"Dear little witch," I cried, and kissed her fragrant hair—"You have brought light into the darkness. I shall offer myself to your father, and by faithful service show my gratitude: but more than that I shall ask him for you."

Her eyes shone. "Speir at him for the place," she said, "and let the second question bide till ye've spoken to mither. Faither loves me—I ken weel: but he's dour and sometimes contrairy, and winna understand. But mither's heart is young yet. She'll help us."

"O winsome little wiseacre," I whispered, and held my open arms out to her.

She sprang up. "I maun leave you," she said. "I want to be alane—to tell the flowers and the birds my secret, but maist o' a' to tell it ower and ower again to masel'. I'll see ye by and by—and maybe ere then ye'll ha'e talked to mither."

She turned and walked lightly away, crooning a song. I watched her longingly as she went, palpitating with life and love, an angel of beauty, the sun on her hair.

For long I sat in a delightful reverie, then I rose and made my way slowly to the house.

Mary loved me!—the moor winds sang for me. They knew our secret.

I found Jean at her spinning-wheel, alone in the kitchen. The moment seemed opportune, so, without any preface, I opened my heart to her.

"You must have seen," I said, "that Mary and I are very warm friends. Indeed we are more than friends, for we love each other, and I would make her my wife; but she will not promise without your consent and her father's. Dare we hope for it?"

She stopped her spinning and took a long breath. "So that's the way o't," she said. "I thocht as muckle, and I'm no' ill-pleased, for I like ye weel. But I dinna ken aboot her faither. He's a queer man, Andra. If ye speir at him he'll want to ken if ye are ane o' the elect, and by your answer ye'll stand or fa'.

"Weel dae I mind his ongoin's when he speired me. A Scotsman's aye practical even in his love-making: but Andra was waur than practical, he was theological. But he couldna help it—that's aye been his weakness. As a maitter o' fact maist Scotsmen are as fu' o' sentiment as an egg is fu' o' meat. But ye've to crack their shell afore ye fin' that oot. An' they'll watch ye dinna. For they're feared that if ye fin' they're saft i' the hert ye micht think they were saft i' the heid as weel. Weel, as I was sayin', he had been courtin' me for maybe a twalmonth. No that he ever talked love—but he would drap into my step-faither's hoose o' a nicht maybe twice a week, and crack aboot horses and craps, and sheep, and kye, tae the auld man, and gi'e me a 'Guid E'en' in the bye-goin'. But aince I catched him keekin' at me through his fingers when we were on our knees at the worship—and though I was keekin' at him mysel' I never let on. But I thocht tae mysel' he was beginnin' to tak' notice o' ane o' the blessings o' the Lord—and so it turned oot, for maybe a month later he brocht me a bonnie blue ribbon frae Dalry; and he cam' to me in the stack-yaird and offered it tae me, kind o' sheepish-like. It was a bonnie ribbon, and I was awfu' pleased; and first I tied it roon my neck, and then I fastened it among my hair. And he looked on, gey pleased-like himsel': and then a kind o' cloud cam' ower his face and he said, 'Eh, Jean, ye maunna set your affections on the gauds o' this earth.' I was that angry that I nearly gi'ed him back the ribbon; but it was ower bonnie.

"Weel, a week or twa went by, and ae nicht in the gloamin' I met him on the road—accidental like. He was gey quate for a time, then he laid a haun' on my airm and said, very solemn: 'Jean, I love ye: are ye ane o' the elect?' My heart gi'ed a big loup, for I guessed what was comin', and juist to gain time I answered, 'I'm no' sure, Andra,' says I, 'but I hope sae.' 'Oh, but ye maun be sure; ye maun be sure. Hope is no' enough,'—and he turned on his heel and went down the road again. Weel, I went back tae the hoose a wee bit sorry, for I liked him weel; and it seemed tae me I had frichtened him awa. But that nicht in my bed I thocht things ower, and said tae mysel'—'Jean, my lass, it's a serious step gettin' married, but it's a lot mair serious remainin' single, and guid young men are scarce, and you are a tocherless lass. What are ye gaun tae dae?'

So I worked oot a plan in my heid. After maybe a week, Andra cam' back for a crack wi' my step-faither, and seein' him comin' up the road I went oot tae meet him. He was a wee blate at the first, but I helped him oot wi't. 'Andra,' says I, 'dae ye mind what ye said the last nicht ye were here?' 'I do, Jean,' says he. 'Weel,' says I, 'I've been thinkin' very hard since then. Ye believe, I hope, in fore-ordination?' 'Certainly,' says he, 'Predestination is a cardinal doctrine.' 'I ken,' I said, 'and it was fore-ordained that you should tell me that you lo'e me. You were fore-ordained tae lo'e me: I was fore-ordained tae lo'e you—and I like ye weel: and if ye let my puir human uncertainty as tae my election stand in the way, ye are fleein' in the face o' Providence wha fore-ordained that we should love each other.' He was a bit ta'en aback, I could see; for he stood quate for a while. Then he turned and said, "I daurna dae that: I daurna. Jean, will ye tak' me?' 'It was fore-ordained that ye should ask me that question,' I answered, 'and it was fore-ordained that I should say "Ay." I'll be a guid wife tae ye, Andra.' And I ha'e been, though even yet he's no' sure if I'm ane o' the elect or no.

"Whiles he thinks I am. I mind the morning after Dauvit was born—I was ane o' the elect then. He sat by the bedside, takin' keeks every noo and then at the wee lamb sleepin' in the fold o' my airm, and repeatin' lang screeds oot o' the Song o' Solomon, wi' the love-licht in his e'e, till the howdie turned him oot, sayin' it was no' seemly for an elder o' the kirk tae be using sic holy words tae a mere woman. A mere woman forsooth! and me a mither! She was a barren stock hersel', ye see.

"But I'm haverin' awa—and no' answerin' your question. Let things bide a wee as they are. Andra thinks a lot o' ye; but he has got tae ken ye better afore he'll judge ye tae be a fit husband for Mary. I'll tell ye when the time is ripe tae speir at him. Meantime the lassie winna rin awa frae ye; and if ye'll tak' the advice o' an auld woman, there's twice as muckle joy in the courtin' days as there is in the level years o' wedded life; sae mak' the maist o' them, and the Lord bless ye baith."

My little sweetheart had been right. Her mother understood.

Later I sought her, and found her alone in the gloaming—the lover's hour.

"And what does mither say?" she asked.

Briefly I told her. She laughed happily:—

"I kent it wad be a' richt."

As she stood before me—her face upturned, her eyes eager, I slipped an arm about her, and would have drawn her to me, but she drew back.

"Dinna spoil it," she said—"maybe the morn"—and she smiled. "I want to keep the wonder o' your first kiss till then: it's a kind o' sacrament."

She laid her hands upon my shoulders, and her words tumbled over each other.

"Love is magical. Since you kissed me I have wakened frae sleep: every meenute has had rose-tipped wings: the silence sings for me, and the moor wind plays a melody on the harp o' my hert. Can ye no' hear it?"

I would have answered as a lover should, but she continued: "No, no! Ye canna hear it. I'm sure there maun hae been a woman wi' the shepherds on the plains o' Palestine the nicht they heard the angels sing. Nae man ever heard the angels sing till a woman telled him they were singing. Men are deaf craturs."

"Mary," I cried, "I am not deaf. I hear the

angels singing whenever you speak"—and I seized her hands.

"Dinna talk havers," she answered, and raced off; but at the corner of the house she turned and, poised on tip-toe, shadowy among the shadows, she blew me a kiss with either hand.

CHAPTER XXI

THE HIRED MAN

THERE was nothing for me to do but lay to heart the advice of my friend Jean. Mary's suggestion that I should offer my services to her father took root in my mind, and next day I broached the matter to him. I began by assuring him of my sense of indebtedness to him and his good wife for all that they had done for me. Money I told him could not repay him ; whereat he shrugged his shoulders and made a noise in his throat as though the very mention of such a thing hurt him.

Then I told him that one of two alternatives lay before me—either to leave Daldowie and endeavour to make my way across the border, or to stay on at the farm and try to repay by service the heavy debt under which I lay. He heard all I had to say in silence, but when I had finished he spoke :

" There's a lot o' places no' as guid as Daldowie. I couldna hear o' ye leavin' us yet. Ye see, Jean—that's the wife—has ta'en an awfu' fancy tae ye ; and as for masel', I like a man aboot the hoose. A man like me gets tired wi' naething but womenfolk cackling roon' him. I think wi' a bit o' experience ye'd mak' no' a bad fairmer. When winter comes wi' the snaw there's a lot o' heavy work to be done feedin' the nowt, forby lookin' after the sheep. Last winter I lost half a score in a snaw-drift, and that is mair than a man like me can afford in sic tryin' times. I was ettlin' to hire a man in the back end o' the year ; but if you like to stop you can tak' his place. I think I could learn ye a lot : and in the lang winter nichts me and you'll be able to ha'e some guid sets to on the dambrod. But a word in your lug. If ye're stoppin' on here ye'd better drap that English tongue o' yours, and learn to talk like a civilised body. It'll be safer. I've noticed that when a Scotsman loses his ain tongue, an' talks like an Englishman, he loses a bit o' his Scots backbane. Maybe in your case the thing will work the ither wey "—and he struck me heartily on the shoulder.

So the bargain was made, and I entered into the service of Andrew Paterson of Daldowie and of Jean his wife. I was already the devoted bond-slave of Mary.

Andrew announced our pact that evening as we sat round the fire. " Jean," he said, " I've hired a man."

Her knitting needles clicked a little faster : " And where did ye get him ? " she asked. " I ha'e seen naebody aboot the steadin' the day, and the hirin' fair is no' till October."

Out of the corner of my eyes I saw a smile on Mary's face.

" Wha dae ye think ? " said Andra. " Bryden here has speired for the job, and as he seems to ha'e the makin' o' a fairmer in him, I agreed to gi'e him a try."

Jean laid her knitting in her lap. " Andra, are ye sure ye're daein' richt ? "

Involuntarily I started. Was Jean about to turn against me ? But there was wisdom in her question, for she knew her husband better than I did. There was irritation in his voice :

" Of course I'm daein' richt, woman. It's like ye

to question the wisdom o' your man. He never does onything richt." He swung himself round on the settle and crossed his knees angrily.

"But," returned Jean, "do ye no' see the risk ye're runnin'? Lag's ridin' through the countryside, and what dae ye think he'll say if he finds that a deserter is serving-man at Daldowie?"

"I ha'e thocht o' a' that, Jean," he replied. "He'll juist hae to keep oot o' sicht when your godless frien' Lag is aboot."

His wife seemed about to raise further objections, but he silenced her: "Haud yer tongue, Jean, and gang on wi' yer knittin'. My min's made up, and I am no' gaun to be turned frae my ain course by a naggin' woman. Let's hear nae mair o't." And then raising his voice he ended: "I'll be maister in ma ain hoose, I tell ye."

This little passage of arms, planned by the shrewd wit of Jean, served but to establish her husband in his purpose. The good wife picked up her knitting again, and for a time there was no sound but the click of her needles. Then, of a sudden, Andrew turned to Mary who, in the semi-darkness, had stretched out her hand and touched mine gently and said: "Mary, licht the cruise and bring the Book."

In this fashion I became a willing servant at Daldowie. The days passed pleasantly. Andrew took a pride in his farm. "A Paterson," he would say, "has farmed here since Flodden. Man, that was an awfu' thrashin' you English gi'ed us yonder; but we've paid ye back tenfold. We sent the Stuarts tae ye,"—and he would laugh heartily. The original little parcel of land had, I learned, been a gift made to an Andrew Paterson after that fateful combat, and each succeeding generation of his descendants had with incessant toil sought to bring under cultivation a few more acres of the unfruitful moor, until now

Daldowie was a heritage of which any man might be proud. The love of his land was a passion in Andrew's blood.

My desire to make myself of use impressed him, and he taught me much agricultural lore. I found, as I had long suspected, that under his dour exterior there was much native shrewdness, and not a little pawky humour. But of that gift he had not such a rich endowment as his wife. In his silent way, he cherished a great affection for her, and though he had never, in my hearing, expressed himself in any terms of endearment, I knew that in his heart of hearts he regarded her as a queen among women. Sometimes he would talk to me of the trials of the hill-men. Of the justice of their cause he was absolutely convinced, and now and then his devotion to it seemed to me to border on fanaticism. He could find no good word to say for the powers that were arraigned against the men of the Covenant, and once, in a burst of anger, he said:

"I ken I can trust the wife, but this colloguin' wi' Lag is a disgrace to my hoose, and nae guid can come o't. She thinks that wi' him for a frien' she's protectin' them she likes best, but I'm thinkin' the Almichty canna be pleased, for what says the Book: 'Him that honoureth Me will I honour,' and ye canna honour the Lord by feedin' ane o' His worst enemies on guid farles o' oatcake—wi' butter forby. Hooever, ye ken her weel enough to understaun' how thrawn she is, and ony word frae me would only mak' her thrawner. Ye're no' mairrit yoursel', and I doot ye ken nocht o' the ways o' women, but that's ane o' them."

I had enough mother-wit to hold my tongue.

Autumn ebbed—and the purple moor turned to bronze.

Winter descended upon the land and the moor

was shrouded in snow; but ere the snow fell, the sheep had been gathered into the lower fold and none were lost. Each short, dark day was followed by the delight of a long and cosy evening by the fireside, what time the baffled wind howled over the well-thatched roof. Andrew and I would engage in doughty combats on the dambrod, while Mary and her mother plied their needles busily: and sometimes, to my great delight, when Andrew was not in the mood for such worldly amusement, Mary would take his place at the game. He is a poor lover who cannot, amid the moves of the black and white men, make silent but most eloquent love, and many a tender message leaped across the checkered board from my eyes to Mary's, and from Mary's to mine. Once on an evening when we had been playing together while her father slept in the ingle-nook, and Jean busied herself with her knitting, Mary brushed the men aside and resting her elbows on the table poised her chin on her finger-tips. My eyes followed the perfect line of her white arms from her dimpled elbows, half-hidden in a froth of lace, to her slender hands that supported the exquisite oval of her face.

" Let's talk," she said.

" Yes, talk," I answered. " I shall love to listen, and as you talk I'll drink your beauty in."

She wrinkled her nose into the semblance of a frown, and then laughed.

" For a book-learned man ye're awfu' blate."

" Ah, sweetheart," I answered, " no man can learn the language of love from books. That comes from life."

" No," she said, laughingly; " no' frae life, but frae love. I'm far far wiser than you "—and she held her hands apart as though to indicate the breadth of her wisdom—" and I learned it a' frae love. For when you knocked at the door o' my he'rt an' it flew open to let you in, a' the wisdom that love cairries in its bosom entered tae. So I'm wiser than you—far wiser." She leaned towards me. "But I'm yer ain wee Mary still—am I no? Let me hear ye say it. Love is like that. It makes us awfu' wise, but it leaves us awfu' foolish. Kiss me again."

Book-learning teaches no man how to answer such a challenge—but love does, and I need not set it down.

Sometimes Mary would read aloud old ballads of love and high adventure—while Andrew and I sat listening, and Jean, as she knitted, listened too. As she read, she had a winsome trick of smoothing back into its place a little lock of hair that would persist in straying over her left ear. That vagrant curl fascinated me. Evening by evening I watched to see it break loose for the joy of seeing her pretty hand restore it to order. I called it the Covenanting curl, and when she asked me why, I stole a kiss, and said, "Because it is a rebel," whereat she slapped me playfully on the cheek, and whispered, "If ye are a trooper ye should make it a prisoner," which I was fain to do, but she resisted me.

Jean took a kindly though silent interest in our love-making, but if Andrew knew, or guessed what was afoot, he made no sign. His fits of depression grew more frequent; but whether they were due to uncertainty as to his own spiritual state or to sorrow and anger at the continued harrying of the hill-folk I was not able to tell, and Jean did not enlighten me, though in all likelihood she knew.

So the happy winter passed, and spring came again rich in promise.

CHAPTER XXII

"THE LEAST OF THESE, MY BRETHREN"

APRIL was upon us—half laughter, half tears—when rumour came to us that the persecutions of the hill-men were becoming daily more and more bitter; but of the troopers we ourselves saw nothing. From what we heard we gathered that their main activities were in a part of the country further west, and we learned that Lag and his dragoons were quartered once again in Wigtown. One morning, when Mary went to the byre to milk the cows, we heard her cry in alarm, and in a moment she came rushing into the house, saying, "Oh, mither, there's a man asleep in Meg's stall."

Her father and I hurried out, and entered the cow-shed abreast. Stretched on a heap of straw beside the astonished Meg lay a young man clad in black. There was such a look of weariness upon his face that it seemed a shame to waken him; but Andrew, whispering to me, "It is ane o' the hill-men," took him by the shoulder and shook him not unkindly. The youth sat bolt upright—fear in his startled eyes. He stared at Andrew and then at me, and in a high-pitched voice exclaimed:

"The Lord is on my side. I will not fear what men can do unto me."

"I thocht sae," said Andrew, "ye're ane o' oorsels: but what are ye daein' in my byre?"

To this the only reply was another quotation from

the scriptures: "The Lord hath chastened me sore, but He hath not given me over unto death."

"Puir laddie," said Andrew, "come awa ben the hoose and ha'e your parritch."

Again the youth spoke: "This is the Lord's doing: it is marvellous in our eyes."

Andrew took him by the arm and led him into the kitchen. He was placed in a chair by the fire and sat looking wistfully and half-frightenedly around him. His face was thin and white save that on one cheek a scarlet spot flamed like a rose, while over his high, pale forehead swept a lock of dark hair. As he held his hands out to catch the warmth of the glowing peat, I saw that they were almost transparent; but what caught my gaze and held it rivetted was the state of his thumbs. Both of them were black and bruised as though they had been subjected to great pressure, and I knew that the boy had recently been put to the torture of the thumbscrews.

Mary and her mother vied with each other in attentions to him. A bowl of warm milk was offered to him, and with trembling hands he raised it to his lips. As he did so I saw the perspiration break upon his forehead. While she busied herself with the preparation of the morning meal, Andrew questioned him, but his answers were so cloaked in the language of the scriptures that it was hard to decipher his meaning.

When he had finished his porridge, which he ate eagerly as though well-nigh famished, Jean took him in hand.

"Now, young man," she said, "tell us yer story. Wha are ye, and whence cam' ye?"

A fit of violent coughing interfered with his speech, but the seizure passed, a bright light gleamed in his sunken eyes, and he said: "In the way wherein I walked they have privily laid a snare for me. I looked on my right hand and beheld, but there was no man that would know me. Refuge failed me. No man cared for my soul. They have spread a net by the wayside; they have set gins for me. Let the wicked fall into their own nets, whilst that I withal escape."

Jean sighed, and turned to Andrew with a look of bewilderment. "The bairn's daft," she said, "beside himsel' wi' hunger and pain. He's had the thumbkins on; look at his puir haun's."

The youth continued in a high-pitched monotone: "Surely Thou wilt slay the wicked, O God. Depart from me, therefore, ye bloody men. Deliver me, O Lord, from mine enemies. I flee unto Thee to hide me."

"Clean doited, puir laddie, clean doited," said Jean. "I'm thinkin', Andra, ye'd better convoy him up to the laft and let him sleep in Bryden's bed. Maybe when he has had a rest, he'll come to his senses."

Andrew put his arm gently through that of the youth and raised him to his feet. "Come your ways to bed, my lad; when ye've had a sleep ye'll be better," and he led him toward the ladder.

As he ascended he still rambled on: "They have gaped upon me with their mouth. They have smitten me upon the cheek reproachfully. Are not my days few? Cease then, and let me alone, that I may take comfort a little," and with Andrew urging him on, he disappeared into the upper room.

In a few moments Andrew descended the ladder and returned to the kitchen. "I've got him safely bedded," he said.

"Ay, puir laddie," answered Jean, as she busied herself clearing away the dishes. "I wonder wha he can be? Maist likely he has escaped frae the dragoons. If they set the hounds on his track, they'll be here afore the day is weel begun."

The thought hardly needed expression. It was present in the minds of each of us; and gathering round the fire we took counsel together. That the lad was in sore need we agreed; but how best to help him was the difficulty. Should the dragoons come to the house we knew that their search would be a thorough one, for though Lag's compact with Jean still held so far as the safety of herself, her daughter, and her husband was concerned, we knew that it would be of no avail in the case of this fugitive. And, further, there was the question of my own presence there, hitherto undiscovered.

The kindly wisdom of a woman's mind was expressed by Jean: "At ony rate there is naething to be done in the meantime but wait and let the lad rest. Maybe after he has had a sleep he will no' be quite so doited, and be mair able to tell us something aboot himsel'."

"Ye're richt, woman," said Andrew. "Meantime, I'll awa' doon the road, and see if there's ony troopers aboot. And you, Bryden, had better gang up to the high field and coont the sheep. Ye'd best be oot o' the road if the troopers should come aboot."

It was partly from solicitude for her welfare and partly for love's sweet sake that I said to Jean, "And what of Mary? May she come with me?"

"Ay!" said her mother, "she micht as weel; but if naething happens, ye'd best come doon within sicht o' Daldowie at dinner-time. If the road is clear, ye'll see a blanket hanging oot in the stack-yard."

Little loth, Mary and I took our departure. As we went we talked of the stranger, but very soon our thoughts glided into other channels; and ere we had reached the high field, the great drab world with all its miseries had been forgotten and we were living in our own kingdom of love.

We found a sheltered nook and sat us down.

"Why do you love me?" said Mary suddenly, crossing her pretty ankles and smoothing her gown meditatively over her knees.

"Because you are the fairest and the sweetest lassie in the whole wide world"—and I kissed her.

"That's awfu' nice—but I doot it's no true. There maun be far bonnier lassies than me. At the best I'm only a wild rose. An' I'd rather you loved me for my soul than for the beauty ye see in me. That will a' wither by and by, and maybe your love will wither then tae. But if ye love me for my soul it will blossom and grow worthier in the sunshine o' your love, and a love like that can never dee."

"And why, my little philosopher," I asked, challenging her, "do you love me? I am all unworthy."

"No, no!" she cried—her eyes gleaming. "I love you, because—because"—she halted, and ticked the words off upon her fingers: "Because you are brave, and big, and awfu' kind, and no ill-looking, and because your blue-grey trusty een kindle a fire in my hert. No, no! That's a' wrong. I love you because—juist because you are you. A puir reason maybe—but a woman's best."

So the morning hours slipped by, and when noon was near at hand we began to saunter down the hill-side.

When we came in sight of the farm we looked eagerly to the stack-yard, and there saw displayed the token of safety, so we hurried down.

When we reached the house we found the fugitive seated by the fire. His sleep had soothed his tired brain, and Jean had been able to discover something of his history.

Two days before, he had been seized by the dragoons

and brought before Claver'se: and with a view to extracting information from him, Claver'se had put him to the test of the thumbscrews. He had refused to speak, and the torture had been continued till God, more compassionate than man, had delivered him from his sufferings by a merciful unconsciousness. As Jean told us his tale he listened, and every now and then interrupted her.

"For dogs have compassed me. The assembly of the wicked have enclosed me. But He hath not despised nor abhorred the supplication of the afflicted. And now," he said, "I must go. Even as I slept the Lord appeared to me in a vision and said 'Arise, get thee hence.' I will lift up mine eyes unto the hills, from whence cometh mine aid."

Jean pressed him to remain.

"No," he said, "I must be gone."

"But you are no' fit to gang, lad," said Jean firmly but kindly. "Ye dinna ken the moors ava. Ye'll be wanderin' into a bog or deein' amang the heather like a braxy sheep."

"Listen," he said, raising his hand, the while his eyes shone, "Listen! Dinna ye hear the voice bidding me go forth?" and he hurried to the door; but he paused on the threshold, and raising his eyes to the roof-tree, said, "Be Thou not far from me, O Lord."

"He's clean daft, Andra," said Jean; "if he'll no' stay ye'd better tak' him awa' and hide him in a kent place. Tell him to stop there and we'll maybe be able to look after him. Meantime," she said, seizing some farles of oatcake and a large piece of cheese, "put this in yer pocket and awa' after him. Maybe the fresh air will bring some sense to his puir heid. An' here, tak' this plaid for him," and she lifted a plaid from a hook behind the door. "He's got plenty o' the fire o' releegion in his hert, but it winna keep his feet warm, and the nichts are cauld. And, Andra, tak' care o' yersel', and dinna be runnin' ony risks. It's a' very weel to dee for the Cause, but it would be a peety if a level-heided man like you were to lose your life in tryin' to save a puir daft wean. Haste ye, man, or he'll be in Ayrshire afore ye catch him."

Andrew sprang after him, turning when some steps from the door to say, "I'll be back before nicht. God keep ye a'."

We stood, a little group of three, just outside the threshold watching the pursuit, and before they twain had passed out of sight Andrew had caught the young man and taken him by the arm, as though to quiet him.

"Losh peety me," said Jean, as she turned to go indoors, "what a puir bairn. I wonder wha his mither is?"

The afternoon dragged wearily on. From time to time I made my way to the foot of the loaning and, hidden by a thorn bush, anxiously scanned the country-side. There were no troopers to be seen.

In the kitchen Mary and her mother were busily engaged with household tasks, and I sat on the settle watching them. We did not speak much, for heavy dread had laid its hand upon us all The hours moved on leaden feet.

On gossamer wings an amber-banded bee buzzed in, teasing the passive air with its drone as it whirred out again. The "wag-at-the-wa'" ticked monotonously. On the hill-side the whaups were calling, and nearer at hand one heard the lowing of the cows. A speckled hen brooding in the sand before the door, spread her wings and, ruffling her breast-feathers, threw up a cloud of tawny dust. Somewhere in the stack-yard a cock crew, and with clamour of quacking a column of ducks waddled past the doorway to the burn-side. When her baking was over, Jean, wiping the meal from her hands, went out into the open. Mary came and sat on the settle beside me, and as I took her hand it felt strangely cold. I sought to cheer her.

After a few minutes Jean returned. "There's naething to be seen ava," she said. "There's nae sign o' the troopers, nor o' Andra. I wish he were safe at hame."

I hastened to assure her that there was nothing to be feared for Andrew. Witless though the demented lad might be, in build and strength he was no match for Andrew, should he be seized with frenzy and endeavour to attack his guide.

"I suppose ye're richt. As a rule I ha'e mair common-sense, but I'm anxious."

Mary joined her counsel to mine. "He'll be a' richt, mither," she said: "it's no' yet six o'clock," and rising, she went out to call the cows. Her sweet voice thrilled the silent air: "Hurley, hurley."

When she had gone I made my way to the foot of the loaning again and from the shelter of the thorn-bush studied the landscape.

It lay, an undulating picture of beauty, in the mellow light of the early evening—purple and golden and green. No dragoons were in sight.

When I reached the house again I found that Jean was no longer there. Thinking that she had gone to search for Andrew, I hastened to look for her, and by and by discovered her standing upon the top of a hillock on the edge of the moor. As I drew near she exclaimed: "Whatever can be keepin' him?" Together we stood and scanned the distance. Far as the eye could reach we could discern no human being. I tried, with comforting words, to still the turmoil of Jean's heart.

"I'm an auld fule," she said, "but when ye've had a man o' yer ain for mair than thirty year, it mak's ye gey anxious if ye think he is in danger. Ye see, my mither had 'the sicht,' and sometimes I think I've got it tae. But come awa' back to the hoose: the milkin' will be ower and it maun be near supper-time."

We returned, and found Mary preparing the evening meal. We gathered round the table, and though each of us tried to talk the meal was almost a silent one. The "wag-at-the-wa'" ticked off the relentless minutes; the sun sank to his rest; the night came, and still there was no sign of Andrew.

The slow-footed moments dogged each other by and still he did not come. When the hands of the clock marked the hour of ten, I rose and went to the door. The night was still; the stars looked down on the thatched roof of Daldowie, heedless of the dread that brooded over it. I strained my ears to catch any sound of approaching footsteps, but all was silent as the grave. I rejoined Jean and Mary beside the fire. They were gazing anxiously into its embers. Mary lifted her eyes with a question flashing from them. I shook my head, and she turned her gaze once more on the glowing hearth.

"Whatever can be keepin' the man?" said Jean, looking up suddenly. "It's nearly ten oors sin' he left us. Mary," she said, turning to her daughter and speaking firmly, "ye'd better awa' to your bed. Your faither'll be vexed if he sees ye sittin' up for him; but afore ye gang, bring me the Book." Adjusting her horn-rimmed spectacles she said, "We'll juist ha'e the readin'," and opening the Book she read the 46th Psalm. When she had finished she took her spectacles off and wiped them with her apron. "I feel better noo," she said. "I ha'e been a silly, faithless woman. Whatever would Andra think o' me, his wife, if he kent the way I ha'e been cairryin' on this day. He'll be back a' richt afore lang. Gang your ways tae bed, Mary."

Mary took the Book from her mother and bore it to its accustomed place on the dresser. Then she came back and standing behind her mother placed a hand upon each cheek and tilting the careworn face upward, kissed her upon the forehead. With a demure "Good night" to me, she was about to go, but I sprang up and, clasping her to me, kissed her. Her cheeks were pale and cold, but the ardour of my lips brought a glow to them ere I let her escape.

Her mother and I sat by the fire so wrapt in thought that we did not observe how it was beginning to fail; but at last I noticed it and picking up fresh peats laid them upon the embers.

"Losh," said Jean, starting from her seat, "what a fricht ye gi'ed me. I thocht I was a' by my lane, and I was thinkin' o' the auld days when first I cam' to Daldowie as its mistress. Happy days they were, and when the bairns cam'—happier still! Ah me!" She lapsed into silence again, and when next she moved she turned to the clock. "Dear, dear," she said, reading its signal through the gathering darkness; "it's half-ane on the nock and he's no' back yet. I'm thinkin' he maun ha'e ta'en shelter in some hidie-hole himsel', fearfu' lest he should lose his way in the nicht. Gang awa' up to the laft and lay ye doon: your e'en are heavy wi' sleep. I'll be a' richt here by my lane. And mind ye this, if, when Andra comes back in the mornin', he has no' a guid excuse for ha'ein kept me up waitin' for him, I'll gi'e him the rough edge o' my tongue. Mark my words, I will that!"

At the risk of offending her, I refused to obey her. "No," I said, "that would not be seemly. I'll keep watch with you. While you sleep I shall keep awake, and when I sleep you shall keep vigil."

"Weel," she said, "you sleep first. I'll waken ye when I feel like gaun to sleep mysel'."

I closed my eyes, and though I fought against sleep, the drowsy warmth overcame me.

When I woke, I felt stiff and cold. The grey light was already beginning to filter in through the windows and beneath the door. The cock was welcoming the sunrise. I looked at the clock. It was half-past four, and Jean was sitting with her elbows upon her knees and her face buried in her hands. She raised her head and looked at me.

" Why did you not wake me ? " I asked.

" I couldna ha'e slept in ony case," she answered shortly. " Listen ! Is that him comin' ? "

Together we listened, but no sound broke the stillness, till once again the cock crew shrilly. I went to the door and threw it open. The morning air smote on my face, and the long draughts which I breathed woke my half slumbering brain. Jean came and stood beside me, and together we looked towards the moor ; but there was no sign of Andrew.

" The morning has come now," I said, " and if he had to take shelter for the night, he will soon be afoot again and ere long we shall be welcoming him home."

" I hope sae," she said. " Meantime, I had better get the parritch ready. When he does come hame he'll be gey near famished, and we'll be nane the waur o' something to eat oorsel's."

We turned to the door again, and as we did so I heard footsteps, and, looking in, saw Mary. Her face was grey with weariness, and dark rings encircled her beautiful eyes. Her quick wit read our faces and ere I could speak she exclaimed, her voice trembling :

" Is he no' back yet ? Whatever can ha'e happened to him ? I maun go and find him," and hastening to the door she gazed eagerly out.

" No," said her mother, " he's no' back yet ; but I'm thinkin' he canna be lang noo."

"Are ye sure, mither, are ye sure, or are ye juist guessin'?" she cried. "Oh, where can he be?"

"Mary," said her mother sternly, "it's time to milk the kye. Gang awa tae your duty, and if he's no' hame by the time the parritch is ready, ye can gang an' look for him; but meantime, control yersel'."

"Oh, mither," she sobbed, "it's faither. He may ha'e slipped and broken his leg, or he may ha'e fallen into a bog. Mither, mither!" and she clasped her hands nervously, "we maun dae something. We canna' bide like this, an' no' ken."

I sought to comfort her with gentle words.

Of that loathly dread which lay most heavily upon our hearts, not one of us spoke. Mary, her heart on fire, had spoken for us all, but her mother did not allow her anxiety to shake her firm common-sense.

"A' that ye say may be true, lassie," she said, "but ye'll no' be as weel able to look for your faither if ye gang withoot your parritch. Get the kye milket, and when ye've had your breakfast, if Andra is no' back, ye'd better gang and look for him."

CHAPTER XXIII

THE SEARCH

DURING the morning meal we discussed what was to be done. None of us knew to which hiding-place Andrew had taken the fugitive. There were, however, two possibilities; he might have taken him to a remote corner of the moor which Mary knew, whither, on occasion, she had aforetime borne food to some hidden fugitive. I had never been to this hiding-place, but I knew the way to the hill-top where my own retreat had been. In the end, we decided that Jean should remain at Daldowie, while Mary made her way across the moor to the one hiding-place and I went to the other. Jean would fain have joined in the search, but we made her see the wisdom of remaining at the farm.

"I suppose you're richt," she said, "but it's dreary wark sittin' idle."

I seized my stick, Mary threw her plaid over her shoulders, and together we were about to set out, when Jean spoke suddenly.

"Can ye cry like a whaup?" she asked, addressing herself to me.

"Yes," said Mary, "I had forgotten; that is the sign—three whaup calls and a pause while you can count ten, then twa whaup calls and a pause again, then three whaup calls aince mair. That," she said, "is a signal that we settled on long ago," and pursing her mouth she gave a whaup call so clear and true that it might have come from the throat of a bird.

"Yes," I said, "I can cry like a whaup. But when am I to use the signal?"

"You had best try it every now and then; for somewhere on the way it may reach the ears of Andra. He'll ken it an' answer ye in the same way, and ye'll ken you've found him."

Mary took her mother in her arms and kissed her. If she had been given to tears I know that her eyes would have brimmed over then; but the brave old woman bore herself stoutly.

"Ye'll tak' care o' yoursels, bairns," she said, "and even if ye shouldna find Andra, be sure to come back afore nicht. If you dinna meet him on the hills, you'll likely find him at his ain fireside when ye get back again."

So we set out. For a time our paths led in the same direction and when we came to the edge of the moor Mary sent her whaup calls sailing through the morning air. We waited, but there was no reply; then we walked on together. She was very quiet, and anything I could find to say seemed strangely empty: but I slipped my arm through hers and she returned its pressure gently, so that I knew she could hear my heart speak. All too soon we came to the place where we must separate.

"That," she said, "is where I found you," and she pointed to a green patch among the heather.

"Come," I said, and we left the path for a moment and stood together there. In the hush of the morning, with no witness but the larks above us, I took her in my arms and kissed her passionately. "Here," I said, "life and love came to me: and happiness beyond all telling,"—and I kissed her again.

She nestled to me for a moment, then shyly drew herself away. "Has it meant a' that to you?" she whispered. "Then what has it meant to me?

It has brocht love into my life, beloved, and love is of God."

I folded her in my arms again, and held her. A little tremor shook her as I bent and kissed her on the brow and eyes and lips. "Flower of the Heather, God keep you," I said. On my little finger was a silver ring. It bore the crest of my house. I drew it off, and taking Mary's hand in mine I slipped it upon her finger and kissed it as it rested there. "For love's sweet sake," I said.

She gazed at her finger and then looked at me archly, her wonted playfulness awaking. "I wonder what faither will say? He'll read me a sermon, nae doot, on setting my affections on the things o' this world; but I winna care. A' I want is to find him; and if he likes he can preach at me till the crack o' doom."

I smiled at her upturned face. "And when we find him, Mary, as find him we will, I will ask him to let me marry you."

A light flashed in her eyes that all morning had been strained and sad. "Let's find him quick," she said. "Noo we maun awa. That is your road, and this is mine. Good-bye, and God bless you," and she lifted her face to me.

I would fain have prolonged the happy moment, but reason prompted me to be strong, so I bent and kissed her fondly, little dreaming of all the sorrow that the future held. At the end she showed herself to be more resolute than I was, for it was she who tore herself away. I watched as she sped lightly over the tussocks of heather like a young fawn, then I turned and took the path she had indicated to me, a path which I had blindly followed amidst storm and lightning once before. Ere I had gone far I turned to follow her with my eyes, and as I watched she turned to look for me. I waved my hand to her, and she waved back to me. The sunlight fell on that dear head of hers and, even across the distance, I could see the brown of her hair and the witching coil of gold set like an aureole above her forehead.

I plodded forward steadily, looking to right and left and from time to time uttering the whaup call. But there was no answer; nor did I anywhere see sign of Andrew. When I turned again to look for Mary she had passed out of sight and, though I scanned the distance eagerly, I could catch no glimpse of her.

My path had begun to lead me up the hills and as I went I was conscious that the strength of my injured limb was not all that I had thought. On the level it served me well enough, but on the slopes the strain began to tell. I was not to be beaten, however, by mere physical pain and struggled on with all the spirit I could command, though my progress was hindered seriously. It was close to noon when I came to the place of the hill-meeting where I had first seen Mary face to face. I clambered down into the hollow. It was a place of hallowed memories. In the hope that Andrew might be near, I uttered the whaup call: but there was no reply. I sat down, and took from my pocket some of the food with which Jean had provided me, and as I ate I pondered. I was not yet half way to my destination and the portion of the road that lay before me was harder far than that along which I had come. I judged that in my crippled state it would be evening before I could reach the loch-side, and to return to Daldowie again that day would be impossible. I dared not go back without having completed my search. To fail of accomplishing my part of the quest would be disloyalty to the friends to whom I owed my life.

My absence for a night would doubtless cause them anxiety, and as I thought of Mary's pain I was sore tempted to abandon my search and turn back to Daldowie at once. But I remembered my debt to Andrew and determined that at all costs I should see this matter through to the end.

Possibly Andrew was lying somewhere in my path with a broken limb such as I myself had sustained, and if I abandoned the search, his death would be upon my head. When I considered what Mary would think of me in such a case, shame smote me; so, without more ado, I set out again and battled on until, as the sun began to climb down the western sky, I found myself within sight of the loch.

Always the twilight hour is the hour of memories, and as I made what haste I could towards the great sheet of water they crowded in upon me. There, on the right, was the hiding-place which had afforded me shelter for so many nights: there on a memorable day I had caught sight of Mary, remote yet bewitching: there, on the other side, was the place where Alexander Main lay sleeping. Then I remembered the mission upon which I had come and uttered the whaup call. The sound was flung back by some echoing rock, but there was no response from any human throat. Again I uttered it, but no answer came; Andrew was not here. I made my way round the end of the loch and sought the little cairn of stones beneath which rested the body of my friend. Taking my bonnet off, I bent reverently above the little mound. He had given his life for me. Had I yet shown myself worthy of such sacrifice? I plucked a handful of early heather, purple in the dying light, and laid it among the grey stones of the cairn. Purple is the colour of kings. Then I stole away, and once more uttered the whaup call; but there was no answer, save that some mere-fowl rose from the surface of the lake and on flittering, splashing wings, furrowing the water, fled from my presence.

I sought the place where I had hidden aforetime and where but for my friend I should have been captured by the dragoons. It was undisturbed. No one, apparently, had made use of it since I had been there. In my weary state and with my aching limb, it was useless to try to return to Daldowie in the darkness. Haply Andrew was already safe, with Mary and Jean, by his own fireside. I pictured them sitting there ; I saw them at the taking of the Book ; I heard Mary's voice leading the singing, and I knew that to-night they would be singing a psalm of thanksgiving. I heard again, as I had so often heard when lying in the garret above the kitchen, the scrape of the chairs upon the flagged floor as the worshippers knelt to commit themselves to the care of the Eternal Father : and I knew that somewhere in his petitions Andrew would remember me ; and his petition would rise on the soft wings of Mary's faith and soar above the high battlements of heaven, straight to the ear of God.

I wondered whether my absence would distress them. Mary, I knew, would be on the rack of anxiety. Her mother, no doubt, would be anxious too : but their anxiety would be tempered by the wise counsel of Andrew who would point out to them, no doubt with emphasis, and possibly with some tart comment on the witlessness of women, that it was not to be expected that I, a lamiter, could accomplish such a long journey in the space between daylight and sunsetting. I could hear him say : " I could ha'e tellt ye afore he started. The lad's a' richt ; but it's a lang road, and would tax even me, an' auld as I am I'm a better man than Bryden ony day."

As I pondered these things the darkness fell, lit by a myriad scintillant stars which mirrored themselves in the depths of the lake so that as I sat there

I seemed to be in the centre of a great hollow sphere, whose roof and floor were studded with innumerable diamonds. For a time I sat feasting my eyes on this enchanting spectacle; then I crawled into my hiding-place and pillowing my head on a sheaf of dead bracken leaves I composed myself to sleep. I slept heavily and when I awoke the hour of dawn was long past. Some old instinct made me push aside the overhanging fronds with a wary hand and peep out cautiously; but there was nothing to be seen except the great rolling hillside. As of old, the laughing waters of the loch called to me, and soon I was revelling in their refreshing coolness.

When I had clambered out I scampered along the edge of the loch till I was dry, then putting on my clothing I sat down and breakfasted. I had not much food left; hardly enough to blunt my appetite, but I hoped that I should be able to make good speed on the homeward journey, and that in a few hours I should once again rejoin the expectant household at Daldowie.

CHAPTER XXIV

BAFFLED

My meal over I went to the loch-side, and dropping on my hands and knees took a long draught of the cool water. Then, raising myself, I uttered the whaup call, but I did not expect any answer and I received none. I looked across the loch to the little cairn that stood sentinel above the sainted dead, and then I turned and made for home and Mary.

I climbed up the slope to my left and scanned the moor. For miles and miles it spread before me, but far as the eye could reach there was no one to be seen. Then the spell of the solitude fell upon me, and I began to understand how, in the dawn of the world, the dim-seeing soul of man had stretched out aching hands in the lone places of the earth if haply it might find God.

The mood passed, and I prepared to haste me on my journey. Taking my bearings carefully, I decided to make straight for Daldowie. The ache in my injured limb had abated and I found that I could make fair speed. My heart was light; I was going back to Mary, and I should find Andrew safe. The larks above me were storming the heavens with their song; my heart was singing too; and soon my lips were singing as well. I sang a love-song—one of Mary's songs—and as I sang I smiled to think that I was practising the art of what Andrew had called "speaking like a ceevilised body."

Midday came, as the sun above me proclaimed, and I judged that already I was half-way home, when suddenly, in the distance, I saw some moving figures. The wariness of a hill-man flung me at once upon my face, and peering through a tuft of sheltering heather, I looked anxiously towards them.

They were mounted men, and I saw that they were troopers. I counted them anxiously. They were searching the moor in open order and I was able to make out a dozen of them. They were between me and Daldowie. Had they seen me? Were they coming in my direction? Breathless I watched. I knew that if they had seen me, they would put spurs to their horses and come galloping towards me. They made no sign—I had not been noticed. I was lying in the open with nothing to hide me but the tuft of heather through which I peered. There was not enough cover there to hide a moor fowl, but close at hand was a bush of broom, and worming myself towards it, I crawled under it and lay hidden.

To the unskilled eye, the distance across the rolling face of a moor is hard to measure, but I judged the dragoons were at least a mile from me.

As I watched I saw them gather together in a cluster. Had they found Andrew, or might it be the poor demented lad whom Andrew had risked his life to hide, or was it some other hunted hill-man? My ears were taut with expectation as I waited for the rattle of muskets; but I was wrong. I saw the troopers fling themselves from the saddles and in a moment a little column of smoke began to steal into the air, and I knew that they had off-saddled to make their mid-day meal. That gave me a respite, and I thought hurriedly what I had best do. Should I endeavour to worm my way further afield until I might with safety rise to my feet and race back to my old hiding-place beside the loch?

Almost I felt persuaded to do so, then I remembered that this would place a greater distance between myself and Mary, and she herself might be in danger. A chilling fear seized me. What was it I had heard of Lag? Was it not that he and his dragoons had gone further west, and were quartered again at Wigtown? If that were so, then possibly the dragoons before me were Winram's men, and the promise of protection given by Lag to the good folk of Daldowie would no longer hold. The horror of it! What could I do? My fears had taken such hold on me that my strength ebbed, and I was as water poured out upon the ground. It was not fear for myself that unmanned me, but a torturing anxiety for Mary's safety. The hour of their midday meal seemed endless. So long as they rested I was safe, and yet, with a strange perversity, I longed for the moment when once again they should mount their horses and continue their quest. Anxiously I looked up at the sun. Already he was past the meridian and I breathed a sigh of relief. In his haste lay my safety, for the close of day would bring the search to an end, for a time at least, and then I could return to my loved one.

At last I saw the troopers climb into their saddles. Was it fancy, or did my eyes deceive me? They seemed to have altered the direction of their search. Spreading out across the moor, trampling every bit of heather under foot, they searched eagerly, but their backs were towards me. I breathed again, for if they did not change their course once more, I should remain undiscovered.

The moments went by on leaden feet, but the sun marched steadily on through the sky. Still the troopers quartered and requartered the same tract of moor, and still, to all seeming, their quest was fruitless.

I found myself wondering what they were looking for. Was it a quest at a venture, or were they searching for the boy who, two days ago, had found shelter at Daldowie? Two days ago! Was that all? It seemed far longer. What was Mary doing now? It was drawing near the time of the milking. Perhaps at this very moment she was out on the hill-side bringing in the cows. Dear little Mary: I could hear her call them home: see her tripping winsomely along the hill-side. My heart cried out to her.

The sound of a whistle cut the air and the dragoons turned their horses. It was the signal for their home-going, and a strange voice which I did not know for mine, though it issued from my lips, said "Thank God."

I watched till the last scarlet coat had disappeared before I ventured to bestir myself and it was not until nearly an hour had elapsed that I ventured to resume my journey. With all wariness, I hurried through the gathering dusk. Ere long I came to the place where the black remnants of the dragoons' fire still lay like an ugly splash upon the moor. I passed it by and hurried on. Only a few short miles now separated me from Daldowie. Before me lay a little hill. Bravely I breasted it, full of hope that once over it I should be within eye-range of home, but when I reached its summit I saw a sight that once again made me fling myself flat on my face. Some two miles away a fire was burning, and clearcut against its light I could see the dark shadows of men and horses. Danger still confronted me. For some reason the troopers were bivouacking upon the moor, right upon the path which I must follow if I would reach Daldowie. There was nothing for it but to steal down the hill-side and seek a resting-place. As I stole away, I bethought myself that in all likelihood they were camping there in order to continue their search on the morrow. With this in mind, it seemed to me that my chief hope of safety lay in hiding myself somewhere on that portion of the waste which they had examined with such care already. So I made for the place where their fire had been, and, using it as a landmark, I struck off at a right angle. A mile away, where the trampled heather proclaimed that it had been well searched, I found a resting-place and lay down to sleep.

Soon after dawn I was awake again. I turned over and peered out cautiously. Nowhere could I see any trace of the troopers, but the morning was yet young, and I judged that it was too early for them to be far afield. I had little doubt that ere long they would come again and I dared not stir from my place lest I should be seen. The morning hours dragged wearily by. The moor was still, save for a trailing wind, and all was silent but for the song of the lark, the cry of the peewit and the melancholy wail of the whaup.

At last the sun reached the meridian, and I ventured forth from my hiding-place. Stealthily I crept along until I reached the crest of the hill, from which I had descried the bivouac of the dragoons. I stretched myself flat upon its summit, and looked anxiously down. The bivouac fire was quenched; there was no sign of horse or trooper. I looked to every point of the compass, but all was vacant moor. Whither the troopers had gone I could not tell, nor did I care so long as they had gone from the path that led me to my Mary.

So, with heart uplifted, I proceeded on my way, slowly at first and cautiously, but gradually gaining speed. By and by I came to the place where they had bivouacked and found close at hand a rush-grown deep pool of water. On hands and knees I lapped the cool liquid, and then I laved my face and hands and felt refreshed and clean. In less than an hour now, Mary would be in my arms. The thought lent new strength to my limbs. Almost I ventured to burst into song again, but I knew that would be madness.

So, though my heart was singing a madrigal, my lips kept silence.

At last I came within sight of the hill where the sheep were pastured. I looked at it lovingly. It was the first thing to welcome me home ; but as I looked I saw no sheep upon it. But what of that ? Probably during the three days of my absence, Andrew had taken them to some other hill-side. I hastened on. Before me lay the green slope from which many a time I had helped Mary to gather in the cows. I scanned it eagerly, half expecting to see her, sweet as a flower, but she was not there. Mayhap at this moment she was busy at the milking. In fancy I heard her singing at her task. Only a few more steps and I should see the kindly thatched roof of that little moorland farm that sheltered her I loved. O Mary mine !

CHAPTER XXV

THE SHATTERING OF DREAMS

LOVE smote me and I ran. In a moment I was within sight of the house. Then horror struck me; the house was gone, and there was but a pointed gable wall, blackened by smoke, and beside it a great dark mass which still smouldered in the afternoon sunlight.

I stood for a moment turned to stone, then dashed forward. The air was acrid with the smell of burning straw. What devil's work had been afoot while I was on the moors ? Had Lag been false to his promise, or had Winram done this thing ? What had happened to Mary, to her mother, to Andrew ? Where could they be ? Were they alive or dead ? As these questions flamed in my tortured mind I walked rapidly round the still smouldering ruins of the house. If murder had been done, surely there would be some sign. Eagerly I looked on every side ; then I peered into the heart of the ruins. Horror of horrors ! God in heaven !—what did I see ? Half buried among the grey-black ashes was a charred and grinning skull. The lower jaw had dropped away and the socket where the eyes had been gaped hideously. I sprang upon the smouldering mass. My feet sank into the thick ashes, which burned me, but I cared not. There was mystery here, and horror ! I stirred the ashes with my stick, and beneath them found a charred skeleton, so burned that no vestige of clothing or of flesh was left upon it. As I stood aghast, the wind descended from the hills and lifted a great cloud of black dust into the air. It swirled about me and blew into my eyes so that, for a moment, I was blinded. Then the wind passed, and with smarting eyes I saw two other skeletons.

Mary !—the heart of my heart, the light of my life, my loved one—Mary was dead ! Tears blinded me. I tried to call her name—my voice was broken with sobbing : my whole body trembled. I stooped and reverently separated the ashes with my hands. What though they burned me, I cared not. Was not Mary dead ? Nothing else mattered.

The fire had done its work thoroughly. There was no vestige of clothing or flesh left upon the bones ; but on one of the skulls, which was surely that of Mary's mother, there was a hole drilled clean, and I knew then that the cruelty of the persecutors had been tempered with mercy. I knew what had happened : Andrew and Jean and Mary—sweet Mary—had been shot in cold blood, and then their bodies had been cast into the blazing furnace of their old home. So this was the King's Justice ! Oh, the cruelty insensate, vile and devilish. I continued blindly to rake among the ashes. Then as they dropped through my fingers something remained in my hand. I looked. It was a ring, half melted by the flames ; the ring I had given to Mary. I pressed it to my trembling lips. My sobs choked me : my heart was breaking.

Half mad with grief I stepped from among the ashes on to the scorched grass. A fit of hopeless desolation seized me. All the dreams which, but a week ago, I had so fondly cherished had vanished into nothingness. Had I anything to live for now ? Would it not be better to go out into the hills and seek some company of fiendish dragoons and declare myself to be a Covenanter—and die as my friends had done? If there were anything in the faith of Alexander Main and of Andrew and Jean and Mary, that would mean reunion with her whom I loved. But what was the good? There was no heaven. It was all an empty lie. There was no God!—nothing but devils—and the earth was Hell.

The mood of anger passed, and there came a storm of grief such as I have never known. Physical pain I knew of old, but this torture of the spirit was infinitely more cruel than any bodily suffering I had ever experienced. I threw myself down on the ground and for a long space lay with my face buried in my hands. I tried to think that as I lay there Mary's spirit was beside me. I spoke to her in little whispers of love and stretched out aching arms to enfold her; but no answering whisper came out of the void, and my arms closed about the empty air. I lay long in my agony.

Then I bethought myself of my state. Here I had found life and hope and love; and now hope and love had been rudely stolen from me, and only the ashes of life remained. Let me up and away and forget! But could I ever forget? Would I ever wish to forget the spell of Mary's voice, the roguish witchery of her eyes, the sweet tenderness of her lips? So long as life should last, I should remember.

I lifted my face to the sky. A myriad stars sparkled there, like the dust of diamonds, and one star shone brighter than all the rest. I called it Mary's star. It was a childish fancy; but it gave me comfort, and of comfort I had sore need. Then I began to consider what I had best do. I should remain no longer in this tortured and persecuted country. It would avail me nothing to remain. Mary was dead: Scotland was nothing to me now.

I rose to my feet. I was chilled to the bone and grief had sapped my strength. My ears caught the sound of trickling water. I was parched with thirst. I made my way to the water-pipe where many a time I had helped Mary to fill her pail, and bending down I let the cool jet splash into my mouth, and washed my hands and face.

I had grown calmer now and was able to think more clearly and to fix my mind upon my purposes. At daybreak I should set out. In a few days I should be over the Border. And if, on my way, I met a company of dragoons, the worst they could do would be the best for me and I should be content to die.

Slowly I made my way to the stack-yard. Here I scooped out a resting-place in one of the stacks, and covering myself up with the warm hay I tried to sleep. But with my spirit on the rack of agony sleep was denied me so, after a time, I climbed out of my hiding-place and kept vigil beside the ashes of my beloved. As I sat with the tears stealing down my cheeks memory after memory came back to me. I recalled the sweet sound of Mary's voice—her dainty winsomeness. I thought of Jean—the warm-hearted, shrewd, and ever kindly: and of Andrew—dour, upright, generous. These were my friends—no man ever had better: and Mary was my beloved. And now I was bereft and desolate. Just there—I could see the place in the dark—she had stood, a dainty shadow poised on tip-toe, and had blown me a kiss with either hand. And now I was alone, with none but the silent stars to see my anguish. What was it Mary had said?—"I wouldna lose the love for the sorrow that may lie in its heart." I had tasted the chalice of love—now I was drinking the bitter cup of sorrow to the dregs.

When morning broke I made ready for my journey. I turned to go, then torn by love stood in tears beside the dear dust of her whom I had lost. Then, as though an iron gate had fallen between my past and me, I strode down the loaning.

CHAPTER XXVI

HECTOR THE PACKMAN

WHEN the rude hand of calamity has blotted the light from a man's life all things change. The sun shone over me—but I resented his brightness. The birds sang cheerfully—but there was dirge in my heart. Now and then a wayfarer passed me—but he seemed to belong to another world than mine. I had nothing in common with him. My soul was among the blackened ruins of Daldowie, where Mary, the light of my eyes, and Jean and Andrew my loyal friends slept, united in death as they had been in life. I envied their peace.

Sometimes as I walked I stumbled—tears blinding me. My life was a barren waste—my heart a desolation. Nothing mattered—Mary was dead. So, in a maze of torturing thoughts I journeyed till, some four days after leaving Daldowie—I have no memory of the precise time—I gathered from a passer-by that I was only seven miles from Dumfries. Before me, huddled together on the left side of the road, was a cluster of cottages. From their roofs steel-blue clouds of smoke were rising. The atmosphere was one of quiet peace, and with my eyes set upon the brown road before me I plodded wearily on. The highway was bordered on each side by a low hedge, when suddenly that on my right hand came to an end and gave place to a green tongue of grassy lawn, which divided the road upon which I was walking from another that swept away to the right. When I came abreast of this grassy promontory, I saw that it was occupied by a man. He sat under the shade of a beech tree; a pipe was between his lips and in his left hand he held a little leather-covered book. An open pack lay beside him. The sound of my footsteps caught his ear and he turned towards me and looked at me with a pair of cold grey eyes.

"A very good day to you," he said, and I halted to return his salutation. "I wonder if you can help me," he continued. "Ha'e you the Latin?" The unexpected nature of the question startled me, awaking me from my torpor, and I asked him to repeat himself. "It's this wey," he said: "this wee bookie is the work o' a Latin poet ca'd Horace, a quaint chiel, but ane o' my familiars. Now I was juist passin' a pleasant half-'oor wi' him, and I ha'e come across a line or twa that I canna get the hang o' ava. But if ye ha'ena the Latin, ye'll no' be able to help me."

"Maybe I can help," I answered, and walking towards him I seated myself by his side.

"It's this bit," he said, laying his forefinger on the place. I took the little volume, and, after pausing for a moment to pick up some knowledge of the context, I suggested a rendering.

"Dod, man," he said, "ye've got it. That mak's sense, and is nae doot what Horace had in his heid. Let's hear a bit mair o't." I proceeded to translate a little more when he stopped me saying, "No, no, let's ha'e the Latin first; and then I'll be better able to follow ye."

With memories of Balliol swelling within me, I proceeded to do as he bade me. I read to the end of the ode and was about to translate it when he broke in:

"I see," he said, "you're an Oxford man; sic'

pronunciation never fell frae the lips o' ane o' Geordie Buchanan's school."

I felt my disguise drop from me before the piercing intuition of this strange wayfarer and for a moment I was at a loss how to protect myself. "Possibly," I said, "my pronunciation may be of the Oxford school, but, be that as it may, you surprise me. One hardly expects to come across a packman who reads the classics."

"No," he said, "there is only ae Hector the packman, and that's me. Ever since I took to the road I have aye carried a volume o' Horace in my pack. Mony a time I ha'e found comfort in his philosophy. I am only a packman, but I ha'e ambitions. Can ye guess the greatest o' them?"

"To own a shop in Dumfries," I said.

A look of distress crossed his face.

"Na, na," he said. "Something far better." He bent towards his open pack and rummaged among its contents, and as he did so I observed—what hitherto had escaped my notice—that he had a wooden leg. His right knee was bent at an angle and his foot was doubled up behind his thigh, as though his knee-joint had been fixed in that position by disease or injury; and the bend of his knee was fixed in the bucket of a wooden stump. "Here they are," he said, and he held up a bundle of small paper-covered books tied together with a tape. "Here they are. Now can ye no' see the degradation it is for a man like me to hawk sic trash aboot the country."

I took the bundle and, looking at the title-page of the uppermost book, read *The Lovers' Dream-Book, being a True and Reliable Interpretation of Dreams by Joseph the Seer*. I looked at the second. It was *The Farmer's Almanac*, and the third was *The Wife of Wigtown*.

"They're what we ca' chap-books," he said. "I

sell them at a penny the piece, but they're awfu' rubbish. Now my ambition is to improve the taste in letters o' the country folk. For mony a year it has been my hope and intention to lay mysel' on and produce a *magnum opus.* Now hoo dae ye think this would look on a title page ?—' Selections from Odes of Horace done into braid Scots by Hector the Packman,' or ' The Wisdom of Virgil on Bees and Bee-keeping by the same author.' Man, I'm thinkin', for a work like that, I micht get a doctorate frae ane o' the Universities. Ay, I maun lay masel' on when next winter comes." He rummaged once more among the contents of his pack, and picked out a pot, the mouth of which was covered with a piece of parchment. " You'll ha'e heard tell o' my magical salve ; an infallible cure for boils or blains in man or beast—it cures as it draws : a soothing balm for burnt fingers : and a cream that confers upon a lassie's cheek the tender saftness o' the rose." He removed the parchment and exhibited the ointment. With his forefinger he transferred a piece of the unguent to the back of his left hand and rubbed it in. In a moment he held his hand up to me—" Did ye ever see onything like that ? Every particle o' it is gone. Think o' the benefit that sic' a salve maun confer upon the human epiderm. I sent the King a pot last year up to London, but I'm thinkin' it has miscarried, for I ha'e never heard frae him yet. Man, there's a widda woman in Locharbriggs : she's maybe thirty-five, but to look at her you would say she was a lassie o' eighteen. What has done it ? Hector's magical salve ! Her complexion is by-ordinar. Nae doot she was bonnie afore, but my salve has painted the lily."

How long he might have rambled on I know not. Our conversation was suddenly interrupted by the clatter of horses approaching at a trot. To our right

I could see dimly the waters of a loch behind a fringe of trees. The sound came from the road which bordered the water. In a moment there swept round the corner of the loch and bore down upon us a little company of grey-coated troopers mounted on grey horses.

So this is the end, I thought, and braced myself for the ordeal well content. At the head of the cavalcade rode a man with a long beard that reached below his belt. I noticed that he wore no boots, but that his feet, thrust through his stirrups, were covered with coarse grey stockings. As he drew abreast of us, the packman, with wonderful alacrity, sprang up and, bonnet in hand, advanced to the edge of the road.

" A very good day to you, Sir Thomas, a very good day," he said.

The horseman drew rein. " Well, Hector," he said, " turning up again like a bad penny! What news have you ? "

" Nane but the best, sir, nane but the best. I'm juist makin' for hame frae the Rhinns o' Gallowa', and a' through the country-side there is but ae opinion—that the iron hand o' Lag is crushing the heart oot o' the Whigs."

" That is good news, Hector, but juist what I expected. Rebels understand only one argument, and that is the strong hand. It is the only thing I put faith in, as mony a Whig kens to his cost."

" Ye're richt, ye're richt, they ken ye weel. May I mak' sae bold as to offer you a truss o' Virginia weed, Sir Thomas," and returning to his pack he picked up a little bundle of tobacco and offered it to the horseman, who took it and slipped it into his pocket.

" A welcome gift, Hector, and I thank you for it. I hope it has paid duty ? "

" Sir," said the packman deprecatingly, " and me a King's man ! "

The rider smiled, and turning his fierce eyes upon me, said, " Who is your companion, Hector ? "

The fateful moment had come, and at that instant my life hung on the thread of a spider's web. But my heart was glad within me. I should find my Mary on the other side. The packman turned towards me : " Oh, Joseph," he said, " he's a gangrel body like masel'. I ha'e been takin' him roond the country wi' me to teach him the packman's job, so that when I retire to devote masel' to the writin' o' books I can hand ower the pack to him."

The quick lie took my breath away.

" Umph ! " grunted the horseman, " and what's he readin' there ? " Suddenly I remembered that I still held the packman's Horace in my hand. " I hope he's a King's man and that he is no' sittin' there wi' some Covenantin' book in his kneive ? Let me have a look at that book, young fellow."

I rose and, approaching him, held out the little leather-bound volume. As I did so I noticed his sharp-cut, flinty features, and a pair of thick and surly lips half-hidden by the masses of hair on his face. He turned the book over and found its title page.

" Oh, I see, somebody's opera ! Weel, he canna' be a Covenanter if he reads operas."

" Na," said Hector, " he's a King's man, and nae Whig. But I maunna delay ye, Sir Thomas, I hope ye'll enjoy the Virginia weed. Guid day to ye, sir."

" Good day, Hector," The horseman urged his horse with his knees, and the company, breaking into a trot, swept past and turned on to the main road which led towards the village.

As the last of the troopers swung round the corner, the packman donned his bonnet, and sitting down spat after the departing calvacade. " Bloody Dalzell," he said, " the Russian Bear—a human deevil. Damn him ! "

The sudden change in the packman's demeanour astonished me. I looked at him searchingly, but he had begun to arrange the contents of his bundle before binding it up.

"Why did you tell Sir Thomas such a string of lies about me?" I said.

He chuckled softly and looked at me, his left eyelid drooping, his right eye alertly wide. "I had ta'en a fancy to ye," he said, "and I was loth to run the risk o' partin' wi' a scholar when a lee micht keep him. Hoo dae I ken that ye're no a Covenanter? I was takin' nae chances. I nearly laughed in his face when Sir Thomas, the ignorant sumph, thocht ye were readin' a book o' operas. That's a guid ane! Mony a laugh I'll ha'e in the lang winter nichts when I remember it. I'm no' askin' ye wha or what ye are. You ha'e the Latin and I jalouse ye're an Englishman: but till it pleases ye to tell me something aboot yersel', I ken nae mair."

As he talked he was pulling his coarse linen covering over his pack. He buckled the broad strap which held it together, and continued: "I suppose ye're makin' for Dumfries. So am I, but I'm no' travellin' the direct road. I'm haudin' awa' roon' by the loch to New Abbey. I aye like to visit the Abbey. They ca' it the Abbey o' Dulce Cor—a bonnie name and it commemorates a bonnie romance."

My interest was awakened, and I asked him to tell me more.

"Ay," he said, "it's a bonnie tale, and guid to remember. I wonder if the widda at Locharbriggs would dae as much for me as Devorgilla did for her man. Nae doot ye ha'e heard o' her. I am credibly informed that she built a college at Oxford, and dootless ye ken she built the brig at Dumfries. But she did better than that, for when her man deid she carried his heart aboot wi' her in a' her travels in a silver casket. She built the Abbey o' Dulce Cor to his memory and she lies there hersel', wi' the heart o' her husband in her bonnie white arms. As the poet has it :

> " In Dulce Cor Abbey she taketh her rest,
> With the heart of her husband embalmed on her breast."

A memory of Mary flamed like a rose in my heart. I choked down my tears and said :

" I have often heard of Devorgilla. If I may, I would gladly accompany you and visit her tomb.

" I'll be gled o' your company," he said. It's no' every day I ha'e the chance o' a crack wi' a scholar. Come on,"—and slinging a stick through the strap round his pack, he swung it on to his shoulder and we set out.

As I walked beside him I studied him. He was tall and thin, and walked with a stoop, his head thrust forward, his neck a column of ruddy bronze.

" Ye're walking lame," he said, " but you are no' sae handicapped as me. This tree-leg o' mine is a terrible affliction. How cam' ye by your lame leg ? "

" I was a soldier once," I said. The answer seemed to satisfy him, though I was conscious that, as I spoke, the colour mounted to my cheeks.

The road upon which we found ourselves wound gently, under the cover of far-stretching trees, by the side of a beautiful loch. On the other side of the road the ground rose steeply up to the summit of a heather-clad hill. Suddenly through a break in the green trees we had a vision of the loch. Its waters lay blue and sparkling in the sunlight. Far off we could see undulating pastures, and beyond them a belt of trees in early foliage. As we stood feasting our eyes the packman exclaimed :

" Noo there's a pictur' that Virgil micht ha'e done justice to. It's a bit ootside the range o' Horace, but

I'm thinkin' Virgil wi' his e'e for a bonnie bit could ha'e written it up weel."

"It's a bonnie place the world," he continued, "fu' o' queer things, but to my thinkin' the queerest o' them a' is man, though maybe woman is queerer. Now there's the widda at Locharbriggs; onybody would think that a woman would be proud to be wife to Hector the packman—a scholar and the discoverer o' a magical salve, wha' some day may ha'e a handle to his name, forby maybe a title frae the King himsel'; but will ye believe me, though I ha'e speired at her four times, I ha'e got nae further forrit wi' her than a promise that she'll think aboot it."

I expressed sympathy and due surprise, and my answer pleased him, for he said: "Man, I'm glad I met ye. Ye're a lad o' sense, and wi' some pairts as weel, for ye ha'e the Latin."

For a time we walked in silence.

Soon we had left the pleasant loch behind us and the road wound in the distance before us. To our left the land was low lying, with here and there a clump of trees. To our right a lower range of hills stretched away to end in a great blue mass that dominated our horizon.

"That's Criffel," he said, pointing to the hill, "and juist at its foot nestles the Abbey o' the Sweet Heart. I ha'e little doot that doon in the village I'll sell a chap-book or twa. Sic trash they are. I maun lay masel' on and get that book o' mine begun."

He was talking on, good-humouredly, when suddenly a shrill cry for help came from a clump of trees on our left. Startled I rushed forward. I reached the edge of the copse and peered in, but could see nothing. The cry came again, with an added note of agony; and, heedless of danger, I rushed into the wood in the direction from which it proceeded. The packman had apparently stayed behind me, for he was no longer by my side. Making what speed I could among the clustering trees, I hurried on. Suddenly I heard footsteps racing behind me. I turned. Close behind me was the fast-running figure of a man. At a first glance I thought it was the packman, but as he rushed past me I saw that this was a beardless man sound in both legs. I could not imagine where he came from, and yet his clothing was strangely like that of my recent companion. I followed the rushing figure and saw that in his hand was a stout stick. Then through between the tree-trunks I saw the cause of the alarm. In an open space in the heart of the wood were four troopers in grey uniform, and I knew that I was about to burst upon some scene of devilry. A few steps more, and I saw a girl tied to a tree. About her stood the troopers. Two of them were holding one of her arms with her hand outstretched: the other two were busy lighting a long match. From the agonising scream I had heard, I knew that the torture had already been once applied. I could see the little spurt of flame as the match flared up, and as I dashed forward my ears were alert to hear her cry of pain. But deliverance was at hand. Into the open space leaped the man who had passed me. His stick swung in the air. Strongly and surely it fell on the temple of the nearest soldier, who dropped like an ox, bringing down a comrade in his fall.

Startled, the others sprang aside, but they were too slow. Twice, with lightning speed, the stick rose and twice it fell, and two more troopers went down. I quickened my pace. The trooper who had been knocked down by the fall of the first soldier sprang to his feet, and flung himself upon the man. Taken from behind he was at a disadvantage and the soldier, lifting him with a mighty effort, hurled him to the ground. Ere he could draw his pistol, I was upon him. My clenched fist caught him full on the chin, and he crashed on his back and lay breathing stertorously.

"A bonnie blow, lad! I couldna ha'e done it better mysel'," cried the stranger.

While I turned to the terrified girl and severed the cords that bound her to the tree, the stranger was kneeling beside the soldiers.

"They're no deid, nane o' them, worse luck! and it will be a wee while before the three o' them that felt the wecht o' my cudgel will come tae, but the fourth would be nane the waur o' a langer sleep," and swinging his stick he struck the recumbent figure a sickening thud upon the side of the head. "That's the proper medicine to keep him quate."

I had been so absorbed in his doings that I had turned my back upon the girl, and when I looked for her again she was nowhere to be seen. When my companion saw that she had gone, he shook his head gravely, saying:

"What was I tellin' ye? Arena women the queerest things on God's earth?"

I looked at him in astonishment; it was Hector after all!

"Good heavens, it's you!" I exclaimed.

"Ay," he replied with a smile, half-closing his left eye: "But haud your wheesht. As the Latin has it: '*Non omnes dormiunt qui clausos habent oculos.*' A trooper can sleep wi' an e'e open. Tak tent, but lend me a haun'."

From one of his pockets he produced a roll of tarred twine. Quickly cutting lengths from it, he tied the feet of the unconscious men, whom we dragged and laid starwise, on their backs, round one of the tree-trunks. He pulled the arms of each above their heads and brought them round the tree as far as possible, tying a cord firmly round their wrists, and carrying it round the bole. The skill he displayed amazed me. Long after they should regain consciousness they would have to struggle hard before they would be able to free themselves. I felt some satisfaction as I thought of their plight. When he had finished his work he surveyed each severely, laying his hand upon their hearts.

"No, there is no' ane o' them deid. They'll a' come tae by and by. But I'm thinkin' they'll be sair muddled. Come awa', lad."

"Let us look for the girl first," I suggested.

"Na, na," said he. "By this time the lassie, wha nae doot can rin like a hare, is half road to Kirkbean. Now if it had been the widda—but that's a different story."

Together we made our way to the edge of the copse. Just inside it I discovered the discarded pack, and beside it the wooden leg and long grey beard.

As my companion adjusted the wooden stump to his knee, he said: "Ay, sic ploys are terribly sair on a rheumatic knee." Then he proceeded to put on his beard, producing from one of his pockets a little phial of adhesive stuff with which he smeared his face. I watched, with an ill-concealed smile. "Noo," he said, "did ye ever see onything cleaner or bonnier? I'm a man o' peace, but when I'm roused I'm a deevil. Juist ae clout apiece, and they fell like pole-axed stirks—the three o' them. Bonnie clouts, were they no'?"

I assured him that I had never seen foes so formidable vanquished so rapidly and completely.

"Ye're a lad o' sense," he said; "that wasna' a bad clout ye hit the last o' them yersel'; but he needed a wee tap frae my stick to feenish him. I like a clean job. Come on," and swinging his pack on to his shoulder he led the way to the road.

The afternoon was drawing to a close when the village of New Abbey appeared in sight. Criffel now stood before us, a great mountain, heather clad and beautiful, like a sentinel above the little township. By the side of the stream, which divided our path from the village, we stopped, and Hector putting down his pack and taking off his coat proceeded to wash his face and hands. Nothing loth I followed suit.

As he was about to hoist his pack on to his shoulder again, he picked up his stick, and handing it to me said: "Feel the wecht o' that." I took it and found it strangely heavy. "It's loaded, ye see," he said—"three and a half ounces o' guid lead let into the heid o't. Juist three and a half ounces—fower is ower muckle; three would be ower little—and ye saw for yersel' what it can dae. A trusty frien', I can tell ye. Naebody kens it's loaded but me and you and the Almichty, forby a wheen sodgers that ha'e felt the wecht o't. I ca' it 'Trusty.' Come on," and, slipping the weighted head of the stick through the strap, he swung the pack on to his shoulders and we made for the village.

When we came to the inn the packman led the way through a flagged passage into a garden at the back. There, underneath a pear-tree, stood a green-painted bench with a table before it. Laying his pack upon the end of the bench, he sat down and pushed his bonnet back; I seated myself beside him.

"Noo," he said, "we maun ha'e something to eat. What will ye ha'e?"

Not knowing what might be available, I hesitated. Guessing the cause of my hesitation, he said: "Dinna be feared: it's a guid meat-hoose and its 'tippenny' is the best in the country-side. As for me, I'm for a pint o' 'tippenny,' and a fry o' ham and eggs. The King himsel' couldna dae better than that."

As he spoke a young girl had come through the door and now stood before us.

"What ha'e ye got for twa tired travellers?" asked Hector. "We want the best; we're worthy o't, and quite able to pay for it forby."

As the packman had foretold, ham and eggs were forthcoming; and having given our order Hector produced his pipe and proceeded to fill it.

When it was drawing satisfactorily he proceeded to point out the beauties of the scene. To the right were visible great grey walls, moss-grown in places, with here and there a bush springing among their ruins.

"That," he said, "is part o' the wall o' the old Abbey. There," pointing to the right, "is a' that remains o' the Abbey itsel'. By and by we'll gang and tak' a look at it."

Soon the girl returned with our food. When we had finished our meal Hector said:

"And noo I maun go and see my frien' the miller. Meantime, I'll leave you in chairge o' the pack, and if onybody should want to buy, you can mak' the sale. I hope ye'll prove yersel' a guid packman,"—with which he stumped off.

In a moment or two the girl came to clear the table. When she had done so, she returned, and looking at me half shyly, said: "Are ye a packman tae?"

"Yes," I answered.

"Oh," she said, "then I wonder if ye ha'e sic a thing as a dream-book in your pack?" I opened the pack, and spread its contents before her. "No, I dinna want onything else but a dream-book," she said. I found one, and, lifting a corner of her apron, she produced a penny which she laid upon the table, and with a finger already between the pages of the book disappeared into the inn.

Left to myself, I drifted into a reverie. Love—the love of a man for a woman, and the love of a woman for a man—seemed the greatest thing on the earth. The packman with his loved one at Locharbriggs; this tavern maid with her sweetheart—for did not her desire for a dream-book tell me that she had a lover—were all under its spell. I, too, had my memories of love,—memories of infinite tenderness—bitter—sweet—torn by tragedy. I tried to banish such thoughts from my mind, for they brought naught but pain, but, try how I might, I found they would return. Nor was it to be wondered at, for at that moment I was within a stone's throw of Devorgilla's monument to her own enduring affection. I was within sight of the place where her haunting love-story had seen its fulfilment. Within the hoary walls of that great fane Devorgilla was sleeping her eternal sleep with the heart of her husband upon her breast. Yes, of a truth was it well said: "Many waters cannot quench love, neither can the floods drown it." Hector would go to the widow, the tavern maid would dream of her lover, while for me, love was nothing but a memory. But what a memory! I was conscious of Mary's presence—her spirit seemed to enfold me in the warm breath of the evening. I almost felt her kiss upon my cheek. Never before, since that day when we had parted upon the moors, had she seemed so near. I slipped my hand into my pocket and caressed the fragment of her ring. I drew it out and pressed it to my lips, and as I did so I heard the stumping footsteps of the packman. Quickly I slipped the ring out of sight and looked towards the door.

Hector came through, carrying a tankard of ale in each hand.

"Drouthy work, carryin' the pack," he said. "Ha'e ye sold onything while I ha'e been away?"

"Only a dream-book to the little maid," I answered.

"Sic trash," he groaned, "sic trash, but they will ha'e them. But wait a bit; I'm gaun to lay masel' on in the back end o' the year. Did ye no' try to sell a pot o' salve ? " I confessed that I had not. " Man," he said, " ye'll no' mak' a guid packman. I could aye sell a pot o' the balm to a lassie that buys a dream-book. But come on : the licht's juist richt for seein' the Abbey at its best."

CHAPTER XXVII

ON THE ROAD TO DUMFRIES

We drank our ale, and leaving the inn turned into the precincts of the Abbey, where for the first time I had an opportunity of gazing upon its ruined splendour. Rarely have I seen such beauty in decay —the mellow light of the evening lending to the red sandstone of the aisles, the choir and the great square tower a rosy hue that made them singularly beautiful. The packman led the way and halted before a richly ornate stone that rested on a pedestal below the great Gothic window. He took his bonnet off reverently and I followed suit, and together we stood in silence. " She lies here," he said, with a break in his voice, and when I looked at him there were tears in his eyes. He sighed as though the stone covered the remains of someone very dear to him. I knew what was in his mind. This brave follower of the open road, this deliverer of maidens in distress, this egotistical packman, and self-styled scholar was an incorrigible sentimentalist. He was thinking, I knew, of Devorgilla's beautiful devotion to her husband, but the widow at Locharbriggs was in his thoughts as well. He turned and laid a hand upon my arm as he donned his bonnet.

" Whaur are ye sleepin' the nicht ? " he asked.

The question surprised me, for I had taken it for granted that we should stay at the village inn. " I suppose," I said, " that I can get a bed in the tavern."

"Nae doot, nae doot," he said, "if so you like, but I never sleep in a bed when I'm oot on the road. It's safer to sleep in the open, especially when ye wear a wooden leg that ye dinna exactly need. Folks are inquisitive. Come awa back to the inn wi' me. You can sleep there if ye like, but I'll come back here. It'll no' be the first time I ha'e slept by the graveside o' Devorgilla."

We returned to the inn where I had no difficulty in procuring a bed. Hector shouldered his pack and took his way back to the Abbey, but he was up betimes and was hammering at my door with his heavy-headed stick before I was awake. We breakfasted and set out for Dumfries.

Hector had lit his pipe and trudged along beside me in silence. Left to my own thoughts, I began to study him. Since we had joined company, he had shown several phases of character difficult to reconcile. In the presence of Sir Thomas Dalzell he had seemed to be an avowed enemy of the Covenanters, yet, when Dalzell and his troopers were at a safe distance, he had displayed contempt and bitter hatred for them. Then there was the attack on the soldiers in the little copse by the roadside on our way to New Abbey. What was he? Was the calling of a packman, like his false beard and his unnecessary wooden-leg, merely a mask? I was puzzled, but I determined that ere our journey should come to an end I would do my utmost to unravel his secret.

When the packman's pipe was empty he returned it to his pocket and broke into song. The mood of sentiment was upon him, and he sang a quaint old song of unrequited love. I failed to make out the words; but I heard enough to know that he was thinking, as always, of the widow.

About an hour after leaving the village we came to the end of a long ascent.

"It's been a stiff clim'," said the packman, "we'd better sit doon and rest a wee." He threw off his pack and we sat down upon some rising ground by the roadside. For a time I sat and drank in the beauty which spread itself before me, but my reverie was disturbed by Hector, who laid his hand upon my knee and said, "I want to talk to you." All attention, I turned towards him, but he was slow to begin. Patiently I waited, and then, half turning so that he looked me straight in the face with his piercing right eye wide open, his left half shut, he said:

"Nae doot ye're puzzled aboot me." I wondered whether he had been able to read the thoughts that had flitted through my mind as we climbed the hill from New Abbey. "I think it is only richt," he continued, "that before we gang ony further, I should mak' masel' clear to you. Maybe when I ha'e opened my heart to you, you'll tell me something aboot yersel' for, if I ha'e kept my counsel, so ha'e you. Rale frien'ship maun be built on mutual confidence; withoot that, frien'ship is naething mair than a hoose o' cairds. Ye ken already that I am no' a'thegither what I seem. I'd better begin at the beginnin'. I'm an Ayrshire man, articled in my youth to the Law and at ae time a student o' Glasgow College; an' lang syne, when my blood was hot and I was fu' o' ideals, I threw in my lot wi' the Covenanters. And I've suffered for it." He pushed down the rig-and-fur stocking on his left leg. "Look at that," he said. I looked, and saw, where the skin ran over the bone, a long, ugly brown scar. "Ye'll no' ken what that means?" I shook my head. "Weel," he said, "that's what the persecutors did for me. I've had 'the boot' on that leg, and until my dying day I'll carry the mark. But I'm no' what they ca' a guid Covenanter. I'm a queer mixture, as maybe you yersel' ha'e already noticed. I canna say that I'm a religious man, and though my heart is wi' the lads that are ready to dee for the Covenant, I fear that I masel' lack grace. Hooever, that's by the way. Lang years sin' I cam'. to this country-side whaur naebody knew me, as a packman wi' a tree-leg, and as such I am kent to maist o' my acquaintances. Wi' my pack on my shoulder I wander through the country-side back and forrit frae Dumfries to Portpatrick, and frae Portpatrick back again to the Nith, wi' chap-books, and ribbons, and pots o' salve, but a' the while I keep my e'en and my ears open. I get to ken the movements o' the troopers, and I hear tell in the hooses o' the Covenanters o' comin' hill-meetings and sic-like, and mony a time I ha'e been able to drop a hint in the richt place that has brocht to nought some crafty scheme o' the persecutors and saved the life o' mair than ane hill-man. If ye like to put it that way, I rin wi' the hare and hunt wi' the hounds. I'm hand in glove, to a' ootward seeming, wi' the persecutors themselves. I foregather wi' sodgers in roadside inns, and it's marvellous hoo a pint or twa o' 'tippenny' and a truss o' Virginia weed will loosen their tongues and gaur them talk. I've listened quately, and mony a time I've let fa' a remark that mak's them believe that a' my sympathies are wi' them and that I'm no' in wi' the Covenanters ava. As a matter o' solid fact, I am sae weel thocht o' by men sic as Sir Robert Grier, Dalzell himsel' and Claver'se, that mair than aince I ha'e been sent by them on special commissions to find things oot; and I've come back and I've tellt them what they wanted to ken, and riding hell for leather they've gane off wi' their dragoons to some wee thackit cottage on the moors. But they've never caught the bird they were after. Somebody—maybe it was me, I'm no' sayin'

—had drapped a timely warnin'; and though I tellt the persecutors nae lee, I ha'e mair than aince gi'en them cause to remember that truth lies at the bottom o' a very deep well. That's my story. I'm a spy, if ye like—an ugly word, but I ha'e na man's blood upon my haun's or on my conscience. And it's dangerous wark, as you may weel ken. Some day ane or other o' my schemes will gang agley, and the heid and haun's, and maybe the tree-leg as weel, o' Hector the packman will decorate a spike on Devorgilla's brig at Dumfries. I wadna muckle mind; for life is sometimes a weary darg, but I'd like, afore that day comes, tae ha'e feenished my *magnum opus.* I maun really lay masel' on and get it begun. It would be a monument by which I micht be remembered.

"Sometimes as I walk my lane alang the roads I think o' things. Here and there I come across a wee mound on the moorland, or maybe by the roadside, and I ken it covers the body o' some brave man wha has died for his faith. Desolate, lonely, and scattered cairns they are. And then I think, that though this is the day o' the persecutors, and though they be set in great power, a day is comin' when a' their glory will be brocht to naething. By and by Grier o' Lag, Dalzell and Claver'se, and a' the rest o' them will pay the debt to Nature, and nae doot they will be buried wi' muckle pomp and circumstance, and great monuments o' carved stane will be set abune them. But in time to come, I'm thinkin', it will no' be their tombs that will be held in reverence, but the lonely graves scattered aboot the purple moors and the blue hills. It's them that will be treasured for ever as a precious heritage. We're a religious folk in Scotland, or at least we get that name—but religion or no', we love liberty wi' every fibre o' oor being, and in days to come, generations yet unborn, wha may be unable to understaun the faith for which the hill-men died, will honour them because they were ready to lay doon their lives in defiance o' a tyrant king. Noo," he said, letting his eyes fall, " ye ken a' aboot me that there's ony need to ken, and it's for ye to say whether we pairt company here or whether we gang on thegither." He drew out his pipe and proceeded to fill it.

For a moment I was at a loss. Was he seeking to entrap me into an open declaration of sympathy with the Covenanters; or was he telling the truth? His confession had been an absolutely open one, so open that if my sympathies were with the persecutors he had placed himself completely in my hands. He had looked me straight in the face with one piercing eye as though to read my soul, while the other was half veiled as though to hide his own. But his voice had rung with fervour as he spoke of the lone graves of the hill-men, and I remembered the fight in the wood. He must have spoken the truth; so I took courage and without further delay told him my story. He listened attentively, and when I had finished he said:

" Ay, the auld packman is richt again. I thocht aboot ye last nicht. Man, I can read fowk like a coont on a slate, and I'm richt gled to hear frae your ain lips, what I had already guessed, that you're for the Cause. If I had thocht onything else, I wu'd ha'e held my tongue."

CHAPTER XXVIII

FOR THE SWEET SAKE OF MARY

WHEN with characteristic self-satisfaction the packman had extolled his own intelligence, he lapsed into silence. As for me, the telling of my tale had reawakened so many sad memories that for a time I sat gazing before me, unable through my tears to see the other side of the road. Hector knocked the ashes out of his pipe, and sighed.

" It is," he said, " ane o' the saddest stories I ha'e ever heard. Sic an experience is enough to mak' a man bitter for the rest o' his days. But if Mary was only half o' what you ha'e tellt me she was, that's no' what she wu'd like to see. It's the prood woman she wu'd be if she knew ye were minded to throw in your lot wi' the Cause. What are ye gaun to dae ? "

" I am making for England," I answered.

Hector shook his head sadly. " I've noticed the same afore," he said, and paused.

" What have you noticed ? " I asked. " I do not understand you."

He looked into the distance, and spoke as though to himself.

" Ay ! It's the auld story. Queer but awfu' human. There was Moses and Peter : the ane the meekest o' men, but he lost his temper twice ; the ither the bravest and lealest o' the disciples, but he turned coward."

" Explain yourself," I said. " I cannot follow you."

"I mean nae offence, but I thocht ye wad hae been quicker i' the uptak'. D'ye no see that men fail maist often on their strongest point? Man, when a man prides himsel' on his strong points it's time to get down on his knees. Ye tell me ye lo'ed the lass—and nae doot ye did. But ye're turning yer back on love, and rinnin' awa'. I'm surprised at ye. If sic a fate as has befallen Mary were to befa' the widda at Locharbriggs, dae ye think I should rest until I had dune something to avenge her. Mind ye I'm no' counsellin' violence, for I'm a man that loves peace. Bloodshed is the revenge o' the foolish. There are better ways than that, and if ye'll throw your lot in wi' mine, I'll show ye hoo ye can dae something for the sake o' her ye loved and for the cause o' the Covenant." I listened in silence and shame. His words were biting into my heart.

He looked at me with eyes that seemed to peer into the depths of my soul. Then I found speech. "Mary," I said, "was to me the most precious thing in all the world. If you can show me how I can render service to the Cause she loved, I am ready to do your bidding."

He thrust out his right hand: "Put your haun' there," he said; "you've spoken like a man. Dae ye mind what Horace says: '*Carpe diem, quam minimum credula postera.*' 'Tak' time by the forelock and never trust to the morn.' A wise word that. Fegs, he was a marvel! In fact he's gey near as fu' o' wisdom as the guid Book itsel'. We'll tak' time by the forelock, and between us, if the Lord wills, we'll dae something for the persecuted hill-folk and strike a blow for Scotland and for liberty. But we'll ha'e to be gettin' on; the day'll no' tarry for us. Let us awa'."

Refreshed by our rest, we rose and took to the road again.

A long descent lay before us and till we had completed it neither of us spoke. But when we reached the foot of the hill Hector suddenly said:

" I've been thinkin' aboot your story. It's wonderfu' what bits o' gossip a packman can pick up on his roonds. Noo, you may be surprised to hear that I kent a' aboot the shootin' o' the minister up on the hills. I heard the story frae a trooper in the inn at Gatehouse. To him it was a great joke, for he saw naething in it but the silly action o' a daft auld man wha's ain stupidity brocht aboot his death. I wonder, if he had kent the hale story as you and me ken it, whether he would ha'e seen the beauty o't. I'm thinkin' maybe no', for to size up a thing like that richtly it maun be in a man's heart to dae the like himsel'. Ay, what a welcome the martyr would get on the ither side!" He paused for a moment, then continued: " And it's queer that I heard aboot you yersel' frae the same trooper. He tellt me that they cam' on the minister quite accidental-like; and that they werena' lookin' for him ava. They were oot on the hills huntin' for a deserter, wha I'm thinkin' was yersel'. They didna find you, he said. As a matter o' fact they believe that ye're deid—he said as muckle. So you may haud yer mind easy, for unless an' ill win' blaws and ye're recognised by ane o' yer fellow-troopers, ye're safe."

We trudged on steadily towards Dumfries. My heart was with Mary, and I did not speak. The packman was silent too—but while I was living in the past he apparently was looking into the future, for he said suddenly:

" It's a dangerous job I'm invitin' ye to tackle—a job that calls for the best wit o' a man, and muckle courage. I'm thinkin' you dinna lack for either, but time will show. Ay: it will that. As for me," he continued, after a pause, " I'm no' a religious man, but hidden in a corner o' my soul I ha'e a wee lamp o' faith. But it doesna aye burn as brichtly as it micht, and mony a time I sit by the roadside and compare the man I wad like to be wi' the man that I ken masel' to be; and it mak's me gey humble. But I aye tak' courage when I think o' Peter. He found the road through life a hard path and he tripped sae often ower the stanes that I sometimes think, like me, he maun ha'e had a tree-leg. But at the end he proved himsel' to be gold richt through, as dootless the Maister kent a' the while." His voice broke, and, looking at him, I saw tears streaming down his cheeks.

"But noo, a word in your ear. We're very near Dumfries noo. We'd better separate there, it will be safer. It behoves ye to ken where ye will fin' a lodgin'.

"In Mitchell's Close at the brig' end there lives a widda woman. She kens me weel. Her door is the second on the left frae the mooth o' the close. Her name is Phemie McBride, and when ye tell her ye're a frien' o' Hector the packman's she'll gie ye a welcome and ask nae questions. We should reach the toon before twa o'clock. You can ha'e bite and sup. I'll leave my pack at my lodgings and syne I'll be awa oot to Locharbriggs to pay my respects to the widda. At six o'clock or thereabouts I'll look for ye at the Toon Heid Port and we'll tak' a walk up the banks o' the Nith thegither. But, a word in yer lug. Dumfries is a stronghold o' the Covenanters; forby it is ane o' the heidquarters o' the persecutors. Lag himsel' has a hoose there—so ye maun be carefu'. Tak' a leaf oot my book, and oot o' the book o' even a wiser man than me—Be all things to all men, and mix neither yer politics nor yer drink. Haud your tongue, and if ye ha'e to speak, keep half yer counsel tae yersel'."

I thanked him and promised to exercise all caution.

"And noo," he said, "for appearance' sake, I maun be Hector the packman, again," and going to a cottage by the wayside he knocked loudly at the door. I walked slowly on and in a moment or two he rejoined me.

With a twinkle in his eyes, he said: "Trade's bad the day. The guid-wife wanted neither a dream-book nor a pot o' salve. But that reminds me, it's gey near three months sin' I saw the widda. Noo you yersel' ha'e kent the spell o' love. I dinna want to touch ye on a sair spot, but if ye were in my place, what wad ye tak' tae yer sweetheart?"

I had no suggestion to offer, and said so.

"Weel," he said, "that's nae help. I'll juist ha'e a look at the jeweller's window in the High Street. Maybe I'll see something there: but failin' that there's aye a pot o' my balm."

"She will not need any of that," I answered. "Your coming will bring a colour to her cheeks without the aid of your magical salve."

"Man," said Hector, "I like ye. Ye're a lad o' promise; I'll mak' a man o' ye yet."

We were approaching another cottage on the outskirts of the town, and once again Hector assumed the rôle of the packman and tapped at the door. When he rejoined me he said: "I ha'e had some luck this time, but no' muckle, because a' I sold was a dream-book. Awfu' trash, as ye weel ken." He groaned as though in anguish of spirit. "And noo," he said, "we'd better pairt company. The brig end o' Dumfries is on this side o' the water."

So we parted, and I walked on ahead, until as I descended a steep hill I saw the end of the bridge before me. I found Mitchell's Close without difficulty and entered it. The houses within it were flinging back the glare of the sun from their white-washed walls. I knocked at the second door on the left, and after a little it was opened by an old woman. Holding the latch in her hand, she stood between the half-open door and the wall as though to block the passage.

"Wha may ye be?" she said. "Ye ha'ena' a kent face."

"I am," I said, speaking low, "a friend of Hector the packman."

She threw the door wide open at once, saying, "Come awa ben." I entered, and immediately she shut and barred the door behind us, and led the way into the kitchen, saying: "Ony frien' o' Hector the packman is welcome here. Can I get ye onything to eat?"

As I had not broken my fast since leaving New Abbey, I was ready to do justice to the meal which she made haste to spread before me. Remembering Hector's warning, I held my tongue, and as she waited upon me the old woman kept her counsel to herself. I could see that she was studying me closely; and when the meal was over she said, suddenly:

"So ye're a frien' o' Hector's, are ye? Whaur's the man noo?"

"When I left him," I replied, "he was making his way to his own lodging."

"Nae doot, nae doot; and by this time I jalouse he's on the road to Locharbriggs."

I smiled.

"If ye are a frien' o' Hector's," she continued, "ye've nae doot heard aboot the widow at Locharbriggs."

"Oh yes," I said. "She bulks largely in his affections."

The old woman laughed heartily. "She does that, the silly auld man, but he'd better look somewhere else, for she winna ha'e him. I ken her weel; she's my dochter."

CHAPTER XXIX

BESIDE THE NITH

When the afternoon was mellowing into early evening I stood upon Devorgilla's Bridge watching the river. Much had happened to me since last I was there. I had drunk deep of joy and sorrow; and as I looked down upon the slow-moving water, memory smote me with both hands. I laid my arms upon the parapet of the wall and stood at gaze, but though I looked before me, my mind was wandering backwards across the chequered, love-lit, blood-stained months that lay behind me. The mood passed and my eyes followed the stream as it issued from underneath the dark arches and flowed slowly on until, in the distance, glistening like a silver band, it swept round a bend and was lost to view. To my right, on the brow of a hill, stood a windmill, its great arms aswing with hesitant gait in the wind. Beyond the windmill the hills sloped down to the river, studded here and there by a copse of trees, or the white gable of a cottage flinging back a ray of sunlight. To my left was the town of Dumfries, with the Sands sloping down from the nearer houses to the river, and the stately spire of St. Michael's Church challenging the sky in the near distance. Beyond, rose a pleasant, tree-crowned hill, on whose slopes I could see the figures of sheep and cattle.

There were yet two hours before I had to meet Hector at the Town Head Port, so, crossing the bridge,

I made for the Friar's Vennel, which I knew to be the main thoroughfare from the brig-end to the centre of the town. It was a busy artery of traffic, lined upon one side by shops and upon the other by comfortable dwelling-places. Some of the houses had gardens, well-kept and orderly. Here and there, between the houses, was a narrow entry and looking down one of these I discovered that it opened into a little court upon each side of which stood small thatched cottages.

I sauntered up the Vennel, and shortly came to the High Street—a broad and roomy thoroughfare. Each side of it was occupied by shops, well-stocked and prosperous-looking, and in the centre of the street were the booths of market-gardeners and fishermen, who were making a brave display of their wares.

Leaving the booths behind me, I continued my journey up the High Street. By and by I came to a wider portion of the street which the inhabitants know as the Plain Stanes. Here was the house of Lag, and I gazed at it curiously. A couple of soldiers stood at the door, from which I judged that Sir Robert himself was in residence ; so, remembering I was a deserter, I did not tarry long, but went on towards St. Michael's Church.

I entered the churchyard and, sitting down under the shadow of one of the gigantic tombstones, I waited until I judged it was time to go and meet Hector.

As I was going out I met a man whom I took to be the grave-digger, and asked him to direct me to the Town Head Port.

"Oh, ye're a stranger in these pairts," he said, as he pointed out the way. I made no answer save to thank him and bid him good evening, and then I hurried in the direction he had indicated.

I found the Port without difficulty and stood just outside it, listening to the cawing of the rooks in the tall trees on the green mound that separated me from the river.

I had not long to wait ere Hector arrived. He slipped his arm through mine, and said :

" Let's awa' doon to the bank o' the water."

He was whistling merrily as we scrambled down the bank, so I judged that the widow had been kind, and ventured to say as much. His only reply was :

" *Dulce ridentem Lalagen amabo dulce loquentem.*"

I asked after her health.

" Oh, she's fine, fine. She was pleased wi' the bonny kaim I took her. Here's a bit o' wisdom for ye, my lad. If ye want to please a woman that ye like, gi'e her some gaud to adorn hersel' wi'. If she's plain and no' weel-faured she'll tak' it as a compliment that ye should wish to mak' her bonnie. If she's bonnie to begin wi', she'll tak' your bit giftie as a proof that ye ha'e noticed wi' your ain een that she's weel-faured and weel-lookin'."

Alas, for me all such joys were things of the dead past.

When we reached the river's edge we walked up-stream.

I have not the pen of a poet, nor has the poet yet been born whose pen could paint with fitting words the glory of the shining Nith. Hector says Virgil could have done it ; but I wonder. There are beauties beyond the range of words. The eye can drink them in ; the soul can interpret them : and as the soul interprets them, so are they revealed to the eye that sees them.

We walked for more than a mile till we came to a lofty eminence, set tree-crowned above the stream. When we had climbed to its summit Hector paused beneath a giant beech tree which stood perilously near the declivity that fell sheer to the river brink. " Look," he said, and pointed down the river. Lit by the rays of the setting sun, it stretched like a ruddy band of bronze into the distance, leading the eye directly to the ruins of the old College of Lincluden with its Gothic window and shattered tower. Beyond, the blue hills raised their brows to the sky, from which, as from a golden chalice, a stream of glory poured.

For each of Nature's pictures there is one divine moment in the day. It was now.

I stood in rapture till Hector touched my arm. "It's bonnie," he said. "I should say ye've naething to match it in England, but we maun awa' hame. Come on," and he led the way across a field to the road. "This," he said, "is the shortest way back to the toon. I ha'e been alang it aince the day already, for it leads tae Locharbriggs, and mair than likely I'll be alang it the morn, for the widda was wonderfu' kind, and though she wouldna exactly gang the length o' namin' the day, she was mair amenable to reason than I've ever kent her afore. So the morn's mornin' I'm makin' my way oot to her again: and maybe I'll be lucky. Ye never can tell, for didna' Virgil himsel' say '*Varium et mutabile semper femina*'—' Woman is a fickle jade onyway ye like to tak' her.' Oh, these auld poets, but they had the wise word every time. Noo that we're comin' near the toon we'd better settle what we are gaun to dae the morn. As for me, I ha'e mony things on haun and my time'll be a' ta'en up. But I'll be free at six o'clock. Ye can spend the day as ye like, and I'll meet ye at that oor at the Vennel Port."

I promised that I should be at the trysting-place at the time appointed.

We were now drawing near the town. By and by we came to the mound known as Christie's Mount, and soon we could see the Plain Stones before us. As we swung round into the lower part of the High Street we heard sounds of revelry coming from Lag's house at the corner of the Turnpike Wynd. We crossed to the other side of the street and looked up. Every window was a blaze of light. From an upper room came the sound of wild voices of men far gone in their cups, and every now and then shouts of laughter. One laugh, a great raucous bellow, dominated all the rest.

"That's Lag himsel'," whispered Hector. "Eh, it's awfu', awfu'. While thae men o' blood are feastin' and drinkin' there, saints o' the Covenant are sleepin' under the cauld sky awa' on the hills."

Suddenly out of the darkness stepped a soldier, who, seeing us gazing up at the house approached, and as he passed scanned us keenly. I nudged the packman with my elbow and at once he led the way up the High Street. He did not speak until we were near the Tolbooth, then he whispered:

"Ay, ye'll min' what I tellt ye; it's true ye've to be carefu' what ye say in the toon o' Dumfries. Dinna forget that. A scarlet-coated loon like yon kens nocht aboot Horace, and he, worthy man, as always, has the richt word for the occasion: '*Redeat miseris, abeat fortuna superbis.*' Ye can translate that literally for yersel', but I'll drap my renderin' in yer lug." Putting his mouth close to my ear he whispered: "'May God bless the puir hill-men, and damn Lag and a' his stiff-necked tribe.' Noo a guid nicht tae ye; I'll meet ye the morn at six o'clock at the Vennel Port."

With some difficulty, for it was dark and the streets were ill paved, I betook me down the Vennel, and crossing the river made my way to my lodgings. My sleep was dreamless, and when I awoke in the morning a sparrow was twittering on the sill. I dressed quickly and went downstairs. In the kitchen, I found the old woman sitting at a well-scrubbed deal table. She had a pair of spectacles on her nose.

and on the table beside her lay an open Bible. She did not raise her eyes at my approach, but continued to read in a sibilant whisper, keeping time to the words as she pronounced them by beating the air with her open hand. I waited patiently until her devotions were finished.

"A good morning to you, sir. Ha'e ye sleepit weel?" she asked.

"Thank you," I replied, "none better. I am sorry that I interrupted you in your religious duties."

"Oh, ye didna interrupt me," she said; "besides, readin' the Book is no' a releegious duty, it's a releegious privilege. Belike ye dinna ken the difference. Nae doot that comes frae bein' a frien' o' Hector's—Hector that is aye haverin' oot o' the auld heathen poets. If he kent as muckle aboot the psalms o' a guid Presbyterian like Dauvit as he lets on he kens aboot Horace, it wad, I'm thinkin', be a lot better for his sowl, the silly auld gommeril. Wantin' tae mairry a lassie a quarter o' a century younger than himsel'! Thank God she's got some o' the sense o' her mither. She winna ha'e him! Noo, lad, yer parritch is ready and I'll juist dish them for ye."

When my meal was over I entered into conversation with her again.

She had a caustic tongue and a good deal of quiet humour, and she reminded me in some ways of Jean at Daldowie; and with the thought of Daldowie came memories of my lost love. The mellow hand of the years upon them may impart to our sorrows a fragrance that mitigates their pain, but the wound in my heart was still a recent one, ready to bleed at a touch.

Almost unable to restrain myself, I picked up my bonnet and going out crossed the bridge and came down upon the Sands. Along their length was stretched a number of booths, and the Sands themselves were thronged with people. Apparently it was a market day. Leisurely, as I had nothing else to do, I joined the crowd—buirdly, well-clad farmers; robust looking farm-servants; sturdy farm wenches with large baskets of butter and eggs upon their arms.

On the outskirts of the crowd a sailor, with a bronzed face and great rings depending from his ears, was putting a monkey through a series of antics to the amusement of the young men and women who stood around him in open-mouthed amazement.

When I had grown tired of watching him I made my way to the Vennel Port, and then I walked leisurely through the main streets of the old town. When I came to its outskirts, just beside St. Michael's Church, I bought some food and making my way to the river-side I followed its course downwards. By and by I came to some rising ground, and climbing up made my way through a rocky gorge and sat down on the soft turf beneath an overhanging oak tree.

After a meal, I stretched myself upon my back, and pulling my bonnet over my eyes composed myself to sleep. When I awoke I remembered that I had promised to meet Hector at six o'clock. By the time I had retraced my steps the appointed hour would be at hand. So I descended to the river bank and made my way towards the Vennel Port.

Six o'clock was striking when I reached it, but Hector was not there. Moment succeeded moment and still he did not come. Impatient I began to walk up and down, crossing the Sands to look at the river where fishermen were busy tempting the fish with their flies. I strolled back again to the Vennel and walked up it for a short distance, descending once again to the Port. There was no sign of Hector, and when the clock struck seven and I realised that an hour had elapsed since I had come to the trysting-place, anxiety assailed me. This was not like the packman. Had some mischance befallen him? He had told me that his was dangerous work, and I knew that he spoke the truth. One false step, and he would be undone. At this very moment he might be in grave danger. Ill at ease, I went up to the top of the Vennel, hoping to meet him. My quest was vain! The clock struck eight: he had not yet appeared. As the time dragged on its leaden way I remembered the long pathetic vigil I had shared with Jean at Daldowie, and though the memory stabbed me to the heart, I hugged it to me. The hour of nine struck on the Tolbooth clock; still there was no sign of Hector. Twilight gathered and deepened; the stars stole out, and still he did not come. When another weary hour had passed I decided that it was useless to wait longer, so, at the last stroke of the hour, I crossed the bridge and made for my lodgings in Mitchell's Close. The good woman of the house had not yet retired to rest, and I was fain to partake of the supper which she had prepared for me.

During the meal I said nothing to her of my anxiety. Hector had warned me to be careful in my speech, and, fortunately, she showed no curiosity as to my doings. When supper was over I bade her good night and went to my room. Before undressing and lying down, I looked through the window. It was a quiet summer night. All the world seemed at peace; but some dazed dread was knocking at the door of my heart and I was sore troubled. Something must have happened to Hector—of that there could be little doubt. For a time I lay awake in a maze of anxiety: and it was not till after midnight had boomed from the Tolbooth clock, that languor stole over me and I slept.

CHAPTER XXX

IN THE TIGER'S DEN

SUDDENLY I woke, startled. Some noise had disturbed me. I listened intently. Nothing stirred in the house. I sat up in bed, and peered into the darkness, only relieved by the fitful light of the moon stealing through the window. What had wakened me? I waited anxiously; then I heard three little taps, clear and metallic, upon the window. I sprang up and looked out, and saw in the dim-lit courtyard the tall figure of a man, who moved forward when he saw me, and I recognised the wooden leg of Hector. Eagerly I undid the window, swinging it back gently on noiseless hinges, and craned forward into the night. Hector put a hand to his mouth, and whispered, " Wheesht! wheesht! " then walked softly to the door of the house. Hastily throwing on some clothes I crept on tip-toe downstairs, and opening the door admitted him to the kitchen.

With uplifted finger he whispered, " Haste ye, and dinna wake the auld woman. We'll talk on the road." As silently as possible I hastened to my room and finished dressing; then, I rejoined the packman. As I entered the kitchen he was lifting the poker from the fireplace. " She'll understand—that's a sign," he said, as he laid it carefully on the top of the table.

" But what," I whispered, " about paying her? "

" Dinna worry on that score," he said; " she kens

me. That's eneuch. There's danger afoot. Come on."

He led the way to the door, which he opened noiselessly and together we passed out into the courtyard.

At the mouth of the close he paused and peered carefully in every direction. Then he turned to me and whispered, "There's naebody aboot." We passed quickly into the street, and, walking close to the houses so that we were in their full shadow, we hurried away.

From the direction we took I judged that our path lay parallel to the course of the river on the side opposite the town of Dumfries. We had walked perhaps a mile before Hector again broke the silence. Still whispering, he said:

"Man, I've had an awfu' day. Horace has the richt word every time: '*Recenti mens trepidat metu*'—'My hert's a' o' a dither wi' fricht.' What's yer name? ye've never tellt me."

For the first time it dawned on me that he did not know my name. He had called me Joseph at the road-end when Dalzell had taken us unawares, but since then the matter had never been mentioned between us. "My name is Walter de Brydde," I said.

"Ay," he said, "but what name was ye kent by when ye were a trooper?"

"I called myself Bryden," I replied.

"That's it. It was you richt enough. Oh, I've had a terrible day. But I had better begin at the beginning, and tell ye the hale story.

"This mornin' I left my lodgings wi' full purpose and intention o' gaun to see the widda. Weel, it's a lang road and a drouthy, so before leavin' the toon I drapped into the Hole i' the Wa', to ha'e a pint o' tippenny. It's a hoose I aye frequent when I'm in

Dumfries. Weel, as I was tellin' ye, I was sittin' in the corner, and I'd juist passed the time o' day wi' the landlord, when in daundered twa sodgers. As soon as I saw the sicht o' their coats, my ears were cocked to catch their words. They were talkin' as they cam' in. The ane was sayin' to the ither: 'I could stake my life it was him.' They sat doon and ordered their yill, and went on talkin'. I didna catch a' that they said, but they hadna been talkin' long ere I guessed it was aboot you. I juist got a word noo and again, but I've pit them thegither. They went something like this :

" 'Aye, at Wigtown, the nicht efter the women were drooned.'

" 'Then what think ye he's daein' here ? '

" 'Oh, I canna tell that.'

" 'I thocht ye had lang syne made up your mind that he had deid on the moors like a braxy sheep. What's this they ca'd him ?—— Oh, ay,—Bryden. What mak's you think it was him ? '

" 'Weel, I saw him yesterday in the High Street. He had a week's growth on his face, and that in itsel' is a disguise, and he walks wi' a limp, which he didna dae when he was wi' us ; but what jogged my memory was a wee jerk he gied his shoothers. I couldna mind off-haun' where I had seen it afore. Hooever, an 'oor afterwards when I was thinkin' o' something else, it flashed across me that Bryden used to move his shoother and his left elbow exactly that wey. So says I to masel', that's the man ; and I went back to the place where I'd seen him. Of coorse he was there nae langer.'

" 'What are ye gaun to dae ? Ha'e ye tellt yer Captain yet ? '

" 'No' me ! I'm no' sae saft. I'm keepin' my een open, an' if he's still in Dumfries I'll be comin' across him ere lang and I'll arrest him on suspicion, and tak' him afore Lag himsel'. Man, there's a price on his heid.'

" Weel, I had learned a lot, and I knew it was you they were after, for I ha'e noticed the jerk o' your left elbow tae. So I made up my mind that afore I should gang oot to Locharbriggs I wad slip across to Phemie McBride's and gi'e ye warning. So I finished my yill and paid my score an' set oot.

" Juist as I was aboot to leave the close-mooth, a dragoon clapped me on the shoother and said :

" ' You're Hector the packman, are ye no ? '

" ' Ay,' says I. ' What of it ? '

" ' Weel,' says he, ' ye maun come wi' me. Ye're wanted.'

" ' Wanted ? ' says I. ' Wha wants me ? '

" ' Sir Robert Grier o' Lag. I've nae doot ye've heard tell o' him.'

" ' Ay,' I answered, ' I ken Sir Robert weel. What does he want wi' me ? '

" ' Come and fin' oot for yoursel',' said he. ' An' ye'd better mak' haste, for if we keep him waitin' there'll be hell to pey. Haste ye ! '

" As we hurried doon tae Lag's hoose in the Plain Stanes, I began to wonder if his summons could ha'e onything to dae wi' the little affair you mind in the woods near New Abbey. I'm sayin' nae mair ; even the darkness may ha'e ears.

" Weel, by and by we cam' to the hoose at the end o' the Turnpike Wynd, and I went up the stair wi' the trooper. He led me into a room, and we waited there thegither. As we waited I heard Lag's voice comin' frae the next room. He was swearin' in a wey the very deil himsel' couldna' ha'e bettered. He was yellin' like ane possessed for cauld water, and as I stood in the room a wee bit drummer boy cam' rinnin' up the stairs wi' a pail o' water that he had brocht frae the Nith. As he passed through the room where I was standin', it went jaup, jaup, jauppin' on the floor. He knocked at Lag's door and syne went in, and I heard the water being poured into a basin. Then I heard Lag shoutin', 'It's no cauld ava. It's boilin', ye wee deevil! Get awa doon to the water for anither pailfu',' and wi' fear on his face the wee laddie raced through the room as shairp as a hare and clattered doon into the street.

"Weel, I waited wi' the trooper in the ante-chamber while the oaths frae the other side o' the door cam' thick and fast. I may say I listened wi' a kind o' admiration. Wi' some folk swearin' is naething mair than a bad habit, but wi' Lag it seems to be a fine art. But that's by the way. By and by the sodger that had brocht me took courage and knocked at the door. It was opened by another trooper. The first trooper gave him a message for Lag, and he shut the door and delivered it, for the next thing I heard was Lag shoutin': 'Well, the packman maun juist bide my time. I'm far ower bad to see him the noo!' so his body-servant cam' oot again and tellt the trooper that had me in haun'. He took me awa' doon the stairs to the kitchen where there was a lot mair sodgers. Weel, ye ken, at this I was gey perplexed. Here was I, haeing promised to ca' on the widda in the mornin', held a prisoner. And I had you on my mind as weel, for frae what I heard in the Inn, you were in danger. So I said to my guard:

"'If Sir Robert canna see me the noo, is there ony need for me to bide here? I'll gi'e ye my promise to come back at four o'clock this afternoon, when I hope Sir Robert will be able to see me.'

"'No, no,' said the sodger, 'that winna dae ava. I'm takin' nae risks.'

"Weel, there was nothing for it but that I should stop where I was, though it was sair against the grain.

Hooever, they produced a bottle o' 'Solway waters,'* and I'm bound to say they didna lack for hospitality. Nothing loth, I took a drappie, and then I took anither, and we began to talk merrily.

"The mornin' slipped by, and still Lag wasna' ready to see me. Every noo and then the wee drummer laddie raced through the kitchen wi' anither pail o' water frae the Nith, and when he had disappeared wi' the water jaup-jaupping ower the side o' the bucket, the troopers would nudge each other and say 'Guid sakes, his feet maun be in hell already,' and the callousness o' their words would mak' me shiver. Fegs, the Latin has it best: '*Horresco referens*'—'It gies me a grue to think o't.'

"By and by the clock struck one and we had oor dinner thegither. I'm bound to say that if the troopers' 'Solway waters' was guid, the victuals were likewise o' excellent quality, and I made a guid meal. It was maybe twa o'clock when the sodger that had been in Lag's room cam' doon into the kitchen. I thocht noo my 'oor had arrived and that I should yet ha'e time to get oot to Locharbriggs afore I was due to meet you. But nae sic luck! 'He's asleep noo,' he said. 'He's managed to droon the pain in Nith water and a couple o' bottles o' Oporto.' Weel, I saw that the outlook was no' very bricht for me; but I made anither attempt to persuade my guard to let me away for an' 'oor or twa, promisin' solemnly that I should return punctually. But he would ha'e nane o't. So there I was, kept a prisoner, and the afternoon dragged wearily by.

"At lang last six o'clock cam', and I knew that if you hadna fa'en into the haun's o' the troopers you would be waitin' for me at the Port o' Vennel. I was sair perplexed. I wondered if I daur bribe the wee drummer to tak' a note to you, and I had

* Smuggled brandy.

framed a suitable epistle in Latin that I jaloused nane o' thae ignorant troopers would understaun'. Then I thocht better o't; for a note to you frae me micht direct their attention to you, and I didna want that. The 'oors o' the evenin' flitted awa' and by and by it cam' to half-past nine, and the sodger cam' doon the stairs again and said: 'Sir Robert is awake noo and wants to see the packman.'

"So I went up the stairs, and as I left the kitchen ane o' the troopers laughingly cried after me:

"'If he wants to put "the boot" on ye, ye'd best offer him your tree-leg. He's likely tae be that drunk he winna ken the differ.'

"The sodger that was his body-servant threw open the door o' his room and said: 'The packman, sir,' and in I stepped as bold as ye like. He was sittin' in a big chair wrapped in a lang flowered goon. His feet rested on twa big cushions and were rolled up in bandages. Juist beside the cushions stood a basin o' water; it was the same, nae doot, that the wee drummer boy had been kept busy fillin'. Lag glowered at me as I cam' through the door, and twisted roon' in his chair.

"'Good evening, Sir Robert,' says I. 'I hope you are feeling better.'

"His brow gathered in a knot, and he growled: 'Wha the devil said I had been ill? I havena asked ye here to talk aboot mysel'. It's you I want to put a few questions to.'

"'I am at yer service, sir,' I said. 'What can I dae for you?'

"'Well,' says he, 'I've had a message from Sir Thomas Dalzell. He tells me that four of his troopers were set on by a gang of ruffians in New Abbey Road twa or three days sin', and seriously mishandled; and he minds that he saw you on the road at Loch End that very day. He jalouses that after he saw you you took the road to New Abbey. What he wants to ken is this: Did you see onybody on the road that afternoon who might have been guilty o' this criminal attack upon the soldiers o' His Majesty?'

"Weel, that was a straicht question, but it wasna to be replied to wi' a straicht answer; so I thocht it wiser to evade the issue, an' I said: 'Sir, can you gi'e me ony further particlers? Hoo mony sodgers were there? What was the number o' their assailants? Where did the attack take place, and what happened to the sodgers?'

"That shook him off the scent, though, for a minute, I was feared that he saw through me, for he said: 'Now, Hector, ye talk like a damned hedge-lawyer. There were four soldiers involved. As far as Sir Thomas can make out, the number of their assailants was six or eight, and the attack took place on the road about a mile and a half from New Abbey. After being knocked senseless, the soldiers were carried into a wood and tied to a tree. They werena found till next day.'

"Now I knew where we stood. Dalzell and Lag had got the scent a' wrang. It wasna for me to gi'e the scent richt. So it didna cost me ony scruples o' conscience to make replies to the facts that he had laid before me. 'Sir Robert,' says I, 'the case baffles me a' thegither. I maun ha'e been very near the wood ye speak o' at the time this attack was made upon the troopers, but I saw nae sodgers on the road, nor did I come across ony six or eight men wha micht ha'e assailed them. As a matter o' fact I met naebody between Loch End and New Abbey, except a puir auld body gatherin' a wheen sticks.' And then an idea occurred to me—for I knew that if Lag or Dalzell couldna lay their hands upon the men wha had attacked the troopers, they would start harryin' every hoose, where there was a likely young man, between Loch End and New Abbey. That would only mean persecution for innocent folk; so, though I was fain enough to save my ane skin and yours, I didna' want others to be punished for oor deeds, and I threw oot a suggestion at which Lag jumped. 'It's only a theory o' mine, Sir Robert,' I said, 'but it's juist possible that this assault on the sodgers was made by the sailors frae some smugglin' craft that micht be lyin' in the Solway ayont New Abbey.'

"'Man, Hector,' he said, 'that's worth thinkin' o'. There was a smuggler reported in the estuary a few days syne. I maun look into that.'

"And then the pain in his feet began to get bad, and he cursed horribly. When he got his breath again, he looked at me and said:

"'And now, Hector, a word in your lug. You're supposed to be a guid King's man, and I have no direct evidence that you are not; but it's a queer thing that when you drop a hint to the King's representatives aboot some hill-man's nest and the troopers gang to harry it, there are nae eggs in it'; and he glowered at me savagely. 'Have a care,' he growled, 'have a care!'

"I thocht it was time to change the subject, and lookin' doon frae his face to his bandaged feet I said: 'I would coont it a high honour if ye wad permit me to try some o' my magical salve on your feet. I can assure ye, sir, it has powers o' a high order; it's used in the Court o' His Majesty the King himsel'.' Wi' that I produced a wee pot o' it oot o' my pocket. 'It will,' I said, 'produce instant relief and ensure for ye a guid nicht's rest. May I ha'e the honour o' tryin' it, sir?'

"'Well,' says Lag, 'I'm ready to try anything. Nobody but mysel' kens the torment I have been suffering. It's fair damnable.'

"Withoot anither word I dropped down on my knees beside him and took off the cauld water bandages wi' as much gentleness as I could: and when they were off and I saw his feet, I kent hoo he maun ha'e suffered. They were the colour o' half-ripe plums and that swollen that if ye put yer finger on them ye left a dint as though they had been clay. I said to mysel', says I, 'Hector, here's a test for yer salve,' so I talked to Lag cheerily o' the wonderfu' cures I had made afore, and a' the while, as gently as I could, I was rubbin' his feet wi' it. When I had been rubbin' for the better pairt o' half an 'oor, he said: 'Man, Hector, ye're nae fule. Ye've gi'en me greater ease than I've had a' day. Did ye say ye made this saw yoursel'?' I told him it was my ain discovery and that nane but me could supply it, but if he would dae me the honour o' acceptin' a pot or twa, he would mak' me a prood man. Then I bandaged his feet and washed my hands.

"'That's fine,' he said. 'Now, Hector, one good turn deserves another,' and taking up a wee bell that stood on a table beside him he rang it, and his body-servant came back into the room. 'Bring a couple o' bottles o' Malvoisie,' he ordered. 'And at the same time fetch that soldier of Sir Thomas Dalzell's wha brought the message this morning.'

"In a few minutes back came the servant wi' a couple o' bottles in his hand and behind him a trooper wi' a bandage roond his heid. I recognised him at aince. He was the fourth that we laid oot in the wood. When I saw him I maun say I got an awfu' fricht; for if ye mind he was the ane that had a chance o' seein' you and me. I thocht tae masel'—Noo, Hector, ye're in a bonnie hole, but neither by act or word did I let on that I was perturbed, and I waited for what should happen next. Lag ordered his man to open ane o' the bottles. Then he poured oot a glass for me and anither for himsel', and turnin' to Dalzell's man, he said :

" 'Can ye tell me if these ruffians that set on you were sailors? and how many o' them were there a' thegither ? '

" The man hesitated for a wee and then answered : 'I'm no clear, sir, whether they were sailors or no'. Ye see, sir, I got an awfu' crack on the heid, and ever since I've felt gey queer like. They may ha'e been sailors ; that I dinna ken, nor am I quite sure hoo mony there were. I min' only o' seein' twa masel' ; but I'm sure o' this, that nae twa sailors nor twa onything else, short o' deevils, could ha'e laid oot four sodgers o' the King's as we were laid oot. There maun ha'e been aboot six o' them. There may ha'e been eight or ten, but I'm no sure ava, sir.'

" 'Well,' said Lag, angry-like, 'that's no muckle help. Could you recognise one o' them if you were to see him again ? '

" I looked at the sodger oot of the corner of my e'e. If I hadna had a wooden leg my knees would ha'e knocked thegither, but I waited.

" 'Yes, sir,' said the sodger, 'I'm sure o't. I could recognise baith o' the men that attacked me.'

" Lag pointed straicht at me. 'Tak' a look here,' he said. 'Have you ever seen this man before ? '

" I looked straicht at Sir Robert and wondered if he was playin' wi' me as a cat plays wi' a moose, and then I turned to the sodger so that he could tak' a guid look at me ; but a' the time I was considerin' what micht be passin' in the crafty mind o' Lag, cauld and cruel behin' his knotted brow. Did he ken the truth ? The sodger looked at me frae heid to foot. The licht in the room was dim, and by way o' showin' that I feared naething, I said : 'By your leave, Sir Robert,' and I lifted ane o' the lichted candles frae the table and held it in my haun' so that the sodger could tak' a guid look at me. He scanned me carefully again and shook his head, saying:

" 'I ha'e never seen this man afore. The man I mind was clean shaved.'

" Wi' that I walked ower to the table and laid the candlestick doon again.

" The sodger saluted and turned to go, but I spoke up: 'Sir Robert,' said I, 'may I examine this puir fellow's heid? I micht by the application o' my magical salve, with whose virtues you are already acquaint, gi'e him some relief.'

" 'Certainly, certainly,' said Lag, now in a good temper.

" So wi' that I took the bandage off the trooper's heid. Ma certie! what a beauty I had put there wi' my ain guid stick. It was the size o' a pigeon's egg, and when I felt it between my fingers I was prood o' my handiwork. But I never let on. I examined it wi' care; then by way o' raisin' a laugh oot o' Lag I said: 'This young man has to thank Providence that he was born wi' a thick heid.' Saying which, I took a little o' the salve and began to rub it on the lump. The fellow winced, but in the presence o' Lag he was frichtened to mak' ony resistance. I put a guid dressin' on the swelling and bound it up wi' a kerchief. He was wonderfu' gratefu', but at a sign frae Lag he went off and I was left alane wi' Sir Robert. He signed to me to sit doon, and passed me a glass o' the Malvoisie. As I took it he raised his glass and said, 'The King, God save Him,' and I, mindin' the advice I had gi'en to you to be a' things to a' men, followed his example and said, 'The King, God save Him,' and under my breath I added to masel', 'God kens he needs it.' Weel, I sat and cracked wi' Lag for maybe half an 'oor and tellt him mair than ane guid story and had a he'rty laugh or twa oot o' him. Then I pushed the glass away, saying: 'By your leave, Sir Robert, if ye're dune wi' me, I'll be obliged for yer permission to return to my lodgings, for I maun be off on the road the morn.'

"He raised nae objection, and said: 'You won't forget to let me have a pot o' that saw.'

"'Certainly, Sir Robert,' I replied, 'you shall ha'e it the first thing in the mornin': or, if it pleases you to send a trooper wi' me you can ha'e a pot o't the nicht.'

"'That's better,' he said. 'And you'll tak' this bottle o' wine, and whenever ye ha'e a wee drap o't, I hope you will think kindly o' Lag. He's a man sorely miscalled in this country-side.'

"'Thank ye kindly, Sir Robert,' says I. 'I shall see that you are supplied wi' my magical salve for the rest o' yer life. And if on yer next visit to London ye should ha'e the chance o' droppin' a word into the ear o' His Majesty, ye micht juist ask him quietly whether he has used that pot I sent him a twalmonth sin'. I'm inclined to imagine, between you and me, Sir Robert, that it never reached His Majesty's ain hand. I think it was stopped on the wey by ane o' the Court ladies wha used it to make hersel' beautiful.'

"He threw back his heid and roared wi' laughter.

"'Man, Hector,' he said, 'ye're a caution. But mair than likely ye're richt. I've been to the Court mysel', and God kens some o' the women there would need a' the magical saws in the world to make them bonnie. I'll juist put it to His Majesty, Hector, and ask him,' and he roared wi' laughter again.

"He rang the bell, and his body-servant cam' in, and he gave orders that ane o' the men was to accompany me to my lodgings to get a pot o' salve. So I set oot, gled as you can weel guess, to be under the open sky aince mair. The sodger wha accompanied me was a douce lad, and by way o' reward for his convoy I gied him a wee bit o' Virginia weed to himsel', forby four pots o' the salve to tak' to Sir Robert.

"Juist as I let him oot o' the door o' my lodging, the clock struck twal, and the soond o' it brocht back to me the thocht that you wad be at a sair loss to ken what had happened to me. I turned things ower in my mind and it seemed to me that Dumfries is no' exactly a safe place for us at the moment. So I decided that in an 'oor or twa, when a' should be quiet, I would slip ower and waken you and tak' ye awa' oot o' danger.

"So here we are. That's the true story o' a' that has happened since I saw you last; and as we are weel oot o' the toon and there's naebody aboot, I think we micht rest oorsels a wee and, juist by way o' celebratin' oor escape oot o' the tiger's den, we micht sample the Malvoisie. I've got Lag's bottle, and I aye cairry a corkscrew."

CHAPTER XXXI

THE CAVE BY THE LINN

WE took turns at the bottle, and found the wine of excellent quality. After a short rest we resumed our journey. The moon had set and from some distant farmyard a cock crew lustily, and I knew that daybreak was not far off.

The wine, or the exercise, or the knowledge that he had escaped from a situation of grave danger, had an exhilarating effect upon the packman, who was now in high spirits. I ventured, while congratulating him upon his escape, to ask where we might be going, for I was at a loss to know. Now and then I heard the sound of running water, and in the grey of dawn I was able to catch a glimpse of a stream to our right, which I thought must be the Nith.

"We're drawing near Auldgirth," he said. "Beyond that we'll come to Closeburn, and no' lang after that we'll be snug hidden in a cave at Crichope Linn."

Soon we came to a bridge, with three arches spanning the brown river. Hector scrambled down through the bushes by the roadside and made his way under the nearest arch, and I followed him. A little grassy bank lay between the pier of the bridge and the water, and here we sat down. The packman unstrapped his wooden leg, and, with some groaning, for the process evidently caused him discomfort, removed his great shaggy beard.

"I'll bury my tree-leg here, for the time being,

but the beard I'll tak' wi' me in my pooch. That's sufficient disguise for me: as for you, you'll be nane the waur o' a bit o' disguise as weel."

He took from his pack a pair of scissors, and set to work upon my beard and whiskers. As he did so, doubt assailed me and I called to him to stop. To be clean-shaven once again was to expose myself to more ready recognition, if it should ever be my lot to encounter one of my former companions among Lag's troopers.

"Ay, lad, ye're richt," said Hector. "I should ha'e thocht o' that mysel'. But never mind, I've no' done muckle damage yet. Were you clean-shaven when you were a trooper?"

"Yes," I answered.

"Weel," he said, "I'll do a bit o' fancy work on your face, and I'll leave your upper lip alane and wi' some o' my magical salve you can dress your moustachios to make you look like a Cavalier. Forby, I'll leave you a wee tuft on your chin, like the King. I'll warrant neither the folk that saw you in Dumfries wi' a fortnicht's growth on yer face, nor the troopers that kent ye as a clean-shaven man, will be likely to recognise you."

When he had finished his work he stood back and looked at me carefully, poising his head upon one side, and as was his wont half closing his left eye. He was evidently satisfied, for, with characteristic self-complacency, he said:

"Man, Hector, ye're a lad o' mony pairts."

Out of his pack he produced a small looking-glass of burnished steel and handed it to me. In the uncertain morning light the reflection of my face was not very distinct, but enough to show that my disguise was effective, for I hardly recognised myself.

"Come on," said Hector, swinging up his pack, and crossing the bridge we continued our journey.

The country had the glamour of early summer upon it. Every bush was crowned with a coronal of green: the fields were smiling with promise: the hill-sides were dimpling with sunny laughter, and the river, which now ran beside us, babbled cheerfully as it sped on its way to the sea.

After a few more miles we saw, in the distance, a long row of cottages flanking our way. Hector suddenly quitted the road, and, hidden behind a hedge, we made a long detour in order to avoid them.

"Yon," said he, "is the village o' Closeburn. The curate's a spy and a tyrant. It behoves us no' to be seen."

Making use of all the cover we could, and continuing our way till Closeburn was left behind, we came out upon a narrow and unfrequented road overshadowed by beech and oak trees. The air thrilled with the song of birds, and the spirit of the hour seemed to have descended upon the packman, for as we trudged along he whistled merrily. By and by we came to the edge of a wood. Just on its margin we crossed a rustic bridge which spanned a little brown rivulet that trickled sinuously in and out between its mossy banks. Following the line of the stream we entered the wood, Hector leading the way. The ground was a great carpet of luscious green, save where it was spangled over with beds of blue speedwell. The foliage of the trees—beech, oak and mountain ash, pine and fir—broke up the rays of sunlight and the air within the wood was delightfully cool. Our path led steadily up from the bed of the stream till it looked like an amber thread meandering through a gorge a hundred feet beneath us. Here and there its course was checked by a quiet pool, so still that one might think the stream had ceased to flow; and where some branch of a bush or tree touched the surface of the water it was garlanded with a ball of tawny froth from which little flakes broke away and studded the surface of the pool like scattered silver coins.

We penetrated deep into the wood—the stream chattering far below us—and at last Hector, half-turning, and saying earnestly "Tak' tent," began to clamber down the slope towards it. I followed, and in a few moments we had reached the edge of the water. Leaping from stone to stone, Hector led the way past a waterfall upon our left which, thin as veil of gossamer and iridescent in the sunlight, fell from an overhanging rock into the burn.

Just beyond us and to the right the stream issued from a defile. Above us, on both sides, the sandstone rocks towered, and looking up from the depths one could see the sky through the leafy screen of foliage that overshadowed us. Carefully choosing every footstep, we continued up the stream. The way, though difficult, seemed quite familiar to the packman.

Suddenly the great sandstone walls which flanked the stream began to close in upon us, rising sheer from the water edge. The stream thus confined into straiter bounds became a broiling torrent. To make progress we were compelled to bestride it, finding precarious foothold in little niches on the opposing walls. After a few more difficult steps the narrow defile widened out and we stood upon the edge of a great broad cup which was being steadily filled by an inrush of water through a gorge at its upper end similar to that along which we had come. In shape the cup was almost circular and looked like a huge misshapen bowl of earthenware. From its sides the sandstone cliffs rose almost perpendicularly, but a few feet above the water was a ledge broad enough to walk upon. It was a curious natural formation. The basin at our feet was deep, so deep that I could not see the bottom. The water leaped into it through the upper defile, churning its nearer edge into yellow froth; but the turbulence of the leaping stream swooned into quietness when it came under the spell of the still water that lay deep and impassive in the heart of the pool. Half-way round its circumference, poised on the ledge and heaped one upon another in seeming disorder, stood a pile of boulders. Hector seized one of them with both hands. He tugged at it vigorously and it moved, disclosing a cleft in the wall of the precipice through which a man might crawl.

"We're here at last," said Hector. "Doon on your hands and knees, and crawl in; there's naething to fear."

I did as he bade me, and, carefully feeling the way with my hands, thrust head and neck and shoulders into the aperture. After the light of the outer world the interior of the cave was impenetrably dark. Steadying myself with my hands, I proceeded to drag my body after me and was about to rise to my feet when suddenly something leaped upon me. A pair of hot hands closed upon my throat from behind and a great weight hurled itself upon my back. I tried to scream, but the lithe fingers gripped my neck and stifled me. There was a clamour in my head as though a thousand drums were rattling; lights danced before my eyes. Again I tried to scream, but my tongue hung helpless out of my mouth and I could hardly breathe. I struggled fiercely, but the hands that gripped my throat did not relax and suddenly I seemed to be falling through infinite space and then ceased to know anything. I remembered nothing until, at last, I felt somebody chafing my hands. Then out of the darkness I heard the voice of Hector say quite cheerfully:

"Ye'll do. Ye'll be a' richt in a minute or twa. Noo I maun ha'e a look at the minister."

"What has happened?" I asked, but Hector did

not reply, so I raised myself and found him stooping over the body of another man lying not far from me.

"Thank God," he said, "I ha'ena killed him. His skull is evidently as soond as his doctrine, and that's sayin' a lot."

"Tell me what has happened?" I exclaimed. "Who is this man?"

"As far," said he, "as I can mak' oot by the licht o' these twa tallow candles, he is the Rev. Mr. Corsane, the ousted minister o' Minniehive. I canna exactly tell what happened afore I cam' into the cave, but juist as your feet were disappearing into the hole, they began to dance in the air, remindin' me o' the cantrips I ha'e seen a man perform when the hangman had him in haun'. I was at a sair loss to ken what ye micht be daein', and I was mair puzzled still when, just inside the cave, I heard a terrible struggling. Hooever, as ye weel ken, I'm nae coward, so in I crawled, wi' my auld frien' 'Trusty' in my kneive. Though it was awfu' dark, I could mak' oot twa men strugglin'. Ane o' them was astride the other and I judged that you were the nethermost. I shouted, the man that had you by the throat let ye go and flung himsel' on me. I caught him a dunt wi' the point o' my elbow juist ower his breist-bane. He reeled back, but when he got his breath he rushed at me again. By this time my e'en were better used to the darkness, so I up wi' 'Trusty' and gi'ed him a clout on the side o' the heid, and here he lies. Then I lichted the candles I had brocht wi' me, and found that he had gey near throttled you deid. By the look o' him I jaloused that he was the Rev. Mr. Corsane, and then the whole thing was plain to me. Maist likely he has been hidin' in this cave—a cave weel kent by the Covenanters—so when you cam' crawlin' in withoot word said or signal given, he maun ha'e thocht it was ane o' the dragoons and like a brave man he made up his mind to sell his life dearly. That's the story so far as I can mak' it oot and I ha'e nae doot it's the true ane.

" But I wish ye would lay your hand ower his heart and tell me I haena killed him, for I wouldna' like to ha'e the death o' sic a godly man on my conscience."

I did as I was requested and I was able to reassure the packman that the man's heart was beating regularly and strongly, although somewhat slowly.

" Thank God," he said fervently. " I'll see what my salve will dae for him," and he opened a pot of his ointment and proceeded to rub it gently into the lump which his stick had raised upon the minister's temple. The effect, however, was far from being immediate. The minister lay with lips half parted and eyes half open, breathing heavily, without signs of returning consciousness. Hector began to show signs of alarm.

" If," he said, " this was only a dragoon I wouldna worry: but this is a minister, a different breed o' man a' thegither. A clout that would dae nae mair than gie a dragoon a sair heid micht kill a minister. He maun be in a bad way if my salve winna revive him."

" Give him time," I said, " and let us see what cold water will do." Crawling out into the open, I leaned over the pool and, filling my bonnet with water, returned to the cave and sprinkled the minister's face copiously. I saw his eyelids flicker as the first cold drop touched his forehead, and a few minutes later he moved one of his hands.

" He's recovering," I said, and taking off my coat I folded it and placed it beneath his head. We waited in great anxiety, and by and by saw other signs of returning vitality. The better part of an hour had elapsed before the minister endeavoured to raise himself upon his elbow, an effort which we gently resisted. Immediately afterwards, with eyes staring up to the roof of the cave, he said :

" Where am I ? What has happened ? "

I motioned to Hector to reply.

" Oh, ye're a' richt, and we are frien's. Ha'e nae fear. Settle yoursel' doon, if ye can, for a sleep: and when you ha'e rested we'll tell you everything."

Without demur the minister closed his eyes again, and we were able to tell from his regular breathing that he had fallen asleep.

Hector rose, whispering behind his hand: " If you'll sit by the minister I'll close the door," and he crawled noiselessly through the aperture and returned, pushing his pack before him, and then closed the opening, cutting off the thin shaft of daylight that had been coming through it.

About an hour later the minister stirred in his sleep, and turning over upon his side opened his eyes and looked at me inquiringly. Hector produced the bottle of Malvoisie with which we had refreshed ourselves on the roadside, and held it to the minister's lips.

" This will refresh you," he said, and without protest he drank. He made some attempt to speak, but Hector forbade him. " No, no, sir, haud yer wheesht a wee langer. Dinna fash yoursel'. We are your frien's. Ha'e nae fear and settle yoursel' to sleep."

Like an obedient child, the minister did so.

The day passed and still the patient slept. By and by Hector went to the mouth of the cave and peered through one of the chinks between the rocks.

" The nicht has come," he said. " It's time we were bedded." Taking up the candle, he searched the floor of the cave. " Dae ye think," he asked, " we daur lift the minister ? Here's his bed," and he pointed to a heap of withered brackens in a corner.

I suggested that it might be an easier thing to carry his bed to the minister, and, stooping down, I gathered up an armful of the leaves, which I spread upon the floor beside him. So gently that he did not stir we lifted the minister on to it, and once more I slipped my folded coat under his head for a pillow. Hector drew off his coat and spread it over the minister's chest, then seizing a corner of his pack he pulled it up, scattering the contents in a jumbled heap on the floor, and spread the canvas covering over the lower part of the minister's body.

"That will keep him warm," he said. "Now you mak' your bed where ye will. I'll keep watch for the first pairt o' the nicht and I'll waken you by and by, and ye can tak' yer turn."

Worn out with the experiences of the previous night and day, I lay down not far off. My neck still ached from the strangling grip of the minister's fingers, and the floor of the cave was a hard bed. But I had lain in many strange places ere this and soon I was fast asleep. Once during the night I awoke and peering through the shadows could discern the figure of the minister on his bracken couch, and, with hands clasped round his bent knees, the packman sitting beside him. But I judged that my time had not yet come, for Hector made no sign and soon I was asleep again.

I awoke cold and stiff as though I had been beaten. Looking towards the doorway I could see a thin streak of light filtering through, and I knew that day had come. Hector still sat motionless: he had kept his vigil the whole night through.

I ventured to upbraid him because he had not kept his word and wakened me in the night to share the watch with him. He laughed.

"It was a kind o' penance," he said. "I ha'e twa things on my conscience that will want a lot o' expiation. *Imprimis*, I felled the minister ; *secundo*, I gi'ed him some o' Lag's wine. In the nicht I've been thinkin' the second is the mair serious transgression. To godless men like you and me, Lag's wine could dae nae hairm, but hoo think ye the wine o' a persecutor will agree wi' the body o' a saint ? As like as no it will turn to gall in his blood and dae him a peck o' hairm."

I laughed quietly. " You may set your mind at rest," I said. " The wine was good. Even though it came from Lag's cellar, it will do the Covenanter no harm."

While we were talking the minister began to move, and in a few seconds opened his eyes. In a moment Hector was bending over him.

" Hoo are ye this morning, sir ? " he said. " I hope ye ha'e rested weel ? "

The minister raised himself upon his elbow, and looked at Hector anxiously. " Thank you," he said, " I have had a good sleep, but my brain is in a strange whirl and my head is very sore. Have I been ill ? "

" A' in good time, sir, a' in good time," said Hector, cheerfully. " You are in nae danger. By and by I'll tell ye a'. Meantime ye maun break yer fast."

The packman rose and going to a shelf of rock on which the candle stood picked up a bowl.

" Here, Bryden," he said. " I'll open the door if you crawl oot and fill this bowl at the linn."

He gripped the movable boulder and swung it round and I crawled out into the open air. The morning sky above me was fleecy with soft clouds ; the air was full of melody ; all the feathered world was awake. Thrush vied with blackbird, blackbird with linnet, and linnet with the far off tremulous lark. I stood on the little sandstone platform above the pool filling my lungs with great draughts of morning air. The haunting beauty of the place—the mystical and impenetrable depths of the pool, the tender foliage above me mirrored on its surface, the soft wind of the morning throbbing with melody —all conspired to cast a spell over me. But I woke from my dream as I remembered the stern realities that beset me. Leaning over I filled the bowl and returned with it to the cave. Hector had already laid out the morning meal, but at the moment a desire more urgent than hunger was upon me.

So I crawled once more into the open air and, quickly undressing, dived into the pool, and swam round it a dozen times. Greatly refreshed I was about to swing myself out, when I saw the shoulders of Hector protruding from the aperture in the wall. He shook his head and smiled at me, saying:

“ You gi’ed me a terrible fricht. I heard the splash and thocht ye had fa’en in. Ye’re a queer chiel ; ye like cauld water a lot better than I do,” and he drew his head back into the cave.

CHAPTER XXXII

TOILERS OF THE NIGHT

THE rest and sleep of the night had done the minister good service ; and though he still complained of considerable pain in the head and bore upon it the protuberant evidence of Hector's skill with his weapon, he was able to join in our conversation. In my absence Hector had told him who we were and what had happened. He had some difficulty in recognising Hector, beardless and lacking his tree-leg, but when the packman had salted his conversation with an apposite quotation from Horace, he had been compelled to admit his identity and had hailed him as an old friend.

Hector's surmise had been correct. The inhabitant of the cave was none other than Mr. Corsane, who, ousted from his charge and compelled to become a wanderer, had made it his headquarters through many a weary month. It was a hiding-place in which he could find shelter alike from the blasts of the storm and from the persecutors. Driven from his manse, his church and his parish, a man with a price upon his head, he did not remain in this cave from week's end to week's end, a craven fugitive. Constantly he had ventured out. Did sickness or sorrow visit one of the homes of his little flock, he was instant in succour, ready to bring to them at all times the spiritual help and consolation for which they looked to him. Wherefore, though he was a minister without a charge, he was not a minister without a people.

When the meal was over I besought Hector to lie down and rest; and being satisfied that the minister was now out of danger, he needed no second bidding.

The weeks and months that followed were full of interest and occupation. As always, in the annals of persecution, an hour had come when the malignity of the tyrants reached its zenith. In a wild endeavour to break the spirit of the persecuted, they applied themselves with increased fury and devilish ingenuity to render the lives of their victims intolerable.

So it came to pass that more and more of the men in the parishes round about us were driven to forsake their homes and take to the moors or the hiding-places among the hills. Little cared the persecutors if the land that should have laughed with rich crops sank into desolation since none were left to cultivate it. The malevolence of the oppressors gave Hector and myself many opportunities of service. By stratagem, and sometimes by force, at great risk, and often after lively encounters, we rescued more than one good man and true from the clutches of the troopers and spirited him away in the dead of night to a safe hiding-place. I may not here set down these high adventures. Some other pen than mine may record them. But for the greater part our deeds were works of peace. All through the months of summer we would steal out from the cave when the twilight came and, making for some farm whose good man had been compelled to flee, we would spend the hours of the night in performing those tasks in the fields which, but for us, would have been left undone.

Toiling all night through, we would steal back to the sanctuary of our cave in the grey dawn, tired, but proudly conscious that we had done something to ease the burden which was weighing upon the heart of some desolate woman. We cut the clover, we mowed the hay, we left it for a day or two to dry and then stacked it into little cocks upon the field, and when the time came, we sheared the sheep and did those thousand and one things that a husbandman does in their due season. We were careful not to be seen, though always when the night was at its darkest, Hector would make his way to the farmhouse or cottage nearest the field in which we were at work and almost invariably he would find upon the window-sill a store of food left for us. For, though the children and the superstitious might imagine that the mysterious labourers in the fields were creatures from another world who accomplished heavy tasks with the wave of a magic wand, the good-wife of the house had more than a shrewd suspicion that they were creatures of flesh and blood who toiled with the sweat on their brows and who had appetites that required satisfaction.

Nor did we confine our work to the farms near our hiding-place. In the course of his wanderings among his flock, the minister would, now and then, hear of a farm more remote that needed our care, and many a night we walked for miles before we reached the fields where our self-appointed tasks lay. I felt, as Hector did, that in this service we were doing something to help the Cause of the Covenant. And as honest work ever offers to a man the best antidote to sorrow, my heart began to be filled with a great contentment. Mary was lost to me. That thought and the sense of desolation which it provoked was ever before me, but my labours for the persecuted were some token of the love I had borne her and I knew that she would understand.

Sometimes, in the darkness, when my back ached beyond endurance as I bent over some unaccustomed task, I would cease for a moment to feel for that little bit of metal lying over my heart that was all that remained of the ring I had given her. And its touch would give me courage and my weariness would disappear.

Hector, I discovered, was a master of all the arts of agriculture. No task seemed too heavy for him, and never have I seen a man so proficient at shearing sheep or with such a subtle way of pacifying a querulous dog. Dogs, indeed, were one of the dangers that beset us, for more than once we spent the night at work on a farm which was in the occupation of the soldiery. If the farm dog had but given the alarm, we might have found ourselves surrounded and shot on the instant, or compelled to flee for our lives. But no dog ever barked at Hector. There was some indefinable understanding between him and the faithful creatures. A startled collie would raise its head and thrust forward its snout as though about to alarm the night, but, at a whisper from Hector, it would steal up to him and rub its head and shoulders in comradeship against his legs. This sympathy between himself and the dogs made for our safety, and there was something else which helped. Most of the troopers were creatures of the grossest superstition, thrilled with an uncanny dread of warlocks, witches, and all the evil spirits of the night. Their bloody deeds by day filled their nights with ghostly terrors, and more than once I have known them desert a farm—upon which they had descended to devour its substance like the locusts—headlong and in fear when they found that the "brownies" had been at work in the fields by night. To them it had become a place uncanny, and they would hastily take their departure, to the no small joy of the farmer's wife and her little children. To the children a visit of the "brownies" was a thing to be hailed with delight and shy amazement.

Once, after a heavy night's work, Hector and I were resting in the early dawn beneath a hedgerow ere we set out upon our long journey to the cave, when I heard the voices of children on the road. I looked through the hedge and saw a little boy leading his sister by the hand. They climbed upon the bars of the gate and surveyed the field before them. Then the quiet of the morning was broken by the shrill voice of the lad, who, pointing to the mown hay, shouted:

"Aggie, Aggie, the brownies ha'e been here," and, leaping down from the gate so quickly as to capsize his sister, who, awed by the mystery, did not burst into tears, he rushed along the road to the house calling at the top of his voice: "Oh, mither, mither, come and see. The brownies ha'e been working in the hay-field and the hay is a' cut. Oh, I wish my faither knew."

We waited till—at the urgent summons of her little son—the woman had walked down the road to the gate and had surveyed our handiwork. We saw her stoop, pick up her children, and kiss them fondly. Then she turned away that they might not see her tears, and, at the sight, our own hearts grew strangely full. We waited until she had taken her little ones home, and then we stole away.

"Puir lassie," said Hector, "puir lassie."

During the day I rarely ventured from the cave, though now and then Hector would fare forth in daylight on mysterious errands of his own. I suspected that he had some tryst to keep with the widow at Locharbriggs, but he did not take me into his confidence. But usually he and I were birds of the night. We were busy folk, and the minister was no less occupied. Messages would come to him mysteriously; how, I was never able to discover; but by some means he was kept informed not only as to the doings and welfare of his own flock, but as to the larger happenings throughout the whole country-side. He knew what men had been compelled to flee from their homes; which others had been haled to Edinburgh and put to torture in the hope that the persecutors might wring from them some confession. He knew the houses which had been touched by the hand of sorrow, and with no thought of self he would steal forth to offer what consolation he could. His quiet bravery impressed me deeply, and I found myself developing a lively admiration for him which rapidly grew into a warm affection.

He was a man of large scholarship; no bigoted fanatic, but a gentle and genial soul borne up perpetually by an invincible faith in the ultimate triumph of the cause for which he had already sacrificed so much, and for which, if need be, he was ready to sacrifice his all.

In little fragments I had from time to time told him my story. I finished it one night as we sat together outside our cave on the narrow ledge above the pool. There may have been some anger in my voice, or some bitterness in my words, for when my tale was ended he was silent for a time. Then he laid one of his hands upon my knee and with the other pointed to the stream as it poured through the gorge into the quietness of the pool.

"See," he said, "the water in turmoil catches no reflection of the sky, whereas the stars are mirrored every one on the quiet face of the pool. So it is with human hearts. Where bitterness and turmoil are there can be no reflection of the heart of God. It's the quiet heart which catches the light."

He said no more, but, ever since, when storms have risen in my soul I have remembered his words and the memory of them has stilled the passion within me.

When the nights were too rough for work in the fields, we would spend them in the cave together. And sometimes Hector, who had a subtle mind, would try to entangle the minister in the meshes of a theological argument, and I would sit amazed at the thrust and parry of wit against wit. These discussions usually ended in the defeat of Hector—though he would never admit it. More than once, at their conclusion, the minister would say:

"We must never forget this; theology is but man's poor endeavour to interpret the will of God towards humanity. It is not for me to belittle theology, but at the end of all things it will not count for much. It's the life of a man that counts; the life, and the faith that has illumined it. Theological points are but sign-posts at the cross-roads, and sometimes not even that. Faith is the lamp that shows the wayfaring man where to set his feet."

As the summer mellowed into early autumn, Hector began to grow restless. I ventured to suggest to him that he was heart-sick for love.

He laughed. "Maybe ye're richt," he said; "but ye dinna imagine that I ha'e managed to live a' these weeks withoot a sicht o' the widda. No, no, my lad."

"And how runs the course of love?" I asked.

"Man," he answered, "I'm gettin' on fine. I verily believe Virgil was wrang when he said 'Woman is a fickle jade.' The widda's no fickle at ony rate. D'ye ken she wears my kaim in her hair ilka day o' the week. It's the prood man I am."

"Then why this restlessness?" I asked.

He laughed as he replied: "Weel, to mak' a lang story short, I am hungerin' for the road. A man that has got the wander fever in his bluid can never be lang content in ae place. I'm bidin' wi' you a week or twa mair, for the time o' the hairst is at hand, but when we ha'e cut a wheen o' the riper fields I'll ha'e to leave ye for a bit. I'll be back inside twa months, and we'll settle doon then for the winter. And when I gang, dinna forget this, I'll keep my ears open for ony news o' what happened at Daldowie, and maybe when I come back I'll be able to tell ye hoo Mary deed."

The mention of Daldowie awoke in my heart a keen desire to accompany him, and I told him so.

"No, no," he said, "no' yet. By and by, if ye like. In the meantime yer duty lies here. You've got to look efter the minister. As ye weel ken, he's a feckless man at lookin' after himsel'. Forby, you'll ha'e work to dae. The hairst winna' be ower when I gang. So you'd best juist bide here."

His arguments were not weighty, but obviously he did not want my company and he had proved himself so good a friend that I shrank from offending him by insisting. So, reluctantly, I agreed to remain behind.

"You will take care," I said. "I fear that Lag has begun to suspect you, and you may run into danger unless you are wary."

He laughed as he replied: "Ah weel, as Horace said, '*Seu me tranquilla senectus expectat, seu mors atris circumvolat alis,*' which ye can nae doot translate for yersel', but which means in this connection, that Hector will either see a peacefu' auld age by his ain fireside wi' the widda, or the black-winged corbies will pick his banes. Man, Horace has the richt word every time."

We did not discuss the matter of his departure again, but continued our nightly tasks in the fields. There was something peculiarly beautiful about our work at this time. The nights were short and never wholly dark. We would steal into a ripening field of corn in the twilight, when the purple shadows lay asleep among the golden grain. As the light of day gave place to the half-darkness of the night, the grain, pierced by the silver shafts of the moon, grew lustrous and shone like fairy jewels. I paused in wonder every time I bent to put my sickle between the tall blades. It seemed almost a sacrilege to cut down such things of beauty.

As the nights were short we could work only a few

hours before the daylight came again ; but always ere it came the slumbering earth was wakened by a burst of melody. When, in the east, one saw a little lightening of the grey shadows, as though a candle had been lit on the other side of some far off hill, one's ear would catch the sound of a bird's pipe, solitary at first and strangely alone. That first adventurous challenge would soon be answered from a myriad hidden throats. Far off, a cock would crow, and then on every side, from the heart of hidden lark and pipit, linnet and finch, a stream of melody would begin to flow over the field. The music increased in volume as bird after bird awoke from its sleep in hedge, and bush and tree, and the choir invisible poured its cataract of song into that empty hour that lies in the hand of time between the darkness and the dawn.

CHAPTER XXXIII

THE GOING OF HECTOR

SEPTEMBER came with all its golden glory and each day Hector became more and more restless. When the month was half sped he left us. One morning on our way home to the cave after a busy night of harvesting he said:

" I'm gaun the nicht." And though I urged upon him that he could not have chosen a worse time, since we had many fields yet to cut, I failed to dissuade him from his purpose. " No," he said, " I can bide nae langer. The fever is in my bluid, and there's nae cure for it but the road."

When night came I accompanied him down the course of the linn and on to the high road. At the last he laid many injunctions upon me, the chief being to take care of our companion in the cave.

" He's a guid man," he said, " but a thochtless. I blame mysel' yet for the crack I gi'ed him on the heid. It seems tae ha'e left him a bit confused. Ye'll tak' care o' him."

When the moment of parting came he took off his bonnet, and gripping me fervently by the hand said:

" I'll be back ere lang, but if I dinna return, I should like ye noo and then to gie a kindly thocht to the memory o' the packman. Maybe I may find a grave under the open sky on the purple moorland; and if that be my lot and ye should be spared for happier days and can fin' the place where I lie, maybe ye'll see that my cairn is no' left withoot a name. But dinna be carvin' ony extravagant eulogy on the stane. Juist put the words 'Hector the packman.' That'll be enough for me—but it's the prood man I wad be, lying in the mools beneath, if ye wad add a line or twa o' Latin juist to let the unborn generations ken that I was a scholar. There are twa bit legends that come ready to my min'; ane is,

" Scire potestates herbarum usumque medendi
Maluit, et mutas agitare inglorius artes.

'He was skilly in the knowledge o' herbs and o' their healing powers, and wi' nae thocht o' higher glory he liked to practise that quiet art'—that's frae Virgil, as ye will nae doot remember an' of course refers to my salve. But there's anither word frae my auld frien' Horace; it's a fit epitaph for a man like me wha's life has never been what it micht ha'e been:

" . . . Amphora cœpit
Institui: currente rota cur urceus exit?

'The potter was minded to make a bonnie vessel; why does naething but a botchery come frae the running wheel?'"

Before I could make a fitting reply he dropped my hand and left me. I stood in the dusk watching him go. He glided into the shadows and soon he had become as incorporeal as one of them. With a sense of desolation upon me, I made for the field where my night's task awaited me, and laboured steadily till the dawn.

As I made my way back to the cave I could not help wondering where Hector might be.

There had been something almost ominous in the manner of his parting. Had he felt the shadow hovering over him?—or was his farewell and his reference to his possible death nothing more than an expression of his curiously sentimental nature?

I could not decide: but I trusted that his natural

caution and his mother-wit, of which I knew something, would carry him safely through.

Consoling myself with this thought, I entered the wood and proceeded to make my way up the bed of the stream.

A week or two passed undisturbed by any eventful happening. Night after night I continued my work in the fields. More than once the minister joined me, lending me what aid he could. But his spirit was greater than his strength, and at last I had to ask him for his own sake, and for the sake of those who counted upon his ministrations, to reserve his energies for their own special work. Recognising his physical limitations, he took my advice.

"Maybe," he said, "you're right. Perhaps it was given to me to be a sower only, and not a harvester. The fields you are reaping were sown by other hands than yours, and mayhap the ripe fruit which in the good Providence of God may spring from the seed I have sown will be gathered by other hands than mine. But it matters little. The thing is to sow honestly and to reap faithfully, so that at the end of the day when we go home for our wages we may win the Master Harvester's 'Well done.'"

Even had he been physically capable of doing useful work in the fields, it would have been unfair to expect him to do it at this time. His days were already full. He was making preparations for a great Conventicle to be held among the Closeburn hills early in October. It was to be a very special occasion—a gathering together of all the faithful to unite in that simple love feast which has inspired with fresh courage and inflamed with new devotion men and women throughout the ages. It was a brave, a hazardous thing to venture on.

I was more than a little uplifted when he honoured me by asking me if I would care to be a sentinel.

His request touched me deeply, and I felt that Mary was smiling upon me with radiant eyes out of the unknown.

A few more days elapsed. Another Sunday came and went, the last before the great occasion. I had spent the day in the coolness of the cave, and the minister had been out about his spiritual duties. I stole out and sitting on the ledge above the pool sat dreaming in the twilight. Far off in the fields beyond the wood I heard a corncrake rasping out his raucous notes. There was a twitter of birds in the trees above me as they settled down to sleep.

As I sat there I was joined by Mr. Corsane, who came through the narrow defile below the pool. He looked weary and somewhat distraught; but though I surmised that some anxiety oppressed him, he did not offer to share it with me, so I held my peace. Soon he retired to rest and when midnight came I set off to my labours. I did not see him on my return to the cave in the morning, nor had he come back by evening when I left again. But when on the morning of Tuesday I came in sight of the pool, I discovered him waiting for me on the ledge outside the cave. He hailed me at once:

"I have been watching anxiously for your return. I am in sore perplexity."

"Can I help you, sir?" I asked.

"If I were younger," he replied, "and could perform the task myself, I would gladly do it; but it is past my power. It is an urgent matter—for it concerns the safety of one dear to me and very precious to the Cause."

"Command me," I exclaimed. "I am ready to do anything I can; only tell me how I may help."

"I have a friend in Edinburgh," he said, "Peter Burgess by name. His life is in danger. I must get a message to him ere Friday. Will you take it?"

"Gladly," I cried. "Trust me—and all the persecutors in Scotland shall not prevent me."

A smile flickered upon his face. "That is a reckless boast," he said. "But I trust you, and thank you."

"I am ready to start at once," I said.

"What?" he exclaimed. "Weary as you are!"

"Certainly," I answered, "one must needs haste. I'll have a plunge in the pool while you write your letter, and after a mouthful of food, I'll be off."

By the time I had bathed and eaten, his message was ready, and with a few last words of instruction I was about to set off. But he called me back.

"Have a care to your goings, my son. Be wary! be brave! I trust you will succeed in reaching my friend ere it is too late; but you cannot be back in time for the great Assembly on Sabbath. I shall miss you."

He raised his hand in blessing, and, secreting the letter about me, I turned, and was gone.

CHAPTER XXXIV

THE FLIGHT OF PETER BURGESS

WHEN night fell I was far away among the hills. I had made good progress and was well content. I should accomplish the journey in good time—of that I was confident—so I crawled into a bed of heather and slept soundly.

In the early morning I was awakened by the call of the moor birds. Before starting on my journey again, I thought it wise to secrete the letter with greater care, so I took off one of my shoes, and, making a hollow in the heel, folded the letter tightly and placed it there. Then I took to the road again.

I had hoped to reach Edinburgh by noon on Thursday, but when I came in sight of the city it was past five o'clock. The journey had proved more arduous than I expected ; but I was still in time. The last long mile accomplished, I reached the city. The moon had risen, and as I swung round beneath the grey shadow of Holyrood I caught a glimpse of the noble brow of Arthur's Seat towering high behind it. I passed the guard of soldiers at the Canongate without challenge, for, apparently, they saw in me nothing more than a travel-stained and dusty wanderer—some gangrel body.

I did not wish to draw suspicion upon myself by asking anyone to direct me to Halkerstone Wynd where Peter Burgess dwelt. But, meeting a boy, I stopped him to ask where I could find the Tron

Kirk, which Mr. Corsane had given me as a landmark. His reply was explicit enough, if somewhat rude. "Follow yer nose," he said, "and ye'll be there in five meenutes," which I took to mean that I was to continue my journey up the hill. Very shortly a large church came into view, and as it took shape in the moonlight a clock in its tower struck ten. I counted the strokes, and, turning, retraced my steps and found at no great distance from the Church, as the minister had told me, the Wynd which I sought. The minister had given me careful instructions, so that when I entered the Wynd I had no difficulty in finding the house in which his friend lived. The outer door stood open, and I entered, passing at once into the confusion of darkness; but I had learned from Hector the wisdom of carrying a candle in one's pocket, and lighting it, I looked around me. I knew that I should find Peter Burgess on the top floor of the house, so, shading the candle with one hand, I began the ascent. Up, and up and up, in never ceasing spirals wound the stair. To me, weary with my journey, it seemed interminable. Between two of its flights I paused, and leaning over the balustrade looked downwards. A chasm, black as pitch and unfathomable to my straining eyes, gaped below me. After a moment's rest I continued my ascent, and by and by, breathless, I came to the top. An oaken door barred my further progress. An iron knocker, shaped like a lady's hand, hung gracefully upon its middle beam. I remember that as I seized it to knock, I held it for a second while I looked at the delicate metal filigree of lace that adorned the wrist. Then I knocked three times—first gently, then more firmly and, as no answer came, more loudly still. At last I heard movements on the other side, and in the flickering candle-light I saw a little peep-hole open, and a voice said "Who is it?" I bent my head to the tiny aperture and said in a whisper "Naphthali," the password I had been told to use. Instantly the peep-hole was closed, and the door was thrown open. "Enter and welcome," said the voice, and I needed no second invitation. I found myself in a narrow passage at the end of which was a room through whose open door a light shone. The man who had admitted me closed and barred the door and then led the way to the room. Then turning to me he said:

"To what do I owe this late visit?"

"I bring," I replied, "a message from a friend, but before I give it to you I must know who you are."

He went to a bookcase that stood against one of the walls and from it withdrew a little calf-bound volume. Opening it he pointed to the book-plate within.

On the scroll I read the legend "Ex libris Petri Burgess," and I saw that the book was a copy of Rutherford's *Lex Rex.* I sat down at once on a high-backed oak chair, and, taking off my shoe, found the letter and handed it to him. He took it with a grave bow, and, breaking its seal, sat down at the black-oak table in the centre of the room.

As he did so, I looked about me. The room was furnished with considerable taste and was lit by two candles which stood in silver candlesticks on the table. Between the candlesticks lay a sheet of paper. Beside them stood an ink-horn and a little bowl of sand in which was a small bone spoon. The light was somewhat uncertain, and to read with greater ease he drew one of the candlesticks nearer to him.

When he had read the letter through, he sat in a fit of meditation, beating a gentle tattoo with the fingers of his left hand upon the top of the table. He read it again, and went towards the fireplace where he tore the missive into tiny pieces and dropped them into the fire. Then he came back to the table.

"Forgive," he said, "my seeming lack of hospitality; you must be worn out and famished. Let me offer you some refreshment."

I thanked him heartily, and in a few minutes he had set food and wine before me.

He joined me in the repast, and as we sat at the table I had an opportunity of studying him with some care. I judged him to be a man over sixty. His face was refined and the delicate line of his mouth which his beard did not conceal bespoke a sensitive nature. He treated me with a courtly grace, asked interestedly as to my journey, and inquired earnestly as to the progress of the Cause in the South. I told him all I knew, and when he heard from my lips how Mr. Corsane, though evicted from his Church, still regarded himself as the shepherd of his people and was constant in his devotion and instant in his service to them, he said:

"Good! good! But how he must have suffered! As for me," he continued, "I have no cave in which to take refuge, so I must steal away like a thief in the night. Please God, ere morning I may find a boat in which to escape to the Low Countries. But you must have bed and lodging; and ere I leave the city I shall see you safely housed with a friend in the Lawn Market."

When our meal was over my host pushed back his chair and said:

"Now I must go." He went to the bookcase, and taking from it two or three volumes put them in the pockets of his coat. Turning to me with a smile, he said: "A fugitive had best go unencumbered; but I should be lost without a book."

He made up a small parcel of food, and then, extinguishing one candle and taking the other from its candlestick, he led the way to the door, and together we passed out. He locked the door from the outside, and lighting the way with the candle, which he still held in his hand, he conducted me downstairs.

When we entered the High Street, we turned and walked up past the Tron Kirk.

The streets were deserted, save for ourselves, for midnight was at hand.

"The Castle," he said, "is just ahead of us, but we are not going so far. This is our destination," and he turned into a narrow Wynd on the right side of the street and passed through an open door just beyond its mouth. In the shadow of the doorway he lighted his candle and proceeded to climb the stair. On the second floor he knocked gently at a door which, after a pause, was opened noiselessly by an old woman.

We entered. My companion whispered a word or two in her ear, and taking a leathern pouch from one of his pockets pressed some money into her hand.

"Be kind to the lad," he said, "he has travelled far."

The old woman looked at me, and with the coins still gleaming in her open palm, said: "Ye can trust me, Maister Burgess. He's no' to peety if he has ane o' my guid cauf beds to sleep on, and a bowl o' parritch in the morning."

Mr. Burgess held out his hand to me in farewell. "God keep you," he said. "And when you see my friend again, tell him I thank him with all my heart. If God will, I shall communicate with him when I reach a place of safety. If not——" and he raised his eyes to the low ceiling and, dropping my hand, turned and was gone.

CHAPTER XXXV

WITHIN SIGHT OF ST. GILES

THE old woman closed the door, and lighting a candle led me to a room and left me. I found that the bed was all that she had claimed for it ; and after my many months of fitful sleep on my bracken couch on the hard floor of the cave, and my weary journey, this mattress of chaff, into which I sank as soon as I lay down, seemed a couch for a king. As I turned over on my side and composed myself to sleep, I had but one regret. Weary as I found myself, it would be impossible for me to get back to the cave in time for the great Conventicle which was to be held among the Closeburn hills upon the coming Sabbath.

My sleep was dreamless, and when I awoke the torch of the sun was blazing outside my narrow window. Having dressed myself, I made for the kitchen, where I found the good-wife busy over the fire. She turned as she heard my footsteps and asked :

" Are ye weel rested ? Ye maun be, for ye've sleepit the better pairt o' twal 'oors. I knocked at your door at ten o'clock ; syne I tappit again at half-eleeven, but for a' the answer ye gi'ed, ye micht ha'e been the Castle Rock. So I juist left ye your lane, and here ye are at lang last, famished nae doot ! " I was surprised to learn that I had slept so long, but the rest had done me good service and I felt greatly refreshed. "There's ae virtue aboot parritch, forby ithers," she said—"a wee bit extra boilin' does nae hairm, which is mair than can be said for ony ither dish except sheep's-heid broth."

When my meal was over I rose to go, and as I did so I offered to pay the good woman for her hospitality.

"No, no," she said, as she shook her head. "Maister Burgess paid your lawin' for ye; and indeed there was nae necessity, for ony frien' o' that saint o' God is aye welcome to a bed and a sup o' parritch frae Betty Macfarlane."

As I had given up all intention of trying to reach Closeburn by the following Sunday, I thought I might with advantage spend the rest of the day in rambling round the historic town. Such an opportunity might not offer again, and I knew that Scotland's story was graven upon the face of her Capital. Under the cover of the night I would begin my journey home. So I walked down the Lawn Market, and descended the Canongate until I came within sight of Holyrood. As I went I admired the lordly houses which flanked each side of the thoroughfare—some of them gaunt, grey and forbidding; others finely timbered; others again turreted and adorned with stone-fretwork that proclaimed the high skill of the carvers' art. I lingered for a time in front of Holyrood, thinking of the tragic career of her whose spirit still seemed to haunt the pile. Then I made my way by the Cowgate to the Grassmarket, where, sombre and menacing—the symbol of the dark days through which this tortured land was passing—stood the scaffold. On that forbidding gibbet I knew that many a brave martyr had met his end. The walls around me had heard the intrepid challenge of their testimonies, while the grim Castle rock, towering above, looked down silent and frowning as though it scorned the cruelties of man to his brother man.

From the Grassmarket I climbed up a tortuous and steep wynd to the Lawn Market again. By this time the afternoon was far advanced, and evening was at hand. In the High Street, not far from the church of St. Giles, I entered a tavern, and having supped I looked at the clock in the Church Tower and saw that it was close upon six. I judged it would be well to set out in another hour. By so doing I should have left the city behind me and be far in the open country ere it was time to sleep; so I settled myself comfortably on a chair in the ingle-nook and called for another pot of ale.

When the clock in the church tower struck seven I called for my score, and, having settled it, made my way out into the High Street. As I came out of the tavern door two officers passed me. I was less than a couple of paces behind them as they walked down the street. Had I willed it so, I could not have failed to catch some fragment of their talk, but my ears were pricked to a lively attention when I heard one of them say: ". . . Among the hills . . . Closeburn." I caught a few disjointed words. " Sabbath . . . three or four thousand . . . a great occasion . . . Claver'se, Lag, . . . something complete . . . no miserable failure . . . Drumclog . . . stamp out . . . no quarter . . . woman or child." A horror so sudden seized me that I stood stock still, and the officers, unaware that I had overheard them, walked on.

What had I heard? The fell purport of the stray words I had caught blazed before me in letters of fire. I knew of the great Conventicle that was to take place among the hills above Closeburn. I knew that every little cottage and every homestead for miles around that held a soul who professed allegiance to the Cause would have its witness there. By some mischance the enemy had learned of the intended gathering, and had plotted a master-stroke to destroy the Covenanters.

The Cause was in jeopardy! Destruction threatened it. And I, Walter de Brydde—one-time moss-trooper, could save it! I alone. My hour had come.

The clock struck, and, startled, I awoke to action.

Forgetful that the news must be carried far, I began to run. Down past the Tron Kirk and on past Halkerstone Wynd and on down the Canongate I ran, until as I drew near the Town Port and saw the scarlet colour of the soldier's uniforms, some gleam of caution returned to me, and I slowed down to a walking pace lest my speed should excite suspicion. I shambled past the sentinels unchallenged, but when I had put a sufficient distance between them and myself, I broke into a run once more and headed for the hills. As I sped along I made a hasty calculation. It was now eight o'clock on Friday evening. To prevent the massacre, I must reach Closeburn not later than midnight on Saturday. That would give time for a message to be spread broadcast by willing couriers in the darkness of the night, and faithful men could be posted to give warning at every cross-road by which the worshippers must pass as they made their way, in the early dawn, to the appointed trysting-place.

CHAPTER XXXVI

FOR THE SAKE OF THE COVENANT

I HAD twenty-eight hours in which to reach Closeburn—time sufficient to cover the distance, if I made an average of three miles an hour. And three miles an hour was well within the compass even of a man lame like myself. Already I saw my task accomplished, and the joy that filled my heart lent wings to my feet. With hands clenched, and chest thrown forward, I raced along until my breathing became a torment and I had to stop. I leaned against a wall by the roadside panting violently, and as I rested, soberer thoughts came to me. This was foolishness!

Not in this way would I ever complete the journey; nor was there need of such impetuous haste. A moderate speed on the level, a steady struggle up the hills and all the speed I could command down them would bring me safely to my goal within the allotted time. I looked back along the way I had come. Far off I could see the light gleaming in the windows of the city, and high up, where a great black mass threw its bulk towards the sky, I saw the red glare of the brazier upon the Castle walls. Already I had travelled far, and when I had recovered my breath, I took to the road again. This time I did not run, but walked steadily.

The moon climbed the heavens, and all the sky was glad with little stars. A gentle breeze had arisen and white clouds were scurrying overhead; but the cool of the wind was as refreshing balm and I plodded steadily on. Hour followed hour, and the moon sank to rest and still I followed the winding road. The first rosy streaks of dawn were warming the eastern sky when I sat down to rest. I was well content. My steady pace had carried me far and though I was weary I was confident. In the daylight I should be able to make better progress than during the darkness. As I rested I became aware that the strength of the wind had increased, and great leaden clouds were beginning to sweep across the sky. Rain began to fall upon my upturned face. The cooling drops were welcome; it would be but a passing shower! Thinking thus I rose and continued my journey. Then the heavens opened and the rain came down in a flood. Blown by the wind it struck my face and hands with missile force and to shelter myself I left the road and crawled under a whin-bush on the hill-side. For a time this gave me protection; but as the storm increased the rain-drops beat their way through the palisade of thorns, and poured mercilessly upon me once more. There was nothing to be gained by resting here. I was losing time. Better up and on! So I took to the road again. The wind had waxed to a tempest and beat direct upon me, so that I had to bend my head and put forth all my strength to fight it. I had not looked for this, but with dogged determination I clenched my teeth and battled on.

On I struggled, unable to see more than a few paces ahead of me; for the rain was like a cloud—so wet that with every step the water streamed from my shoes. Should I ever reach the end of the journey? I would though I fell dead! It was for Mary's sake.

Hour after hour passed, and at last the storm began to abate. The fury of the rain lessened, and the downpour settled into a drizzle. The sky began to clear. There were breaks in its leaden vault through which a white tuft of cloud thrust an infrequent pennon, and by and by the sun broke through the dull veil that had hidden it, and the rain ceased.

Still the wind blew upon me with such force that every now and then I was brought to a standstill. When a lull came between one and the next more stern blast, I would run a pace or two ; but only to be baffled again when the wind had gathered strength. I cast an anxious look up to the sky ; the sun was visible now, but there was no vigour in his rays. It seemed as though the rain had quenched his fire, and that instead of looking into the heart of a furnace I gazed upon a ball of grey ashes. But what gave me pause and filled me with sudden dread was his place in the sky. He was already well past the meridian. The steady progress of the night, in which I had taken such satisfaction, counted for little set against the small tally of the miles covered since the dawn. The agony in my heart whipped me to greater effort, and I tried to run. But the wind seized me, and smote me with mighty buffets so that I had to desist and content myself by making what poor speed I could. On and on I trudged—hour after hour boring my way head downwards against the relentless wind, ashamed to count my paces, for I knew that the tale of them, as each minute slipped past, was less than a quarter of what it would have been if fortune had not turned against me. I had left the moorland track now and was upon a stretch of better road, sheltered in some fashion by trees upon either side. They broke the sterner fury of the blast and the better surface of the road made speedier progress possible. Spurring myself to the effort I sprang forward. Suddenly, to my joy, I saw on the hill-side above the road a little white cottage. I dragged myself up the slope, sodden and weary, and as I drew near I noticed the iron tyre of a cart-wheel leaning against the side of the house, and near by a rusty anvil. I knocked at the door, which was opened immediately by a young woman.

" What's yer pleesure ? " she asked.

" Something to eat—and the time o' day," I answered.

" It's past five on the nock, an' if ye'll come awa' ben ye can ha'e some provender."

She led the way into a large kitchen, and as she busied herself in setting oat cakes and ale before me I warmed myself by the fire. I was in no mood for delay, so I ate some of the food hastily, stored a little in my pockets, drank my ale, and called for my score. As I paid her I asked the distance to Moffat.

" Eight miles and a bittock, and the first bit is a' uphill—an awfu' road: but easy after ye pass the Beef-tub."

My heart sank, the hour was late—far later than I had thought, and I had still far to go.

Bidding my hostess good day I hurried to the door, threw it open—and walked into the arms of two troopers. Taken unawares I was startled, but quickly recovering myself I bade them good day and tried to pass them.

" No' sae fast, young man—no' sae fast. Ye're in a de'il o' a hurry," said one of the troopers—a towering brawny giant—as he seized me by the coat.

" Unhand me," I cried. " What right have you to interfere with a loyal subject, engaged on his lawful occasions ? "

" Hear tae him, Sandy," said my captor. " He talks like a mangy lawyer. 'Lawful occasions !' We'll see aboot that. What are ye daein' here ? "

Eager to satisfy the man, and in the hope that by doing so I should be permitted to continue on my way, I answered :

" I am a traveller on my way to Dumfries—I have been caught in the storm, and sought shelter and refreshment in this house "—and I tried to wrench myself from his grasp.

"A gey thin tale. Whit think ye, Sandy? As like as no' he's a Covenanter." And Sandy grunted "Umphm."

Again I tried to shake myself free—but the giant flung his arms about me, and lifting me up, struggle how I might, as though I had been a child he carried me back into the kitchen and thrust me roughly on a chair.

The woman of the house looked on open-eyed.

"Whit ken ye o' this man?" said the trooper, turning towards her, but all the while keeping a firm hold of me.

"Naething mair than yersel," she answered. "He cam' tae the door a bittock syne, and asked for something tae eat—and he peyed his lawin' like a gentleman."

"Umphm," growled my tormentor; and Sandy standing beside him answered "Umphm."

"Bring us something tae drink, Mirren, Solway waters if ye hae them. We're fair drookit," said my captor. "As for you," he said, tightening his grip on my arm, "we'll ha'e to look into your case. Sandy—fetch a tow."

Sandy followed the woman into another room, and in a moment returned with a rope in his hand.

"What does this mean?" I shouted. "You have no right to interfere with me—and when I reach Moffat I shall lodge a complaint with the Officer Commanding."

"Shut yer jaw," bellowed the giant, and shook his fist at me.

I sprang up—my clenched left fist smashed into his face, and the blood streamed from him—but still he held me.

Sandy sprang to his aid, and though I struggled like one possessed I was quickly overpowered, flung roughly on the chair and bound there. The rope that surrounded me, and held my arms close to my sides, was drawn so tightly that I could hardly breathe.

They ran it round the back of the chair and under the legs shackling each ankle. I was helpless. As he bound me the giant cursed me soundly, pausing only to spit blood from his foul mouth.

"Ye blasted hound! Ye're no' what ye pretend. We'll mak' ye talk in a wee. Eh, Sandy?" And Sandy, binding my ankles, answered "Umphm."

When I was tied securely they stood away from me and surveyed their handiwork.

"Umphm," said Sandy—as he poured out a glass of Solway waters from the bottle which the woman had brought, and raised it to his lips. The two sat down by the fire—the bottle between them—and for a time turned all their attention to its contents. I tried to move—but I was gripped as in a vice. I was in sore case. I cared not what happened to myself, but there was my message. I alone could prevent the massacre on the morrow, and now the proud hope I had cherished of doing service to the Covenant was brought to naught. Was there a God in heaven, that such things could be? I was not left long to my thoughts.

Suddenly the giant rose, and standing over me glowered into my eyes as he shouted:

"Are ye a Covenanter?"

Temptation assailed me. If I denied the Covenant, I could with a firmer claim demand to be set free—and then I might yet carry my message through. "No" was upon my lips—but it died unspoken there. I heard the notes of a flute on a heather-clad hill-side: saw again a heap of smouldering ashes where a home of love had been. I could not deny the Covenant.

Firmly I answered "I am"— and in the gathering shadows I saw the radiant face of Mary smiling upon me—as she blew me a kiss with either hand.

"Umphm," said Sandy, "I thocht as muckle."

"So ye're a Covenanter, are ye?" roared the giant. "I'll learn ye! Wull ye say 'God save the King?'"

"God save the King," I answered promptly. "I am a loyal subject and a Covenanter."

"Ye lie," he shouted. "The Covenanters are a' rebels. Wull ye tak' the Test?"

In the cave at the Linn I had heard Hector repeat the involved sentences of the Test with scorn upon his lips, and I knew that this half-drunken trooper could not possibly find his way through them; so I answered:

"If you can put the Test to me you shall have my answer."

Sandy—with the bottle in his hand—looked over his shoulder and laughed softly. The giant turned upon him. "Whit the deevil are ye lauchin' at"—and then turning to me, "I'm nae scholar—and I canna min' the words, but if I canna pit the Test to you I can pit you tae the test—and by heaven I will." A look of fiendish cruelty swept over his hard face.

"Try him wi' the match," said Sandy.

"Ay—that'll test him."

While Sandy busied himself about my fastenings to free my left arm for the ordeal, the other trooper was trying to make the long match he had unwound from his head-gear take light. It wa sdamp and would not burn. I watched in a strange state of abstraction. Only a few minutes ago the vision of Mary had smiled upon me. Pain and torture were nothing to me now. Let them do their worst!

"It winna burn: it's wat," said the giant. Throwing the match on the floor, he gripped my left arm savagely and pushed back the sleeve of my coat.

"Rax me a live peat," he said, and Sandy picked one up with the tongs and handed it to him. He seized the tongs, and held the peat against my arm just above the wrist where the blue veins showed. "That'll mak' ye talk, ye dog," he shouted. But no word escaped my lips. My eyes sought the distance

—and there I saw the face of Mary—twin tears upon her eyelids. The pain was swallowed up by the joy.

"He's a dour deevil," growled Sandy.

"Ay: but we'll ha'e him yelling for mercy yet. The peat's gaen cauld. Gar it lowe, Sandy."

Sandy bent his head and blew upon the peat. It began to glow again—but I did not flinch.

"Rax me anither," said my tormentor, letting the first fall and relaxing his grip of my arm. For a moment he turned to watch his companion pick up another glowing peat—and in that moment I eased the ropes about my right arm with my left hand. They slipped upwards and my right arm was free.

My tormentors did not observe it when they came to me again and applied the torture to my left arm once more.

Again Sandy lowered his head to blow upon the peat—and in that instant my right arm shot out like a steel spring, my fist crashed into his jaw and he fell in a heap, knocking the legs from under the giant, who fell heavily upon him.

"Ye clumsy lout!" he cried, as he rose in drunken fury, and as Sandy lay motionless he kicked him savagely with his heavy boots in the chest.

The kitchen door opened softly, and for a moment I caught a glimpse of the woman's frightened face: then she withdrew.

"Get up—I tell ye," roared the giant, kicking the recumbent figure again.

My blow could have caused him only temporary damage—but this savagery of the giant would kill him.

My eyes were on Sandy. His pallid face grew ashen: his chest was raised from the ground in a curve like a bow as he took a convulsive breath: blood and froth bubbled at his lips—and he lay still, his ashen pallor deepening.

Fear seized the giant. He dropped on his knees

beside the body. " Get up, Sandy my lammie "— he said, drunken tears falling down his cheeks. " Ye're no' deid. " Ye'll be a' richt in a meenute. Get up, lad. Say ye're no' deid."

But Sandy lay motionless.

" You have killed him," I said.

" You lie," roared the trooper, springing to his feet and facing me. " You did it—an' ye'll pey for 't."

He seized me by the throat, and readjusted my fastenings—binding me cruelly tight. Then he took a long draught from the bottle, and sat down. I watched him as he took a knife from his pocket, and ran his thumb along its edge.

" I'll bluid him like a sheep," he muttered, as he bent down and tried to sharpen the blade on the hearth-stone.

I knew I could expect no mercy from this frenzied, half-drunken brute.

A prayer stole up from my heart—not for mercy, but for the safety of the hill-folks on the morrow, and for the pardon of my own sins. Only a shriven soul could hope to be reunited with my beloved :—please God, Mary would be waiting for me on the other side.

The trooper rose and came towards me.

" I'll bluid ye like a sheep," he snarled, and seizing me by the hair swung my head over to one side.

Death stared me in the face, and, let me set it down for the comfort of those who live in daily terror of death, at that moment I felt no fear.

" Like a sheep," he mumbled—and swung his arm back for the blow ; but at that instant he crashed forward carrying me before him, and his open knife clattered on the floor.

" Thank God—oh, thank God," whispered a woman's voice, as she drew me, still bound to the chair , from under the heavy body of the giant. In a trice she had cut my bonds—and was chafing my numbed limbs.

" Ha'e I killed him ? " she asked anxiously.

I looked at the giant. He was breathing heavily—and a long gash on the back of his head was spurting jets of blood.

" No," I said—" only stunned him. I owe my life to you."

" Ay. Tae me an' the tatie-beetle," she answered, pointing to her weapon on the floor. " But haste ye. Tie him up afore he comes tae."

I bound him, hands and feet, with a grim satisfaction, and left him lying on his face.

The woman watched me anxiously, urging me to greater haste.

" And now," I said—" what of you ? You must escape."

" Oh, I'll be a' richt," she said, leading the way to the other room. " My man will be back in an 'oor. Tie me in a chair—and gag me : and I'll tell a bonnie story when Peter comes hame."

I did her bidding quickly, pouring out my gratitude with fervent lips.

As I was about to gag her with her kerchief, she forbade me for a moment, and said with tears in her eyes :

" God forgi'e me ! My mither was a Covenanter—an'—I mairrit a trooper."

I bent down reverently and kissed her bound hands.

" You have done a greater service to the Covenant than you know," I said, then springing up I dashed from the house into the gathering darkness.

I had lost two precious hours—but by the mercy of God I was still alive, and I should carry my message through.

I raced down the slope to the road, and turned my face to the long ascent. The wind had abated, and I could make better progress. The cold air stung my burnt arm, but as I set my mind to my task the pain ceased to trouble me.

With hope still rising within me I struggled on—breaking into a steady, mechanical trot. As the woman had said, the road was very bad, but, after my strange deliverance from death, nothing could daunt me, and I fought my way on. The stars were looking down upon me now, and I looked up at them with a grateful heart. At last I reached the top of the hill, and the long descent lay before me. I paused for a moment to regain my breath, and saw far below me that tender light which always hangs in the sky, when night comes, above the habitations of men, and I knew that I was looking down on Moffat. As though the light were a beacon which beckoned me, I started to run down-hill.

My stiff limbs warmed to their work and soon I was running with some freedom. On and on . . . splashing through the pools of water that lay in the path, with eyes strained ever towards the gleam in the sky ; on, and on . . . with clenched teeth and parted lips through which my hurrying breath issued with the poignant sound of a sob. On, and on . . . the rhythmic sound of my footsteps throbbing through my brain. Faster now, for the light was drawing nearer ; on, and on . . . till just without the confines of the little town I turned to the right lest the sound of my racing feet should awake suspicion. Skirting the township cautiously, I came out upon the road again beyond it.

On, and on . . . fear and desire lending speed to my feet ; and behind me the town clock striking ten. God help me !—a score of miles still lay before me ; had I strength to accomplish the task ? The perspiration broke out upon me, and for very weariness I reeled as I ran. At last I came to the place where I must leave the highway and take to the open country. It was harder going thus, but the way was more direct and every moment was precious. On, and on . . . until my mind divorced itself from my body, and in a mood of abstraction contemplated the running figure alongside which it sailed so easily. On, and on . . . the mind holding itself aloof and regarding with a kind of pity the struggles of the tired body that was plunging headlong across the fields. Suddenly I was conscious that something other than myself was running along beside me . . . keeping step with my step, measuring its paces with my paces, neck and neck with me. What ghostly companion was this ? I looked to the right and left but saw nothing, and, as I looked, the sound of the attendant footsteps ceased and I heard nothing but the tick-tack of my own feet. On, and on . . . crashing through the hedges, leaping over the low dykes, stumbling in the ruts of the ploughed fields, wading the little streams, . . . still I pressed on. I was panting wildly now, so that my breath whistled as the wind whistles through a keyhole in winter. Nothing mattered: come life, come death, I should carry the tidings through. Once more the ghostly feet were audible, keeping time with my own—pit-pat, pit-pat, step for step. I flung my arms to right and left, but they touched vacancy, and the ghostly footsteps ceased. On, and on, . . . until a heavy languor stole over me and filled me with the hunger of sleep. My eyelids drooped, so that for an instant I did not see the ground before me, and I stumbled and almost fell. I sprang erect and shook myself. Sleep meant death—not for myself, but for thousands of others who had grown to be dear to me, and on and on I ran. But the things that a man would do are conditioned by the strength which God has given him, and the body, though an obedient slave to the mind, sometimes becomes a tyrant. My limbs were heavy—no longer things of flesh and blood, but compact of lead. On, and on . . . knowing nothing now but that my task was a sacred one, deaf to the sound of my own footsteps, blind to the things around me, on and on I reeled till sleep or something akin to it, seized me, and for a time I raced on unconscious of what I did. Stumbling, I fell to spring up again wildly alert. I should win through or die ! On and on—and on and on . . . till I sank helpless to the ground.

I slept: I dreamed:—

It was a peaceful Sabbath day. In a hollow among the hills above Closeburn a great gathering of men and women and children was assembled to keep the feast. On a low table covered with a fair white cloth stood the sacred elements. Behind the table I saw my friend of the cave at the Linn standing with a look of rapture on his face. The gathered people were singing a psalm, when, suddenly, there was a loud alarm. The posted sentinels came hot-foot with cruel tidings on their lips. But it was too late. From north and south and east and west, on horses at the gallop, poured the dragoons—Claver'se's men, Lag's men, Winram's men, Dalzell's men, all with the blood-lust in their eyes—and in a moment that peaceful hollow was a bloody shambles. Muskets rattled on every side; men, women and children fell. Through and through that defenceless company the wild troopers rode, spurring their horses to their sickening task, trampling the women and children underfoot, shooting the men with their bullets or beating them down with the stocks of their muskets. Screams and wild blasphemy rent the air that but a moment before had been fragrant with the melodies of love and adoration. Lag himself I saw spur his charger over a tangled mass of dead and dying right at the sacred table. The horse leaped, spurning to the ground the Bread and Wine, and the man of blood, swinging his sword high, brought it down upon the head of the sainted minister, who fell cleft to the chin. And I, by whose failure such deeds of blood had been made possible, lay bound, a prisoner, hand and foot.

CHAPTER XXXVII

"OUT OF THE SNARE OF THE FOWLERS"

A BLAZE of light as though the sun had sprung full armoured to the height of heaven smote upon my eyes. I opened them, but in that brilliant glare I could see nothing, though I heard voices about me:

"Wha' think ye he can be?"

"He hasna got a kent face," a woman's voice replied. "Some puir gangrel body nae doot. But what can he be daein' off the high road?"

I let the light filter through a chink between my eyelids, and when I could bear its full brightness I opened them and looked around me. A little group of five people bent over me—an old man, holding a lantern, an old woman, and three young men whom I took to be their sons.

As I looked round there came to me out of the depths some memory of the happenings of the night. I wondered dimly if the tragedy of which I had been witness were reality or dream. Who could these people be? Were they some chance Samaritans who had come upon me bound hand and foot, and delivered me from the hands of the persecutors? As I wondered I heard the old woman say to her husband:

"Think ye he can be a hill-man? sic another as we found in the laigh field after Rullion Green."

Hill-man! hill-man! the words burned themselves into my torpid brain. I gathered all my strength, and raising myself so suddenly that they fell away from me startled, I cried, " For the love of God, tell me, are you hill-folks ? "

" What o' that, what o' that ? " asked the old man cautiously.

Then I threw discretion to the winds. " Tell me," I cried, my voice breaking, " are you hill-men, for I bring tidings that will brook no delay."

They gathered round me again and looked at me with anxious eyes.

" Oot wi' it, lad," cried the old man, almost as excited as myself, and with what speed I could I told them all. Breathlessly they listened. " God in heaven, save us," groaned the old man as I finished, and then, turning to his sons he cried : " Boys, it's yours to carry the message through. Awa' wi' ye ! Post men at the cross-roads, scatter the news far and wide, and the Cause may yet be saved."

Like hounds from the leash the lads sprang away into the darkness. With failing sight I saw them go, then I sank back again wearily and knew no more.

Long afterwards I was conscious in a dim kind of way of being lifted from the ground and borne gently over what seemed to be an interminable distance ; but I was too drowsy and fatigued to care what was happening to me. When I opened my eyes I found myself lying on a soft bed in a small farm kitchen. A glowing fire was on the hearth and its pleasant warmth pervaded the room. The good man of the house brought me a drink of something hot, which put new life in my veins and I was my own man again.

I would fain have talked to my rescuers, but they forbade me, and I sank once more into a drowse, but ere I slept I heard, as I had heard so often in the old house at Daldowie, the good man opening the Book and saying, " Let us worship God by singing to His praise a part of the 124th Psalm."

I slept deeply, and when I awoke it was late in

the Sabbath afternoon. When they heard me stir the kindly folk showed themselves assiduous in those little courtesies which mean so much to a weary man. When I essayed to rise the old man was at my bedside to lend me aid, and when I had risen he brought me water wherewith to wash myself. The cool liquid took the stains of travel from my face and hands, and at the same time purged me of weariness. On my left arm, where the torture had been applied, was an ugly red sore all blisters at its edges. I looked at it with a kind of pride. It was the brand of the Covenant upon me. The old man bound it with a buttered cloth, to my great comfort.

The blind was drawn down over the window so that the light within was restful. I took my seat upon the settle and the farmer's wife spread a meal before me, and as I ate they questioned me. From them I gathered that when they came upon me lying in a stupor in the fields, they were themselves upon their way to the hill-meeting. They had some ten miles to travel, and as they had to measure their speed by the speed of the good-wife, they had set out soon after midnight. I asked anxiously whether they had news of what had taken place, and whether their sons had succeeded in spreading the alarm sufficiently widely to prevent the Covenanters assembling. To this the old man replied:

"I dinna ken for certain, but ye may tak' it frae me that the troopers found naething but an empty nest. We'll be hearin' later on, for the lads will be back ere long." He stirred the peats with a stick, and continued: "Man, it's wonderfu', wonderfu'; a' foreordained. If I were a meenister what a graun' sermon I could mak' o't!"

By and by night fell. The good-wife lighted the candles, and when another hour had elapsed the three lads returned. There was joy on their faces; and there was joy in every heart in that little house when they told us how their mission had sped. With the help of many others they had spread a warning so far afield that no Covenanter came within a mile of the assembly place. Then they told us how, when their task was fulfilled, they had watched unseen the cavalcades of the dragoons invading from every point of the compass the quiet sanctuary among the hills. And they told too, with some glee, of the wrath of the soldiery when after riding like hell-hounds full tilt from every side they plunged into the hollow only to find that their prey had escaped them.

Early next morning I arose, and would have taken my departure, but the good man forbade me.

"If ye maun go, ye maun," he said, "but it will be kittle work travellin' by day. The dragoons are like to be sair upset after the botchery o' yesterday and nae doot they'll be scourin' the country lusting for bluid. So, ye'd better bide here till nicht comes and the hawks are a' sleepin', and ye'll win through to yer journey's end in safety."

His words were wise, and, though I knew that my continued absence might cause Mr. Corsane anxiety, I decided to take his advice. When the night fell and the moment of farewell came, the old man took me by the hand:

"God keep ye," he said. "Ye ha'e done a great thing for the Covenant. Years hence, when these troublous days are a' by, the story will be told roond mony a fireside o' the great race ye ran and the deliverance ye brocht to the persecuted."

With the sound of kindly blessings following me through the darkness, I set out and, long ere the dawn, was safely concealed once more in the cave above the Linn.

Mr. Corsane gave me a hearty welcome. I assured him that I had delivered his message in good time, and then told him of all the events which had followed. My story filled him with astonishment. He himself had been warned by Covenanting sentries who challenged him as he was stealing in the early dawn towards the trysting-place, and he had returned to the cave and waited in a tumult of anxiety. But little had he imagined that I had brought the news.

"I never doubted your loyalty," he said, "but this deed of yours has thirled you to the Covenant for ever," and he laid his hands upon my shoulders and let them rest there for a little space.

CHAPTER XXXVIII

THE PASSING OF ANDREW AND JEAN

THE land was in the iron grip of winter. No longer was there any work for me in the fields, so that I was driven to spend nights and days in idleness. For a man to rest from his labours may be a pleasant thing for one weary, whose heart is at ease; but my inactivity of body served but to fan the embers of my hopes, and I was tortured by lively flames of hope which would flare up within me only to expire vacuously choked by the cold ashes of reality. Mary was dead; my life was desolate!

On a morning in mid December I crawled out upon the sandstone ledge above the pool. The air was crisp and dry, so that my breath issued from my mouth like a cloud of smoke; and, as I breathed, the chill of the atmosphere bit into my blood. The sky above me was blue, like a piece of polished and highly tempered steel; and only a few irresolute beams of sunlight filtered through the gaunt branches of the trees on the heights above me. The stream, where it poured into the pool, was festooned with dependent sword-points of ice; and the pool itself, except in the centre where the slow-moving waters still refused the fetters of winter, was shackled in ice. A robin was perched on a tree above me—his buckler the one spark of warmth, his song the one note of cheer.

I had paced up and down the narrow ledge several times when I heard the sound of footsteps. In the clear air they rang like iron upon iron. Alert, I listened to discover their direction. They came from down the stream. Someone was making his way along the course of the rivulet towards the pool. Could it be a dragoon on a quest at a venture, or was our retreat discovered? Quickly I hurried round the edge of the pool. There was no time to slip into the cave without discovery—the footsteps were too close at hand. A spear of ice, and a stout heart could hold the defile below the pool through which the intruder must pass before he could reach the cave. If I held the gorge, the minister would have time to make good his escape. His life was of greater worth than mine.

A glow pervaded me: the lust of combat was upon me. Life was sweet: but to die fighting was to die a death worth while, and the poignard of ice which I held in my hand was a man's weapon. I peeped into the defile: the further end was blocked by the body of a man who, with face bent downward, was choosing his footsteps with care. It was no soldier in the trappings of war—but a countryman. The man raised his face and I could have shouted for joy: it was Hector! He saw me at once, and waved a hand to me, and, hot with expectation, I awaited his coming. Soon he had squeezed his way through, and stood beside me. I offered my hand in welcome, and as I did so remembered that it still held my murderous weapon. I dropped it on the instant and it fell into the pool, its sharp end cutting a star-like hole in the sheet of ice. The packman laughed as he took my hand.

"So, so," he said, "ye thocht I was a trooper. A puir weapon yon! Gi'e me 'Trusty,'" and he struck the rocks with the head of his stick so that they rang. "And hoo is a' wi' ye?" he continued—"and the meenister?"

I had no need to reply, for at that moment he emerged from the cave.

Our first greetings over, we hustled the packman into the cave. We spread food before him, and as he ate we plied him with questions. One question was burning in my heart: but I knew the answer, and had not the courage to put it; and as the minister was hungering for news, I gave place to him and held my peace.

How fared the Cause in the west country, and were the hill-men standing firm? That was the essence of his questioning. And Hector, with eyes glowing so that they shone like little lamps in the darkness of his face, told him all. The cruelties of the persecutors had reached their zenith: but neither shootings, nor still more hideous tortures threatened, could break the proud spirit of the Covenanters. As he talked, Hector's voice thrilled until his last triumphant words rang through the cave like a challenge and a prophecy.

"Ay," he cried, "though the King's minions heap horror upon horror till every hill in the South o' Scotland is a heather-clad Golgotha, the men will stand firm: and generations yet unborn will reap the harvest o' their sacrifice."

He ceased, and so deep a silence fell upon us that through the rock wall I could hear the splash of an icicle as it fell into the pool. The minister's bowed head was in his hands. Awe and reverence fettered my tongue. Then Hector spoke again. He had taken his pipe from his pocket, and was filling it with care.

"And noo," he said, turning to me, "I ha'e news for you." A question sprang to my lips, but before I could shape a word Hector held up his hand. "You maun ask nae questions till my tale is done. You can talk yer fill by and by: but hear me in silence first." I nodded my head, and he began.

"You mind I tellt ye, before I left, that when I went west I should try to fin' oot what happened at Daldowie. Weel, on the road to Wigtown, I held away up into the hills, and by and by I cam' to the auld place. It stood there—what had been a bien hoose and a happy home—a heap o' ruins, ae gable-end pointin' an angry finger tae the sky. I looked amang the ruins, for I minded what you had seen there; but I saw naething but ashes and charred stanes, save that Nature, a wee mair kindly than man is, had scattered a flooer or twa oot o' her lap in the by-gaun and they were bloomin' bonnily there. By and by I took the road again, and though I got as far West as the rocks below Dunskey, where the untamed waves hammer the cliffs like an angry stallion, I gathered nane o' the news I was seekin'. But on the hame-comin' I dropped into the Ship and Anchor at Kirkcudbright, and as I sat ower a pot o' yill I heard a couple o' troopers haein' high words. What the quarrel was aboot I dinna ken, but it ended by ane o' them springin' up and ganging oot o' the door. As he went, he half turned and said, wi' a laugh: 'Ye deserve what the guid-wife o' Daldowie gied Claver'se.' Whereat the dragoon left behin' let a roar o' laughter oot o' him and took a lang pull at his yill. When he set it doon he laughed again, and I jaloused that his anger had passed. So I drew oot my pipe and tobacco, and I offered him a fill. He took the weed gledly, and then I drew in to his table and asked him to ha'e a drink. I ordered 'Solway waters,' for I ken hoo they can lowse the tongue, and when they cam' I clinked glasses wi' him, and by way o' settin' suspicion to rest, I drank to the King. Soon I had him crackin' away merrily. But I didna learn muckle frae him till I had plied him wi' mair drink, and then his tongue got the better o' his discretion. Suddenly he said wi' a laugh, 'I deserve what the guid-wife o' Daldowie gied to Claver'se, dae I? We'll see aboot that, my lad!' and he laughed again. I had got my opening.

"'That seems to be a guid joke,' I said. 'If it's worth tellin' I should like to hear it.'

"'Oh,' he answered, 'it's a graun' joke; but for guidsake dinna be lettin' on tae Claver'se I tellt ye. It's a sair point wi' him.'

"Little by little I got the story frae him in fragments mair or less disjointed. But since then I've put it thegither, and I'll tell it in my ain way.

"Ae morning last April Claver'se and his troopers were oot on the moors a mile or twa to the west o' Dalry, when they saw twa men comin' towards them. Ane o' the men was chasin' the other up and doon amang the moss-hags, and the troopers put spurs to their horses and sune had them surrounded. When Claver'se looked at them he recognised in ane o' them a young Covenanter wha' had escaped twa nichts afore frae a barn near New Galloway where he had been flung after a dose o' the thumbikins. The other was a much aulder man. The younger o' the twa was clean demented: and they could get nae sense oot o' him—juist a screed o' haivers whenever they questioned him. The auld man was as dour as a rock—and would gie nae account o' himsel', but it was enough that he had been seen chasin' the daft lad on the moors, belike wi' the intention o' concealin' him in some hidie hole. Weel, Claver'se was for shootin' the auld man oot o' hand if he wouldna speak, and said as much; but a' the answer he got was 'I'm ready, sir. Ye can dae nae mair than kill my body,' and he took off his bonnet and looked undaunted up at the sky. Weel, just then ane o' the troopers drew up alangside Claver'se and spoke to him. He had recognised the man as Andrew Paterson o' Daldowie, and tellt Claver'se as much.

'O, ho!' said Claver'se, 'the old fox! So this is the guid-man o' Daldowie. I think we had better tak' him hame to his ain burrow. Maybe we'll find other game there.' So wi' that they tied Andrew and the lad to the stirrup leathers o' twa troopers and made for Daldowie—maybe ten miles awa.

"As they drew near to Daldowie they saw a woman standin' in the doorway lookin' into the distance under the shade o' her hand. She dropped her hand, and made a half turn, and then she saw them comin'. Wi' that she rushed into the hoose and closed the door: but nae doot she was watchin' through a crack, for when they were near enough for her to see that her guid-man was a prisoner, she cam' oot again and stood waitin'. When they drew up she threw oot her airms, and like a mither that rins tae keep her bairn frae danger, she ran towards her man, callin', 'Andra! Andra!' But at a sign frae Claver'se ane o' the dragoons turned his horse across her path and kept her off. Then Claver'se louped frae his horse, and tellin' ane o' the dragoons to lay hold on the woman, and calling half a dozen to follow him, drew his sword and walked in at the open door.

"Inside they made an awfu' steer, pokin' here and searchin' there, nosin' even into the meal barrel and castin' the blankets off the beds after Claver'se himsel' had driven his sword through and through them. Then ane o' the troopers spied a ladder in the corner, and up he goes into the loft, and Claver'se follows him. Then they cam' doon again, Claver'se leadin' and no' lookin' pleased like. He stalked oot o' the kitchen into the open air. Juist then the daft laddie let a screech oot o' him, and Claver'se flung up his heid. 'What the devil is he yelling about?' he cried. 'I'll stop his girning!' and wi' that he shouted an order and twa sodgers ran forward and cuttin' the thongs frae his wrists, dragged him tae the wall o' the hoose. They cast their hands off him, but stood near enough to keep him frae runnin' away. He looked at the dragoons wi' a simple look on his face, and then his e'en wandered away to the blue hills in the distance,—'From whence cometh mine aid,' he said. But he spoke nae mair, for, wi' a quick 'Make ready: present: fire!' Claver'se let his sword drop, the muskets crashed, and the boy fell deid. 'A good riddance,' said Claver'se, spurning the body with his foot. 'There's enough daft folk in the world,' and he laughed.

"There was a sudden turmoil among the men, and the soond o' a woman's voice. The guid-wife was strugglin' to free hersel', and as she did so she shouted, 'Inhuman deevils! Is there nae milk o' mercy in yer herts? What has the puir lad done that ye should murder him?' But a word frae her husband quieted her, 'Jean,' he said—that was a'; but she stood quite still and struggled nae mair, though the tears streamed doon her face. Then Claver'se made a sign and Andra was unbound and led before him, and at the same time the troopers let go their hold o' the woman and she cam' and stood beside her man. 'Daldowie,' says Claver'se, 'you have long been suspected of consorting with and harbouring the hill-men. I have caught you red-handed to-day in the act of succouring one of them; and in your house I have found proof that you have sheltered fugitives from justice. What have you to say for yourself?' Andra looked his judge straight in the face. 'The facts are against me, sir; but I ha'e dune naething for which my conscience rebukes me, and I am ready to answer to God.'

"'More cant! More cant!' roared Claver'se. 'You have to answer to me, the representative of the King. God only comes into the question later,' and he laughed as though he had said a clever thing.

'Will ye tak' the Test? Will ye swear allegiance to the King?' "

" 'Time was,' said Andra, 'that I would gladly ha'e sworn fealty to the King in things temporal; but in things spiritual I am answerable to a Higher than ony Stuart. I was a loyal subject, like a' the hill-folk, till the Stuarts broke their ain pledged word: and ye canna' expect a Scot, least o' a' a Galloway man, tae turn aboot like a weather-cock, when it pleases the King to turn.'

" 'Damnable treason,' shouts Claver'se. 'Don't you know that the King is above the law, and reigns by Divine Right?'

" Andra shook his head, but his wife answered: 'Ay, so the Stuarts say, but they waited till they got to England before they blew that bubble. Weel they kent there were ower mony jaggy thistles in Scotland for that bag o' win' tae last long this side o' the border.'

" 'Woman,' says Claver'se, angrily, 'be silent,' and turning to Andra he said: 'You know you have forfeited your life: many a man has died for less; but I would not be hard on you. Will you be done with the Covenanters? Say the word and you are free. Refuse'—and he waved his hand towards the body o' the lad. Andra followed the gesture wi' his e'en. Then he looked at Claver'se again—wi' nae sign o' fear on his face. 'You ken my answer, sir, I canna.' And as Claver'se turned angrily away the guid-wife threw her airms aboot her husband's neck and sobbed, 'Oh, Andra, my ain brave man!' The dragoons had loosened their hold o' him, and he put his airms aboot her, and patted her heid. 'Dinna greet, lassie,' he murmured, 'dinna greet. Death is naething: only a doorway that lets us ben the Maister's hoose. I'll wait for ye yonder; the pairtin' will no be lang.'

"Claver'se had turned to the dragoons and was rapidly gi'eing them orders. Twa sodgers laid hold on the woman and tried to drag her awa' frae her man, but wi' her face buried on his shoulder she clung to him sobbing. Wi' his ain hands he took her airms frae his neck, and haudin' her face between his palms, kissed her. 'My ain Jean,' he said, 'God keep you. You ha'e been a guid wife tae me,' and kissing her again he left her and took his place by the wall o' the hoose. The firing party was ready. Claver'se half raised his sword to gi'e the signal; then he checked himsel' and turned to Andra.

"'An' you will,' he said, 'you may have five minutes to make your peace with your Maker.'

"'I thank you,' replied Andra, 'but that's settled lang syne.' Claver'se's blade rose sharply in the air. 'Ready,' he shouted—and the sword fell, and as its point struck the ground, Andra Paterson o' Daldowie passed ower unafraid.

"The smoke had no' had time to blaw frae the muzzles o' the muskets ere Jean had broken frae her captors, and flung hersel' on her knees beside the body o' her man. She raised his heid and held it in her lap: and bendin' ower kissed his face. 'Andra,' she cried, 'Andra—my ain bonnie man! Waken, Andra! waken! and speak to me. Andra! Andra! Canna ye hear me? It's me—Jean, yer ain wee lass: ye mind, Andra, ca'in' me that lang syne afore Dauvit was born. Andra, speak to me! Juist ae wee word, Andra!' She paused, and stared wildly at the upturned face. Then bursting into tears she sobbed, 'Oh, Andra, my ain dear man, the faither o' my bairns, they ha'e killed ye.' As the tears streamed doon her cheeks she took her kerchief frae her neck and spread it ower his face. Then lovingly and tenderly she laid his heid doon and spreadin' her open hands abune it said, 'Ane o' the elect noo.'

"Then she rose tae her feet. As she did so she noticed the body o' the lad, and wringing her hands knelt doon beside it. 'Puir wee laddie,' she said. 'God comfort your mither, wherever she may be,' and she bent ower and kissed his broo. Then springing up she faced Claver'se and the dragoons. He was pacing up and doon restlessly, sword in hand. Clenching her fists she shook them angrily at him. 'May God in heaven pey ye for this day's wark. Inhuman fiends! Are ye men born o' women—or spawn o' the de'il?' and leaping forward sae suddenly that Claver'se hadna time to throw himsel' on guard, she seized his sword and wrenched it frae his grip afore he knew that she was on him. She swung up the blade, and brocht it wi' a crash upon his heid. It was sic a blow as would ha'e cleft him to the chin, if she had had skill wi' the weapon. But it turned in her haun' so that she struck him wi' the flat o't, and he fell senseless to the ground. And then she turned on the troopers—ae woman against twenty armed men—striking richt and left, stabbing, lunging, and thrusting till she had scattered the hale troop, aghast at her onslaught, and the mischief she had dune their leader. But her triumph was short. Four o' the troopers plunged their spurs into their horses and rode her down, and as she lay stunned ane o' the troopers dismounting put his musket to her heid and fired."

CHAPTER XXXIX

FALSE HOPES

THE tears were streaming down my cheeks.

I could contain myself no longer. "Then, Mary is alive," I cried. "Thank God! thank God!"

The packman raised a warning hand, and in a steady voice which, to my fevered ears, sounded harsh and cold, said: "Haud yer wheesht till I feenish the story." And with the sudden hope that had sprung up in my breast quenched like a watered flame, I knitted my hands together and waited.

"Weel," he went on, "after they had murdered the guid-wife, the troopers gathered roond Claver'se anxious-like, for he looked deidly. But when they had sprinkled water on his face, he began to come tae himsel'. By and by he opened his e'en and looked aboot him dazed like.

"'What has happened?' he said; then, memory coming back, he cried: 'Whaur the devil is the old hell-cat? Blow her brains out.' The sergeant saluted and said, 'Your orders ha'e already been carried out, sir.' Wi' that Claver'se pulled himsel' thegither and sat up. But he was a' o' a dither. He couldna staun' by his lane, but there was enough o' the de'il left in him to gi'e orders to set the steadin' on fire and burn it to the ground. When the place was a' in a blaze and the roof had fallen in, he sent off others to round up the cattle and the sheep and drive them to Kirkcudbright.

" 'Nothing like making a clean job o't,' he said. Then wi' the help o' the sergeant he mounted his horse, but his heid went licht again and he couldna sit in the saddle. So there was naething for it but to cairry him back to heidquarters. The sergeant and maybe a dozen dragoons were left behind to see that the fire didna gang oot till the bodies were completely destroyed. The rest set oot for heidquarters, taking it in turns to cairry Claver'se on a stretcher they had knocked thegither, while others drove the cattle behin'.

" That is the story," said Hector, " as the trooper telled it to me. Though my heart was heavy, I forced up the ghost o' a laugh when he had feenished and said, ' So that was what the guid-wife o' Daldowie did to Claver'se. Weel, weel, a bonnie tale ! ' Then I plied him wi' mair drink, for there was something else I wanted to ken, aboot which he had said naething. And when he had primed his pipe aince mair I said switherin'-like, as though I were tryin' to mind something : ' Let me see. I think in my traivels I ha'e visited Daldowie. If I'm no wrang I aince sold a ribbon to a bonnie lass there, wha I took for the dochter. Did ye see onything o' her when ye were up by ? ' The trooper shook his heid.

" 'No,' he said, ' I saw naething o' ony bonnie lass, and it was as weel for her, for in the mood that Claver'se was in he would ha'e made short work o' her tae. Are ye sure ye're no' mistaken ? ' he asked.

" ' No, no,' I said, ' I'm no mistaken. If I min' richtly the lassie's name was Mary.'

" ' Weel,' he replied, ' I saw naething o' her while I was at Daldowie. But I'm thinkin' that if she happened to be hidin' onywhere aboot she wad be discovered by the sergeant and the men that were left behin', and mair than likely they'd mak' a clean job by feenishing her tae. Hooever,' he said, ' if it'll be ony satisfaction to ye, I'll speir at ane o' the men wha' was left behin' wi' the sergeant. And if ye're here the morn, at this time, it will gi'e me pleesure tae drink the health o' the King wi' ye again and I'll then be able to tell ye what ye want to ken.'

"Wi' that he rose, and I pressed anither truss o' Virginia weed in his hand and promised to wait for him in the inn the next day. So off he went, but at the door o' the parlour he turned and flung a kiss to the servin'-maid wha was keekin' through the ither door after him. When I had had anither pipe, I found a bield bit in a field, and, wi' my heid on my pack, I settled myself to sleep. I was in great hopes o' hearin' mair when I met the trooper again: but in the grey dawn I heard the soond o' horses coming alang the road, and peepin' through the hedge I saw Claver'se at the heid o' his dragoons makin' for the hills. The trooper I had cracked wi' was among them. That is the last I ever saw o' him, and as they didna come back tae the toon that nicht, I didna learn what he had to tell. But I turned the thing ower in my mind and said to mysel', 'Ane o' twa things has happened—either Mary cam' back and was ta'en by the troopers and martyred like her father and mother, or she escaped and is somewhere in hidin'.' And I said to myself, 'Hector, if the lassie's leevin', it's for you to find her.' So I shouldered my pack and set oot for the west again. I wandered frae hoose to hoose, frae cottage to cottage, frae clachan to clachan, aye wi' the ae quest in my mind, aye wi' the same question on my lips, and keepin' my ears wide open to hear some whisper if I could o' bonnie Mary Paterson.

"I went west as far as the sea. On my road back again I passed here and there and everywhere. But frae Portpatrick to the brig end o' Dumfries I saw neither sign nor heard a word o' her."

He ceased, and a silence fell upon us, so heavy that our hearts were crushed and not one of us dared speak. At last I rose, and crept out of the cave. I stood on the ledge above the frozen pool and felt the ice gather about my heart. Was Mary dead or not? This awful uncertainty was harder to bear than the knowledge I had believed was mine. I slipped my hand into the pocket over my heart and drew from it the fragment of her ring. It lay glistening faintly in the light in my open hand, and then I could not see it for my tears. Mary was dead! I sat down and buried my face in my hands. My soul was in the depths.

CHAPTER XL

I SEEK A FLOWER

MANY a time in the weeks that followed I pondered over Hector's story. Andrew—dour, stout-hearted, and faithful—and Jean—shrewd, loving, and whimsical—had borne themselves valiantly in the hour of doom, and the darkness of the tragedy was illumined by the thought of their high heroism. My sorrow was flushed with pride, though the pride was akin to tears; but ever in my mind there was a torturing doubt. Reason urged me to believe that Mary was dead. But love, and desire which is the child of love, bade me hope on.

More than once I laid bare my heart to the minister, and from his wise words I gained much solace; but, though he would not say so, I knew that in his heart he believed that Mary had fallen into the hands of the troopers and been done to death like her father and mother.

A day came when I could bear the suspense no longer. Inaction served only to increase my torture of mind. I must seek Mary myself.

I told my companions what I purposed. With one voice they tried to dissuade me. They pointed out that such an enterprise was beset with hazard and might lead to death. Little did they know that death had no terrors for such a love as mine, and that I would have counted it a pleasant thing when weighed against the unquenchable torment that burned in my breast. So I beat down all their objections until, convinced that I was set in my purpose, they ceased to oppose me and planned means whereby I might the better carry out my quest. It was from Hector that the most useful suggestion came.

"Ye micht," he said, "gang through the country as a packman, but frae what I mind o' your puir success at New Abbey, you wouldna fill the pairt." His eyes twinkled. "Besides," he continued, "I feel that I ha'e a proprietary richt to ony customers there are to be had in Galloway, and you micht be interferin' wi' my business—an affront I couldna weel thole. Better pose as a puir gangrel body, wounded, if ye like, in the wars. Yer game leg is evidence eneuch o' that, and when ye come to a toon or a wee bit clachan, ye can aye turn an honest penny by singin' a sang. I mind ye tellin' me Mary was a bonnie singer. Belike ye min' some o' the songs she sang—dootless weel-kent auld Scots sangs. If she were to hear ye singin' ane or ither o' them, mair than likely, oot o' curiosity, she would come oot to see wha it was that was singin' ane o' her ain sangs. If ye keep yer e'en open as weel as yer ears, wha kens but what ye may find her. Besides, the disguise o' a puir gangrel body is hardly likely to be seen through by ony dragoons ye may come across, for ye can aye, if ye like, if ye imagine there are troopers aboot, sing a King's song, sic as 'Awa, Whigs, awa!' and they'll never suspect ye o' bein' a Covenanter. And dinna forget this; if ye ever want word o' Hector the packman, ask at Phemie McBride's. She'll no hae forgotten ye, and she'll aye be able to tell ye where ye'll find me. If ye will gang, gang ye must; but ae last word o' advice I would gi'e ye—dinna be runnin' yersel' into needless danger and aye remember that a guid ash stick laid on tae the heid o' a trooper will mony a time thwart an evil deed devised in his black he'rt. There's nae ither man I would dae it for, but I'm makin' ye a present o' 'Trusty,'" and he pressed his own stick into my hand.

So, just as the darkness had closed in, one January night I set out. Hector and the minister accompanied me to the edge of the wood and, with many good wishes and the blessing of the saintly man still ringing in my ears, I took the road. Before morning broke I was close to Lincluden Abbey, and, under the shelter of its hoary walls, I lay down and rested for a while. I slept till the late afternoon and, having refreshed myself with food, which I procured from a cottage near, I took the road again in the twilight and, avoiding the town of Dumfries that lay on the other side of the river, I made for the heart of Galloway.

Day after day I wandered—hither and thither—not blindly, but of set purpose. Sometimes I travelled upon the high road, and at other times I would leave it and take to the less frequented by-paths in order that no little sequestered cottage might escape me. Here, there and everywhere I sought—one day close down by the sea, the next far back in the solitary places of the hills, questing—questing—questing—but ever without avail. Sometimes, when in a village street I would essay to sing one of the sweet old songs which I had heard so often fall golden from the lips of her I loved, memories of happier days would surge over me, and for very pain my voice would falter and I would cease to sing.

And though, over and over again, the sound of my singing would bring women, old and young, to the open doors of their cottages, my hungering eyes never caught a sight of that face for which they longed. Sometimes a girl, standing in the doorway, pitying my poor attempt at melody, would join her voice to mine and lend to my singing a beauty that it lacked; but though my ears were ever alert for the lute-like voice of Mary, they were never gladdened by the sound for which they ached.

And once on a day I stood blinded by tears beside the ruins of Daldowie.

Day followed day, and still I wandered on. Week after week found my quest still fruitless, and at last I stood upon the confines of the land where the sea expends its futile thunder upon the black rocks by Corsewall point. I had reached the uttermost limit of the journey I had set myself, and my journey had been in vain. So, with a heavy heart, I turned, crushing down the sudden desire that had risen within me to make an end of it all by hurling myself into the sea. The temptation was sore upon me—for life gaped empty before me—but something within me shouted "Coward," and I crushed the impulse down.

On my homeward way I made greater speed than I had done upon my outgoing. Still I searched, and still my search was vain. At last when April had come with laughter and tears and all her promise of summer, I was within sight of Dumfries once more.

I had cause to remember Dumfries. I knew that within its gates danger might await me, but danger had ceased to have any terrors for my stricken heart. At the most, discovery could only mean death, and death was preferable to a life without her whom I loved. When the town came within view I quickened my steps and in the late afternoon I descended the hill that led down to the bridge. As I approached it I was tempted to turn aside and seek the house of Phemie McBride at once, for I remembered Hector's parting words; but some impulse to stand again upon the spot where Fate had descended upon me, all bloody in the uniform of a Sergeant of Dragoons, drove me onward.

When I reached the bridge I stepped into the little alcove where aforetime my destiny had been so strangely moulded, and leaning over looked down upon the rushing stream. My eyes followed the water as it flowed into the distance. Suddenly my gaze was arrested by a crowd which I saw coming along the Sands. At such a distance I was unable to see clearly, but I could make out mounted men and the gleam from their trappings told me they were dragoons. In their wake was a crowd, and as I watched I saw it grow steadily. Men and women and children dashed out of the streets and alleys which opened on to the Sands and joined the rabble behind the troopers. Discretion bade me have a care, but curiosity impelled me and I crossed the bridge and descended to the Sands. Already a throng of folk who had seen, in the distance, the approaching company of troopers, had begun to assemble and I mingled myself with them. The soldiers were advancing at a walking pace and from this and the presence of the rabble at their heels I knew that they had prisoners. Ere long the sound of the horses' hoofs was audible and rumour began to be busy among the people around me.

"What's a' the steer?" asked a woman who had just joined the crowd, her shawl slipping back from her head on to her shoulders. Her question was addressed to the crowd, and out of it somebody made answer.

"It's the troopers. They say they've ta'en twa Covenanters, a man and a woman, somewhere ayont the Kingholm."

Steadily at a march the soldiers approached us. With necks craned eagerly forward we tried to get a glimpse of the prisoners.

"Wha are they?" asked a voice; but to this there was no answer, for the cavalcade was almost upon us. Just as it came to the Port of Vennel the officer turned in his saddle and rapped out a few words of command. The company divided into two, the front half coming to a halt, and I saw that tied to the stirrup leather of one of the troopers was a man. Wheeling to the right, without pause, the second half of the company continued its march. The crowd broke and ran across the intervening space to catch a closer glimpse of the female prisoner. Almost against my will I was carried on by the surge of the people. I could not see the woman's face, but the sunlight fell upon her hair, and—God in heaven! it was chestnut brown, and over her forehead, where the light struck it, it shone like burnished gold. My heart shouted within me, but something—was it the finger of God?—was laid upon my lips and they were still. Rudely flinging men and women aside, I sprang forward that I might see the woman's face. It was Mary in very deed—Mary, in the hands of the persecutors, beautiful as a flower, pride in the poise of her head, courage in her dauntless eyes.

CHAPTER XLI

IN THE HANDS OF THE PERSECUTORS

I REINED in the impulse that seized me to spring forward and attempt a rescue. That way lay madness, and the failure of all hope to effect my purpose. If I adventured it I knew that I should be shot down like a dog and that Mary would go to her fate unsuccoured. Wisdom lay in waiting to see how events would shape themselves. If, at the last, I found that Mary was being taken to Christie's Mount to be martyred on one of the gibbets there, then I should not stand quietly by and see a merciless vengeance wreak itself upon her. If I could not rescue her, I should die with her.

I mixed with the crowd again and was borne onward as it surged up the Vennel. In the press I was thrust so near to Mary that, had I stretched out my hand, I could have touched her, and though my eyes sought her face and feasted upon it, I tore myself away lest she should see me and in a moment of recognition betray us both. The cavalcade breasted the hill up to the High Street and as we went the crowd grew as every shop door added its unit. Here and there a high window was thrown open suddenly and the head of a man or woman would appear, with eyes downcast, to see what was going on in the street below. More than once I heard a word of pity fall from unseen lips.

The company swung into the High Street. Eager

new-comers thrust themselves forward and broke the line of my vision so that it was difficult to keep Mary in sight, but I watched for the aureole of gold set among her chestnut hair, and seeing it my heart beat high again.

By and by we came to the Tolbooth and the cavalcade halted. There was a loud knocking at the door which, in a moment, was thrown wide open, and two of the dragoons rode in with Mary between them. Then the door was shut in our faces. The crowd hung uncertain for a little space, then it began to disperse slowly till only a handful of curious idlers was left gazing vacantly at the prison. Of them I was one, but though my body was idle my mind was working at fever heat. Mary was in the Tolbooth! That meant, at the very least, that no immediate travesty of justice was to be perpetrated upon her. Perhaps, like the women at Wigtown, she would be given a trial, and it might come to pass that she would be found blameless and set free.

As though in answer to this thought the great oaken door swung open again. With eyes almost starting from their sockets, I watched to see her come forth. But no; my hopes that had been soaring in the sky crashed headlong to the earth. The dragoons that had led her in rode forth and the door closed behind them. The company formed up and set out for its quarters and I was left gazing at the door as though a spell were upon me. Suddenly it flashed upon me that to stand there with eyes riveted upon the Tolbooth was to draw attention to myself; so I turned slowly away and walked, as though I were a casual wayfarer, down the High Street again. By the time I had reached the head of the Vennel my mind was set. Mary must be saved. I should rescue her or perish in the attempt. A hive of schemes swarmed in my brain, and my mind was perplexed and divided. Then I thought of Hector. He, if anyone, could aid me: but time was precious and where could I find him? Then I remembered Phemie McBride, and quickening my pace I hurried down the Vennel. Near the Vennel Port a crowd was assembled and when I came to the edge of it I found that my way was blocked by the press of the people. As I stood waiting for a break through which to worm myself, I overheard two boys talking together on its outskirts:

"Ay, I'm tellin' ye, I ha'e juist seen a man shot."

"Get awa'!"

"Ay."

"Tell me aboot it."

"They stood him up on the Sands and six sodgers stood afore him and took aim at his breist."

"Was he feart?"

"De'il a bit!"

"Get on."

"He never even trem'led. But ane o' the young sodgers was gey shaky. Then the captain cried 'Fire' and they a' shot thegither. The man gied a kin' o' jump in the air and fell in a heap."

"Deid?"

"Ay, deid, but no quite, for ane o' his legs gied a bit shake, and scraped the grun'. Weel, the captain took a lang pistol oot o' his belt a' covered wi' siller, and bendin' doon pit it to his heid and fired."

"Behin' his lug?"

"Ay, behin' his lug."

"Eh, I wish I had been there!"

"Weel, never mind, ye'll come the morn wi' me."

"Whaur tae?"

"Tae the College pool and see them droonin' the woman."

"Are they gaun to droon a woman?"

"Ay, they are that."

"As shair as daith?"

"Ay, as shair as daith," and he drew a wet finger across his dirty neck.

"Hoo will they droon her?"

"They'll pit her in a poke wi' twa channel stanes and they'll fling her richt into the pool."

"Will she sink?"

"Ay, richt eneuch."

"I'm comin'."

"Come on, and I'll show ye the bluid o' the man they shot; maybe we'll fin' a bullet."

My fingers itched to be at the throats of these carrion-crows of the streets, to whom Mary's extremity and mine was nothing more than an occasion of amusement.

My heart cried within me—"O my beloved!" and I pulled myself together and began to force a path through the rabble and by and by succeeded in reaching the Vennel Port. Quickly I crossed the bridge and made for the cottage of Phemie McBride.

I knocked anxiously at the door. Would she remember me and—would she know where Hector was? As these doubts and fears were racing through my mind, the door was opened just far enough to allow the good woman to protrude an inquiring face. She looked at me penetratingly; then recognition dawned:

"It's you, is it?"

"Where's Hector?" I answered brusquely.

"Come awa' ben," she said, "and see for yersel'," and with that she threw the door wide open to allow me to enter. I sprang past her, and there, sitting by the kitchen fire, his pipe aglow and his well-thumbed copy of Horace in his hand, sat the pack-man. He sprang to his feet and grasped me warmly by the hand.

"Man," he said, "ye couldna ha'e come at a

better time. I'm fair graivelled by this passage in Horace. Can ye gie me the sense o't ? "

" To perdition with Horace," I shouted. " Mary's in the Tolbooth of Dumfries and I want your help."

The book fell spinning from his hand and lay face down on the floor.

" In the Tolbooth o' Dumfries ! " he exclaimed. " Wha tellt ye that ? "

" I saw her enter less than an hour ago with my own eyes," I said.

Hector stooped, and, before replying, picked up his book. " In the Tolbooth o' Dumfries," he said slowly. " Guid sakes ! I thocht the lassie was deid. Ye're sure it's her ? "

" As sure," I answered, " as I am that I am speaking to you."

" Weel," he replied, " if that's so Horace maun juist bide a wee. This is a maitter that wants con-siderin'. Come awa' to my room," and he led the way to the chamber in which, close on a year ago, I myself had slept.

CHAPTER XLII

IN THE TOLBOOTH OF DUMFRIES

THAT night, as the town clock spoke the hour of nine with its silver tongue, any casual wayfarer passing the Tolbooth might have seen an old, bowed woman knocking timorously at its oaken door. Under the shawl which covered her head and enveloped her to the feet she held a letter, sealed with a large seal. After she had knocked for a second time, the door was partially opened and a hurried conversation took place between her and the jailer. She handed him the letter and, in order the better to read it, he admitted her within the door. Its contents satisfied him, for, at once, he led the way to a cell and taking the great key from a chain that hung at his belt, he unlocked the door and threw it open.

"Mary Paterson," he called, "are ye sleeping? Here's yer auntie come to see ye wi' the special warrant o' the Shirra' himsel'. I never kent the like o' this afore, but I ha'e his warrant for it sealed wi' his ain seal."

There was no response. So, seizing the old woman rudely by the shoulder, the jailer thrust her forward and closed the door behind her. As the key grated in the lock he growled through an iron grille set in the solid wood: "Ye ha'e half an' 'oor thegither: no ae minute langer."

I listened anxiously until I heard his footsteps die gradually away: then with arms outstretched I stepped forward into the darkness.

"Mary, Mary," I cried, in a loud whisper, and out of the darkness a voice spoke:

"What trick is this? Wha are ye? I ha'e nae aunt that would visit me. In a' the world I am alane."

The sadness of that dear voice, once sweet with witchery, unmanned me, but I knew that every minute was precious and that there was need to make haste. "Mary," I said, "it is Walter, your own beloved."

There was a pause, then a sob, and the sweet voice said brokenly: "It canna be. My loved ane is deid lang syne. Are ye someane come here for his ain ill ends?"

"Mary," I said, "where are you? Come to me! come and lay your hand on my face and you will know that it is I indeed."

There was a movement in the cell, and in the darkness a little hand touched me timidly. I seized it in both my own, and smothered it with kisses. Then I drew a shrinking figure towards me and took Mary, my own loved one, in my arms. She nestled to me sobbing gently, for she knew that I was in very deed her lover come again.

"Beloved!" I whispered. "Little flower of the heather." Oh the rapture of that long embrace for which my heart had hungered through so many weary months! "Dear heart," I whispered, with my lips set close to her little ear, "I have come to save you. Be brave, do what I bid you and all will be well."

"To save me?" she said. "Oh, it's no' possible."

"Yes," I answered, "all things are possible to love."

Quickly, in whispers, for the minutes were rapidly fleeing, I explained my plans to her. Wrapped in the great shawl with which I had disguised myself, she was to impersonate the old woman who had come to visit her, and, when the jailer returned, to quit the dungeon with him and make her way to freedom and to safety.

"Once you are out of the Tolbooth," I said, "hurry to the Townhead Port. By the side of the Moat Hill you will find an old man waiting for you. He will be smoking a pipe. Trust him; and he will take you to a place of safety."

I wrapped the shawl about her. It covered her, from head to foot. Then she clung to me once more while I hurriedly whispered the little words of love with which my heart was full, and heard her sweet whispers in return. Suddenly she disengaged herself from my arms, and seizing me by the hand, said:

"My love, my love, it canna be. Why did I no' think o' it afore. I am escaping, and you are to be left behin'. No, I wunna, I canna dae it."

"What a foolish little Mary you are!" I murmured, as I clasped her to me once again. "Feel this," and I guided her fingers along the rough edge of a file I had concealed about me. "Within an hour of your escape I shall be with you. There is only one iron bar to file." I turned her head and made her look at the little window set in the wall high up near the roof of the cell, through which the uncertain light of the moon sent a faint beam. "I knew all about this cell before I came into it. The friend to whom I am sending you has been here himself. He remembered that there was but one bar to the window. He it was who told me how I should escape. So, sweetheart, be brave. On you all depends. If you love me, do what I ask and we shall both soon be free."

She gave her promise as the silence was broken by the sound of the approaching footsteps of the jailer.

"Be brave," I whispered, as I kissed her lips. She clung to me in a brief storm of sobbing, but let her arms fall as the key grated in the lock. The door was thrown open, and the light of a lamp trembled athwart the darkness.

"Come on, auld wife," growled the jailer: "the time's up. Ha'e ye ta'en yer fareweel o' the lass? I jalouse you'll no' see her again till she's swingin' at the end o' a tow."

There was no answer but a burst of sobbing from Mary, who turned from me. I sank back into the darkness of the cell, while she walked bowed as though with age and sorrow towards the open door. She passed through, the door clanged behind her and the key grated in the lock. With ears pressed tight against the door I listened eagerly to the sound of their retreating footsteps. Would she escape, or would some mishap reveal her to the jailer? My heart, that was in a tumult of suspense, bounded for joy when at last I heard the massive oak door close with a hollow clang on the doorposts. My loved one was free, and I—well, what did it matter? I had held her in my arms once again: I had kissed her sweet lips and with that memory to uphold me I could go bravely to my death. But hope beats high in the heart of youth. I ran my finger over the stout file which I had brought with me. In an hour—or at most two—I should be at liberty.

I had learned from Hector that the jailer would make a round of the Tolbooth at ten o'clock, now near at hand. On the last stroke of the hour on the town clock a beam of light came through the grille in the door and a voice said: "Is a' richt wi' ye?" I answered in a whisper. Whether all was right or not the jailer did not trouble to ascertain, for, with a grunt, the light was withdrawn from the grille and the sound of his footsteps faded away in the distance.

I threw off the woman's garments that encumbered me.

The moment had come for action. The window,

with its solitary bar, was set high above my head, and groping anxiously over the wall below for any means by which I might raise myself up to it, I found a few chinks, but none of them large enough for the purpose. Rapidly and noiselessly I scooped some of the mortar from between several of the great stones, and in a few minutes had succeeded in clambering up to the window and laying hold of the upright bar with my left hand. The wall was a thick one, and the outer sill of the window sloped down at a sharp angle from the bar. I recognised that once the bar was severed I should have little difficulty in squeezing myself through the window. Confidently I set to work, beginning at the top of the bar and filing on the inner side. I soon discovered that the iron was weather-beaten and rusty, and as the dust of it fell upon my left hand, tightly clasped about the base of the stanchion, I rejoiced to find that my task was proving easier than I anticipated. But when the bar was filed nearly half through at the top, the cramped position in which I was compelled to work began to weary me, and I dropped down upon the floor of the cell to rest. When I climbed up again, I passed the file to the outer side of the bar and set to work on it at the base. My hope was that when I had filed the stanchion half through, top and bottom, I might be able to break it. The tool bit into the iron, and I worked feverishly. Suddenly there was a snap—the handle of the file was left in my hand—the blade slid down over the sloping sill ere I could catch it, and I heard it drop with a tinkle in the street below.

For a moment I hung there in despair. I was left with nothing but my naked hands, and what could they do against a stout iron stanchion and thick stone walls. I threw my whole weight upon the bar and sought to break it through ; but strive as I might it would neither bend nor break. A second time I tried, but still without avail. Its sharp edges tore my hands so that they were wet with blood, but, hardly conscious of physical pain, I continued to struggle with it. My efforts were fruitless, and from sheer exhaustion I was compelled to desist. I hung for a moment on the edge of the sill, and then dropped down into the cell. My shaking legs refused to support me and I sank in a heap on the ground, bathed in perspiration, with panting breath and parched tongue. As I lay there I remembered how I often watched a bird beating its wings vainly against the bars of its cage, and a great pity for all wild things made captive rose within me. Picking myself up I groped my way round till I reached the door. I felt for the grille. Its bars were thin and rickety, but even if they were removed my arm alone would scarcely go through that tiny aperture. I began to examine the door, passing my hands carefully over it in the hope of finding the lock. The lock was upon the other side! Escape in this direction was impossible, so I fumbled my way round until I stood beneath the window once more. I climbed up to make another attack upon the stanchion. Still it resisted me, and, at last, for very weariness I was compelled to desist and drop down to the floor again. The town clock struck one. A few short hours—I could count them up on the fingers of one hand—and I should be discovered, and discovery meant death. Well, Mary, my Mary, was safe, and my sacrifice was a very little price to pay for that. I had held her in my arms; I was content to die. As I sat in the dark, memory after memory of the things that had befallen me chased each other through my brain. Some were memories of unspeakable happiness, others were memories touched by pain, but even those of pain were made fragrant by the knowledge that my loved one was free.

In Hector's keeping she would be safe from harm. Hector—warm-hearted, beloved adventurer—I could trust her to him.

Once again the silence was broken as the town clock pealed out the hour of two. As its last note was dying I heard a muffled thud above me. I looked up quickly, but could see nothing except the faint beam of light which came through the window, blocked by that tantalising bar. What had the sound been? Was it some phantasm of my disordered brain? My senses were alert again, and I dragged myself once more up to the window. I peered out. Across the street I could see the roofs of the houses, but of the street itself I could catch no glimpse.

My ears had deceived me; there was nothing to be seen or heard. I had taken hold of the iron stanchion to steady myself, and the grip of my hand upon it awoke in me a fresh desire to put it to the test. Perhaps it needed only one more effort to break it! I would try. With legs wide apart I planted both my feet flat against the wall, and, bracing the muscles of my thighs until they were tight as bowstrings, I flung the whole weight of my body upon my outstretched arms, and, with breath held, pulled. Suddenly the beam of light that came through the window was broken by a moving shadow, as though a bird had flown across it, and almost in the same instant something struck me sharply on the chin, then fell between my extended limbs to the floor. In an instant I had dropped down into the cell and on hands and knees was groping for the missile. As I did so, something touched my face, and putting my hand out I caught a piece of cord. This guided me at once to the object of my search, and seizing it I discovered, to my amazement, that it was a book. The cord was firmly tied about it so that I could not open it; but there was no need for that. Its size and the smoothness of its leather cover told me that it was the copy of Horace which was Hector's constant companion. The darkness about me glistened with a thousand stars. Hope sprang on tip-toe in my heart again. Hector was just outside, and I should yet escape.

The cord ran up from the volume into the air towards the window, and, instinctively, I began to pull it in. From the weight of it I knew that there was something upon the other end. Foot by foot, yard by yard, as a seaman passes a cable through his hands, I hauled in the string until I heard a little metallic click as the object attached to it struck the stanchion set in the window, and the string became taut. Seizing the cord in my teeth, I scrambled up the wall. There on the sloping sill, one edge touching the iron bar, lay my file. I gripped it and would have fallen to work upon the stanchion at once, but I saw that I had not yet come to the end of the cord, which ran over the outer edge of the sill and disappeared from sight. So, unlooping the file from the running knot in which it was held, I continued to draw in the cord. As it came up I saw it thicken and knew that my faithful henchman in the street below was sending me a rope. Placing the file between my teeth, I hauled the rope in feverishly till at last the lower end of it was in my grip. I dropped it into the cell behind me and with new strength, but with infinite care, I set myself again to my task upon the bar. Now at the bottom, and now at the top I worked, the iron dust falling in little jets and trickling over the sill. Was it fancy, or was I working with greater skill ?—the file seemed to bite more deeply and more easily into the iron. First on one side of the bar, then on the other, I worked, changing from top to bottom, or from bottom to top, as too long work in one position cramped me. Rasp, rasp . . . I felt the bar vibrate like a violin string in the hand that held it. Rasp, rasp, rasp . . . and a puff of wind from the outside blew the iron dust into my mouth and eyes. What cared I for that ? Rasp, rasp, rasp . . . and the top of the bar was cut so thin that I could break it through. I gripped the file in my teeth and, seizing the stanchion high up with both my hands, threw all my weight upon it. It bent just above its base, but did not break, and where its iron fibres were at tensest strain in the bottom of the groove which I had already cut, I set the file to work once more. The iron gave like crumbling bread before the teeth of the file, till the bar was so thin that with one hand I could bend it in whichever direction I pleased. One strong pull towards me, one mighty thrust outwards, and the stanchion broke with a snap so sudden that the hand which held it shot out through the window. I steadied myself with my left hand on the inner edge of the sill; then I dropped down on tip-toe and seized the rope. As I did so, my fingers touched the volume which had brought me to safety. Breaking the string which bound it, I slipped it into my pocket. It would never do to leave it, neither would it do to leave behind me the disguise I had worn. I gathered up the bundle and tied it tightly about with the cord, the end of which I took in my teeth. Then with the rope round my neck I swarmed up the wall to the window. To my joy, when I reached it, I found that in my efforts to break the bar I had bent the lower end inwards. The stump, thus curved, would give a securer hold to the rope upon which I was about to trust myself. It seemed hardly strong enough to bear my weight, but its length was ample, far greater than I should need. So I doubled it over the stump of the stanchion and having passed it out over the sill, began to worm myself through the window. Slowly and painfully I pushed my way through, and at last my head and the upper part of my body were beyond the aperture. I bent forward, gripping the rope as far off as my arms could reach, and throwing my weight down upon my hands so that the rope was taut, I wriggled myself through until I felt my toes were touching the inner edge of the sill.

Now had the moment come for all my courage. Slowly moving my hands one beyond another, I disengaged my feet from the inner edge of the sill and for a moment hung head downwards. Would the rope hold ? If not, I should crash upon the pavement beneath me, a broken, lifeless mass. But it held ! As I felt my toes slipping down the slope of the sill, I twisted my body to one side so that my feet and legs described a half-circle, and for a moment I swung to and fro against the wall like the pendulum of a clock. Then I lowered myself quickly. Before the last of the rope had run through my hands my feet were upon the ground, and I was free. Somewhere a voice, close beside me, whispered, " No sae bad. No sae bad." Turning, I saw Hector. He patted me on the back, and then whispered anxiously, " I hope you ha'ena forgot to bring my Horace ? " I could have screamed with laughter, but all I did was to nod my head with vigour. Then I took the cord from between my teeth and proceeded to haul upon it. The bundle at its end caught for a moment as it was passing through the window, and then fell, a dark mass out of the heights above, and I caught it as it fell. Hastily I put it into Hector's hands, and seizing the lower end of the rope jerked it once—twice—thrice. The loop above disengaged itself from the stanchion, and in its fall struck me upon the upturned face.

The town-clock struck once. " Half-fower," whispered Hector. "For God's sake let us hurry." Quickly I coiled the rope up into a hank. Hector seized me by the arm and half dragged me across the street to a close mouth. When I tried to thank him he stopped me.

"There's nae need o' that. Awa' wi' ye to Lincluden. Haste ye! Below the big window ye'll fin' a flicht o' steps. The second moves when ye step on it: but never mind—that's naething. The fifth seems firm: but it's no'. I'm the only man that kens that. Shove hard at the left-hand bottom corner—and crawl in when it swings roun', and stop there till I come for ye. Mary's a' richt and in safe hands. Dinna fash yersel' aboot her; but gi'e me the rope. I lifted it off the Provost's drying-green, and though I may be a liar, I'm no' a thief yet and I maun put it back. Awa' wi' ye like a hare."

I needed no second bidding. Hurrying along under the shadow of the houses, I soon found myself in a little lane which ran down to the edge of the water. I made for the Staked Ford, crossed the river hot-foot there, and hot-foot raced on my way. Dawn had not yet begun to break when I reached the Abbey. Once within the shelter of its walls I had no difficulty in finding the steps of which Hector had told me. The second moved as I trod upon it, but I remembered his caution and hastened to the bottom. Then I turned, and kneeling on the last step I pushed hard against the fifth as he had bidden me, and it swung round. I crawled into the cavity beneath it and, turning, drew the step into place again. Then on my hands and knees, for there was not sufficient room to do more, I crawled on until I found myself in a spacious passage.

CHAPTER XLIII

BY THE TOWER OF LINCLUDEN

UNDER my feet was dry crisp sand, and knowing that I was in perfect safety I lay down at full length. I could sleep here undisturbed. Mary was in good hands: I had Hector's word for that, and ere long I knew that I should see her again and be able to claim her for my very own. When I was able to tear my thoughts away from the enchanted dreams of our reunion, I fell upon sullen doubt. We should be in daily peril so long as we continued to remain in Scotland. There was nothing for it but to escape from this tortured land. But how? I knew the ports were watched, and I had heard how the roads that led to the border were patrolled by the dragoons. Mary's escape and mine would spur the persecutors to measures more stern. At whatever risk, we must attempt to get to England. There lay safety. And then I thought of Hector. Hector, the resourceful, the indomitable, would find a way; and with this thought in my mind, I settled down to sleep.

How long I slept I cannot tell, but when I awoke and felt the sand beneath me and, reaching out, touched upon either hand rough walls of stone, I thought for a moment that I had been buried alive. Then I remembered where I was.

I crawled along the passage until I was beneath the steps. A faint little feather of light came through the chinks between them and from its tenuousness I judged that it was night. I must have slept all through the day. Cautiously I swung round the step and crawled out until I stood within the precincts of the Abbey beneath the Gothic window.

The sky was studded with stars. I judged that I might with safety go further afield to stretch my limbs, so I stole out of the Abbey and walked across the level lawn until I came to the edge of the river. It moved silently through the darkness, so slowly as to seem asleep, and I thought of my own quiet Avon. I walked along the bank to the point where the Cluden steals silently into the bosom of the shining Nith, to flow on with it, one and indivisible, to the sea.

I followed the course of the stream downward until the black, still surface of the College pool lay at my feet. As I stood there I listened to the faint murmur of the river as it flowed at the foot of the banks beneath. There was love in its language, and I, whose heart was aglow with love, could hear and understand. The Nith was whispering to the Cluden, adrowse in its arms, such little tender messages as soon I should be whispering to my beloved. I drifted away upon the soft wings of reverie to a land of dreams, but I was brought back suddenly by hearing afar off the sound of the town clock. I counted its strokes. It was midnight. Midnight! and there was no sign of Hector; nor had I yet seen Mary! What could have happened to them? Had disaster befallen them, and were all the high hopes which I had formed doomed yet to be brought to the ground? I dared not think so, and, to rid myself of my fears, I threw off my clothing and with a running leap plunged head foremost into the College Pool. The coldness of the water stung me like a lash, but there was refreshment in it, and with hope once more on tip-toe, I yielded myself to the enjoyment of the moment, and swam until the stiffness left my limbs. Then I made for the bank again, and when I had dressed sought my hiding-place. Sometime ere dawn, I imagined, Hector would come to me, with news of Mary. With this hope in my mind I sat in my gloomy vault waiting patiently. Hour after hour went by, and still he did not come, and at last sleep overcame me and I sank into dreamland again. When love sits on the throne of a man's heart, dreamland is his empire, and on winged feet I wandered with Mary at my side, through the meads, flower-dappled, of that bewitching land. Then I woke again, and realised that it was a dream and that nothing surrounded me but darkness.

Once more I crawled beneath the stair and peeped out. It was broad day, but still Hector had not come. Then fear seized me. Had he fallen into the hands of Lag and been done to death ? Was the price of my freedom to be his life, and if he had been taken, where was Mary ? I had his assurance that she was in a place of safety. There was comfort in that knowledge. But the comfort was alloyed by the thought that I had no knowledge whatever of her whereabouts and that she was lost to me. I was almost tempted to throw caution to the winds, and quit my hiding-place in broad daylight to go in search of them both. I stretched out my hand to seize the step and swing it back, and then discretion returned to me and I refrained. Any rashness now might bring to nothing all we had accomplished. I must wait. There was nothing for it but patience and unwavering trust. Every hour that dragged its weary length along was leaden with torpor. Would the day never come to an end ? Hector, I knew, was not likely to come to me save under the screen of the darkness, and the darkness seemed very far off. The longest day, however, draws sometime to a close, and at last the rays of light stealing through the chinks in the stair-case ceased to be burnished spears and were transmuted into uncertain plumes of smoke. The hour of twilight had come; soon darkness would envelop the earth, and with the darkness Hector might come. I crawled out of the confined space in which I was lying and sought the deeper part of the passage. As I did so, I heard a grating sound. Someone was moving the step. It must be Hector! Yet in that moment of tense expectation I kept a grip upon myself and did not move. If, instead of Hector, it should prove to be some murderous pursuer on my track, I knew that in this darkness, to which my eyes through long imprisonment had become accustomed, I should have the advantage and might fall upon him unawares. A voice spoke and my fears were set at naught. The packman had come!

"Are you there?" he asked.

"Yes," I answered.

"Ha'e you got my Horace?"

"Confound Horace and all his works! Where is Mary?"

"Mary, the bonnie lass! she's a' richt. Ye micht trust me for that. Ye'll be seein' her in less than half an 'oor. Where's my book?"

I handed him the volume, and though I could not see him I guessed from the sound of the leaves fluttering through his fingers that he was examining it carefully.

"It seems to be nane the waur, except that the corner o' ane o' its braids is broken. Man, it's a lucky thing for you that I'm a scholar, and carry Horace wi' me. When I got tired o' waitin' for ye at the trysting-place, I thocht that something must ha'e gane wrang, so I gaed doon to the Tolbooth to ha'e a look for mysel'. I got a terrible shock when I struck my foot on the file you had dropped. I thocht a' was up then; but it didna tak' me lang to mak' up my mind. At first I thocht o' flingin' the file through the window, then I thocht that if I missed it would mak' an unco' clatter and micht waken somebody, so I fell back upon Horace and he served. I put the book through the window at the second shot, which is no' bad for an auld man, as ye will dootless admit; and here ye are in safety. Mony a time Horace has fetched me oot o' the dungeons o' despondency, but I never kent him help a body oot o' the Dumfries Tolbooth afore."

The garrulous fellow would doubtless have continued longer in a like strain, but I would have none of it. My heart was crying for my loved one. "Tell me," I exclaimed, "where is Mary?"

"Come on," he said with a laugh, "and see for yoursel'."

He led the way out into the open and I followed close behind him. As we emerged a man approached us out of the darkness. I started and laid a hand upon Hector's arm.

"There's naething to fear," he said. "It's only the minister frae the cave at the Linn. He's come to mairry you."

"To marry me," I exclaimed. "Who has arranged it?"

"I ha'e nae doot," answered Hector, "Mary and you arranged it lang syne on the braes at Daldowie. A' I ha'e dune is to mak' your arrangements possible."

My heart was full.

The minister greeted me warmly, and together the three of us made for the summit of the little knoll beside the Abbey. While Mr. Corsane was congratulating me upon my escape and upon the rescue of Mary, the packman had turned his back upon us and was gazing earnestly towards the mouth of the Cluden. As we talked he interrupted us suddenly by saying:

"They're coming noo, I can see them." Along

the edge of the bank below us, three figures were moving. Soon they had begun to ascend the knoll.

"Mary's there," said Hector, "and the twa wi' her are the good-man o' Nunholm and his better three-quarters."

I sprang towards the advancing figures and calling "Mary," clasped her in my arms. There are moments too sacred for speech. I could only kiss her. Then linking my arm through hers I helped her to the top of the mound.

There in the aisle of the trees with the light of the kindly stars filtering through and falling on the ground with a holier radiance than ever streamed through the east window of a cathedral, the minister made us one. He could not unite our hearts. That had been done long ago. He could only join our hands.

Hector, as ever, proved himself to be a friend in need, for, when the moment came for me to place a ring upon Mary's finger, I realised with a pang that I had none. But Hector slipped one into my hesitating hand, whispering, "It was meant for the widda." The simple service was soon over, but ere he gave us his blessing the minister said:

"In quieter times, when I, please God, am restored to my parish, your marriage will be registered in the records of my church at Minniehive: meantime I declare you man and wife in the sight of God and according to the laws of this realm." Then he raised his hand to bless us.

I turned to embrace my wife; but Hector was before me. He kissed her loudly upon both cheeks, and as he yielded her shrinking form to me said: "Nae need o' my salve there. They're as saft as the damask rose."

"For ever, dearest," I whispered, as she clung to me.

"My ain dear man," she breathed; and on her warm cheek close pressed against my own I felt a tear. I folded her in my arms.

"My children," said the minister, drawing near us, "I must leave you now, and get me back to my hiding-place: but may He who brought joy to the wedding feast at Cana of Galilee company with you all the days of your lives. Good-bye." He turned, and was gone.

"Now," said Hector, "we maun hurry. We ha'e a lang road to travel afore daybreak. Come on."

Together we began to hasten down the hill, and soon were at the edge of the river close to the mouth of the Cluden. The good wife of Nunholm and her husband led the way. I took Mary in my arms and carried her through the water behind them. No man ever bore a burden more precious. Her arms were about my neck. In mid-stream I paused and, bending, kissed her. I had forgotten Hector behind us.

He sighed. "Ay. It mak's me jealous. I wish the widda was here. But ye've a hale life-time o' that afore ye, so haste ye, for we're no oot o' danger yet."

Mary smiled proudly up at me in the moonlight. "Nae danger maitters noo. But let us haste."

When we came to the bank on the other side, the farmer led the way to a hedge and we passed through a gap into a field across which we hurried together. In a few minutes we found ourselves beside a little farm-house.

"Come awa' ben," said the farmer's wife, throwing the door open. "It's no' a very grand wedding feast, but it'll dae to set you on the road, and it shall never be said that the guid-wife o' Nunholm lacks in hospitality."

We entered the kitchen and found an ample supper

awaiting us. Mary had endeared herself, and little wonder, to these good folks during the two days she had spent with them, and they were full of anxiety for her safety.

We made all the haste we could through the meal, and when it was nearly over the door was thrown wide to the wall and a shock-headed lad thrust his body in. The farmer turned to him: " Is a' richt, Ebenezer ? " he asked.

" Ay, faither, there's no' a trooper between here and Dumfries."

We finished our meal, and bade the good wife and her husband an affectionate farewell, the former insisting on Mary's wrapping herself in her own best plaid.

" Ye've a long road to travel, lassie," she said, " and ye maunna catch cauld. Tak' it as a keepsake, and if ye're ever back in these pairts, dinna forget tae come and see me."

I thanked the good man and his wife for their kindness to us, and, Hector leading, we went out into the night.

CHAPTER XLIV

"QUO VADIS, PETRE ?"

Ere the darkness had given place to the dawn we three were lying in a copse of hazel bushes not far from the Castle of Caerlaverock within a stone's throw of the sea. On leaving Nunholm we had made a detour so as to avoid the town, and struck the road to Glencaple far outside its boundaries.

The journey, made in stealth, had been without adventure. Hector led the way; Mary and I followed close behind him arm in arm. We had spoken little; Mary and I hardly at all, for the touch of her arm in mine, tender as a caress, was more eloquent than speech; but Hector found time to tell all he had done since the moment of my escape from the Tolbooth.

For him the intervening hours had been crowded. He had gone to the cave at the Linn to fetch the minister to marry us: but he had also devised a means to help us back to England, and it was for this end that he had brought us to the place where we were.

"There was juist ae thing I failed to do, for I hadna the time," he said. "I intended to speir again at the widda, for I should ha'e been a prood man tae ha'e been mairried at the same time as yoursels. But the widda maun juist bide my time. She's kept me waitin' lang enough. She'll maybe appreciate me a' the mair if I keep her waitin' in turn. Nae doot she'll miss me, for I'm comin' wi' ye as far as the Isle o' Man. Ye see this affair will mak' a terrible steer in the toon o' Dumfries ; and it will be safer for me to be oot o' the road till the storm blaws by. Forby, it will gi'e me the chance o' introducin' my magical salve to the Island. Anthony Kerruish, the maister o' the *Sea-mew*, tells me that it is no kent there, and besides if I had a quate six months in the island I micht get on wi' that *magnum opus* o' mine."

Mary and I were delighted to learn that he was coming with us, for well we knew that he could stay behind only at grave risk. As we thanked him, with full hearts, for all he had done, he held up a deprecating hand.

"Hoots," he said, "I've dune naething: and in ony case I took my fee o' Mistress Bryden's cheeks." He laughed quietly as he stole out of the copse.

Dawn was breaking. The dark shadow of Criffel was turning to a ghostly grey, and on the face of the water we could see, about half a mile away, a little barque lying at anchor. Hector lit a candle, and taking off his bonnet passed it in front of the light twice. Then he blew the candle out. His signal had been seen; a little answering light flashed for a moment on the deck of the barque, and was gone. Then a man dropped into the boat that nestled under the lee of the barque, and began to pull towards the shore. As he drove the boat on to the sand we slipped out of our shelter. I took Mary in my arms, and, wading out into the tawny water, I placed her in the boat. Then I jumped in. Hector, close behind me, flung a leg into the boat: then I heard him sigh so deeply that I thought he had bruised himself. I turned, and saw him withdraw his leg, and seize the boat by the prow. With a mighty shove he sent her off the sand into the deep water, and stood erect gazing after her.

"Good-bye," he said, with a tremor in his voice, as he took off his bonnet.

"Good-bye?" I exclaimed doubtingly. "What do you mean? I thought you were coming with us?"

"So I was," he answered. "But I remembered Peter: and I'm gaun back. My work's no' feenished yet." And with that he splashed out of the water and disappeared into the copse.

But we saw him again. When we were safely on board the barque, and the anchor was up, and the skipper and his men were setting their sails to the breeze, Mary and I stood on the poop and looked anxiously back to the little wood by the water-side. A figure came out of the shadows and waved a hand. We waved back in answer, and the figure disappeared.

CHAPTER XLV

ON THE WINGS OF THE SEA-MEW

THE wind and the tides favoured us, and the little barque took to the sea like the bird whose name she bore.

Before us a rosy path, painted by the rising sun, stretched into the distance. The soft winds of the dawn filled the brown sails and carried us onward, and the little waves patted the sides of our boat as though they were the hands of the sea-maidens, come from out of the deep to cheer us on our way.

We sat together in the stern of the boat, our feet resting on a heap of tarry cordage. I had wrapped her plaid about her to keep my Mary warm—and under its folds I had made her hands captive in one of mine.

"I can hardly believe it," she said. "It is amaist ower guid to be true: to ha'e you by my side, my ain man, when I thocht you were deid."

"And I," I answered, "thought that I had lost you for ever. Many a time, of a night, I have looked up at the stars and chosen the brightest of them, and called it Mary's star: because I thought it must be your dwelling-place. And all the while you were not dead at all."

"And were you really very, very sorry when you thocht that I was deid?" she asked, with a twinkle in her eyes.

"Mary!" I exclaimed, "how can you?" And

as there was no one to see but a following gull which hung above us, I kissed her. "But tell me," I continued, "what happened to you after we parted on the moors—and how came I to find this among the ashes of Daldowie," and I drew out the fragment of her ring and showed it to her.

"My ring!" she cried. "The ring you gave me! Did you fin' it there? Oh, laddie!" and she nestled against me so tenderly that, in that happy moment, the weary months of pain through which I had lived seemed as nothing.

Then she told me what had befallen her. She had gone to the hiding-place, but found no trace of her father; and after seeking for him far and wide, but without avail, she had decided to return home. On her way back she discovered troopers out upon the moor between herself and home, and she had been compelled to hide for the night among the heather. It was not until late on the following afternoon that she had ventured to steal back to Daldowie, only to find her home in ashes. As I had done, when I returned upon the day following, she had found three skeletons among the ruins, and, with horror of heart, she had counted that one of them was mine.

"I leaped," she said, "among the ashes, and though they burned me cruelly, I brushed them aside frae the face that I thought was yours to see your smile again. But a' I saw was red embers and fleshless bones. Oh, sweetheart—how I cried!" And she buried her head upon my shoulder and sobbed for a moment. Then she raised her face and smiled.

"You maun think me silly. I'm greetin' noo for joy, I cried then for sorrow. As mither used to say—'Women are kittle cattle'—aren't we?" and she smiled, until the light in her sweet eyes dried the tears as the sun dries the dew from the heather bells. "And I suppose," she added, "that's when I lost my ring—though I didna miss it till I had left Daldowie far behin' me."

"And where have you been," I asked, "since then? Both Hector and I searched the length and breadth of Galloway for you, but without avail."

"Oh, fie," she said. "Ha'e you no' been tellin' me that you thocht I was in the Kingdom of Heaven—and you looked for me in the Kingdom o' Galloway," and in the playful notes of her voice I heard the echo of her mother's.

"Where was I?" she continued. "Weel, I was within three miles o' Dumfries a' the time. Ye see, when I left Daldowie, I didna ken where tae go. I ran for miles and miles ower the hills, till I could run nae langer; and then the dark fell, and I lay doon among the heather and cried mysel' to sleep. But when the mornin' cam' I sat up and said to mysel', 'Mary Paterson—you maunna be a fool.' I spoke it oot lood—and it sounded sae like mither's voice that I began to greet again, and I went on greetin' till I could greet nae mair, and then I felt better." She looked at me roguishly. "And after that," she went on, "I set oot for Dumfries. I thocht if I could reach the Solway I micht wade across it to England, but—I'm thinkin' noo that I've seen it, I would ha'e been drooned in the attempt." She laughed, and the gull above us, with its yellow legs apart, and its tail stretched tensely fan-wise, dropped down and touched the sea with its beak, and having seized its prey, wheeled round on wide wings and floated above us again.

"Food I got frae kindly cotters, and when at last I reached Dumfries I set oot to mak' for Glencaple. But when half-way there I sat doon by the road and began to think, and then for the first time I missed my ring, and thinkin' o' the day when you put it on my finger and o' a' the love you bore me, I fair broke doon and cried like a bairn. I was greetin' sae sair that I didna notice a lady dressed in black until she was standing beside me. Very gently she asked me what ailed me, and the look in her face made me feel that she had kent sorrow hersel'—so I tellt her everything. Before I was finished she was greetin' as sair as mysel', and then she slipped her airm through mine and drew me to my feet and kissed me. 'I am but a poor widow,' she said, 'whose husband and sons have died for the Covenant: but the widow's cruse never runs dry, and you are welcome to a share of whatever the Lord sends me.' She led me to her bonnie wee hoose, set in a plantin' o' beech trees on the Glencaple road, and she has been a mother to me, and I a daughter to her ever since. Sometimes we would shelter fugitive hill-men—and often I ha'e ta'en them food—and it was for that, for I was caught red-handed, that I was made prisoner and thrown into the Tolbooth."

"And that," I said, taking up the tale, "is how you come now to be sitting, my wife, beside me." I kissed her beneath her little shell-like ear.

"Behave yoursel'," she said with mock sternness. "The captain will see you!"

"And what if he does?" I asked, as I repeated the offence.

"Did you see me on the road to the Tolbooth?" she continued.

"Yes," I said, "that is where I saw you. Just when hope seemed utterly dead—you came."

The woman in her spoke: "Did I look feart?" she asked.

"Not a bit; you looked as brave as you are."

She laughed as she replied, "I'm gled I didna show it, for mither would ha'e been ashamed o' me if she knew, but in my hert I was as frichtened as a bairn."

" Never mind," I said, " you have nothing to fear now. You are mine for ever."

" For ever," she answered. " That's a lang, lang time ; are ye sure ye'll never get tired o' me ? "

" Sweetheart," I answered fervently, " long ago you told me to love you for your soul. I have learned to do so, and such a love can never die " ; and as the captain's back was turned and there was neither sea-gull nor sailor-man to see, I took her winsome face in both my hands and smothered her with kisses.

CHAPTER XLVI

SUNSHINE AFTER STORM

THE morning after we had waved our farewell to Hector saw us safe in the Isle of Man. Here, through the kindness of the skipper of the *Sea-mew,* we found a lodging until such time as he could arrange for us a passage to England on some barque that was sailing thither. Two days later we were on board the *Kitty-wake,* which carried us safely to the port of Liverpool. On the outskirts of the town, in the little village of Walton, in a cottage behind the old church we found a lodging with the good woman to whom the master of the *Kitty-wake* had commended us.

Now that I was back in England I determined to seek a reconciliation with my uncle and guardian. With some trepidation I wrote him a letter telling him of all that had befallen me, asking his pardon for the anxiety I must have caused him, and craving permission to bring my wife to see him in the old home. It was a hard letter to write, hard and perplexing, and when it was completed I was far from satisfied with it. But Mary, who helped me with wise words, assured me that unless his heart were of adamant it would melt him. So I dispatched it, and waited anxiously for a reply. A fortnight passed, and there was no answer; but one morning when the third week was drawing to a close a post-boy on horseback knocked loudly at the cottage door and I heard him ask: "Does Walter de Brydde, Esquire, live here?" I rushed to the door and received the missive from his hand. " Four shillings to pay, sir," he said. Gladly I paid the fee, and gave him something wherewith to slake his thirst at the nearest tavern. Raising the butt of his crop to his cap, he dug his heels into the flanks of his horse and was off.

I hastened into Mary's room. The letter was heavily sealed with red wax and the superscription upon it was in writing that I did not know. All excitement, I broke the seal. The letter was from the firm of notaries which for generations had conducted the affairs of our family. They begged to inform me that my letter had been handed to them in their capacity as notaries in charge of my uncle's affairs. They regretted to announce that some seven months ago he and his lady had died of a fever within a few days of each other, the wife predeceasing her husband. As my uncle had died without issue, they had the honour to inform me that the estates passed to me as the next heir male. They noted with satisfaction that I had taken unto myself a wife and they looked forward with pleasure to making the acquaintance of my lady at no distant date. They took the liberty of enclosing for my immediate necessities a draft upon their agents in Old Hall Street in the city of Liverpool, and they trusted that as early as should be convenient to myself and my good lady we would return to Warwick and take up our residence in the old manor. They ventured to hope that the long and amicable relations which had existed between my family and their firm would continue. They assured me of their devoted services at all times, and they had the honour to subscribe themselves my humble and obedient servants.

We read the surprising document with heads pressed close together, amazement fettering our tongues. Suddenly Mary drew away, and clasping her hands, exclaimed :

"I'm sorry."

"Sorry?" I said. "Why? The silly old man and his wife were nothing to you."

"Oh no, it's no' that. I cam' to you a tocherless lass wi' naething to gi'e ye but my love—and noo ye're rich."

"Sweetheart!" I cried: and dropping the letter with the draft upon the table, I took her in my arms and drew her towards me. "Your love is more to me than all the riches of the Spanish Main. Gold is but dross: love is of God, and eternal."

She slipped an arm about my neck, and laid her head upon my shoulder.

"Ye can kiss me," she said—and added roguishly as she smiled at me—"if ye like."

So it came to pass that within a fortnight of receiving the letter we arrived at Warwick, making the journey, as became our state, in a hired carriage with postilions. The needle-women of Liverpool had done their work well, and as I looked at the dainty figure, all frills and furbelows, beside me in the carriage I almost felt that I had lost the Mary I had learned to love at Daldowie. But the light in the pools of her eyes, the aureole above her forehead, and the smile on her bewitching face as she said, "Now, behave yersel'. Ye maunna crush my new goon," told me it was Mary still.

CHAPTER XLVII

THE END; AND A BEGINNING

A YEAR has passed, and once again it is the month of May. My little flower of the heather, transported from the hill-sides of Galloway and set in the kindlier atmosphere of this southern clime, has blossomed into a flower of rare beauty. She has not a peer among the ladies of Warwick, and that is saying much.

Sometimes, as we sit together on the green lawn that slopes down to the quiet Avon, and think of all the things that befell in the days that are dead, we wonder if they were all a dream. Yet in spite of what she suffered among them, Mary sometimes whispers to me that her heart is sick for the grey hills of Galloway, for the sting of the wind on her cheeks, for the cry of the whaup in her ears; and I find it hard to comfort her. But I think she will never again be sick at heart for the hills of heather, for a new joy has come into her life and mine. A week ago the wonder happened.

When, in the early dawn, the good nurse brought me the news as I paced in a fever up and down my study floor, I was all ardent, as any man would be, to see my Mary and her child on the instant. But the nurse bade me curb my impatience, telling me that Mary was asleep. So I made my way out to the lawn, and, leaning on the retaining wall, gazed down upon the Avon. Early roses wet with dew were pouring their incense into the still air, and I plucked me a handful for Mary. As I stood by the wall with the flowers in my hand I chanced to look up the river towards the bridge, and on it I saw a man upon whose shoulders was a pack. Lighting my pipe, I sat down upon the garden seat with the heap of roses beside me. As I sat there I heard a little voice that I had never heard before. Through the open window, my child was joining its little cry to that of a jubilant bird, and my heart was glad within me and the whole sun-kissed earth was ringing with melody. O Mary mine!

The sound of footsteps upon the carriage-drive made me turn, and I saw—Hector.

I rushed to him with hands outstretched. "Hector!" I cried, and shook him warmly by the hand.

"Ay, it's me richt eneuch. I got your letter. Ye were wise to write in Latin—but, man, your construction's awfu'—gey near damnable. Ye should mak' mair use o' the ablative absolute. I was pleased tae hear frae ye, though, and things being mair settled up yonder I juist thocht I'd tak' a daunner into England to pit you richt on ane or twa points o' syntax. An' hoo's your good lady?"

"Mary is splendid," I said. "She has just this morning given birth to a daughter."

"My best respects to her and my felicitations upon this great event; but I'm sorry—I'll juist tak' the road again and gang awa' hame. I couldna ha'e come at a waur time."

"My dear Hector, what do you mean? Mary would never forgive me if I let you go." And, dropping into the language which I knew he loved, I slipped my arm through his and said, "Com awa' intae the hoose."

To-night I have been penning the final pages of this my book, with Hector sitting at his ease in a leathern chair reading a volume from the well-stocked shelves of the study. And I—because my hand was weary, or because my heart was aching for a sight of Mary—stole up to her room a moment since. She was lying in the great carved oaken bed, with the light from the candles in their silver sconces falling upon her dear face and the glory of her hair as it lay outspread on the lavender-scented pillow. I bent over her, and slipping an arm under her shoulders kissed her, and she pushed down the white coverlet with her pretty hand to let me peep at our daughter lying asleep in the fold of her arm.

"Isn't she bonnie?" she whispered. "I think we'll ca' her Jean."

"Flower o' the heather and little heather-bell," I said, and gathered them both in my arms.